Mindbender

Sovereign of the Seven Isles: Book Three

by

David A. Wells

MINDBENDER

Edited by Carol L. Wells

www.SovereignOfTheSevenIsles.com

To Heather and Toby

NORTHPORT

BLACKSTONE KEEP

HEADWATER

BUCKWOLD

NEW RUATHA

GLEN MORILLIAN

THE GREAT FOREST

WARRENTON

SOUTHPORT

HIGHLANDS REACH

ISLE OF RUATHA

KAI'GORN

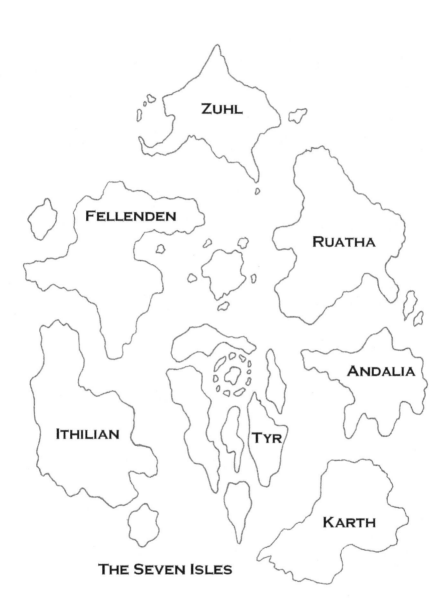

ZUHL

FELLENDEN

RUATHA

ANDALIA

ITHILIAN

TYR

KARTH

THE SEVEN ISLES

Mindbender

Chapter 1

Isabel stood on the balcony that jutted from the side of the fortress island many hundreds of feet above the ocean. It was a calm day with clear blue skies and gently rolling seas. Under other circumstances the view would have been peaceful and beautiful. The gentle breeze was cool but not uncomfortably so and the sounds of seagulls could be heard in the distance as they soared over the surf looking for their next meal.

She tried to focus her mind on the numerous problems at hand but inevitably found herself thinking about Alexander. It had been several days since she and Abigail had been summoned before the triumvirate and they were both anxious for news. The serving girl who brought food to their well-appointed prison cell was pleasant enough but she wasn't privy to the inner workings of the fortress island, let alone the intentions of the triumvirate.

Last Isabel had heard, Alexander was in the Reishi Keep along with Jataan P'Tal. Although she had great faith in Alexander, she worried that even with the Thinblade powered by the magic of the skillbook, he might not be equal to the battle mage. The thought of losing him was one she was not willing to entertain and yet it intruded into her mind with maddening insistence.

Whatever troubles he was facing, she had a few of her own to consider. She and Abigail were still prisoners. The possibility of escape from the fortress island was unlikely. The Reishi Coven and the Sky Knights, as the wyvern riders called themselves, had revealed little of their purpose—save for their intention to prevent the Sovereign Stone from falling into Phane's hands.

Then there was the matter of the poison coursing through her veins. She had only a few weeks to live, unless Magda was telling the truth about Mage Gamaliel's magic, and provided that the magic actually worked. Her own predicament only brought her back to her worry for Alexander. She knew that his love for her was true and complete. She had felt it when their souls bonded during their escape from the netherworld. If she died, it would crush his spirit. His will to fight was tied to his love for life and that was bound to his love for her. She had to find a way to convince the witches to save her from the poison—if not for herself, then for Alexander.

Abigail stopped pacing behind her and came to stand silently next to her on the balcony. They'd spent most of their time at the fortress island together and had bonded as friends and sisters. Both shared the same resolve to secure their freedom and return to Alexander's side to see this war through to the end.

Abigail had been pacing since breakfast. Isabel left her to it. She had just as much to worry about, if not more. The revelation that she and Alexander were Reishi had hit her hard. The first night after that unwelcome revelation, she had cried herself to sleep. The Reishi had killed her oldest brother, burned her home to the ground, and hunted her family across all of Ruatha.

She had good reason to hate them.

Isabel suspected that Abigail had come to some new understanding but waited patiently for her to speak.

"What if they're right?" Abigail asked. "What if Alexander and I are Reishi?"

Isabel thought about it for a moment before she said, "I don't know. It's hard to tell how the Reishi Protectorate might respond, let alone the people of Ruatha."

Abigail frowned. "I hadn't thought about that, but I see what you mean. The Protectorate might become less of a threat and the people of Ruatha might decide that we're their enemy. After all, the Reishi brought about the fall of the House of Ruatha during the war." She shook her head to bring herself back to her original concern. "What happens when Alexander finds the Sovereign Stone? Do you think he might be able to use it?"

Isabel looked at her sharply. Until now the Sovereign Stone had been nothing but a terrible threat to the future because of the power it would confer upon Phane if he found it first. Isabel hadn't considered the possibility that Alexander might be able to use it.

She shook her head slowly. "I don't know, but it's worth thinking about. If we had the power of the Sovereign Stone, it might tip the balance in our favor. I wonder how the witches would react to that."

Abigail gave her best mischievous grin. "I doubt they would be pleased, but then I don't really care." She paused to look out over the ocean. "I wish we knew where Alexander was," she said in a small, worried voice.

Isabel took her hand and gave it a squeeze. "He's all right, I can feel it. Besides, a number of Sky Knights returned just after breakfast, so I'm hoping we might have another conversation with the triumvirate today. I'm sure they have news to report."

They both stood at the balcony railing in silence for a long time. The frustration of being trapped when so much was happening in the world was maddening.

There was a tap at the door, then the bar was removed and the bolt thrown. A large, burly guard pulled the door open to admit Wren, their serving girl. She was a waif of a thing, maybe five and a half feet tall and a hundred pounds dripping wet. She had fair skin and wispy dirty-blond hair that was always slightly disheveled. Her big eyes were deep blue and she had freckles across her nose and cheeks. She was innocent to the point of naiveté. Isabel and Abigail had both taken a liking to her in spite of the fact that she was working for the enemy.

"Mistress Isabel, Mistress Abigail, I have your lunch," she said as she entered, balancing a covered tray on one hand. The guard closed the door behind her and bolted it shut.

Isabel smiled. "Wren, how many times do I have to tell you to call me Isabel? I'm not your mistress."

Wren flushed a bit and nodded. "Yes, Mistress," she said as she went about the task of laying out their meal.

Isabel and Abigail shared a smile.

Wren was fragile and friendly and terribly eager to please. She went out of her way to ensure that the meals she brought were well prepared, always warm and consisted of food that her two charges preferred. Isabel had to admit that she and Abigail ate well despite their lack of freedom.

They had tried to engage Wren in conversation a number of times but she was usually not very forthcoming—not out of a desire to withhold information but more from a pronounced sense of deference. It was clear that the witches had impressed upon her the need to provide excellent service. That simple fact gave Isabel a measure of hope that there was still a chance for an alliance with these people.

"Please, sit and share a meal with us, Wren," Isabel said with a warm smile.

"Oh, but I couldn't, Mistress," Wren said. "I'm just a serving girl. It's not my place to sit with high-born ladies." She looked down as she spoke.

Abigail laughed and Isabel smiled with a gentle chuckle. Wren looked up with alarm until she saw the genuine mirth on their faces and she couldn't help but smile slightly.

"I was born on a ranch and grew up herding cattle," Abigail said. "I'm not 'high-born' by any stretch of the imagination."

"I grew up riding patrol in the Great Forest of Ruatha, sleeping on the ground and eating trail rations," Isabel said. "You don't have to be afraid of us, Wren. We'd like to be your friends."

A look of puzzlement mingled with hope ghosted across her face. "Why?" she asked simply and earnestly.

Isabel shrugged. "Because we could use the company and you seem like a nice person."

Wren hesitated for a moment. "You're so different from anyone here. People here are always worried about position and appearance. None of the important people would dare be caught talking to a servant except to give orders." She shook her head. "I've often wondered what it would be like to live in a place where people could do what they want instead of what they were born to do."

"What do you mean, born to do?" Isabel asked.

"We're all born into our place here. The mission of the Reishi Coven is so vital to the world that we must all accept our place and do our part to protect the future from the Reishi Prince," Wren said.

Isabel and Abigail shared a look. "Please sit with us. We know almost nothing of your ways and customs. Would you tell us about your home?" Isabel said, motioning to a chair at the sturdy dining table.

Wren blinked a few times and slowly sat down, clasping her hands on the table and studying them like she thought she was guilty of some transgression.

Isabel and Abigail took their seats at the square little table and helped themselves to lunch. There was smoked fish, roasted bison, and freshly baked hard rolls with a wedge of soft spreadable cheese. It was simple fare but it was well prepared and there was plenty of it. Isabel figured the people of the fortress island must have limited sources of food, hence the reliance on fish as a main staple of their diet. She fixed a plate of food for Wren and set it in front of the waifish serving girl.

Wren looked up wide-eyed with just a hint of panic. "I can't eat your food. I would get in trouble."

Isabel shrugged. "We won't tell if you won't," she said as she popped a piece of smoked fish into her mouth.

Wren looked at the food, then at Isabel. "You promise?" she asked.

"Of course," Isabel said nodding.

Wren looked to Abigail.

She smiled warmly. "We won't tell a soul."

Wren hesitated for a moment more before she took a small piece of roasted bison and spread some cheese on it. She closed her eyes and savored the flavor of it as she chewed.

"Meat is scarce, so the servants aren't allowed to have any," she said. "It's delicious." She didn't make a move to have any more.

Isabel stabbed a good-sized slice from the serving tray and put it on Wren's plate. "Eat," she said around a bite of bread with cheese.

Wren lost all reluctance. She ate her fill, savoring every bite like it was a treasure. When they finished the meal she sighed with satisfaction. "That is the best meal I've ever had, except at festival—twice a year we have a big feast that lasts two days. Everyone gets to eat whatever they want during festival."

"Can you tell us more about the fortress island?" Isabel asked.

"What would you like to know?"

Isabel had a few important questions in mind but she didn't want to spook the child with overtly military questions, so she opted for more general inquiries.

"How many people live here?" Isabel asked.

"Just over five thousand," Wren said. "The triumvirate is careful to ensure that our population doesn't expand past the space available in the fortress. Our population has been pretty constant for the past two thousand years. That's one of the reasons everyone is born into a position. Families are permitted to have children to fill the positions of those who die from age or accident. Of course, there are always a few hundred extra people who fill in here and there where they're needed."

"So you're expected to be a servant for your whole life?" Abigail asked, a little taken aback by the concept.

Wren nodded earnestly. "My grandmother was a servant. When she got old, my parents were permitted to have me so that I could fill her position."

"Is that what you want to do with your life?" Isabel asked.

Wren hesitated before she looked down at the table and shook her head ever so slightly. "I should be going. The kitchen will expect me to return with your tray soon." Isabel's question seemed to frighten her.

Abigail leaned in and spoke softly, gently. "What do you want to do with you life?"

Wren looked down at her empty plate and took a deep breath before she answered. "I want to sing," she whispered softly. She looked up quickly like she'd said too much. "You won't tell anyone, will you? Please, they wouldn't understand. Everyone has a place and each of us is needed where we are. The future of the Seven Isles depends on the Reishi Coven and the Sky Knights. We must all play our parts to protect the world." Her words sounded like they were regurgitated platitudes she'd heard so many times that they had become ingrained in her understanding of the world.

"Your secret is safe with us," Abigail said. "Perhaps someday I'll be able to introduce you to a friend of mine. He's a very good singer. I'm sure he'd be happy to teach you." Abigail found that she had been thinking about Jack a lot since the Sky Knights had scooped her up from the shore of the Reishi Isle.

"You know a singer?" Wren asked with a hint of awe. "There are only four singers in the fortress island and two apprentices. They're held in very high esteem and they look so joyous when they're singing."

"My friend's name is Jack. He's the Master of the Ruathan Bards Guild," Abigail said.

Wren blinked a few times. "I've read tales of the bards of old. They used to sing for the sovereign before the war. Ruatha must be a truly wonderful place if there's a whole guild of bards."

"Ruatha is home," Isabel said. "We both miss it and hope to return soon, provided the triumvirate decides to release us."

Wren looked down. "You've been so nice to me. And I'm sure the triumvirate will decide to let you go soon. They're very wise. When they make decisions that are a burden to others it's just because they have such a terrible responsibility and they must put their duty first."

She cleared the table and picked up her serving tray, balancing it on her left hand.

"Thank you for sharing your meal with me," she said. "If you need anything, just let me know and I'll do what I can for you."

She knocked on the door and a few moments later it was unlocked and opened by the guard in the hall. Wren gave them a timid little smile before she left and the door to their comfortable prison cell was closed again.

Isabel and Abigail went out onto the balcony. "I've been keeping an eye on the comings and goings of the Sky Knights," Isabel said. "With a population of over five thousand they could easily have several hundred wyverns here. That would be consistent with my observations. They're constantly rotating patrols of two. Enough to keep eyes on every inch of the Reishi Isle's coastline at all times."

Abigail whistled quietly. "A few hundred Sky Knights would do wonders for our army. With them on our side, we could prevent Andalia from landing any more troop transports."

Isabel nodded, "I was thinking the same thing. We need to do whatever we can to win them over."

"I agree," Abigail said. "If what they've told us about their purpose is true, they should realize that we all have a better chance against Phane if we stand together."

Chapter 2

Not long after Wren left, there was a firm knock at the door followed by the grating of the bolt. Three guards stood in the hall.

"The triumvirate has summoned you. Come with us," the leader of the detail said.

They wound through the passages of the fortress island until they came to the now familiar audience room. The grandeur of the massive chamber was still impressive. The high ceilings, the long raised bench facing the gallery, and the high windows all served to create an air of authority.

Magda, Cassandra, and Gabriella sat in their places behind the bench. Two chairs in front of the bench awaited the prisoners. A woman dressed in the riding armor of the Sky Knights was standing off to the side, her arm resting in a sling and a slightly bloodstained bandage was wrapped around her shoulder.

Isabel and Abigail walked to their chairs without a word and sat down.

"Thank you for joining us," Magda said. "We have just received a report from our forces at the Reishi Keep. It would seem to verify much of your story but it also presents us with a dilemma. This is Mistress Constance. She commands the flight of Sky Knights that was assigned to prevent your friends from entering the Keep."

"It appears that she has failed," Gabriella said sternly.

Constance didn't flinch or react but instead stood stoically in her place.

"Mistress Constance, please recount your report for our guests," Magda said.

"Yes, Mistress." She spoke without meeting anyone's eyes and her words carried no emotion. "The invaders entered the Keep by stealth in the night. Once they were inside, we chose to wait for them to exit before we made our attack. The next morning, another group of invaders led by Commander P'Tal of the Reishi Protectorate assaulted past our guard force and entered the Keep as well. We posted guards and overwatch patrols all around the Keep.

"Some time passed before we encountered the invaders again. They were in one of the three main towers when the Reishi Gate opened and Prince Phane emerged on horseback. He wielded terrible magic against my Sky Knights and against the Keep itself, destroying the observation deck that joined the three towers and releasing a netherworld beast of terrifying capability from one of the towers.

"In the ensuing chaos, the invaders came to the bridge that I guarded. One calling himself Alexander Reishi held out the Sovereign Stone, which was glowing softly, and proclaimed himself to be the Seventh Sovereign of the Seven Isles."

Isabel and Abigail shared a look of both concern and triumph. Alexander had the Stone and he was bonded to it. The claim that Abigail and Alexander shared Reishi blood was clearly true.

"A few moments later Commander P'Tal attacked me with a javelin that nearly killed me. The invaders crossed the bridge and entered the tower containing the master Gate. We did not see them again. Some time later Phane fled the Keep with a small number of others. Just before he reached the wood line, a single member of his party broke off and went northwest into the wilds. We focused our attack on Phane and fought a running battle but the Reishi Prince's magic was more than we could match. He made it to a ship concealed in a cove and fled toward Andalia.

"When we returned to the Keep and entered to search for the invaders, we found a terrible demon in the master gate room. It killed several of my riders. We saw no evidence of a battle and the Reishi Gates had been deactivated, so we can only assume that the one called Alexander has bonded to the Stone and that he fled through the master Gate, to where we do not know."

Isabel's mind raced. If the Gates had been active for any length of time, there was a good chance that Phane had moved an army into Ruatha. He would've known that the Gates would awaken with the return of the Sovereign Stone. He would have been ready to seize the opportunity. If her assumption was correct, then Alexander would not have gone to Ruatha—so where then? She ticked off the islands one by one in her mind. She ruled out Andalia and Karth. He probably wouldn't have gone to Zuhl. That left Tyr, Fellenden, and Ithilian. If the Reishi Protectorate was indeed loyal to him because of his bonding with the Stone, then Tyr was the most likely choice.

"Thank you, Mistress Constance," Magda said. "Please remain to clarify any questions that may arise."

Constance nodded her assent and remained where she stood.

"A great many things have come to pass that we did not foresee," Magda said. "The Seven Isles are in great peril. The Sovereign Stone cannot be allowed to fall into Phane's hands and yet it is loose in the world. Phane, no doubt, knows this and is taking steps to bring it under his control. I have brought you here to humbly ask for your help. The Sovereign Stone must be brought here and placed under our care. Only here can it be safeguarded against Phane and his dark minions. Please, any insight you may have into young Alexander's likely actions would be of great service to the future and may be the only course that will preserve his life."

Isabel and Abigail shared another look. By unspoken agreement Isabel turned back to Magda and replied to her plea. "What you ask is treason. I have sworn my life and my love to Alexander and I will not betray him for any price. More importantly, if the report we just heard is true, then Alexander *is* the Sovereign of the Seven Isles and you owe him your allegiance. Further, if he is bonded to the Stone, then he is our best hope for defeating Phane."

From the looks on the triumvirs' faces, Isabel could see that she was telling them truths that they didn't want to hear. She pressed on.

"Phane is the enemy," she said. "Since the day he woke from his long sleep, he's hunted my husband. His agents murdered his brother and burned his home to the ground. Alexander will never surrender to the Reishi Prince and he will not rest until he has rid the world of the threat that Phane represents. Even as we speak, war is ravaging the Seven Isles, yet you're fixated on Alexander and the Sovereign Stone. Your resources would be better spent fighting Phane's armies rather than obstructing and harassing your one true ally. Join with us. Help us."

The three witches were quiet for a long moment until Cassandra broke the silence. "Perhaps some of what you say is true, but there are still many questions to be answered before we would consider such an alliance. Alexander is far too young to be an arch mage and yet by all accounts only an arch mage can bond with the Stone. How is it that he was able to accomplish such a thing?"

Isabel frowned. She was out of her depth. There was so much she didn't know about the history of the Reishi Empire and their ancient magic that she could only guess at an answer. But she did know Alexander. That would have to be enough. She considered the consequences of revealing some of his unique talents and decided that the risk was worth the potential gain.

"He is a very powerful wizard," Isabel said. "Only a week after he survived the mana fast, he was able to send his awareness from Glen Morillian in Ruatha to the Isle of Karth. Through this clairvoyance he was able to both see and hear the proceedings of a meeting between Phane and the Reishi Army Regency. I know little about magic but as I understand it, such a feat is beyond even the most accomplished mage. Perhaps the Sovereign Stone responded to his power even though he has not yet undertaken the mage's fast."

"I find that difficult to believe," Gabriella said with just a hint of derision.

Isabel ignored her tone. She needed to win them over. "So did his parents and the wizard that guided him prior to the mana fast. I can attest from personal experience just how powerful his magic is—Alexander was able to send the essence of his being into the netherworld through a rift torn within my own mind and bring me back from the darkness. Is such a feat within the realm of any typical wizard's power? If you doubt me, I can tell you the names of the shades."

"That won't be necessary," Magda said.

Gabriella still didn't look convinced.

"Where would he take the Stone?" Cassandra asked.

Isabel shrugged. "The plan was to return to Blackstone Keep and secure the Stone within the Bloodvault where Phane would be forever denied his prize. After hearing your Sky Knight's report, I suspect he's changed his plans."

"Where would he go?" Gabriella demanded.

Isabel smiled without any humor. "I don't know. From the sounds of things, the Reishi Gates awoke when the Stone returned to the world of time and substance. Phane probably sent his army from Karth to Ruatha, so Alexander wouldn't have been able to return home without being surrounded."

"The Stone must be returned to our care," Gabriella said. "We will find Alexander wherever he is hiding and then he will surrender what he stole."

Abigail laughed derisively. "You think he's hiding? Not a chance. He's doing everything he can to raise an army and rally anyone with the wisdom to listen to his cause. If he wanted to hide, he would have stayed in Glen Morillian, or Blackstone Keep for that matter—but he didn't. He chose the most dangerous course possible because it was the only path he could see that would preserve the Seven Isles from Phane. Every moment you work against Alexander is a moment you serve Phane."

"How dare you speak to us with such impudence!" Gabriella said, standing with anger. She raised her hand as if preparing to cast a spell.

Isabel shot to her feet and interposed herself between Gabriella and Abigail.

"If you strike us down, you doom any chance of an alliance," she said.

"Phane has bested your Sky Knights in every encounter. You have no hope of protecting the Stone here. The moment he learns you have his prize, he will come and you will deliver the world into darkness."

Magda placed her hand on Gabriella's outstretched arm. "Hold, Gabriella. We still have much to consider."

"I concur," said Cassandra.

Gabriella reluctantly lowered her hand and took her seat with a visible effort.

Isabel thought she saw something else in Gabriella's countenance. She thought she saw hate. Again, she wished she had Alexander's sight. He would know the truth of these three.

She remained standing. "If you truly serve the Old Law, then you and my husband have the same master and the same enemy. The people of Ruatha are fighting for their lives against Phane's armies. Help us. The time for patrols over the Reishi Isle has ended. Now is the time to wage war. Come with us to Ruatha and lend your strength against our common enemy."

"You speak with passion and conviction," Magda said. "I'm convinced that you speak the truth as you know it. I'm equally convinced that you and Alexander stand against Phane. I'm less convinced that the Stone is where it belongs.

"As a gesture of goodwill I suggest we should permit them to move freely about the island as guests," Magda said to the other triumvirs.

"I concur," Cassandra said.

"I disagree," Gabriella said. "We should hold them and offer their lives in trade for the Sovereign Stone once it has been located."

Cassandra shook her head. "Such a course diminishes the possibility of an alliance that we may sorely need in the near future."

Magda nodded. "You will be assigned new quarters with locks on the inside of the doors," she said to Isabel and Abigail. "You will be given free access to the common areas of the island. I would ask that you not attempt to leave the island and that you respect the Old Law while you are our guests."

"Thank you," Isabel said. She'd made progress. It was enough for now. "May I enquire about the antidote given to you by Mage Gamaliel?"

"Of course," Magda said. "I understand how urgently you must wish to be rid of the threat of death but we don't yet fully understand the nature of the item. I'm sorry, but we must continue to study it for a while. You have my word that we will administer the magic before the poison becomes fatal. Until the threat becomes urgent, we believe there is greater wisdom in further investigation. I hope you understand."

"In truth, I don't," Isabel said. "But, I'm willing to accept your assurances that you won't permit the poison to kill me."

"If there's nothing else, the guards will show you to your new quarters," Magda said.

Abigail stepped forward. "If we are truly your guests, then I would ask that our weapons be returned to us. I give you my word that I will harm no one except in defense."

Magda looked to her two counterparts for their input. Cassandra nodded reluctantly but Gabriella shook her head angrily.

"Your possessions will be delivered to your quarters," Magda said. "We will hold you to your word."

***

The guards led them to a new suite of quarters on a higher level of the fortress island. The main sitting room was easily forty feet square with ten foot ceilings. The wall opposite the entrance had five arched windows looking out onto a wide balcony with several chairs around two tables and four comfortable-looking lounges lined up along the windows. The central window held a double door that opened outward. Heavy curtains of dark red velvet hung over each window, save for the central door, which had its curtains tied open. A large dining table that could seat a dozen people occupied one side of the room, and a sturdy low table surrounded by well-cushioned chairs and plush couches filled the other. There was a stand-alone fireplace in the center of the room with a chimney that rose directly up into the ceiling. Doors on either side led to small but comfortable bed chambers, each containing a large bed with plenty of blankets, a small table with a lamp, a chair, and an armoire.

Most importantly, the hallway door had a sturdy bar, locking pins at the top and bottom, and a bolt that secured the room from the inside. They were no longer prisoners . . . or at least their prison had just expanded substantially. With free access to the fortress island, they could gather vital information about the capabilities of the Sky Knights and the Reishi Coven.

Not long after they had made a thorough inspection of the rooms for anything out of the ordinary, they heard a knock at the door. Two men stood outside with their packs and weapons. Abigail was greatly relieved to have her bow back. Everything else was replaceable—but her bow, a gift from the Guild Mage of Ruatha, was priceless both in terms of gold and for the capability it gave her on the battlefield.

"I'm starting to feel a little better about our situation," she said to Isabel when the men left.

Chapter 3

"Alexander cannot possibly be capable of wielding the Sovereign Stone with sufficient power to stand against Phane," Gabriella said once they had retired to the triumvirate's private council chamber.

"Yet he was able to bond with the Stone," Magda said. "He may well be our best hope against the Reishi Prince."

"We must also consider the truth of history," Cassandra said. "The Reishi failed. Their model of government led to war and horror. Can we permit the Reishi Empire to rise again, knowing that they will surely succumb to the seduction of power and lead the world back into darkness?"

"What are you suggesting?" Magda asked.

"Perhaps we should look for a way to destroy the Stone and end the Reishi line permanently," Cassandra said.

Magda took a deep breath and let it out slowly, taking a moment to consider the suggestion before shaking her head. "That course would be a betrayal of our commitment to the Old Law. Alexander and his family did not violate our rights. They merely took action to accomplish the same end that we're striving for. How can we justify killing them?"

"They killed a number of our Sky Knights and trespassed on the Reishi Isle," Gabriella countered.

"I know you have suffered a great loss, Gabriella, but I would ask you to set your grief aside and view our dilemma through the prism of our common duty," Magda said. "Ultimately, I fear necessity will guide our hand. The facts are indisputable. Phane must be defeated. Alexander has bonded with the Sovereign Stone and he is fighting to defeat Phane. Our choice seems obvious to me."

"I disagree," Cassandra said. "Phane will destroy the boy and take the Stone. It's only a matter of time until we are all lost. We must bring the Stone here where we can protect it."

"I agree," Gabriella said. "Whether the Reishi line is permitted to survive or not is less important than protecting the Seven Isles from the Sovereign Stone."

"I suggest we locate Alexander and offer him an exchange—his wife and sister for the Stone," Cassandra said.

"I agree," Gabriella said.

Magda hesitated, searching the faces of her sisters. She acquiesced with a sigh. "Very well. But I would ask that I be the one to present the offer."

They both nodded agreement.

"And if he refuses?" Magda asked. "We may find ourselves with two enemies. While I agree that Alexander is unlikely to pose a threat with magic, he does command an army and he has demonstrated control over the Reishi Gates."

"If he refuses, then we may have harder choices before us," Gabriella said. "I am loath to suggest such a thing, but these are desperate times. We may find that a demonstration of our resolve is in order."

"What are you suggesting?" Magda asked.

"Killing him would be counterproductive because he is standing against Phane, but killing his wife or sister would demonstrate our commitment and perhaps motivate him to accede to our demands." Gabriella delivered her explanation in the most reasonable-sounding terms.

Magda felt a chill run up her spine. "Or, such an action may drive him to wage total war against us as his wife suggested."

"I see a third option," Cassandra said. "Isabel is in need of an antidote for her poison. We could tell him that the magic sent by the Guild Mage failed to work and offer her return so that he can seek an alternative remedy."

Gabriella nodded. "That option preserves the threat while reducing the potential of creating a committed enemy. I concur."

"Very well," Magda said. "I disagree, but I will carry out the will of the triumvirate. First, we must locate Alexander and for that we will need the combined strength of the entire coven."

She wondered about the report given by Isabel of Alexander's ability to see across the Seven Isles with his clairvoyance. Such power was indeed formidable if her account was accurate.

"I will make the necessary preparations for the scrying," Cassandra said.

"I will summon the sisters to the scrying well at midnight," Gabriella said.

***

Isabel and Abigail had just settled into their new quarters when they heard a knock at the door. Wren stood in the hall with a tray of food and a timid smile.

"I'm happy that the triumvirate has decided to free you," she said as she placed the large tray on the main table. Dinner was a thick and hearty stew with big chunks of bison, potatoes, carrots, and onions served with half a loaf of bread and a large lump of butter.

Isabel motioned to a chair and Wren reluctantly took a seat with them after she checked to make sure the door was closed and bolted. Abigail dished the stew and took her seat across from Wren.

"There's a lot of talk about you," Wren said. "The rumor is that the Sovereign Stone was taken from the Reishi Keep and it's loose in the world." Her eyes were wide as she spoke. "The coven is meeting in the gardens tonight but they won't say why."

"What are the gardens?" Isabel asked. She was eager to learn anything she could but kept in mind that Wren was loyal to the Reishi Coven.

"The top of the fortress island is a plateau," Wren said. It's covered with gardens, some for food and some for people to walk through. In the center is the scrying well. That's where the sisters go when they want to discuss something important or cast a powerful spell."

"What do you think they're planning to do?" Abigail asked.

"If I had to guess, I'd say they're going to try to locate the Sovereign Stone," Wren said. "The whole point of the Reishi Coven and the Sky Knights is to protect the Seven Isles from the Stone. After all this time, someone just slipped in and took it right out from under their noses. I've never seen the sisters so afraid."

Abigail and Isabel shared a look. Isabel made a mental note to be more wary of the triumvirs. They clearly had an agenda. Her hopes for an alliance waned.

"We'd like to take a look around the island," Isabel said. "Would you be our guide?"

Wren looked up excitedly. "I'd love to. When I was younger I used to explore everywhere I could. I know the island as well as anyone. I just have to return your tray to the kitchen first."

Isabel and Abigail followed her to the kitchen and waited in the dining area for her to finish her tasks. They drew more than a few looks from the Sky Knights and others eating dinner. Some looked on with curiosity, others with thinly veiled anger, and yet others with a hint of fear.

Isabel idly wondered how many of the people here had lost someone to Alexander's sword as they tried to prevent him from retrieving the Sovereign Stone. Then there was the matter of their collective pride. They had lived for the purpose of safeguarding the Stone only to have it taken in spite of their best efforts. Winning them over as allies might prove to be difficult.

She was glad to have her knife strapped to the back of her belt. She was starting to wonder if they had been safer locked away in their comfortable cell. The triumvirate said they were guests, but she wasn't entirely sure that everyone else on the island agreed.

They didn't wait long before Wren came out of the kitchen. She threaded through the dining hall looking at the ground like she was trying to be invisible. The Sky Knights and tradesmen in the hall ignored her, until she stopped in front of Isabel and gave her a timid smile. A few of the Sky Knights seemed to take note that the young serving girl was associating with the enemy.

Isabel started to wonder if they were putting Wren at risk. The last thing she wanted was for the innocent young woman to be harmed because she was friendly with her and Abigail. They left the hall quietly. Both Isabel and Abigail noted the Sky Knights who had the most unfriendly looks on their faces.

The fortress island was bigger than it seemed it should be. The entire interior was riddled with halls, passages, chambers, and staircases leading this way and that. It was apparent that the original interior architecture was very old, but there were many passages that had been carved later to accommodate a larger population.

Wren led them through a meandering course that she followed with casual familiarity. They followed silently, taking note of the many rooms and large halls they passed. Some areas of the community served as marketplaces, others were reserved for quarters, while still others were set aside for the wyverns.

She led them up a staircase onto a semicircular platform that jutted out of a high wall overlooking one of the launch bays. It was an observation deck for watching the wyverns come and go.

The chamber below was enormous. It stood open to the elements on one side and was easily three hundred feet across with an arched ceiling a hundred feet high. The giant launch deck reached into the fortress island nearly five hundred feet with numerous passages leading out, some sized for men and others large enough to accommodate the passage of wyverns.

"This is the eastern launch deck," Wren said. "There are four in the island. Each can launch up to five Sky Knights at once but usually they only launch two at a time."

Motion over the ocean caught their attention, and Wren pointed excitedly. "Look! There's a patrol coming in."

Two wyverns glided gracefully toward the gaping opening in the side of the fortress island. They were separated by about fifty feet, with the one on the right slightly behind the other. Mounted on each was an armored Sky Knight. From the floor below, a horn sounded and a number of men took positions on the side of the deck. The two wyverns coasted in under the cover of the giant vaulted ceiling, flaring their wings to slow themselves before landing gently in the middle of the deck.

Teams of handlers raced to each of the giant flying steeds. The Sky Knights dismounted and gave their wyverns an affectionate pat on the neck before heading off the deck, unbuckling their armor as they walked stiffly toward the barracks built into the sides of the giant chamber.

The handlers went to work quickly. They removed the tack and saddles and gave each wyvern the hindquarter from some large beast. The wyverns ate their snacks in one bite but didn't seem to pose a threat to the handlers. They behaved much the way a well-trained horse does with a familiar stable master.

Until now Isabel had never thought about the graceful beauty of the beasts. When they were trying to kill her, she saw them as monsters. Now, they were nothing short of magnificent. They had long powerful necks that met their bodies where their broad, leathery wings extended from the shoulder. Their rear legs were powerful and ended in talons that could grasp prey much like a raptor. They were easily big enough to snatch a full-grown horse from a field and carry it off without ever touching the ground. Their tails were long and powerful, ending with a flat-bladed bone spike. From nose to tail each beast was at least eighty feet long, with wings spanning over fifty feet when fully extended.

As the two wyverns returned to their stables, another two were led out of the interior of the fortress and calmly allowed a team of handlers to saddle and harness them. Once they were ready for their patrol, two Sky Knights dressed in armor came out of the barracks area and carefully checked all of the buckles and clasps. Once they were satisfied, they mounted up and strapped themselves in place. It looked like their armor was designed to strap into the saddle so they couldn't fall off even if they were knocked unconscious. Given how high they flew, it seemed like a reasonable precaution to Isabel.

The departing patrol waited patiently until a horn blew from a position at the edge of the opening. Once the launch signal was given, the wyverns thrust up their wings, lifting themselves and their riders thirty or more feet off the deck. The second flap of their mighty wings sent them forward toward the edge of the launch deck and a fall of a thousand of feet to the ocean below. They locked their wings into a soaring position and slipped out into the sky not ten feet off the deck where they passed the edge.

It all seemed so routine and yet so breathtakingly awesome at the same time.

"How many wyverns live here?" Isabel asked with just a hint of awe in her voice.

"Last count was four hundred and thirty-eight, but there's a brood of eggs that should hatch any day now," Wren said. "There are five Sky Knights who've lost their steeds in the past several weeks. They'll get the first chance to bond with a newborn. After that, the senior trainees will vie for the rest. Those selected by the remaining newborns will be promoted to the rank of Sky Knight. Those who are not selected will be given another chance with the next brood."

"How many trainees are there?" Abigail asked.

"Right now there are twenty-eight," Wren said. "But the triumvirate just announced an expansion of the training academy and ordered the breeders to increase the number of wyverns allowed to mate. Our biggest constraint is space. The wyverns can breed more quickly than the academy can train new Sky Knights, especially since we have a limited population to choose from. Aside from that, we only have space for five hundred wyverns at the most."

"They're impressive creatures," Abigail said. "It must be a thrilling experience to ride one."

Wren nodded with excitement. "During festival, the Sky Knights give people rides just so we can see what it's like. Last summer I got to go up. It was amazing. I've never felt so free in all my life."

They heard boots on the stairs behind them and turned to see three Sky Knights approaching. They looked angry.

Chapter 4

"What is your purpose here?" the first demanded. Isabel recognized him from the dining hall.

Wren looked timid and afraid but didn't back down. "We were just watching the patrols launch," she said.

"Silence, girl! I wasn't talking to you!"

Wren seemed to withdraw into herself as she stepped back. Her face went scarlet.

Isabel and Abigail positioned themselves so they would be ready to fight if it came to that. They were trapped. The staircase in front of them was filled with three big men wearing armor and armed with short swords. The low wall to their back was the only thing standing between them and a fall of seventy feet.

Isabel stood tall and didn't flinch despite the hammering in her chest. "As she said, we were watching the patrols arrive and depart."

"You have no business here," the Sky Knight said. It was clear that he was the leader. The other two stood behind him just at the top of the staircase and remained silent.

"I wasn't aware this was a restricted area," Isabel said.

He looked a bit flustered but quickly regained his sense of moral outrage. "You should still be locked in a cell," he said. "You and your accomplices killed two of my friends and my steed."

"They'd still be alive if they hadn't attacked us," Abigail said.

Isabel cringed inwardly. Abigail was sometimes a bit too brash. These men were caught up in their grief and anger. They were spoiling for a fight and Isabel was hoping to talk them out of it.

"You trespassed on the Reishi Isle," he shouted. "You should have all been killed!"

"The triumvirate thinks differently," Isabel said calmly. "Mistress Magda assured us that we would be treated as guests. Are you trying to make a liar out of her?"

He started to say something but stopped short while glaring at her with pure hatred. "Maybe you're just clumsy and you fell," he said with an undercurrent of menace. "It's a long way down and no one here would much care if you two turned up dead."

He reached for Isabel. Rather than back away from him as he expected, she stepped into his guard and grabbed his wrist, pulling him closer as she slipped her knife free and brought the point up to his throat. In the same moment, Abigail stepped past him and kicked one of his friends in the chest, sending him tumbling down the stairs. Then she deftly drew the leader's short sword from his scabbard while Isabel held him at knife point.

When the third man drew his sword, Isabel shifted the leader between herself and him, then walked him backwards into his friend. She released his arm as he lost his balance and the two of them tumbled down the long staircase.

Isabel and Abigail raced down the steps with Wren in tow. Isabel scooped up one of the guards' short swords as it clattered to a stop at the base of the stairs. All three men were injured and bruised—one had a broken arm—but they were all still alive.

Wren backed up against the wall at the base of the stairs as Isabel and Abigail surveyed the men. The first staggered to his feet and reached for his sword but it wasn't there. Abigail grinned and waggled the short sword at him mockingly. A mixture of hatred and embarrassment contorted his face. He snatched the sword from the scabbard of his broken-armed friend and faced them, just as Mistress Constance rounded the corner behind him.

"Warrick!" she shouted.

He stiffened but didn't turn his back on Isabel and Abigail.

Constance stalked past him and stopped in the space between the points of raised blades, surveying the situation with a calm air of command.

"They attacked us," Warrick said. "I claim the right of challenge."

"Silence," Constance said calmly. She turned to Wren. "What is your name, child?"

"I'm called Wren, Mistress," she said with wide eyes and a bit of a tremor in her voice.

"You're Tovi's daughter."

"Yes, Mistress."

"Tell me what happened here. Speak only truth," Constance commanded with calm assurance.

"Yes, Mistress," Wren said. "Our guests asked that I show them the island. I brought them here to watch the patrols. It's one of my favorite places, so I thought they would like it. Knight Warrick and his men came up the stairs behind us and threatened to throw them off the balcony."

"You lie, girl," Warrick shouted.

Constance slowly turned a glare on Warrick and he shrank back a bit and fell silent.

"Please continue, Wren," Constance said gently.

"Knight Warrick reached for Lady Isabel's throat, but she and Lady Abigail were faster. They knocked them down the stairs and took their swords. Knight Warrick regained his feet and drew his friend's sword just as you came around the corner."

"You're a traitor, girl," Warrick growled.

Wren swallowed hard and seemed to shrink in on herself again.

"Lady Isabel, do you agree with Wren's account?" Constance asked.

Isabel lowered her sword and looked Constance in the eye. "Yes," she said calmly but firmly.

Constance appraised her for a moment. She was clearly a woman accustomed to command. With a nod she turned her back to Isabel and Abigail and faced the three Sky Knights.

"I understand your anger, Warrick, but your actions are unacceptable. First, Lady Isabel and Lady Abigail are guests by order of the triumvirate. If you or any of your associates cause them to feel unwelcome in any way, I will see to it that you never ride again. Second, Wren is under my protection. Harm her and I will challenge you myself to single combat." She paused to drive home the likely outcome of such a challenge. From the look on his face it was clear that he understood. "Third, you attacked a force of unknown capability from a position of weakness. That was foolish. Learn from the mistakes you made here today. Now, take your men and attend to your injuries. I will accept the bruises to your bodies and your pride as sufficient reprimand for your transgressions."

Constance turned to Isabel and Abigail. "Please, return their weapons to them. You have my word they will not bother you again."

Isabel and Abigail flipped the swords around and held out the hilts for the Sky Knights to take. Warrick gave them a look of smoldering hate. His friends looked more embarrassed than anything. Mistress Constance watched them hobble off down the hall until they turned the corner before she faced Isabel and Abigail again.

"Warrick lost his steed attempting to stop your husband from entering the Reishi Keep," Constance said matter-of-factly. "Two of his close friends never returned from that battle. He feels guilt that he was not at their side when they fell and grief for their loss. I say these things not to excuse his actions but to explain them. If you choose to take this matter to the triumvirate, as is your right, they will be punished severely."

"I don't think that will be necessary," Isabel said. "But hear me clearly, Mistress Constance, Wren has offered us her friendship freely and honestly. I will not have her harmed for being my friend. I will view any retaliation against her as an attack against me and mine and respond accordingly."

Constance smiled gently. "Then it would seem that she has two protectors." With that, she turned on her heel and strode off down the hall.

Wren was quiet as she led them back to their quarters. When they arrived at the door she stopped and looked up timidly, her wispy hair floating around her head like a halo. She was clearly shaken by the violent turn the evening had taken.

"Thank you," she said. "I'm honored to have you as friends."

Isabel smiled. "Thank you, Wren. We're a long way from home and this would be a very lonely place without you."

Abigail gave her a hug, then held her out at arm's length. "If anybody gives you any trouble, you let us know right away."

Wren nodded seriously.

Abigail smiled. "Good night, Wren."

They bolted the door to their quarters and did a quick sweep of their rooms to ensure that they were alone. Isabel went out onto the balcony and found Slyder perched on the railing. She rubbed under his chin and he leaned into her affections.

"It's going to be a long night," she said softly. "We have some work to do before we can rest."

Slyder stood and unfurled his wings to stretch before taking flight.

"What do you have in mind?" Abigail asked.

"I'm going to look in on the witches," Isabel said. "Wren said they're gathering tonight. I want to know what they're up to."

She took a seat in one of the comfortable low chairs in the sitting room and relaxed. As she had so many times in the past, she tipped her head back, closed her eyes, and linked her mind with Slyder. A moment later she was soaring high over the ocean, gradually gaining altitude in wide circles. She reached the level of the plateau top and still she climbed. Fires surrounding the gathering place of the witches came into view. Isabel circled silently a hundred feet overhead, watching as the witches gathered.

They assembled in a circular amphitheatre. A well filled to the brim with still water occupied the center. The top ring of the seven steps leading down to the well was flush with the ground. Each ring was three feet wide and three feet deeper into the ground than the one encircling it. Torches burned brightly around the outer ring, but the light dimmed toward the center.

Magda, Cassandra, and Gabriella, each wearing a simple white robe, stood in a triangle around the well. On each of the steps radiating away from the central well stood a ring of women. There wasn't a single man anywhere on the surface of the entire plateau. Once the women had all assembled, over a hundred in total, they began chanting in unison. It was a light and airy verse that they repeated over and over. Isabel thought she could feel the power being drawn to them and focused into the three at the center of the coven.

Magda, Cassandra, and Gabriella joined hands and started chanting another verse. The power reverberated through the air with every word. Isabel circled higher and remained silent.

The night-black surface of the water in the well began to shimmer, slightly at first, and then it started to glow. The witches all around continued chanting, but the triumvirs fell silent, continuing to hold each other's hands and forming a triangle over the well with their arms.

The surface shifted and moved as the three witches focused the power of their entire coven into their spell. Gradually the surface of the water began to reveal an image. It was blurry and unfocused at first but became sharper as the seconds passed.

Isabel almost lost her connection with Slyder when she realized the image was of Alexander. He was sitting at a table inside a large tent. To his right were Jack and the man who'd been hunting them for months, Jataan P'Tal.

Around his neck, Alexander wore a glowing blood-red ruby cut into a teardrop shape and suspended from a heavy gold chain. Isabel had to remind herself to remain detached. She was almost overpowered with relief at the sight of her love alive and well.

The view shifted and a man wearing a breastplate and sitting on Alexander's left came into focus. He was a good-looking man with strong features, fair hair, and grey eyes. Isabel looked closer through the keen eyes of her forest hawk and saw the crest emblazoned on his breastplate. It was the family crest of the House of Ithilian.

Alexander had gone to Ithilian.

The witches seemed satisfied with the results and allowed the spell to lapse. The water went dark and the women began to disperse without a word.

Isabel returned to her own body and opened her eyes. Abigail was sitting in a chair nearby waiting patiently.

"He's alive and well on Ithilian," she said with a broad smile.

Abigail took a deep breath and released it slowly as she closed her eyes. "Ithilian has the only other Thinblade known to exist. That would make them powerful allies."

Isabel nodded. "There's more. Jataan P'Tal and Jack were sitting to his right. Jack looks good, by the way," she said with a knowing smile.

Abigail almost blushed before she changed the subject. "How could you tell they were on Ithilian?"

"The other man at the table wore the Ithilian family crest," Isabel answered and then fixed Abigail with a deadly serious look. "Alexander is wearing the Sovereign Stone and it's glowing."

Abigail closed her eyes and shook her head. "I have met the enemy and it is me," she whispered.

"Nonsense," Isabel replied. "Your blood has nothing to do with the quality of your character. Alexander has a good heart. I know that with the same certainty that I know water is wet."

"I don't doubt Alexander," Abigail said. "I've just spent the past several months running from the Reishi only to discover that I am Reishi. It's a lot to take in."

"This may be the best news we could have gotten," Isabel said. "If Alexander can access the knowledge and wisdom of the Stone, we might be able to turn the tables on Phane. At the very least, it looks like Alexander has a battle mage watching his back."

"Provided Commander P'Tal can be trusted," Abigail said cynically.

"I think he serves the Reishi," Isabel said. "If that's the case, then Alexander is his master. If Alexander can forgive him, then I can."

"He's the one who sent the assassin to kill Darius," Abigail said. "It'll take me some time to get used to the idea of forgiveness. That's never been one of my strong suits."

As they retired for the night, Isabel felt more hope than she had in quite some time. With certainty about Alexander's well-being and confirmation that he had bonded with the Stone came a sense of calm purpose.

She was Lady Reishi.

Her duty to the people of the Seven Isles had just magnified and multiplied. She could no longer think in terms of protecting only the people of Ruatha. She had an obligation to safeguard the lives and liberty of every innocent person in the entire Seven Isles. She drifted off to sleep with the firm resolve to bring an army of Sky Knights to her husband's side.

Chapter 5

They started early the next day. Isabel made it a priority to learn as much as possible about the workings of the fortress island. She and Abigail explored the place in a methodical way, both to familiarize themselves with the layout and to determine any military vulnerability. She was both impressed and concerned that she couldn't find any significant weakness.

The entire island was nearly completely self-sufficient. The only real exception was the meat brought in by hunting parties of Sky Knights that snatched up bison from the range on the Reishi Isle. Aside from that and the fish they caught, everything else was produced within the giant stone plateau. The gardens on the top were efficient and well tended. There were several openings at the water level that allowed for fishing boats to come and go with ease. The vessels were mostly sturdy longboats designed for use in the immediate area—they weren't suitable for travel across the open ocean.

Isabel wanted to talk to the triumvirate but she was politely informed that they were too busy to see her. Witches of lower rank seemed to regard them with curiosity, although they wouldn't engage in any form of meaningful conversation.

Few of the Sky Knights would talk to them and the ones that did weren't interested in having a conversation either. It was clear that the majority of the people in important positions regarded them as the enemy, but then they were so isolated that they had no doubt formed an "us versus them" mentality regarding the entire Seven Isles.

The serving staff and trade class that kept the island running smoothly were far more friendly and forthcoming. Aside from those directly involved with the mission of the fortress island, the rest of the people were just living their lives in the only community they'd ever known.

Through Wren they learned about the political structure of the fortress island. The triumvirs were the highest authority on the island. They commanded the coven and the Sky Knights as well as set and enforced the laws of the community. Each triumvir won her seat by challenging and defeating a sitting triumvir. In this way they ensured that the most powerful of the coven were the leaders. The witches served as constables and arbitrators. They were widely regarded as wise, evenhanded, and fair in their judgments.

The Sky Knights were commanded by witches as well. The Air Commander was in charge of the entire army and all of the support personnel necessary to care for the wyverns. Subordinate to her were four Flight Commanders, each in command of about a hundred Sky Knights. Each flight had four wings of about twenty-five led by a Wing Commander. Within each wing were a number of squads which were typically led by Sky Knights or witches chosen for the position based on demonstrated merit.

They were a well-ordered and disciplined military force that clearly took great pride in their capability. The more she learned about their history and sense of duty, the more Isabel came to understand the shame they felt for letting the

Sovereign Stone return to the Seven Isles. They had a long tradition of seeing themselves as the guardians of the world against the tyranny of the Reishi. Their entire reason for existence was to prevent Phane from getting the Sovereign Stone. They had long believed that he would be unable to retrieve the Stone from the aether. The wild card that Alexander represented had dealt a serious blow to their confidence and wounded their pride. It was clear to Isabel that they would go to great lengths to redeem themselves.

She worried about that. They knew where Alexander was and might take it upon themselves to confront him. She couldn't be certain how that confrontation might end, but she suspected that the witches would not be happy with the outcome. Alexander's power was growing. With the Sovereign Stone and the Reishi Protectorate behind him, he was a significant threat. Added to that was the high likelihood that he would be successful at negotiating an alliance with Ithilian. The combined forces of Ithilian and Ruatha would be formidable. Isabel only hoped that she could convince at least two of the triumvirs of the wisdom of an alliance.

Wren had become a constant companion and a genuine friend. She was very naïve, but she had a heart as big as a house and was eager to hear any story of the Seven Isles that Isabel or Abigail was willing to tell. Occasionally, they would catch her singing softly under her breath as she went about her tasks. She had a clear and bright voice with perfect pitch and excellent range.

At dinner several days after they were given their new quarters, Wren seemed hesitant about something. When Isabel asked if she'd been threatened, she shook her head emphatically.

"No one has bothered me since that day," she said. "I think Mistress Constance made it known that I was to be left alone. Since she's a Flight Commander, her word counts a lot, especially with the Sky Knights."

"You seem nervous about something," Abigail said.

"I'm more excited than nervous," Wren said. "The eggs are hatching. Already the first five have chosen. I think the rest will hatch tonight and I want to go watch." She stopped herself short as if she had revealed too much.

"May we come?" Isabel asked.

"Of course, but please don't tell anyone," Wren said. "I know a place where we can see the hatchery. I don't think anyone else knows about it, and I'm not really supposed to be watching."

Isabel and Abigail chuckled softly. "Your secret is safe with us," Isabel said. "Would you get in serious trouble if we got caught?"

Wren shrugged. "I don't know. They might be pretty mad but there aren't any laws against it, so I think they would just close off access and give me some extra work to do for a while."

***

She led them through a winding series of passages and corridors until they came to a door that looked like it was seldom used. Wren was careful to look both ways to ensure that no one would see them enter before pushing the door open and slipping into the dark room. She held her candle higher to illuminate a storage room lined with shelves filled with sealed containers of food. She threaded her way through the shelves until she came to the far corner. She carefully pulled a bin out from under the shelving and set it aside. There was a crack in the wall beyond. It was about two feet wide and only four feet high.

"It's kind of a tight fit," Wren said. "And we have to douse the light, so it'll be really dark until we get to the hatchery. Please be as quiet as possible so they don't hear us." With that, she squatted down and made her way into the darkness.

The passage led through the solid stone of the fortress island for several dozen feet and made a sharp turn before opening onto a ten-foot-wide natural stone shelf that jutted six or seven feet out from the wall. Past the edge of the shelf, the stone sloped down at a steep angle into a large chamber about forty feet below. It was a natural cave that had been adapted to the purpose of birthing wyverns.

The circular floor was about a hundred feet across. The walls sloped up and away from the floor to the ceiling nearly eighty feet above. Oil lamps on high posts formed a ring around the entire chamber. In the center was a clutch of very large eggs surrounded by a ring of stones. A number of hopeful trainees stood around the clutch of eggs, waiting for the next one to hatch.

At the entrance to the room on the far wall stood a number of Sky Knights, handlers, and a woman who wore the same rank insignia as Mistress Constance. They watched for a few moments before one of the eggs started rocking back and forth. A crack formed and the egg toppled over, abruptly widening the crack and releasing the baby wyvern within.

It flopped around as it tried to make its legs work, then stumbled out of the ring of stones and past the first hopeful trainee. He shied away as the baby wyvern squawked at him. The other trainees shifted position to form a circle around the hatchling. They kept a distance of about ten feet and were very disciplined in their behavior. They didn't try to draw the wyvern's attention but instead waited for the wyvern to choose. They didn't have long to wait. After a bit of clumsy stumbling around, the baby locked eyes with one of the trainees. The young man smiled with pure joy and walked straight up to the wyvern. The baby nuzzled him on the chest and he led his new steed to the entrance where he was congratulated by the Sky Knights and assigned to a squad. He led his wyvern out of the hatchery, and the remaining trainees returned to their posts around the clutch of eggs, waiting for another to hatch.

Isabel shared a look with Abigail and they both looked over at Wren. She had an expression of pure joy. Her eyes sparkled and she was smiling gently.

Two more eggs started to move. The trainees held their positions, waiting for the hatchlings to emerge. As the first egg cracked, Isabel and Abigail both heard a noise behind them. They turned and saw a man with a sword. He said nothing as he lunged at Abigail.

She was sitting cross-legged, close to the edge of the stone shelf. As the tip of the blade came for her, she twisted and lay over to avoid the strike. At the same time, she grabbed the man by the wrist and pulled, remembering Anatoly's training in hand-to-hand combat. He always told her to use an enemy's weight and motion against them. She pulled with all her might and spun her feet around to kick at the man's shins. He toppled over on top of her and went over the edge, but not before grabbing a handful of Abigail's tunic and dragging her over with him.

They slid down the steep sloping wall of the hatchery, struggling to right themselves so they would land on their feet instead of their heads. As they slid, two eggs cracked open and two baby wyverns stumbled out into the world. The trainees were torn between the two new hatchlings and the commotion at the edge of the chamber.

Wren sat in wide-eyed shock at the suddenness of the attack.

Isabel drew her knife and slipped over the edge, sliding to the floor below so she could stand with her sister.

Abigail and her attacker regained their feet at the same time. He still had his short sword. She drew her knife and backed away from him toward the center of the chamber. There was shouting off in the distance. Sky Knights started running toward the intruders.

The attacker charged Abigail. She blocked his slashing strike, but just barely. Rather than engage, she spun away from him and ran for the center of the chamber, hoping the onrushing Sky Knights would protect her from the sudden attack.

Isabel landed and rolled to her feet. She didn't call out to their attacker but instead charged him from behind. He heard her footsteps and whirled to meet the attack but was just a moment too slow. Her attempt to stab him in the lung from behind slashed his arm as he spun. He couldn't get his sword around fast enough but he was able to land a hard backhand.

She went down but regained her feet quickly, coming up in a crouch to face him. Abigail stopped and whirled around to see Isabel and the man squaring off. She heard the shouts of running Sky Knights and the squawk of a baby wyvern behind her as she charged back toward the enemy.

He turned to face her rather than expose his side by attacking Isabel. Isabel circled as the man with the sword lunged at Abigail. She blocked the stabbing strike with her knife but left herself open for the thrust-kick he delivered into her abdomen. She fell backward, doubled over and gasping for breath. Isabel charged again but she was just a step too far away to land a solid blow. He raised his sword for a kill strike against Abigail when the entire chamber filled with brilliant light. The Flight Commander stood at the edge of the ring of stones with her hand outstretched. A bolt of white-hot fiery magical energy stabbed out from her hand and burned a hole three inches in diameter through the man's chest where his heart used to be. He stumbled backward and collapsed.

There was a moment of stillness. Isabel sheathed her knife and raised her open hands as she started forward. One of the hatchlings had stumbled through the ring of trainees and clumsily made its way straight toward Abigail. When she opened her eyes, the baby wyvern was looking straight at her from a distance of about a foot.

Her vision cleared and they locked eyes. A sudden and unexpected feeling of protectiveness and love for the hatchling washed over her. In spite of her pain, she rolled onto her knees and smiled at her new steed. It nuzzled her and she gently hugged its head to her breast. When she looked up, there was a cordon of Sky Knights surrounding her and Isabel.

The Flight Commander strode through the circle of armored men and stopped a few feet from Abigail. The commander was tall and stocky for a woman. Her hair was dirty-blond and braided. Her eyes were dark brown and her face was tan and weathered. She appraised the situation for only a moment before she nodded.

"I am Mistress Bianca. You have much to explain, but right now you must feed your hatchling. This is Knight Raja. He is your squad leader and will teach you how to care for your wyvern. The first days of a wyvern's life are critical. Go with him and do as you're told."

Abigail blinked in surprise but then she looked at her hatchling. He was ugly and gangly but she realized she loved the beast and would do whatever she could to protect him. She looked at Isabel, who nodded for her to go with the Sky Knight.

She got to her feet with a wince from the pain in her gut and turned to Knight Raja. He stood about six feet tall and had a stocky build. His arms and chest were muscular and he wore a neatly cropped beard on his strong jaw. He appraised Abigail for a long moment.

"Come with me," he said. "Your wyvern will follow." He turned on his heel and strode off with Abigail and her hatchling in tow.

Mistress Bianca turned and faced Isabel. "Explain your presence here."

"We were watching the hatching," Isabel said.

"From where, exactly?" Bianca asked. "This chamber is supposed to be closed except for the main entrance."

"There's a stone shelf about forty feet up the wall," Isabel said pointing. "Abigail and I were watching the eggs hatch when we were attacked by surprise." Her mind was racing. The attack could not have been random. He had to have followed them. Then there was Wren—Isabel had given her word that she would keep the young woman's secret.

"I see," Bianca said looking up to the platform above. "How did you get there?"

"There's a crack leading from a storeroom to the platform," Isabel answered without elaborating.

"How did you come to discover this in the few days you have been permitted to roam our halls freely?" Bianca asked.

Isabel looked her directly in the eye and said, "I prefer not to say."

Bianca frowned like a woman who was unaccustomed to being refused. "Ah," she said with sudden understanding. "Mistress Constance told me you've befriended your serving girl. She will not be punished, although her secret passage will be sealed."

"Who is this man?" Isabel asked, pointing to the dead man who had tried to kill them.

"He is one of the trade class," Bianca said. "I don't know his name, but I will before nightfall. You will be required to provide a full report of this incident to a constable. She will determine if any sanctions are warranted."

Isabel nodded. "I will honor your law. And what about Abigail? What happens to her?"

Bianca shrugged. "She will be trained as a Sky Knight."

"I don't understand," Isabel said. "We've been treated like pariah by the Sky Knights since we got here and just like that you accept her into your ranks?"

"She's bonded with a wyvern," Bianca said. "Our law is clear. Wyvern hatchlings choose their riders. The circumstances of the bonding are unimportant. I suspect there will be those who object, but short of intervention by the triumvirate, the hatchling's choice is final."

Isabel smiled. "Good. I'm confident that Abigail will make an excellent Sky Knight. Thank you for saving her life. I'm afraid I was a step too slow to stop him."

"You're welcome," Bianca said. "I'm told you are a queen and Abigail is a princess. It would not do to have either of you murdered while you are guests of the Reishi Coven."

A Sky Knight escorted Isabel back to her quarters. Abigail wasn't there, but Wren was waiting in the sitting room. She shot to her feet when the door opened. The look of panic and worry on her face turned frantic when only Isabel entered.

"Where's Abigail?" she said. "Is she hurt?"

Isabel smiled reassuringly. "Abigail's fine, maybe a little beaten up but she'll be all right."

"I was so worried," Wren said. "I don't know how that man knew where we were or why he tried to kill you." She looked down. "I'm sorry I ran. But I didn't know what I could do to help you."

"Hush, it's all right," Isabel said. "You didn't do anything wrong. I'm afraid Mistress Bianca figured out your secret passage though. I suspect they'll seal it off."

Wren nodded. "I don't care about that, I'm just glad you and Abigail are okay."

"I do have good news," Isabel said. "At least I think it's good news. Abigail bonded with a wyvern. Mistress Bianca says she'll be trained as a Sky Knight."

Wren looked at her with stunned amazement. "That's wonderful! I'm so happy for her."

"Me too," Isabel said. "Now, it's late. Your parents are probably wondering where you are. Go home and we'll talk more tomorrow. I'm sure Abigail will have some stories to tell us about her new friend."

Chapter 6

Alexander strode into the permanent encampment with Conner Ithilian at his side and a throng of people following behind. It was a well-ordered and clean camp. Roads were clearly marked and well traveled. Oilskin tents were lined up in neat rows and organized in clusters. The soldiers were well equipped with serviceable-looking weapons and armor that was well maintained. These men were disciplined soldiers who took their profession seriously.

Conner led them to the center of the camp and ordered an officer to provide tents for Alexander's Rangers and offered Alexander his father's tent. Apparently it was customary for deployed legions to maintain a well-appointed command tent in the event that the King arrived unannounced. It was a comfortable tent easily big enough to house a dozen men or more. A large bed sat opposite the entrance and the floor was lined with carpets. There was a table and furnishings but the place was cold and unused. Clearly it had sat empty for many months. Alexander had Lucky put Anatoly in the bed and ordered Boaberous to remain with them. Then he and Jataan and Jack went to the command tent to talk with Conner.

Conner was waiting with the mage and another man dressed in full battle armor.

"Please, share a meal with us," Conner said, motioning to the table as they entered. "I'll have food delivered to your tent for your men, and my healer will see if he can assist your injured friend."

Alexander took the seat at the head of the table which drew a look from the older man in plate armor, but no objection. Jataan and Jack took seats to his right. Conner sat at Alexander's left, followed by the mage and general.

"Lord Reishi, allow me to introduce Mage Dax, my chief advisor, and General Brand, my Second," Conner said.

"Thank you for your hospitality, Prince Conner," Alexander said. "This is Jataan P'Tal, General Commander of the Reishi Protectorate, and Master Jack Colton, the Bard of Ruatha." At the mention of Jataan P'Tal's name, Mage Dax stiffened perceptibly and his colors flared with anxiety. Commander P'Tal was known to the man. Alexander decided to ignore the concern for now in the hopes that their conversation would ease any tensions.

"It has been many generations since anyone came through the Reishi Gate," Conner said. "We were expecting an all-out invasion. When we saw a small party come through, we feared that Phane had come to force our hand. In truth, I don't know what to make of your arrival."

Alexander smiled and nodded. Conner Ithilian's colors were clear and steady. He was a man who spoke his mind without guile or apology. Alexander decided he liked him.

"I come in search of allies against Phane," Alexander said. "War has broken out across the Seven Isles. No corner of the world will be spared. Those who love life and liberty must stand together, or the future will suffer greatly for our failure."

"I have many questions that must be answered before I can take you to meet my father," Conner said.

"Ask what you will, I will answer what I can," Alexander said.

"If I may," Mage Dax said.

Conner nodded.

"It is well known that the Sovereign Stone was lost during the Reishi War. How has it come to be in your possession?"

Alexander smiled gently. He had asked Chloe to remain hidden when they arrived. He spoke to her without speaking. "I believe a grand entrance is in order, Little One."

In the center of the table she buzzed into a bright, scintillating ball of light and materialized in midair. She hovered two feet off the table, surveying the representatives of Ithilian before she locked eyes with an astonished Mage Dax.

"Hello, Mage," Chloe said. "My Love asked me to bring the Sovereign Stone out of the aether, so I did."

Mage Dax blinked several times as if he wasn't quite sure that what he was seeing was real. Chloe flew over, landed on Alexander's shoulder and sat down cross-legged.

"You're a fairy," Mage Dax whispered with an undercurrent of awe.

Conner and General Brand sat stock-still.

Chloe shrugged. "Of course I'm a fairy."

Alexander smiled slightly.

"How can this be?" Mage Dax asked. "The fairies withdrew from the world after the Reishi War. No mortal has even reported seeing a fairy in the past two thousand years, let alone bonding with one as a familiar."

"My Love convinced my mother that the world needed our assistance," Chloe said. "I volunteered to sacrifice my immortality for the opportunity to experience mortal love." She looked at Alexander with a smile. "I am very happy with my choice."

General Brand spoke into the stunned silence. He was a big man, gruff and plainspoken, clearly an experienced combat soldier with many years of command. He reminded Alexander a bit of Anatoly. "Our reports say that the Reishi Protectorate is serving Phane. How is it that the General Commander of the Reishi Protectorate is here with you if you are not in league with Phane?" There was no anger or antagonism in his tone, just the matter-of-fact question of a general officer.

Alexander nodded to Jataan to answer the question.

He cleared his throat. "I serve the Reishi Sovereign. Until last night I believed that Prince Phane was the last of the Reishi line and performed my duties accordingly. When I saw Lord Reishi take possession of the Sovereign Stone, I realized my error. At this time I have not yet had an opportunity to communicate the truth of the situation to the soldiers and agents of the Reishi Protectorate, so they are still acting on behalf of Prince Phane."

"How is it that you were able to bond with the Stone?" Mage Dax asked.

"The Reishi are a branch of the Ruathan line," Alexander said. "I am of the Ruathan bloodline and so I am also Reishi."

"I see," Dax said. "Prince Conner, I believe we have ample evidence of

Lord Reishi's truthfulness. And the fact that he has bonded with a fairy is proof positive of his moral character. I recommend we make haste for the palace in the morning."

Conner nodded and stood up, offering Alexander his hand in friendship. When Alexander stood to shake his hand, his cloak slipped off the hilt of the Thinblade. Conner's eyes went wide and his hand went to his sword.

"You have my father's sword," he said with alarm.

Mage Dax stood, quickly muttering the words of a spell. General Brand drew his sword, and Jataan P'Tal suddenly had a knife in each hand.

"Stop!" Alexander commanded. Everyone froze. He unbuckled his belt and held the hilt of the Thinblade out to Conner.

"Have you ever held your father's sword?" Alexander asked.

Conner frowned and nodded.

"How did it feel?"

Conner hesitated for a moment. "Like it was made for my hand."

Alexander nodded knowingly. "Grasp the hilt of my sword, but do not draw the blade."

Conner's frown deepened but he did as he was told. When he grasped the hilt, an unsettled look ghosted across his face and he released it quickly.

"It feels like a snake writhing in my grasp."

"That's because this is the Ruathan Thinblade. This sword is bound to my line just as your father's sword is bound to yours."

"My apologies, Lord Reishi," Conner said. "It looks exactly like my father's sword. When I saw it, I feared the worst."

"You're right to be cautious," Alexander said, extending his hand to Conner.

They spent an hour sharing a meal. Conversation revolved around the histories and traditions of Ithilian and Ruatha. Both islands were similar in size and resources. Ithilian had vast farm and range land. They grew grains and vegetables, cultivated orchards and vineyards that covered miles of hillsides, and raised beef, bison, and sheep. In the high central mountains, they mined iron, copper, and silver. In the west, they quarried fine marble. The people were prosperous and industrious. They had a united government that recognized the sovereignty of the Old Law and respected the individual.

Conner spoke of the political infighting that was a staple at court but dismissed the power of the political class to do any real damage to the well-being of the people because of the protections of the monarchy. Alexander wanted to hear more about their system of government, but the meal ended and he had other things to do that were more pressing.

He retired to his tent and found Anatoly sleeping soundly. Lucky said that a healer of considerable power had visited and cast a number of spells over the big man-at-arms. He was optimistic about Anatoly's recovery and believed he would be able to ride by morning. After a brief discussion about the events of the evening, Alexander laid out his bedroll next to the bed.

Jataan frowned and stepped forward. "Surely, you're not going to sleep on the floor when there's a bed for you to use."

"Anatoly needs it more than I do," Alexander said as he pulled up a carpet to reveal the dirt below. He positioned a meditation pillow and carefully drew a magic circle around it.

"You are Lord Reishi," Jataan said.

"So? Anatoly needs it more," Alexander replied. "I'll be fine on the floor. I'm going to meditate for a while before bed. See to it that someone checks on Lieutenant Wyatt."

Chloe buzzed into existence and flitted up to eye level. "Are you going to leave again, My Love?"

"Yes, Little One," Alexander said. "The magic circle will protect me from wandering spirits."

"I know, but I still don't like it when you leave. I feel lonely when you're gone."

"I have to do this, Chloe," Alexander said. "I need information and Ruatha needs to know that I have the Stone. If they believe Phane has it, they may do something unwise."

"I understand," she said as she landed on his knee. "I just don't like it." She sat down cross-legged and looked up at him.

Alexander smiled at her and closed his eyes. With his all around sight, he could see Jataan P'Tal watch him for a long moment before sending Grudge to check on the Rangers.

Alexander cleared his mind. He had a lot of thoughts insisting on his attention, but he put them aside one by one and found that place of empty-mindedness that led to the firmament. When he found his awareness floating on the ocean of potential, he listened to the song of creation for a moment. What he heard made him anxious. There was greater discord and fear in the collective consciousness of the world than he had ever heard before. He suspected the increased angst was the result of the armies that had just invaded Ruatha and Fellenden.

He coalesced his awareness high above the Reishi Gate on Ruatha. What he saw intensified his anxiety. There was an army of at least ten legions of Reishi Army Regency. They had come through the Gate the night before and were busy establishing a defensive encampment and organizing for an attack.

Alexander moved his focus to Blackstone Keep. The world rushed by with impossible speed and abruptly he was in Kelvin's workshop. The Mage was nowhere to be seen. He floated over to his message board. There were two numbered messages.

"Isabel and Abigail have been taken by the Reishi Coven. I have assurances that they are both alive and well. I have sent an item of great power that I believe is Isabel's best hope for surviving the poison."

Alexander read the message twice. The weight of worry that had burdened him since he last saw his wife and sister lifted and relief flooded into his soul.

They were alive.

Everything else paled in the face of that one simple truth. He turned his attention to the second message. It was more hastily written.

"The Reishi Army Regency has invaded through the Gate. They are led by three wizards and they have a scourgling. Since the Gates are open, I can only assume that Phane has recovered the Stone. There is great fear within the ranks of your army. Please send word when you see this message."

If the first message lifted his spirits, the second troubled him deeply. A scourgling under the control of an advancing army would be nearly unstoppable. Alone, it might be contained, but with troops behind it, the Ruathan Army would have little chance against it.

He floated in the Mage's workshop for a time, thinking about his options. There was so much to do and all of it was important. He decided to finish with his clairvoyance before pondering his next move. With a thought, he brought his focus into the sleeping room. There were three Rangers sound asleep awaiting his message.

Alexander picked one and gently moved into the sleeping man's consciousness and manifested in his dreams. He found himself standing on a trail in the Great Forest. The Ranger rounded a corner riding hard and came to an abrupt stop in front of Alexander. He dismounted and approached tentatively.

"Ranger, I am Alexander, and I come with messages for the Guild Mage and General Valentine," Alexander said.

"Lord Alexander, I'm happy to see you," the Ranger said. "What messages can I deliver?"

"I have recovered the Sovereign Stone, and much to my surprise, it has bonded with me," Alexander said. "The Gates opened when the Stone came back into the world but I closed them as soon as possible and they are now under my control. The invading army will receive no reinforcements through the Gate. Fellenden has been invaded by Zuhl. I am on Ithilian seeking an alliance. I will send word before I return."

"I will deliver your message, Lord Alexander. Your words will give our soldiers hope," the Ranger said.

"In the battles that come, protect the people. Buildings can be rebuilt," Alexander said and then extracted his awareness from the mind of the sleeping Ranger. He floated up and saw the man come awake and hastily pull on his boots.

Alexander thought of Fellenden and his focus shifted across the entire Seven Isles. The world rushed by impossibly fast and then he was floating high above the island. A great army filled the gently rolling fields surrounding the Gate. They had separated into two forces—two legions surrounded the Gate and eight legions had moved a small distance before making camp for the evening. Alexander wondered what Zuhl wanted with Fellenden. He feared that he would find out all too soon.

Next, he shifted his focus to the Angellica and came to float high over her mast. She was holding position between Ruatha and the Reishi Isle. Alexander pushed into the interior of the ship and found Captain Targa sleeping in his quarters. He gently entered the man's dreams and instructed him to make best speed for Southport. He also told him to inform Kevin of the invasion force that had arrived through the Gate.

He saved his final target for last because he was worried about having his awareness scattered into the firmament. He knew that the fortress island was guarded by magic. If Isabel was there and he tried to look in on her, he would fail. So he focused his awareness on Slyder. Again he moved with terrific speed, stopping abruptly just outside the fortress island. Perched on the railing of a balcony was Slyder.

Alexander carefully drew closer until he was floating just a few feet from the balcony. He peered through the windows and saw Isabel and Abigail sitting at a table with a young woman with wispy dirty-blond hair. They were talking like friends. Alexander spent several minutes simply looking at his wife and sister. They were alive. He couldn't be sure if they were safe, but their room was well appointed and comfortable-looking. They might be prisoners, but they were being treated well.

The weight lifted even more. His greatest worry and all of the uncertainty that went with it vanished and left him with a feeling of hope that swelled within him and buoyed his soul. With a great sense of relief, he returned to his body and opened his eyes.

Lucky was snoring gently. Anatoly was sleeping soundly, as well. Jack sat at the little table working on a story or a song. Jataan sat watching Alexander.

"Isabel and Abigail are alive and well," he said softly.

Jack looked up quickly with hope and expectation.

"I saw them," Alexander said. "They're on the fortress island where the wyvern riders live. They both look well."

Jack closed his eyes tightly for a moment. "Thank you, Alexander. That's wonderful news. I'll sleep much better tonight."

"Lord Reishi," Jataan asked. "Of whom do you speak?"

"My wife and sister were abducted by the wyvern riders that guard the Reishi Isle," Alexander said. "We feared the worst, but I've just seen that they're alive."

"Forgive my inquisitiveness, Lord Reishi, but the more I know the better I can protect you," Jataan said. "Is your wife the one in the light green dress who stood with you on the balcony in New Ruatha when you tried to kill me?"

"That's her," Alexander said with a smile. "Actually, it was her idea to take a shot at you. The Guild Mage tried to talk her out of it, but she wouldn't hear it."

"Then the blond woman who tried to kill me on the glass bridge with her very fast bow is your sister," Jataan said.

Alexander chuckled. "That's Abigail. The bow was a gift from Mage Gamaliel. She's good with a normal bow but with that thing, she's dangerous."

Jataan's face grew grave and serious. "If you say that you can see them at such distances, then I believe you. But if they are at the fortress island, then their safety is in question. The Reishi Coven controls that island and commands the Sky Knights. They were established by Malachi Reishi's wife shortly after the Reishi War to prevent Prince Phane from retrieving the Sovereign Stone. They blame the Reishi for the devastation wrought by the war and seek to prevent it from ever happening again. I have had dealings with them in the past. They are formidable and very dedicated to their duty as they see it. I believe they will attempt to offer your wife and sister in exchange for the Sovereign Stone."

Alexander felt the anxiety flood back into him. "What would they want with the Stone?" Alexander asked. "They can't use it."

"They don't want to use it," Jataan said. "They want to make sure that no one else, especially Prince Phane, ever uses it again. They fear the power it represents and believe that the world would be safer if that power was destroyed."

Alexander shook his head as he remembered a lesson from his childhood. His father said that power is like a hammer. It can be used to beat someone's brains out or it can be used to build a house. The hammer didn't know or care. What really mattered was the intent of the person holding the hammer.

"Will they harm Isabel or Abigail if I refuse?" Alexander asked.

"That's hard to say," Jataan said. "They are ruled by three witches of great power who never make any decision of consequence without the consent of at least two. They may or may not be open to reason. I would recommend a contingency plan."

"Did you have something in mind?" Alexander asked.

"Once we arrive at the capital city of Ithilian, I will call my agents together to swear allegiance to you. I can assess their capability at that time. If they have the necessary talents, I will put together an assault team and send them to retrieve the Lady and Princess Reishi."

Alexander nodded. He wanted to do much the same thing but he had a few other concerns that were more pressing. He felt a pang of guilt at considering anything more important than Isabel and Abigail but quickly reminded himself to be driven by emotion but ruled by reason. As long as they were alive and safe, they were of less urgency than the death and destruction that was about to engulf both Ruatha and Fellenden. He needed to find a way to protect his people from the ambition of two different tyrants.

"Put together your strike force but don't send them without my order," Alexander said. "I would prefer to win the Reishi Coven over to our side than face yet another enemy. We have enough to worry about as it is."

"As you wish, Lord Reishi," Jataan said.

"I'm going to be unavailable for a while," Alexander said. "We'll be leaving early tomorrow, so I suggest everyone get some sleep."

"Where are you going, My Love?" Chloe asked.

Alexander tapped the Stone resting against his chest. "In here. I have some questions and I'm hoping the Reishi Council can answer them. I won't be long."

He touched the Stone and concentrated. It took only a few moments and he was standing in the darkness surrounding the council table. The previous six Reishi sovereigns were all there as if they had never left.

Balthazar stood and smiled at Alexander. "I see that you are still alive and well. How can we help you?"

Alexander sat down and gave the sovereigns a report. "One day has passed. I've closed the Gates and traveled to Ithilian to seek an alliance. A large part of Phane's army on Karth has moved through the Gate into Ruatha and an army from Zuhl has moved into Fellenden. There are a number of important issues that I wanted to discuss with you before I decide what to do next.

"First, my wife and sister were abducted by soldiers riding wyverns. These soldiers call themselves Sky Knights and are commanded by an organization called the Reishi Coven. They are holding Isabel and Abigail against their will on the southernmost fortress island that sits off the coast of the Reishi Isle.

"Second, Malachi created a device called the Nether Gate. As I understand it, this device opens a portal to the netherworld much like the Reishi Gates open a portal between two places in the Seven Isles. The shades are loose in the world and I believe they are trying to find and open this Nether Gate."

Five of the six previous Sovereigns looked stunned. Malachi looked smug. Balthazar broke the long silence that followed.

"How could you be so irresponsible, Malachi?"

Malachi was defiant. "The Seven Isles rebelled against me," he spat. "I had no choice. I needed an army to keep my power."

Demetrius shook his head sadly. "I failed you, my son," he whispered. "And through you I have failed the world."

Darius, the Fourth Sovereign shook his head. "You're wrong, Son. Malachi failed us all. You ruled with wisdom and fealty to the Old law. We can only bear the burden of responsibility for our own choices."

"I'm sure the issue of your wife and sister are more worrisome to you, Alexander, but I believe the issue of this Nether Gate is more urgent," Demetrius said. "I suggest you command Malachi to reveal all he knows about this device."

Alexander turned to a defiant-looking Malachi with a glare. "Tell me all you know about the Nether Gate."

Anger filled Malachi's countenance. "I created it in a secret, underground fortress in the northwest mountains of the Reishi Isle. It has three keystones that must be used together to activate it. Once the portal is open, the one who activated it can call forth any creature from the netherworld. Everything that passes into this world is bound to serve the one who activated the Gate."

"Where are the keystones and what do they look like?" Alexander asked.

"Each is a black stone pyramid three inches on a side," Malachi said through clenched teeth. "Each stone must be physically placed into the Gate itself by the same person in order to open it. Once open, it will remain open until one of the stones is removed. As long as the one who activated the Gate is alive, the portal will only allow creatures that he calls forth to pass. But if the one who activated it dies, then any creature that finds the portal within the netherworld can pass through it without restraint or control. As for where the keystones are," he shrugged indifferently, "how should I know? I've been trapped in the aether for two thousand years. They could be anywhere by now."

Alexander looked at Malachi like he was trying to figure out how to kill someone who was already dead.

The other sovereigns sat staring at Malachi with looks of shock and horror.

"Where were the keystones when you died?" Alexander asked as calmly as he could.

"Two were hidden in the Reishi Keep, the third was secured in a secret chamber inside the fortress where the Gate itself was located," Malachi said.

"So all three are probably still on the Reishi Isle," Alexander said.

Malachi shrugged defiantly. "Could be."

"How do I destroy the Gate?" Alexander asked.

"How should I know," Malachi said. "I never tried to destroy it."

Alexander turned to Balthazar. "Will the Thinblade be able to cut it?"

"Possibly, but I doubt it," Balthazar said. "I designed the Reishi Gates so that the Island Kings would not be able to use the Thinblades to destroy them. If this Nether Gate is made with a similar process, then I suspect it will be impervious to the Thinblade."

"I believe the better approach to this problem would be to find one of the keystones and place it beyond the reach of the shades," Demetrius said.

"I agree," Balthazar said. "When last we spoke, you mentioned a Bloodvault keyed to your line. Perhaps that would be the safest place for the keystones once you locate them."

Alexander nodded in thought, then asked, "What can you tell me about the shades?"

"They have no physical form in this world but are capable of possessing those of weak moral character, people bearing a burden of guilt or those in despair," Demetrius said. "They are cunning and intelligent, not to be underestimated. Once a shade is in possession of a person, it is very difficult to drive it out while the host remains alive. They delight in causing harm and will go to great lengths to remain in the world of time and substance."

"How can I destroy them?" Alexander asked.

Malachi laughed with a tinge of insanity. "You can't."

"They can be confined within a magic circle like any other creature from the netherworld," Demetrius said. "They can be banished back to the darkness by one of sufficient strength and talent, although attempting to do so can be very dangerous because it leaves the one casting the banishing spell open to possession. Another theoretical possibility would be to open a rift to the netherworld in close proximity to the shade. Since they do not belong here, their presence creates an imbalance. That imbalance would cause them to be drawn into the rift . . . theoretically. However, I know of no attempt to open a rift to the netherworld actually succeeding."

"It may also be possible to create a vessel to trap and contain them," Balthazar said. "An enchanter of sufficient power and imagination may be able to accomplish such a feat. I believe I would have been able to create such an item during my later years."

Alexander thought for a long moment. He needed to talk to Mage Gamaliel. If anyone alive could create a vessel to imprison a shade, it was the Guild Mage. He also needed to find the keystones or at least one of them. He had no idea how he was going to go about doing that. Maybe his clairvoyance would help him, but for some reason he doubted it. He decided he had enough information about the Nether Gate for now.

"What can you tell me about the fortress islands?"

Dominic Reishi, the Second Sovereign sat forward. "I created them to provide an airborne defense against naval attack. Each is an artificial island called up out of the ocean floor by magic. They are shielded against scrying or clairvoyance and are designed to withstand a siege. Each has the capability to be completely self-sufficient for several years. They are also virtually immune to magical assault. They were designed to house a flight of five hundred wyverns along with their riders and handlers. They do have a weakness that you can exploit, however. Within a hidden and shielded chamber located deep under the Reishi Keep is a map room of the Seven Isles. From this map room, the one bound to the Stone may destroy any of the fortress islands on command. I built this feature in as a failsafe in the event of treachery."

Alexander smiled. "That might become useful. Is there a secret way into the fortress islands?"

Dominic shook his head. "I'm afraid not. I considered the idea but for purposes of security, I decided against it. The only way in is by air or by sea."

Alexander grinned a bit as he turned to Malachi. "I thought you might like to know that the Reishi Coven was founded by Aliyeh Reishi, your wife, for the purpose of preventing Phane from getting his hands on the Sovereign Stone."

Malachi turned red with anger and started to speak, but Alexander stopped him with a raised hand. He sat fuming while several of the other sovereigns chuckled.

"I always like Aliyeh," Demetrius said. "She had a good heart and took her duty seriously."

Alexander turned back to Balthazar. "I just have one more question for the time being." He paused for a moment as the magnitude of his question weighed on him. "What is the secret of Wizard's Dust?"

Balthazar took a deep breath and let it out. "That is the question at the heart of it all, isn't it? I will tell you if you wish, but I encourage you to wait until you are ready to make use of it. You do not have the necessary talent or power to create Wizard's Dust, so knowing the secret may prove to be a liability without providing any benefit."

"What talent is required?" Alexander asked.

"Alchemy," Balthazar said. "An alchemist mage or an arch mage of any talent is required to create Wizard's Dust. The process is tedious and somewhat time-consuming. Unfortunately, simply understanding the process is not enough, you must also have the right magic to power the process."

"Very well," Alexander said. "Phane must not learn the secret or the world will fall. I don't fully understand the scope of his power and he may have ways of drawing the knowledge out of my mind without my awareness or consent, so I see the wisdom of your advice.

"Nevertheless, I'd like to make plans for the future. My childhood tutor and lifelong friend of the family is a master alchemist. How can I help him rise to the level of mage?"

Balthazar smiled and nodded his approval. "I can provide you with a series of experiments and formulas for him to work through. Each will push him to expand his understanding and develop his connection to the firmament. He will need a well-equipped workshop in order to proceed and the processes are complex, so I doubt it would do any good to teach you at the moment. Just know that the secret is here when you're ready and that I commend your wisdom in allowing it to remain a secret for now."

Four sovereigns nodded their agreement while Malachi shook his head in disbelief and contempt.

Alexander stood. "Thank you for your counsel." He turned and strode into the darkness. When he opened his eyes, everyone else save Jataan and Chloe was asleep. The commander sat at the table watching him. Chloe flitted up to eye level when he opened his eyes.

She spoke in his mind. "You're back, My Love. Did you find what you needed?"

He smiled at her and nodded. "I believe I did, at least for now," he said to her without speaking.

"Jataan, you should get some rest," Alexander said as he arranged his bedroll and lay down.

"Now that you are back and safe, I will," Jataan said. "Lieutenant Wyatt reports that his quarters and meals are good. He will be ready to ride at dawn. I've taken the liberty of assigning a Ranger guard detail at the entrance of your tent for the night."

"I doubt it's necessary but I've come to value caution," Alexander said as he closed his eyes.

Chloe curled up on his pillow a few inches from his face.

Chapter 7

When Alexander woke the next morning, Chloe was sitting cross-legged not six inches from his face watching him sleep. He smiled at her.

"Good morning, Little One," he said to her without speaking.

"Good morning, My Love," she replied. "There is much commotion in the camp."

Alexander sat up and saw that Anatoly was asleep and breathing deeply, Lucky was just waking, Jack was already up and out of the tent, and both Jataan and Boaberous were outside as well.

Alexander rubbed the sleep from his eyes and pulled on his boots. Even though he'd slept well, he still felt tired. The past few days had offered little time for rest. When he strolled out of the tent into the early dawn, he saw his Rangers eating breakfast around a set of cook fires. Jack and Boaberous had joined them, but Jataan was standing just outside the tent with his hands clasped lightly behind his back.

"Good morning, Lord Reishi. The Rangers tell me they have breakfast ready if you're hungry."

"Have you eaten?" Alexander asked.

"Not yet," Jataan said.

Alexander nodded and started for the cook fires. Jataan followed him like a shadow. Breakfast was oatmeal with nuts and honey. Alexander ate quickly and had the Rangers make up two more bowls for Lucky and Anatoly. Jataan frowned slightly when he saw Alexander head back to the tent with breakfast for his friends, but he didn't argue.

Lucky was checking Anatoly's bandages and smiled appreciatively when he saw the steaming bowl of oatmeal.

"How're you feeling?" Alexander asked Anatoly.

Anatoly glared at Jataan and then looked at Alexander. "My wound is mostly healed but I'm still a little stiff. Mostly, I'm confused. Why is he here?" Anatoly asked, looking hard at Jataan.

Alexander sat down on the side of his bed and handed him the other bowl of oatmeal. He held up the softly glowing Sovereign Stone and shrugged. "It turns out the Reishi line is descended from the Ruathan line. When I picked up the Stone, it bonded to me—and Jataan switched sides."

"That's a bit hard to swallow," Anatoly said suspiciously. "Are you sure we can trust him?"

Alexander shrugged. "As sure as I can be. His colors tell me I can and he helped fight off the Andalians. He seems pretty intent on protecting me."

Anatoly didn't look convinced.

"I understand your reluctance to trust me, Master Grace, as well as your understandable animosity toward me," Jataan said. "However, I assure you that I serve Lord Reishi and no other. I have offered him my life in recompense for the crimes I committed against his family and that offer stands. He may order my death at any time and I will end my own life on his command without protest."

"Huh," Anatoly said. "I suppose I'd rather have you on our side than trying to kill us. But it may take some time for me to warm up to the idea."

Jataan bowed. "Quite understandable," he said as Boaberous Grudge entered the tent.

"Him, too?" Anatoly asked.

Alexander nodded. "Apparently, the whole Reishi Protectorate will come to serve me once they learn that I've bonded with the Sovereign Stone."

"That could be useful," Anatoly said around a mouthful of oatmeal.

Alexander spent the next half hour recounting what he'd learned through his clairvoyance and by visiting the Reishi Council, except the part about the keep on the southern island of Ithilian. He was concerned that Phane might have some means of listening in and he needed whatever information he might find in the keep too much to risk it.

Lucky and Anatoly were both happy and relieved to learn that Isabel and Abigail were alive and well. After breakfast they went out to find the Rangers tending a small herd of horses. Conner Ithilian strode up to Alexander.

"I have an honor guard of a hundred men waiting outside the encampment," he said. "Your Rangers are preparing the horses my stable master has provided. We should be ready to ride within the hour." He looked past Alexander to Anatoly. "How are you feeling, Master Grace? I trust my healer took good care of you?"

Anatoly stepped up and offered his hand. "I'm feeling much better, thank you. Your healer doesn't require me to swallow noxious liquids," he said with a grin and a sidelong glance at Lucky, who smiled gently at seeing his friend well enough to needle him about his potions. Anatoly's injury had been severe. Lucky would never admit it, but he'd been worried that Anatoly might not survive.

***

The three-day ride to the capital city, also named Ithilian, was quick and uneventful. They rode hard each day. Since they were a large party numbering over a hundred riders and flying the banner of the House of Ithilian, no one interfered with them.

The countryside was rich and lush. Spring came early on Ithilian, so the crops were in full growth. Many of the vegetables were being picked and the orchards were heavy with fruit. The herds were fat and well tended.

Aside from the warmer climate, the place reminded Alexander very much of home. The people were industrious and behaved with a sense of responsibility for their lands. The soldiers in Conner's honor guard were respectful toward the people and took care to avoid damaging crops, livestock, or land.

It was clear that the Old Law was understood and respected here. Alexander began to feel hope for building an alliance. He knew from experience that you could learn a lot about a people's leaders by the way the people behaved. The citizens of Ithilian worked hard and took care of their own.

In the middle of the afternoon on the third day of travel, they crested a rise and got their first glimpse of the capital. It was a sprawling city spread out on the plains surrounding a rocky hill that rose a thousand feet high. The central hill overlooked the confluence of two large rivers that joined to continue their journey to the ocean several days' travel away. Dozens of bridges spanning the rivers joined the three sections of the city together.

The palace rested on top of the central hill and was surrounded by steep forested slopes on all sides. It was made of white marble that glistened in the sunlight. Streamers fluttered in the breeze off the soaring spires atop the conical tower caps. It was every bit the castle that Alexander had always envisioned when his mother told him stories as a child. Unlike Ruatha, Ithilian had been a seat of power for over four thousand years. New Ruatha was an impressive city with its glittering plateau encrusted with buildings, but Ithilian presented a romanticized view of power that only served to heighten the authority of the king.

"I've always loved this view of the city," Conner said.

"It's beautiful," Alexander replied quietly.

They rode on into the city itself. The main roads were well traveled and well maintained. The flagstones were heavy and fit together with exacting precision. Crowds of people parted with a nod of deference for Conner and his retinue. They paid little attention to Alexander and that suited him just fine. He had learned that battle and warfare was as much about information as it was about manpower or magic. The less the enemy knew of his whereabouts, the safer he was.

They followed the wide street through the center of town past shops and through marketplaces until they arrived at the base of the central hill. A low stone wall surrounded it with a road on the outside and forest on the inside. A break in the wall allowed access to the single road that wound up through the untamed forest to the palace on top.

It was almost a jarring transition to go from bustling city to the calm and peace of ancient trees and wild underbrush. When they emerged from the woods, they were greeted by a manicured garden that surrounded the sprawling white marble palace. Many of the flowers were in full bloom and displayed an explosion of colors that stood in stark contrast to the bright white of the palace's outer wall.

As they rode through the open gatehouse, Alexander noted that the walls were easily forty feet thick. It was a military structure first and foremost despite the light and unthreatening façade it presented. Within was a small city with a smaller keep built on the highest point of the enclosed seat of government. All manner of structures filled the capital fortress and each was made from the same white marble. While they were all well maintained, it was clear that the place was ancient. Many of the structures had probably been constructed during the rule of Balthazar Reishi.

Conner led the way to a large stable where their horses were turned out into a lush green paddock. After a brief conversation with the stable master, Conner returned to Alexander and his friends.

"Your packs and gear will be taken to your quarters in the family keep," Conner said. "I'm told my father is in council. If we hurry, you'll have the opportunity to address the assembly."

Alexander sighed as he thought to himself how useless nobles usually turned out to be, but there was no help for it. They would expect to be a part of the decision-making process if only to assuage their egos, and they were always more cooperative if their importance was acknowledged.

The honor guard was dismissed and Conner was left with his personal valet. He led Alexander and his friends through the streets until he came to a fork in the road. One branch led to the keep overlooking the entire valley, the other led to an impressive-looking building constructed on the next highest point on the hilltop. It was a round building about two hundred feet across with a domed top supported by a circle of pillars.

"Lord Reishi, my aid will show your people to your quarters," Conner said. "We should go to the assembly hall so you can meet my father."

"Jack, I'd like you to come with us," Alexander said.

Jack nodded.

"I'd feel better if you had someone to watch your back," Anatoly said. "No offense, Prince Conner, but we've had more than our share of threats and this is unfamiliar territory."

"I concur with Master Grace," Jataan said. "I will accompany you."

"That's not exactly what I had in mind," Anatoly said.

Alexander smiled at the big man-at-arms as he put his hand on his shoulder. "I'll be all right with Commander P'Tal. Take a look at our quarters and get some rest. You still look a bit worse for wear."

Anatoly nodded with a frown. "We'll be waiting for you."

Alexander, Jataan, and Jack went with Conner to the assembly hall. The building became more impressive as they got closer. The pillars were easily seventy feet tall and ten feet in diameter. The entire place was built with polished marble. The outside wall was interspersed with tall windows that let in the light of day. Conner led them up the broad steps to the entrance and into a foyer. He strode across the marble floor to the double doors across from the entrance. On either side of the doors stood a guard in polished battle armor, each with a spear at his side. They opened the doors as Conner approached, but one dropped a spear across Alexander's path as he attempted to follow Conner through the door.

"Weapons are not allowed in the assembly hall," the guard said. "You'll have to surrender your sword until your business is concluded." His tone was respectful but unwavering.

Alexander smiled pleasantly at the man and opened his cloak to reveal the hilt of the Thinblade. "Make an exception," he said.

The guards stared at the Thinblade but remained silent.

Conner put his hand on the shoulder of the man barring Alexander's path. "He may pass with his sword," Conner said, "by my command."

"As you wish, My Prince, by your command," the guard said as he stepped back and allowed Alexander to pass with a respectful nod.

The interior of the assembly hall was constructed like a circular amphitheatre with a single podium standing on a raised marble platform in the center. Radiating away from the floor were levels of circular balconies that rose toward the domed ceiling. Light was provided by hundreds of windows cut into the dome and paned with fine, faceted crystal that caught the light and diffused it into the chamber.

The balconies were filled with men and women of rank. On either side of the room on the lowest balcony was an extended platform that jutted out over the floor below by ten feet or so. Each of these platforms held an oversized chair.

Conner stopped at the threshold of the floor and waited while the man at the podium spoke about the need to respect the autonomy of each province.

"The man to the right," Conner said quietly as he motioned to the man sitting on the platform, "is my father, King Abel Ithilian."

King Abel looked distracted as he watched the man at the podium speak.

"To my left is the Chancellor of the Assembly, my uncle Cassius Ithilian," Conner said. "He's the political leader of our nation. He's responsible for enforcing our laws and guiding the course of the assembly, while my father is responsible for commanding the army and presiding over the courts to ensure that the Old Law remains supreme over all other laws."

The man at the podium noticed Conner and Alexander and stopped his speech. "Delegates, Chancellor, Your Majesty, I yield the floor to Prince Conner." With a bow he withdrew to an alcove near the exit on the other side of the chamber.

With a look, Alexander commanded Jataan and Jack to remain where they stood while he followed Conner to the podium.

"Father, Uncle Cassius, Delegates, I come with urgent news of great importance to our people and to the people of the Seven Isles," Conner said with a kind of practiced ease that only comes from experience in public speaking. "Four days ago the Reishi Gate came to life and a small party came through."

There was a murmuring among the delegates as they discussed the unprecedented news. The Chancellor gaveled the chamber back into attentive silence.

"Please continue, Conner," he said.

Conner nodded respectfully to his uncle before continuing. "After speaking with our guest, I determined that we must travel here immediately so that the assembly can hear his message. It is my privilege and honor to present Lord Alexander Reishi, the Seventh Sovereign of the Seven Isles."

Conner stepped aside and Alexander stepped up to the podium. The silence within the room was palpable. The shock and disbelief Alexander saw as he evaluated the colors of the delegates was only overshadowed by their fear. He surveyed the room calmly and took note of the muddy and dark colors of Cassius Ithilian, the Chancellor.

His gaze settled on Abel Ithilian, the King. He was a man of courage and conviction. He watched Alexander with inquisitive eyes that seemed to see right through him. Alexander wondered if he wasn't the only one in the room with magical sight. He nodded to Abel deferentially and then drew the Sovereign Stone from under his tunic. The softly glowing large red stone came to rest on his chest and the chamber gasped collectively.

"I am Alexander Reishi and I am at war with Prince Phane," he said clearly. The chamber carried his words to every corner. "I serve the Old Law. Phane serves only his own ambition. I have come to offer Ithilian an alliance."

Alexander stopped and waited. A moment later the chamber erupted into debate. He ignored the delegates and focused on Abel. He was an older man, probably in his midfifties. His short dark hair was greying around the edges. His slate-grey eyes conveyed intelligence and piercing insight. His hand rested lightly on the hilt of his Thinblade. He didn't react to the announcement but seemed to be waiting for others to raise the inevitable questions.

The Chancellor obliged by gaveling the chamber into silence. "You must understand how fantastic such a claim sounds. Can you offer us any proof of your statements?" He seemed smug. Alexander could see in his colors that he didn't believe a word Alexander had said.

"Of course," Alexander said without any ire. "You are wise to seek the truth before passing judgment. I will need the assistance of King Abel to offer the proof you require."

Again the chamber erupted into murmuring.

The Chancellor gaveled the chamber silent again and spoke before Abel could respond. "I simply cannot permit such a thing. For all we know you are a very creative and well-spoken assassin come to murder our King. With the grave events that have recently come to light, we must err on the side of caution. I move that we take this man and his companions into custody until we can ascertain the truth of his claims. If he speaks the truth, I'm certain he will be gracious enough to forgive us our precautions."

The chamber responded with a chorus of "ayes" as the delegates concurred with the Chancellor's motion. A moment later the far door opened and twenty men wearing plate armor and armed with spears, large round shields and short swords flooded into the room. They fanned out in a semicircle and began to advance toward Alexander. With his all around sight, Alexander saw Jack flicker out of sight. Jataan was suddenly standing at his side with his hands casually clasped behind his back.

Conner stepped in front of Alexander and faced the advancing soldiers. "Hold!" he commanded. They stopped in place. Conner turned to his father. "I gave him my word as Prince of Ithilian that he would be welcomed as a guest in our home. Will you allow this assembly to dishonor our House?"

Abel smiled slightly before he stood and made his way down the staircase from his platform to the floor. Alexander surveyed the room with his all around sight and saw that the Chancellor was furious that the King had allowed Conner to countermand his order. He wondered idly at the political dynamic in this place. It was clear that every member of the assembly was ambitious and many were corrupt but no more so than any other collection of nobles he had encountered.

Abel strode up to Alexander and nodded politely to him. "You've made a bold claim. How may I prove your truthfulness?"

Alexander smiled in return. "Stab me with your Thinblade."

The assembly gasped. Jataan took a step forward. All eyes were on Alexander. He placed a hand on Jataan's shoulder and shook his head slightly to stay the battle mage, then he stepped forward and stood with his hands held open and palms up at his sides.

"Draw your sword and stab me," Alexander commanded.

"You are unarmed and pose no threat to me," Abel said. "To do such a thing would violate every principle I hold dear."

"I know and I'm glad of that," Alexander said. "I make this demand only because I cannot be harmed by any of the Thinblades and quite honestly, you are the only man here that I need to convince."

Abel hesitated and then shook his head. Alexander sighed and tossed his cloak back to reveal the hilt of his Thinblade and then drew. With a fluid movement quicker than anyone could react to, he swept his blade around and sliced a chunk the size of a man's head off the marble podium. It slipped to the ground and broke into several pieces. The crash reverberated around the sudden silence in the great chamber. Alexander held up his bare arm for all to see and brought the Thinblade down forcefully against his forearm. It bounced away without even touching. The room gasped.

Abel gave him a strange look. "I believed that all of the Thinblades were lost except mine," he said.

"Three remain," Alexander said as he returned his sword to its scabbard. "A week ago, I was the King of Ruatha. When I recovered the Sovereign Stone, I discovered that the Reishi are descended from the House of Ruatha and so I am heir to both Houses." He fixed Abel with a firm look. "Draw your sword and push it through my hand," he commanded as he held up his left hand.

Abel dismissed the soldiers arrayed around the room with a gesture, then turned to Alexander. He considered for a long moment before he drew his Thinblade. It was identical to Alexander's in every way save the bond to his bloodline. He gently and carefully raised the point to Alexander's palm and slowly pushed against it. The blade stopped like a steel blade against stone. Alexander reached out and slapped the edge of the blade, but it didn't cut him. He held up his hand to the assembly for all to see.

The room fell dead silent until a delegate stepped forward. "Even if we accept that you are heir to the Reishi line and have found and bonded with the Sovereign Stone, we have no reason to accept your rule."

Alexander smiled and stepped up to the now damaged podium. "I have not come to demand your fealty. I have come as a servant of the Old Law in the hopes that the people of Ithilian serve the same master as I."

Another delegate stepped forward. "The Reishi were the cause of the war. Your bloodline brought darkness to the world for two hundred years. Why should we trust you to serve the Old Law when the last Reishi Sovereign betrayed it so completely?"

Alexander turned to the delegate and nodded deferentially. "It is true that Malachi Reishi betrayed the Seven Isles and enlisted the aid of the netherworld through the dark magic of necromancy. It is equally true that his son Phane has followed the same path of personal ambition and power lust as his father. For two hundred years, they waged war on the innocent people of the Seven Isles and they deserve your contempt for that. It is also true that the Reishi presided over eighteen centuries of peace, prosperity, and advancement like nothing ever seen before or since. If you wish to judge the Reishi honestly, then you must take into account both the accomplishments and the crimes of the entire Reishi Empire."

Yet another delegate stepped forward to speak. "We have no wish for war. If we choose neutrality, will you honor our choice?"

"I will, but Phane will not," Alexander said. "He will never stop until all who draw breath serve him. You will not be spared this war. The only question you have to answer is this: Will you ride out and meet the enemy or will you cower in your beds until the enemy sets fire to your homes?"

Another delegate from across the chamber spoke. "His words are true. We've already received Phane's demands. When we refused, he abducted Princess Evelyn and demanded that we acknowledge the secession of Grafton Province."

Alexander looked to Abel. "Is this true?"

Abel nodded with his jaw clenched. Conner took a step toward his father and they shared a look of fear and loss.

"We were discussing our options when you arrived," Abel said. "Evelyn was taken two nights ago. Yesterday we received a message that she would be held in Grafton as insurance against an invasion. I have reports that Grafton is being reinforced from the sea by armies from Karth and Andalia."

"Phane controls Karth outright and the House of Andalia has sworn allegiance to him," Alexander said. "Andalian Lancers are in control of the southernmost territory of Ruatha, and an army of ten legions moved through the Reishi Gate from Karth to Ruatha five days ago."

"It would seem that Phane is moving much more quickly than we expected," Abel said. "Perhaps his impatience will be his undoing. His resources can't be unlimited. He may be overextending himself."

"We can hope," Alexander said, "but I doubt it. His army on Karth is vast, and Andalia has long ruled by force. I'm afraid that our enemies have more soldiers than we do and there are other concerns as well. Phane is not the only threat."

The delegates were listening with rapt attention to the discussion. Alexander realized that there were some details he wasn't ready to share with the general public. He knew that the delegates were probably loyal to Ithilian but they were nobles, so they really couldn't be trusted with information of great importance.

"What other threats do you speak of?" Abel asked.

Alexander took a deep breath and let it out slowly. "Zuhl has invaded Fellenden with a massive army. I don't know his purpose but I doubt it will help us."

Abel thought about it for a moment and then looked around like he suddenly remembered he was standing in the assembly hall. "We have much to discuss. I would be honored if you would join me at my table this evening. Perhaps a meal will lessen the weight of our burden somewhat." He turned to his brother. "Cassius, I would welcome your presence as well."

With that, they left the assembly hall, surrounded by a royal guard of twenty well-trained and well-equipped soldiers. It was a short walk to the keep. Abel spoke of his city and the style of architecture used in its construction. It was clear that he wanted to wait until they were safely within the walls of the family keep before speaking of anything of importance.

Chapter 8

The keep itself was a castle made of the ubiquitous Ithilian white marble with high walls and soaring towers. Alexander listened politely as Abel explained how the stone was quarried, finished, and transported. Once inside the keep, Conner showed Alexander to his rooms. They were in a secure wing of the keep, almost wastefully spacious and richly appointed. Alexander had seen so many palaces and seats of government in recent months that he was becoming immune to the sense of awe that he'd felt the first time he had set foot in the palace at Glen Morillian.

Anatoly met him in the entry hall. "They gave us enough space to house a small army but it's secure enough and easily defended. How'd the assembly meeting go?"

"As well as can be expected," Alexander said as he unclasped his cloak. "Turns out Phane is making inroads here as well." He quickly recounted the events of the meeting, then found his lavishly furnished quarters and washed the road grime off before changing into his finery.

Boaberous and the Rangers, with the exception of Lieutenant Wyatt, stayed in the quarters while everyone else went to the King's table for dinner. It was informal but there were still quite a number of people there. King Abel and his wife, Queen Sofia sat to the left and right of Alexander who was given the seat of honor at the head of the table. Abel introduced his advisor Mage Lenox and his senior military commander General Kishor. Conner and Cassius were there as well.

The meal was excellent. Ithilian produced a wide range of food crops and the chef was an accomplished cook. Alexander enjoyed the meal and spoke freely of Ruatha and his home. By an unspoken agreement, the more important subjects were avoided until the meal was cleared away and wine was served.

"You mentioned other threats," Abel said.

Alexander nodded. He spent a few minutes explaining the threats posed by Phane and Zuhl, then told them of the Reishi Coven and the abduction of Isabel and Abigail. Finally, he explained what he knew of the shades and the Nether Gate while being careful not to reveal where he believed it was located. Mage Lenox listened intently with a look of alarm.

"Lord Reishi, forgive me, but much of what you say is hard to believe," Mage Lenox said. "I have studied magic for many more years than you have lived and I have never heard of a wizard sending his mind into the netherworld, let alone providing a conduit for the shades to reach this world. Such a thing is beyond imagining."

"I agree, but it's the truth nonetheless," Alexander said. "I can name the shades if you wish."

Mage Lenox blinked. "No. That won't be necessary. The shades are terrifying creatures and I have no desire to draw their attention."

"Alone, they are frightening enough, but with the possibility that they could open the Nether Gate, they may be a greater threat to the Seven Isles than Phane," Alexander said.

"I agree," Mage Lenox said. "Perhaps we can be of some assistance. The head of my order is very talented at divination. He may be able to determine the whereabouts of one or more of the keystones you spoke of."

"That would be very helpful," Alexander said. "My hope is that the keystones have been taken from the Reishi Isle and are scattered around the Seven Isles, the farther apart the better. With my wife and sister's abduction and the invasion of my homeland, I have other matters I would rather attend to first."

Alexander paused for a moment, considering how much to reveal about the adept wizard's keep in southern Ithilian. The colors of everyone at the table were clear and bright except for Cassius Ithilian's. He had the muddy and cloudy colors of a self-absorbed narcissist—Alexander didn't trust him. He decided to proceed with caution.

"What can you tell me about Grafton Province?" he asked.

Abel nodded to General Kishor. The ranking officer of the Ithilian Army cleared his throat. He was a man of medium height and sturdy build with powerful arms and a broad chest. His eyes were dark brown and his white beard was close cut as was his greying hair.

"Grafton is comprised of the southern island and a portion of the land holdings around Grafton city proper on the mainland," Kishor said. "The area around the southern island is teeming with sea life, and the people who live there are skilled fishermen. The interior of the island is very rugged and mountainous. It's avoided because it's rumored to be haunted by an ancient magic, but more practically, there are a number of dangerous predatory creatures that reside in the rocky heights. Additionally, there's very little of value in those mountains that warrants the risk of traveling through them.

"The bulk of their population actually lives on the mainland within the city. Most of their forces are stationed there and they have a substantial fleet of merchant ships and fishing boats that routinely make port there. Most of our iron and copper is imported from Tyr through Grafton."

"Where are they likely to hold the princess?" Alexander asked.

"I would guess they'd take her to Lighthouse Keep on the southern tip of the island," Kishor said. "There's a small fortress on a high bluff overlooking the ocean that doubles as a lighthouse. It's the most easily defendable position in all of Grafton and the most inaccessible."

"I take it the approaches by water would be easy to spot," Alexander said.

"Yes, and the roads are also easily guarded," Kishor said. "The island has a single road that runs along the coastline. It runs over the southern bluff farther inland but there are a series of switchbacks on each side that can be seen from the keep."

"What about over the mountains?" Alexander asked.

"There's no path or road and the terrain is treacherous," Kishor said. "Of greater concern are the ganglings and the revenant, as well as the persistent rumors of some form of haunting within the mountains that seems to revolve around the ancient ruins of a long-dead wizard's keep."

Alexander schooled his reaction carefully to avoid any hint of interest. He suspected that the ruins were exactly where he needed to go for answers about his magical calling but he didn't dare reveal as much. He couldn't afford to let that information get to Phane before he found what he was looking for. And he also didn't want to show weakness by revealing his limited understanding of his own calling.

"I've had encounters with ganglings before but I've never heard of a revenant," he said.

"A revenant is a most terrifying creature," Mage Lenox said. "It's believed that they were created during the Reishi War by Malachi Reishi himself. They're larger than a man and have large wings, sharp claws, powerful strength, and a crown of bone horns protruding from a hairless head. They feed on blood, and it's said that a person who survives the bite of a revenant will slowly transform into one of the foul creatures. If there is an antidote to the curse of the revenant's bite, it has long been lost. Revenants of extreme age are said to develop the ability to create illusions in the minds of their victims.

"The people who live on the island speak of seeing a revenant on the hunt from time to time. It doesn't venture into the villages that ring the small island, but there are many stories of those who strayed from the safety of the coastline never to be seen again."

"I may be able to learn something more of these creatures if Malachi Reishi actually did create them," Alexander said. "Normally, I would dismiss the story of a haunting but recent events have opened my mind to such possibilities. What can you tell me about the ruins and the restless spirits surrounding it?"

"Over the years some brave or foolish souls have ventured into the mountains in search of what treasure might be found in the ruins," Mage Lenox said. "Those who returned reported many unexplained sightings, from dragons to shadows that move on their own. Many attribute these phenomena to the revenant but there is some evidence to suggest that there are other forces at work. In most reports, the intensity of the sightings increases closer to the ruins. Aside from the high mountains to the west, the central region of Grafton Island is the most remote and unexplored part of Ithilian, so it's hard to say for certain what resides there."

"If your daughter were returned safely, do you have the military strength to bring Grafton back under your control?" Alexander asked Abel.

"Absolutely," Abel said. "The latest reports say there's less than a legion of enemy troops there with more soldiers arriving every day. I can muster three legions without drawing soldiers away from the outlying garrisons or the Reishi Gate."

Alexander hesitated for a moment before he continued. His next question was the most important. The future rested on King Abel's answer. "Lord Abel, will you accept my offer of friendship and alliance against Phane?" Alexander held the King's eyes firmly with his own while he waited for an answer.

Abel didn't hesitate. "I will, but my word on the matter is not final. An alliance must be confirmed by the assembly. As for your friendship, I welcome you to Ithilian and into my home."

"Thank you, Lord Abel," Alexander said and then turned to Cassius. "Chancellor, I urge you to support this alliance within the assembly. I'm confident that the delegates will follow your example in this matter."

"Of course, Lord Reishi," he said. Alexander schooled his reaction when he saw the Chancellor's colors flare with deceit. "I will give this alliance you propose my full-throated support and urge the members of the assembly to stand behind it as well."

"Thank you, Chancellor," Alexander said politely. He wanted to strike the man down for his deception but dismissed the irrational desire out of hand. Cassius Ithilian would undo himself with his treachery in time. Alexander wondered how much damage he might cause before he was revealed for the traitor he was. Then a thought occurred to him. He heard his father's voice from a lecture long ago: "Deception is the most powerful weapon on the battlefield. If you can make your enemy believe something, you can make him take the action you want." Perhaps Alexander could use Cassius to his advantage. If the Chancellor was in league with Phane, he might prove invaluable as an agent of disinformation.

Then another thought occurred to him and his blood ran cold. He had revealed the presence of the shades and the existence of the Nether Gate. If that information fell into Phane's hands, he might be able to bind the shades to his will, find the keystones, and open the Nether Gate before Alexander could stop him. He silently chided himself for his error in judgment. He knew from Cassius's colors that the man couldn't be trusted, but he hadn't considered the possibility that the Chancellor was already in league with Phane.

"Lord Reishi, if I may," General Kishor said. Alexander nodded for the general to continue. "You spoke of an army from Zuhl invading Fellenden. Can you estimate their numbers?"

"I'd say at least a hundred thousand," Alexander said.

General Kishor's eyes went a bit wide. "Fellenden will fall to such an army very quickly. They are not a single nation but rather a collection of territories and city-states. Without an organizing authority to marshal a defense, they won't stand a chance."

"We're trading partners with many of the territories of Fellenden," Abel said. "They'll appeal to us for our help in the face of such an enemy, and I'm inclined to offer what assistance I can."

"I understand," Alexander said. "If there weren't two enemy armies on Ruatha, I'd send an army to Fellenden myself, but as it stands, I can't spare the troops. Something has been troubling me though. Why Fellenden? What do they have that Zuhl wants?"

"Iron Oak," Mage Lenox said. "Zuhl is rich in minerals and stone. Their fisheries are the most productive in the world, but they have little in the way of timber. The Iron Oak forests of Fellenden could be used to build a fleet of ships. Zuhl could realize his lifelong dream of establishing an empire under his name that spans the entire Seven Isles."

Alexander frowned. "I don't know much about Zuhl."

Mage Lenox nodded. "That's understandable. Zuhl is a very secretive and paranoid ruler. My understanding of his domain comes mostly from conversations I've had with the head of my order, Mage Jalal. He's used his magic to learn about many of the more powerful figures in the Seven Isles. Zuhl is a necromancer mage of great power. His most significant achievement is a spell that he uses to prolong his life span through the sacrifice of another. By some accounts, Zuhl is over seven hundred years old, yet he looks like a man of about twenty-seven."

Alexander was astonished. He knew that the mana fast led to a longer life. Many of the Reishi Sovereigns had lived for four hundred years or more, but he'd never heard of anyone living for seven centuries.

"The House of Zuhl was the first to fall during the Reishi War," Mage Lenox said. "Zuhl has spent the better part of his life spreading the story that the suffering and hardship experienced by the people of Zuhl is the fault of the Reishi. He has actively promoted the story that Phane will return to enslave them. Through such propaganda, he has kept his people in a state of constant war, pitting one territory against the other. The result is a large population of battle-hardened and quite ruthless soldiers. They have a culture of rule by violence, with utter contempt for weakness. Killing is glorious and battle is the greatest endeavor. The people of Zuhl see conquest as the only alternative to enslavement. They hate the Reishi with irrational passion and have lived for the day when they could fight in the final battle of the Reishi War."

"That's unsettling," Alexander said.

"Yeah, but we might do well to introduce Zuhl to Phane," Anatoly said.

General Kishor chuckled. "I was thinking along the same lines. I'd much rather they chewed up their forces against each other. Might buy us some time to build up our strength and consolidate our positions."

Before anyone could suggest a concrete course of action, Alexander steered the conversation away from any firm decisions. He wanted to present a range of possibilities without settling on any one path so that Cassius wouldn't be able to warn Phane if he was indeed in league with the Reishi Prince.

"For my own admittedly selfish reasons, my heart tells me to go to the fortress island and rescue my wife and sister," Alexander said. "Can you shed any light on the Reishi Coven or their Sky Knights?"

"We're well aware of them," Kishor said, "but we've had few dealings with them. They do not interfere with ships unless they stray too close to the Reishi Isle. Our merchant-vessel captains understand the dangers and stay well clear."

Alexander nodded and yawned. "Forgive me. I'm afraid the past few days of travel have made me weary. I think it would be wise to put off any final decisions until tomorrow."

"Lord Reishi," Mage Lenox said. "I have one question of importance, if I may?"

"Of course," Alexander said.

"Legend says that the Sovereign Stone holds the secret to Wizard's Dust," Mage Lenox said. "Is this so?" He sat forward with intense interest.

With his all around sight, Alexander saw Cassius sit forward a bit as well.

"It is," Alexander said. "Unfortunately, the process is difficult and time-consuming. While knowledge of the secret will probably decide the outcome of this war, I'm afraid it will be of no help in the immediate future. Furthermore, I can't risk allowing Phane to learn the secret, so I've decided to share it with no one for the time being."

Mage Lenox looked conflicted and deflated at the same time. "I see the wisdom in your decision. Perhaps we could be of assistance. I'm certain that every member of my order would provide any and all support within our power."

"I have no doubt," Alexander said. "In time, the secret will be revealed, but for now it's simply too dangerous."

Mage Lenox sighed. "I understand. Please know that I do not ask for myself. We have many young apprentices of great potential, but it's been years since we've discovered a cache of Wizard's Dust. I'm afraid our order is aging and shrinking in number."

"I sympathize," Alexander said. "The same is true for the Wizards Guild on Ruatha. All I can offer for now is my word that your order will be revitalized."

"Lord Reishi," Queen Sofia said. "It's quite clear that you have the weight of the world on your shoulders. Many people's lives depend on your decisions. I ask you to remember that one of those lives is my Evelyn. She's innocent and full of life. She doesn't deserve to be used like a piece on a board game."

"I understand your heartache," Alexander said. "I'll do what I can to help you get your daughter back, but she may have to wait until other matters are resolved."

Sofia blinked and a tear slipped down her cheek but she nodded her acceptance and then stood. "Thank you all for sharing a meal with us. The hour is late. Good night." She spoke clearly but it was plain to all that she was terrified for her daughter and struggling to maintain her composure.

Chapter 9

As they left the dining hall, Alexander spoke silently to Chloe. At his request, she had not revealed herself since their arrival in the city. "Little One, please follow Chancellor Cassius and see if he makes any report to our enemies."

"Of course, My Love," she replied within the confines of his mind. "I don't like him. Even without dirty colors, there's something about him that makes me uncomfortable."

"He values power over all else," Alexander said. "Don't let him see you and don't risk your safety, Little One."

Once back in his quarters, Alexander sat down in one of the chairs in the central sitting room that served as the hub for his guest chambers. The Rangers and Boaberous were there and it was clear from the remains of their dinner that they had eaten well. He motioned for everyone else to take seats around the low table.

"Any thoughts?" Alexander asked.

"I don't trust Chancellor Cassius," Jack said.

"Yeah, I hope I didn't reveal too much about the shades and the Nether Gate," Alexander said. "I don't know if Cassius is in league with Phane or not. The last thing I want is Phane getting his hands on that Gate."

"You didn't mention anything specific," Lucky said, "and we might gain some invaluable information from Mage Jalal about the keystones."

"I hope so," Alexander said. "I'd feel a lot better with one of those keystones in our possession. Oh, before I forget, I'd like to give the wizards a gift." Alexander took the vial of Wizard's Dust out of his pouch and handed it to Lucky. "Can you separate this into individual vials, each with enough for a mana fast?"

Lucky carefully took the vial and set it on the table. "Of course," he said. "I imagine such a gift will create quite a bit of goodwill." He dug around in his bag and came out with a little wooden box that held over a dozen empty glass vials. Within a minute he had measuring spoons, a small scale, and a little glass funnel arrayed on the table before him. He set to work filling eleven glass vials with Wizard's Dust and then slipped each vial inside a small metal tube with a fitted screw top. One by one, he assembled eleven doses of Wizard's Dust sufficient for one mana fast each.

Alexander told him to keep the small amount of the potent magical dust that was left over. Lucky packaged it carefully and put it back into his bag along with the rest of his equipment. Alexander took the eleven, metal-encased glass vials and slipped them into his potion pouch along with his vial of night-wisp dust, his vial of fairy dust, and a jar of healing salve.

"Lord Reishi," Jataan said, "there are many who would kill you for the contents of that pouch. I recommend that you do not reveal what you possess. Nations have gone to war over lesser quantities of Wizard's Dust."

Alexander nodded his agreement.

"What do you think our chances are of convincing King Abel to loan you a couple of legions?" Anatoly asked. "I'm sure your father could use some help right about now."

Alexander nodded. "I was thinking the same thing. When I looked in on them a few days ago, the Reishi Army Regency hadn't started moving yet, but they might be at the outskirts of New Ruatha by now. We have about the same number of troops north of the Great Forest as they moved through the Gate, but they have that scourgling with them. I just hope the wizards can defend against it or New Ruatha might be in trouble."

"I suspect King Abel would be much more willing to lend his soldiers if his daughter was safe," Jack said.

"I agree," Alexander said. "What's more, I'd like to destroy the army Phane sent before they can gain a foothold here. Ithilian produces a lot of food and I don't want a prolonged battle to jeopardize their crops. We may need the supplies to survive the winter."

There was a knock at the door. Jataan nodded to Boaberous. The giant opened the door to a valet who looked slightly startled at the sheer size of Lieutenant Grudge.

"Lord Abel sent me to invite Lord Reishi for an evening drink," he said.

Alexander stood and headed for the door. "Get some rest," he said to his friends. "We may have to move tomorrow."

Jataan P'Tal followed him without a word. The valet stepped in front of him. "Lord Abel requested only Lord Reishi," he said.

Jataan nodded. "I'll wait in the hall," he said.

The valet didn't quite know what to do with the battle mage but he led the way when Alexander nodded for him to proceed. They wound through the halls of the keep until they came to a nondescript door. The valet knocked, paused for a moment, and then opened the door to a small reading room with a little balcony. The furniture was comfortable but not overly lavish and it looked well used. The shelves were lined with books of all kinds and the lighting was ample for reading. Two comfortable-looking chairs sat on the balcony with a small table between them. A silver tray held a crystal bottle of spirits and two heavy crystal glasses.

Abel stood in the middle of the room with a grave look on his face. "Please come in," he said.

Alexander entered and Jataan took a position in the hall with his back to the wall opposite the door and stood casually with his hands clasped lightly behind his back.

"I was hoping we could have a private conversation," Abel said. "The walls have ears and there are precious few whom I trust."

"I understand all too well," Alexander said as Abel led him out onto the balcony.

"Mage Lenox has spelled this room to prevent others from eavesdropping."

Alexander nodded. "A wise precaution," he said as he took a seat and allowed Abel to pour him a glass of the fine dark liquor.

The King sat down and sipped from his glass. "This is my favorite blend," he said before taking a deep breath. "The assembly will not approve of the alliance you propose." He sighed. "My brother cannot be trusted."

"I know," Alexander said.

Abel looked at him quizzically and nodded. "Your insight is excellent. Cassius is three years older than I, yet our father chose to give me the Thinblade and the throne. Cassius has never forgiven either of us for that. He is ambitious and will turn any situation to his advantage, up to and including jeopardizing the whole of Ithilian if it suits his purpose."

"I fear it may be much worse than you know," Alexander said. When Abel looked him in the eye, he continued. "He may be in league with Phane. I've learned from painful experience that Phane often uses bribery and promises of reward to enlist the aid of those who can help him achieve his ends."

"It pains me to say so, but I wouldn't put it past him," Abel said. "If Phane offered him the Ithilian throne, I have no doubt that Cassius would pay any price."

"What is the extent of your power as King?" Alexander asked. "And what powers reside with the assembly and the Chancellor?"

"As King, I'm responsible for ensuring that all governing bodies adhere to the Old Law and for defending against foreign enemies," Abel said. "That's one of the reasons that the abduction of my daughter is so insidious. By using her as a shield, they force me to choose between my child and my duty.

"The Chancellor is elected by a vote of the assembly from within their ranks. He is responsible for administering the apparatus of government and managing the daily operation of the constables and corps of builders. Laws are enforced by the constables through investigation, apprehension, and detention of criminals. The Chancellor has great latitude as to which laws he chooses to enforce. Through the corps of builders he controls how various construction projects will proceed, who will be hired to perform the work, and from where the materials will be procured. In many ways he has far more power than I do.

"The assembly is comprised of delegates elected by local communities. They each serve a term of six years per election and are responsible for enacting the laws that the Chancellor is responsible for enforcing."

"What about the Old Law?" Alexander asked. "How do you ensure that the laws enacted by the assembly don't contradict the Old Law?

"I am responsible for the judiciary," Abel said. "All crimes are brought before a court presided over by a judge appointed by me. The first duty of a judge is to ensure that the Old Law is enforced. In cases where a law of the assembly is found to contradict the Old Law, the judge has the authority to dismiss the case and refer the law to me for review. If I find the law to be incompatible with the Old Law, I have the power to strike it down.

"Generally our system of governance works well. There are many factions all vying for power which tends to prevent the concentration of too much power in the hands of any one faction."

"I find many aspects of your system appealing," Alexander said. "On Ruatha, the petty nobles control the majority of the lands through hereditary title. As you might imagine, they often lose sight of the needs of the people in favor of their own pursuit of power. I can see how a system where those who make the laws are beholden to the people would place a limit on abuses."

"It does have its advantages, but it's also difficult to get things done quickly," Abel said. "The delegates are always looking for a benefit that they can bring back to the people they represent, even to the point of holding the greater good of Ithilian hostage. I'm afraid that's what will happen with your proposal for an alliance. While I control the army, any formal alliance must be sanctioned by a law passed by the assembly. They will all want something for their vote. Because the matter is so urgent, they will expect to extract a high price for their support. My brother will also be working behind the scenes to ensure that he has enough votes against us to prevent passage until he gets what he wants."

"And what is that?" Alexander asked.

"Control over the judiciary," Abel said. "In recent years, I've struck down a number of laws that would have allowed the government to take property from the people in the name of the greater good. They were little more than thinly disguised schemes to steal from innocent citizens in order to empower and enrich those in government."

Alexander shook his head. "The Old Law is more important than a formal alliance."

Abel sighed heavily. "I'm greatly relieved to hear you say that." He looked at Alexander with a little smile. "It's good to have a friend who understands that being King is far more about duty than privilege."

Alexander raised his glass. "I couldn't agree more."

They sat in silence for a few minutes enjoying the late spring evening and their newfound camaraderie when the darkness was shattered by the sudden appearance of Chloe. She buzzed into existence a few feet in front of Alexander in a scintillating ball of white light. Abel's eyes grew wide. Chloe ignored him and floated up to face Alexander.

"He's a bad man, My Love. I followed him. He went straight to a wizard and commanded him to send word to Phane. The wizard crushed a stone and a moment later the imp that serves Phane appeared out of the darkness. He told that noxious little demon that you were here with the Sovereign Stone and he would be able to tell Phane your plans tomorrow." She buzzed into a ball of light again for a moment. "The imp said it would be back for his report tomorrow evening and then it disappeared in a cloud of darkness."

"Thank you, Little One," Alexander said. "This is Abel. He's my friend. Abel, this is Chloe, my familiar."

Abel blinked a few more times before he found his voice. "I'm most pleased to meet you, Chloe. I've read stories about fairies but I never imagined I would have the privilege of actually meeting one of your kind."

Chloe smiled and buzzed into a ball of light, then flitted over to Alexander, landed on his knee, and sat down cross-legged.

"I'm afraid I asked Chloe to see what your brother did after dinner," Alexander said.

Abel nodded sadly. "We were friends when we were boys. He used to be a good person, but somewhere he discovered an insatiable ambition. Now, we're more like rivals than friends."

"I hate to suggest the possibility, but Cassius may have been involved in your daughter's abduction," Alexander said softly.

Abel looked at Alexander with a stricken expression. He closed his eyes as sadness, betrayal, and rage flashed across his countenance. When he opened his eyes, he appeared resolute. "Without irrefutable evidence, I have no power to act against him." He thought for a long moment before shaking his head. "Our law makes no provisions for a situation such as this. The father in me wants to strike him down, but I must be King before father, and as King, I cannot act without proof to present to the constable."

"Perhaps there's a better way," Alexander said. "He will report to Phane what we decide to do after tomorrow's discussions. I suggest that you and I decide on our course of action now and tomorrow we put on a show for the benefit of your brother and his new master."

Abel smiled. "We'd have to keep things between us until our plans are in motion, otherwise he'll get wind of it."

They talked for another hour, carefully laying plans and choreographing the elaborate deception they'd devised. Alexander walked back to his quarters feeling a bit of mirth at the power he was going to wield against Phane. It wasn't force or magic or the will of the masses but a simple ruse that might be able to buy Ruatha the time she needed to save her people while at the same time securing Ithilian against Phane's invasion.

Before going to bed he took a piece of charcoal from the hearth and drew a magic circle on the stone floor of the balcony. His clairvoyance had become predictable and reliable. He had a process that worked every time he put it to use. Within a few minutes, he found himself floating on the firmament. The cacophony of the music of creation was discordant and fearful. War was engulfing the Seven Isles and people were dying. Alexander shoved the sadness of human tragedy aside and focused his will. His awareness coalesced high over Ithilian.

He moved with blinding speed until he was hovering over the city of Grafton, which was about the size of Southport. There were encampments on its outskirts. About two thousand Andalian Lancers and another three thousand heavy infantry from Karth were deployed around the city.

Alexander shifted his perspective. Now he was high over Grafton Island. He could see the ring of lights from the communities that dotted the coastline; the mountainous interior was dark. He searched until he found the ruins. They were broken and crumbling but still somewhat intact. He wanted to explore the place with his clairvoyance but couldn't in the dark. Even with his magical sight, he still needed light to see by.

He moved to the south point of Grafton Island and floated slowly around the keep. It was a simple stone structure made from granite blocks. There were three outer towers that formed a triangle with thirty-foot-high walls spanning the distance between them. The southernmost tower served as the lighthouse. The two towers on either end of the north wall faced toward the road and the interior of the island. A gatehouse with a heavy portcullis served as the only entrance to the courtyard and stables within the walls.

He floated up over the interior of the keep and saw a single large building inside the walls with one high tower that rose above all of the exterior towers. The keep was well manned and well defended. Alexander moved in closer and saw men wearing the distinctive armor of the Reishi Army Regency. Not surprisingly, Princess Evelyn was in the first place he looked for her—the top room of the central tower. She was unharmed but clearly afraid, as well as angry. She stood at the open window looking out to the north. Alexander wished she was sleeping so he could leave a message with her, but he didn't have time to wait for her to go to bed.

He shifted his awareness to Ruatha and went straight to Kelvin's workshop and the message board. There was a single, hastily scrawled message: Enemy moving to assault New Ruatha.

Alexander went to the sleep room and found one Ranger sound asleep. He entered the man's dreams and gave him the message he wanted delivered to his father and the Guild Mage.

With all of his tasks complete, he made one last stop outside the fortress island. Isabel and Abigail were in their room sitting comfortably and talking over a cup of tea. Alexander floated there for a time just taking strength from the knowledge that his wife and sister were alive and well. When he returned to his body, Chloe was sitting on his knee watching him, and Jataan was sitting at the table watching as well.

Alexander winked at Chloe, then touched the Sovereign Stone. A few moments later he was in the Reishi Council Chamber. He took his seat and apprised the Reishi Sovereigns of the events that had passed since the last council meeting.

"You are wise to enlist the aid of Ithilian," Balthazar said. "They have excellent resources and will be an invaluable ally, especially if you can ensure that Phane doesn't gain a foothold on the island."

"I need information about another one of Malachi's creations," Alexander said. "A creature called a revenant." He turned to Malachi. "Tell me all you know of these creatures."

Malachi smiled. "I'm glad to see my works are still alive in the world. I created the first revenant by breeding a demon with a virgin witch. She died during childbirth, of course. Probably for the best," he said smiling. "I'm sure she would not have appreciated the beauty of her offspring. It feeds on the life force of dying creatures. Any who survive the bite slowly transform into a revenant themselves. As I recall, the one I created developed a taste for blood, which I thought was odd since it didn't need to eat for sustenance. They're very strong and frighteningly quick. As they get older, their power increases. Eventually, they can read the mind of a human within a few dozen feet and even project images into the mind's eye. They seem to enjoy feeding on those who are feeling fear, so they tend to play with their prey before they eat. Feeding gives them the ability to quickly regenerate any injuries, so the more life force they've recently consumed, the more difficult they are to wound."

"How do I kill it?" Alexander asked.

"Cut off its head or pierce its heart," Malachi said. "Although, the latter option won't actually kill it, just render it helpless. I found that decapitation followed by burning its entire body is the only sure way to permanently destroy a revenant."

"Why would you create such a creature?" Demetrius asked.

Malachi shrugged. "Because I could. And because they served my purpose of punishing those who betrayed me."

"What about those bitten but not killed?" Alexander asked. "How do I cure their affliction?"

"Kill the revenant that bit them before the transformation is complete," Malachi said offhandedly. "Once they fully transform, they cannot be saved."

Alexander left the Reishi Council and found Chloe and Jataan exactly where he'd left them. He stood and stretched. It was late and he was tired, so he went to his room without a word. Chloe followed him and curled up on the pillow near his head.

Chapter 10

He woke just after dawn the next morning with a mixture of excitement and trepidation. Today would set in motion a number of important plans that would decide the fate of many. He reviewed the plans he and Abel had agreed upon and emerged from his bedchamber to a sitting room full of Rangers and his friends.

"A valet delivered an invitation for you and your companions to attend a late breakfast to be followed by a King's Council meeting," Jack said. "It seems that there will be a number of important people in attendance. Perhaps your finery would be in order."

Alexander grimaced. He'd put on his riding clothes as a matter of habit and went back to his room to change into the more formal attire that he wore when he needed to impress people who thought they were important.

When they entered the dining hall, all eyes turned to him. The room was full of people that Alexander didn't know. He'd brought Anatoly, Lucky, Jack, Jataan, and Lieutenant Wyatt with him. Chloe remained out of sight. Jataan had sent Boaberous on an unspecified errand. Alexander guessed it had something to do with the Reishi Protectorate. Wyatt had sent his Rangers to visit with the Ithilian military to learn what they could about their tactics and weapons.

Alexander stopped just inside the door and scanned the room with his second sight. He saw a mixture of colors from the clear and bright hues of King Abel and his son to the expansive auras of three wizards to the muddy and guileful colors of the delegates and the Chancellor.

Before he moved any farther, Jack stepped up on his right side. "Lords and Ladies, Chancellor and Delegates, Wizards and Generals, King Abel and Queen Sofia, it is my privilege and honor to announce Lord Alexander Reishi, Seventh Sovereign of the Seven Isles," he said in a clear voice that carried to every corner of the room.

Alexander smiled inwardly at the introduction. Not six months ago he was a cattle rancher. He still had more ties to that life than he would ever have to this one.

The reaction to the announcement was mixed. Abel and his family smiled warmly, the wizards and generals showed reserved respect, while the more self-important of the delegates could barely disguise their envy and contempt. Whatever the reaction, Jack's announcement put everyone on notice that Alexander had claimed the position of master of the room.

Lady Sofia raised a glass and tapped it with a spoon to draw everyone's attention. Once the room fell silent, she said, "Please be seated and breakfast will be served."

There was a general commotion as everyone found their place at the long table. Abel motioned to Alexander to sit at the head of the table, which drew looks from some of the delegates. Once everyone was seated, a flurry of servants entered from all sides like a well-coordinated attack. They brought platters of bacon, sausages, and sliced ham, large porcelain serving bowls heaping with scrambled eggs and hash browned potatoes, baskets filled with biscuits, sweet rolls, and crusty loaves of bread, pitchers of fresh juice, and kettles of steaming hot tea.

Alexander enjoyed the meal. It was warm and hearty and well prepared. After the dishes were cleared, Abel stood and looked to him for permission to proceed. Alexander nodded.

"The King's Council will come to order," Abel said before he sat back down.

Everyone's attention turned to the head of the table.

"I have invited you all here to apprise you of the situation faced by the Seven Isles," Abel said. "Prince Phane has conquered Karth by force and rules Andalia by proxy. He has invaded Ruatha where even now battle rages and innocent lives are being destroyed. He has seduced the Governor of Grafton Province and is landing troops on the mainland of Ithilian. Yet our troubles don't end there. Fellenden has been invaded by a massive army from Zuhl. All of the Seven Isles is at war or soon will be. Lord Reishi has risen to stand against those who would trample the Old Law. He is a natural ally for our people, and so I have decided to throw the weight of the House of Ithilian behind his cause without reservation.

"Lord Reishi and I spoke late into the night. After careful consideration, we have determined our course of action. Lord Reishi will depart for the Gate tomorrow accompanied by Prince Conner. They will make the Gate legions ready for battle and then travel through the Gate to assault the Reishi Army Regency on Ruatha.

"General Kishor, you will assemble your three legions to the west of the city and prepare to move north to join the Gate legions as soon as possible. We will send out a call to arms to all provinces of Ithilian. All will be expected to contribute to this struggle. I will stay here and negotiate a settlement with Grafton Province. I am prepared to acknowledge their sovereignty in exchange for the safe and immediate return of Princess Evelyn and assurances that they will not assemble any more than one legion of soldiers.

"The battle on Ruatha will be fierce, but with the aid of Ithilian's soldiers, Lord Reishi assures me that victory is certain. Once the enemy has been routed from Ruatha, we will consolidate our forces and pour into Fellenden to destroy the invaders from Zuhl and restore security within the mainland of our most important trading partner."

Abel stopped talking and the table fell dead silent for several moments. Alexander appraised the colors of the men in the room. The wizards and soldiers were all clearly willing to do what they could to stand against the enemy, but the colors of the delegates and the Chancellor reflected schooled rage and indignation.

"Surely you don't mean to form an alliance with Lord Reishi without the consent of the assembly," Chancellor Cassius said with a little more rancor than even he wanted to display.

Abel responded with the smooth and easy delivery of one skilled in the art of political infighting. "Cassius, you assured me that you would place your full support behind an alliance with Lord Reishi against our common enemy. Has the assembly rejected your counsel?"

The room again fell silent. Alexander watched the colors of the

Chancellor twist and contort as he fought to maintain his composure.

"As I'm sure you well understand, Lord Abel, these things take time. Surely you don't want to act without giving the voice of the people a full hearing."

"I'm afraid that this is a matter of war more than one of alliance," Abel said. "While I fully agree that any formal declaration of alliance should only be made once the people have had a full hearing, the domain of war is mine alone. Swift action is necessary or we will quickly find ourselves surrounded on all sides by conquered lands with nowhere to turn for aid."

"A few days are all we need for a thorough debate," Cassius said. "Surely the world will not fall for the delay of a few days." His tone was now completely in control and he spoke with almost syrupy condescension.

"Time is of the essence," Abel said. "Our legions will attack the Reishi Army Regency forces on Ruatha in seven days." He stood to punctuate the end of the meeting. "Mage Jalal, Lord Reishi has requested a private meeting to consult with you on a point of magic. General Kishor, I need to discuss the details of your troop movements."

Mage Jalal stood and bowed formally to Alexander. "Lord Reishi, I am at your service."

Some of the delegates were hotly discussing the sudden change in circumstances. They were alarmed at the speed with which events were moving and their apparent lack of input into important decisions. Alexander watched the Chancellor slip out of the room in the commotion of the meeting's adjournment.

Everyone in the chamber froze when an alarm bell tolled high overhead in one of the towers.

The doors burst open and a squad of palace guards hurried in and made a straight line to King Abel.

"Lord Abel, there's a dragon!" the squad leader said breathlessly, his face pale white. "It's landed on the outer battlements."

"Do not attack!" Alexander commanded. "Take me there at once."

The squad leader looked to Abel.

He nodded. "Take us there quickly."

A procession of soldiers and wizards strung out down the hall following Alexander as he ran through the keep with the palace guard. Jataan was a step behind and to the left. When they emerged into the morning breeze, Alexander surveyed the scene. It wasn't a dragon—it was a wyvern. It had landed on a round corner tower of the outer wall of the family keep. There was a wide pathway along the top of one outer wall that led to the corner tower and then away along another wall. Soldiers were arrayed on both walls facing the wyvern and its dismounted rider.

"Hold!" Alexander called out to the soldiers. They stopped their slow advance and held their positions a good fifty feet from the intruder.

"Jack, Abel, please come with me," Alexander said. Jataan fell in behind him without a word.

"Stay hidden and stay close, Little One," he said to Chloe without speaking.

"I am here always, My Love," Chloe replied within his mind.

Alexander scrutinized the rider, who was standing calmly at the foot of her steed. She looked middle-aged and beautiful, with strawberry-blond hair and an unmistakable air of authority. More than that, her colors radiated power with the same intensity of a mage, yet somehow different.

The cluster of soldiers parted to allow them through. Jataan put a hand on Alexander's shoulder and brought him to a stop.

"This is unwise, Lord Reishi," Jataan said. "Her name is Magda. She is the first triumvir of the Reishi Coven. I have had dealings with her in the past. Her power is not to be underestimated."

"I understand," Alexander said. "She's the one who took Isabel and Abigail." He turned and strode toward her with the confidence of a king.

From somewhere behind him, he heard Jataan say, "There's another high in the sky."

Alexander cataloged the piece of information and brought his full focus to bear on the moment. He surveyed his surroundings through his all around sight. Mage Jalal and Mage Lenox had moved to stand with the cluster of soldiers on the wall. Magda stood still and proud, wearing riding leather that made her look more like a soldier than a witch.

Alexander stopped ten feet from her. "You abducted my wife and sister. Return them and I will spare your home." Alexander felt rage boiling within him. He reminded himself to be ruled by reason but driven by emotion. The old refrain taught to him by his father so many years ago schooled his desire to strike her down and reminded him that battlefields come in all forms.

She surveyed Alexander calmly and then turned to Jataan P'Tal. "Commander P'Tal, it's good to see you again. You're looking well."

"As are you, Mistress Magda," Jataan said politely. "Lord Reishi has spoken. You would do well to accede to his demands."

"I must say, Jataan, I was surprised to learn that you have chosen to serve young Alexander here," she said like an elder speaking about a wayward child.

"Lord Reishi is bonded with the Sovereign Stone," Jataan said. "His age is of no consequence."

"Did you help him steal it?" Magda asked.

"No. In fact, I was sent by Phane to kill him the moment he retrieved it from the aether," Jataan said. "When I witnessed Lord Reishi bond with the Sovereign Stone, I realized I was serving the wrong master and my duty became clear."

She turned back to Alexander with a little smile. He could see in her colors that she had a certain arrogance about her, no doubt the product of leading a powerful coven of witches and an army of Sky Knights. More importantly, he saw a basic goodness and respect for life tempered by a fierce loyalty to her duty.

Magda then turned to Abel. "You are the King of Ithilian and bearer of the Thinblade."

"I am," Abel responded.

"Do you stand with young Alexander?" she asked.

"I do," Abel said. "I have only known Lord Reishi for a short time, but I have come to think of him as a friend. What's more, my daughter was recently abducted by forces in league with Phane, so I understand with intimate clarity the pain you've caused him by taking his wife and sister. Your tactics are akin to those of Phane."

"Perhaps, but sometimes the stakes are so high that distasteful things must be done for the good of all," Magda said.

"Sounds like the rationalization of someone who believes they're morally superior to other people," Abel said. "You would do better to obey the Old Law."

She turned back to Alexander. "Isabel and Abigail think very highly of you," she said. "They are both formidable women. You should be proud of them."

"I am. Now bring them back to me," Alexander said calmly but firmly.

"I give you my word that they are both alive and well," Magda said. "We're treating them with appropriate respect and have provided them with comfortable quarters."

"I know," Alexander said. "I looked in on them just last night."

"Impossible," Magda said with a tinge of ire mixed with worry.

Alexander described their room in detail. He told her where it was within the fortress island, how it was furnished, and commented on the young waifish-looking girl who'd been sharing a meal with them the first time he'd used his clairvoyance to find them.

Magda's eyes widened a bit and some of the color drained from her face. Her colors showed just a hint of fear. "How can this be? The fortress islands are shielded against magical vision."

Alexander smiled and tapped the Sovereign Stone glowing softly as it rested against his chest. "I also had a conversation with Dominic Reishi the other night. He was the Second Sovereign, as you may recall. He built the fortress islands, so he had a few very interesting things to say about them. For example, did you know that the holder of the Sovereign Stone has the power to destroy any of the fortress islands on command?"

"That can't be," Magda said with rising alarm.

"I have no desire to destroy your home and everyone you know and love," Alexander said. "But if you harm either Isabel or Abigail, I will."

"Enough of this! I will not be threatened by a child," Magda said. "I have come to offer you a trade. Give us the Sovereign Stone so we can ensure that it will never fall into Phane's hands and we will return Isabel and Abigail unharmed."

Alexander regarded her calmly in spite of the rage boiling up within his soul. "Your offer is rejected," he said firmly. "But I have a counterproposal. Join with me in service to the Old Law and help me destroy Phane. Those who stand against him must work together or we will all fall."

"Surrender the Stone and we will help you against Phane," Magda said.

"Why do you want the Stone? You have no one who can use it and no way to guarantee that Phane can't take it from you," Alexander said. "Could it be that you and yours have stood watch over it for so long that your egos are bruised at having lost it to a child?"

Her face flushed, but Alexander was watching her colors more closely. There was something there in the background of her consciousness that he didn't quite understand. Then it hit him, and everything made more sense. She was delivering a message that she didn't fully believe in.

"Isabel is dying," she said.

Her colors flared with deception. Alexander listened without reacting.

"We tried the magic given to us by Mage Gamaliel and it failed. Perhaps you could find a way to save her if she were returned to you."

"Don't lie to me, witch," Alexander said with an undercurrent of menace in his voice. He spoke calmly but his awareness heightened and sharpened the way it always did when he was in a fight. The stakes of this battle were far more important to him than his own life.

Magda was clearly shocked at his immediate rejection of her lie. She looked at him with a renewed wariness. "There is more to you than we suspected."

"Isabel has not been given the magic that could save her life," Alexander said while his eyes glittered with golden rage. "If she dies in your care, I will shatter your home into gravel and scatter it into the ocean. Give her the magic. Save her life, not because I command it, but because you know it's the right thing to do. Holding her hostage is the kind of tactic I would expect of Phane. Are you no better than he?"

Magda turned to Jataan with a familiar little smile. "I can see why you have chosen to serve him rather than Phane." She looked down for a moment in thought as if she was fighting a battle within her own psyche. She nodded and looked up.

"Allow me to explain," she said. "The Reishi Coven and the Sky Knights are ruled by a triumvirate. I am one of three. We act only when there is agreement by two or more triumvirs. I was in favor of exploring an alliance as Isabel suggested. Cassandra and Gabriella, the other triumvirs, were in favor of forcing your hand by using your loved ones as leverage. It's clear to me now that this course is a mistake. There may be another way, but you will like it even less."

"I'm listening," Alexander said.

"The wife of the Reishi Sovereign must be a witch," Magda said. "Isabel is an impressive woman but she cannot be Lady Reishi. Tradition demands it, but more importantly, there are practical considerations. The Lord Reishi must have a mate who has the power to stand with him in battle. Furthermore, there is the issue of longevity. You have survived the mana fast—you will live nearly two hundred years, more if you survive the mage's fast. Isabel will die in less than a hundred years."

Alexander was struck by the inescapable logic of the second part of her reasoning. He dismissed the idea that Isabel couldn't stand with him in battle because he knew from experience that she could and would. While he was considering the implications of Isabel growing old while he remained relatively young, Magda made her offer.

"Forsake your vows to Isabel and choose a witch from within the Reishi Coven as your wife," Magda said quietly. "It's the only way to create the alliance you seek."

Alexander was slow to react because he couldn't quite make sense of what he'd just heard. The idea of giving up Isabel was so foreign to him, so incomprehensible, that he was stunned with momentary confusion as he tried to reconcile Magda's words with his feelings. When the truth of her statement finally penetrated into his mind, he started to reach for his sword. Before his hand touched the hilt, Chloe buzzed into existence not three feet from Magda's face. The witch's eyes went wide and her mouth fell open. Chloe flitted up to within a foot of her and shook her finger in the face of the triumvir of the Reishi Coven.

"Their vows cannot be unmade," Chloe said with scolding anger. "They were given freely out of love and nothing else. There was no thought of alliance or power, only love. They cannot be unmade and you would be wise to heed my warning. Their vows were witnessed by the Fairy Queen herself and she will be most unhappy if you interfere."

Alexander stayed his hand and calmed Chloe without speaking to her. She gave Magda one last very stern look before flying into an orbit around Alexander's head.

Alexander smiled at the uncertainty in Magda's aura and on her face. Fairies were creatures of legend. They represented an omen of luck and good fortune for those blessed by their friendship. The significance of Chloe's presence wasn't lost on Magda.

"Isabel spoke of the fairies, but I didn't believe her," Magda said quietly. "Such a story is so fantastic and unlikely that I dismissed it as subterfuge. Still, the problem remains. Cassandra and Gabriella will insist that you must marry a witch in order to be recognized by the Reishi Coven as Lord Reishi."

"Then make Isabel a witch," Alexander said. He knew what her next objection would be and was prepared for it.

"We don't have the necessary Wizard's Dust," Magda said. "And even if we did, the process is difficult and dangerous, possibly even deadly."

Alexander smiled. The hook was set. He reached into his pouch, withdrew three vials of Wizard's Dust and walked up to Magda, holding them out for her.

"One for Isabel, one for Abigail if she wants it, and one for the triumvirate to use as you see fit," he said. "Think of it as a token of my goodwill in the hopes that we can become allies against Phane in spite of our initial disagreements."

Magda was stunned. She blinked at the three vials he held and cautiously took them, then very carefully opened one to confirm the contents. Her face went slightly pale. "How is this possible?"

Alexander held her eyes with his and very deliberately tapped the Sovereign Stone resting against his chest.

"You will give Isabel the magic to save her from the poison and then you will guide her through the mana fast," Alexander said. "She is strong, smart, and determined. She will survive and then your conditions will be met."

Magda smiled in wonder. "My sisters are going to take some convincing, but I'm confident that Isabel will be permitted to endure the trials. However, I cannot guarantee the outcome."

"I know," Alexander said. "I've been through it myself. Give her the guidance she needs and she'll do fine."

"You understand that this will take some time," Magda said. "Then there's the issue of Abigail and her training."

"What do you mean?" Jack asked before Alexander could speak.

Magda regarded the bard curiously for a moment, then said to Alexander, "You claim the highest seat of royalty in all the Seven Isles, yet you surround yourself with people who would speak out of turn."

"On the contrary," Alexander said. "Master Jack Colton, the Bard of Ruatha, is one of my most trusted advisors and he's also Abigail's friend. He shares my concern for her well-being and he knows that I welcome his input on any matter. What exactly is Abigail being trained to do?"

"It seems that she found her way into a wyvern hatchery and bonded with a newborn wyvern," Magda said. "She is being trained as a Sky Knight."

Alexander chuckled. "That sounds like Abigail. Train her well." Alexander allowed his smile to fade and became deadly serious. "I'm entrusting you with the two people that I love most in this world. Teach them what they must learn and send them safely back to me."

"I make no promise save this: I will do what is within my power to protect your wife and sister. I can offer no more."

Alexander held her gaze for a moment before he slowly approached so he could speak for her ears alone. "With Isabel at my side, I have every reason in the world to fight for life and liberty. Without her . . ." his voice trailed off for a moment. "Well, let's just say I have less to live for."

She smiled gently, almost fondly. "I understand."

Alexander fished around in his pouch and produced the medallion of Glen Morillian. "This belongs to her. She'll know it came from me. Tell them both that I love them."

Magda took the medallion and slipped it into her riding armor. "I will deliver your message."

Alexander stood silently and watched the wyvern grow smaller as it gained altitude and distance. Jack stood next to him, resting his hands on the battlement of the castle wall.

"Do you trust her?" Jack asked quietly.

After a moment of thought, Alexander nodded. "For her part I do, but there are other forces at work in the fortress island. Isabel and Abigail are still in danger, but hopefully, they have an ally in Magda."

As they walked back to the cluster of soldiers standing with Mage Jalal and Mage Lenox, Abel chuckled. "That ought to stir up gossip in the city for a while."

"I imagine," Alexander said. "In fact, that might work to our advantage. Let's keep the reason for her visit a mystery for the time being. People's speculation about the matter will only serve to enhance the value of my offer of alliance."

Abel laughed. "I like it. When faced with uncertainty, the delegates will always err on the side of caution."

"Hopefully, they'll see an alliance with me as the cautious move," Alexander said just before they reached the cluster of soldiers.

"Quite an impressive visitor," Mage Jalal said. "May I enquire as to her purpose here?"

Alexander smiled graciously. "I'm afraid it's a personal matter. Is there somewhere we could speak in private?"

Abel turned to the leader of the squad of soldiers. "Sergeant, escort Lord Reishi and Mage Jalal to a private conference room."

The room they arrived at was simple but functional. It contained a sturdy table surrounded by heavy oak chairs. There were no windows and only a single door. Light was provided by a number of brass oil lamps lining the walls. It looked like a place where military officers met to plan their duty rosters.

Jack, Lucky, and Anatoly tagged along. Jataan was silently present as well, never asking permission nor accepting orders that put his charge out of reach.

He stood silently near the single door with his hands clasped easily behind his back.

"Thank you for meeting with me, Mage Jalal," Alexander said, once everyone had found a seat. "I'm told you may be able to help me locate the keystones used to activate the Nether Gate."

Mage Jalal was a very old man. His hair was white and shoulder length. His beard was white as well and reached to the middle of his chest. He moved with stiffness and deliberate care, but his eyes were clear and his voice was strong.

"Straight to the point," he said. "I like that. So many who aspire to power speak endlessly about issues of no importance in order to avoid facing the hard choices. Yes—in fact, I have already done so. When Mage Lenox brought the issue to my attention last night, I went to work on the problem immediately.

"The Nether Gate itself is located in the northwest mountains of the Reishi Isle. One of the keystones is there. The second keystone is located on Tyr, more specifically on the central island of Tyr. The third stone is beyond my vision. I will continue to look for it, but I believe it is being shielded against magical detection."

"A shade must have found one of the keystones already," Alexander said. "That makes the keystone on Tyr a priority. We can hope that the third is permanently out of reach, but for all we know Phane already has it. Thank you, Mage Jalal. This information is invaluable. If you learn the whereabouts of the third keystone, send word of it to me immediately."

"Of course," Mage Jalal said. "Can we be of any further assistance?"

"You can," Alexander said. "Master Alabrand here is an alchemist. I suspect he would like to use a laboratory before we depart tomorrow."

Lucky smiled broadly. "You read my mind."

"I will see to the arrangements myself," Mage Jalal said.

Alexander took three vials of Wizard's Dust from his pouch and set them on the table before the Guild Mage. "One last thing," he said. "Select your three most promising apprentices and guide them through the mana fast."

Mage Jalal blinked in surprise. He reverently took one of the vials and opened it carefully. A smile slowly grew across his wrinkled face. "This is a gift of immeasurable value. It will revitalize our order and renew faith that the path of an apprentice will eventually lead to the trials. Thank you, Lord Reishi."

"You are most welcome, Mage Jalal," Alexander said. "In time, I hope to have more to offer, but for now this is all that I can spare."

After meeting with the Mage, Alexander returned to his suite of rooms for lunch. Abel joined him there. A small army of serving staff brought a well-prepared meal with plenty of food for all of Alexander's friends.

"I've spoken with General Kishor," Abel whispered to Alexander as they stood out on the balcony while the servants set the table. "He understands his orders."

"Good. What about Conner?" Alexander asked.

"I've written him a letter," Abel said as he handed over a piece of parchment sealed in wax with the glyph of the House of Ithilian. "He's young. Subterfuge is not his strong suit. I fear that he might inadvertently give us away."

Alexander nodded as he slipped the letter into his pouch.

Boaberous returned after lunch with over two dozen men and women from all walks of life. Alexander wasn't sure what to make of it as the throng filed into his sitting room. There were soldiers, craftsmen, traders, merchants, a delegate, and even a constable.

Jataan stood up and all of the newly arrived guests immediately fell silent and attentive. He surveyed them for a moment before he turned to Alexander.

"Lord Reishi, I have instructed Lieutenant Grudge to round up all of the members of the Reishi Protectorate that he could locate on short notice and bring them before you so that they might see the Sovereign Stone and offer you their loyalty and service."

Alexander stood and withdrew the Sovereign Stone from his tunic. There was a wave of murmuring among the crowd and then, as one, they all went to a knee.

Alexander frowned at the display of submission. "Rise," he commanded. "I am Alexander Reishi and I have bonded with the Sovereign Stone. Phane Reishi is my mortal enemy. He is a necromancer and a murderer. He has nothing but contempt for the Old Law and seeks total power over the lives of all. Spread the word through any means you have at your disposal that Phane is the enemy of the Reishi Sovereign.

"On another front, Lord Zuhl has invaded Fellenden with a massive army. Use what resources you have to learn his intentions and military strengths and weaknesses. The people of Fellenden are suffering under his invasion. When the time is right, I intend to make war on him as well."

Jataan spent some time speaking with each one of his operatives. He received their reports and gave them more detailed instructions. Most importantly, he impressed on each one the importance of the coming struggle. This moment in history was what the Reishi Protectorate had been waiting for. Their long exile was at an end. The Reishi line was reborn and the ancient and sacred purpose of the Reishi Protectorate was once again in need of their service.

Alexander made a point of circulating among the members of the Protectorate as well. He wanted to meet some of these people who had just weeks ago been the enemy. Most were driven by a sense of loyalty to their purpose. Their colors revealed little in the way of personal ambition or corruption. They were people who lived for duty to a cause greater than themselves, a cause that they could believe in. Alexander remembered Jack's assertion that people wanted to believe in something larger than themselves. The Reishi Protectorate was living proof of that.

Even with all of the challenges he faced, Alexander couldn't help but feel better about the odds of success. Knowing that Isabel and Abigail were alive and relatively safe was a huge relief that freed up his mind to focus on other matters.

***

They rode out the next morning at dawn, accompanied by Prince Conner and his royal guard of a hundred soldiers. The bells on the towers all around the city tolled to honor the soldiers who would soon face battle. Not a soul in Ithilian was unaware that their army had been committed to the war against Phane. Alexander smiled to himself at the theatre of it all.

Once they were well outside of the city and out of view of anyone who might be watching, Alexander called a halt.

"Conner, your father and I have agreed on a strategy that is quite different from the one we announced to the world," Alexander said. "He wrote a letter for you and asked that I give it to you once we were well away from the city." Alexander produced the folded piece of parchment stamped with the seal of Ithilian and handed it to Conner.

The Prince of Ithilian read the letter and a fierce smile spread across his face. "I like this plan much better," he said. "But I don't understand why I was excluded until now."

"Your uncle Cassius is in league with Phane," Alexander said gravely. "He may have helped the enemy abduct your sister."

Conner's face went crimson red and fury flashed in his eyes. "I'll kill him for this," he said with coiled rage. "He has never supported my father, but this is treason. Why isn't he in chains as we speak?"

"Because I asked your father to let him continue with his treachery," Alexander said. "He's far more useful to us as a conduit of disinformation. If he were arrested, it would alert the enemy that their plans have been compromised. If our ruse works, it will accomplish two things. First, the forces in Grafton Province will drop their guard because Abel has indicated a willingness to meet their demands. Second, the enemy on Ruatha will adjust their strategy to defend against an army coming through the Gate behind them. Hopefully, that will buy my father some time to protect the people of New Ruatha and Northport."

Anatoly chuckled. "I'm glad to see you were paying attention during your strategy lessons."

"I must caution you, Lord Reishi," Jataan said, "Prince Phane has ways of spying at a great distance. It would be wise to not speak of this again."

Alexander knew as well as anyone how valuable information was. He had used his unique magical talents to gather information time and again. He nodded to Jataan. "Point taken," he said, then turned to the Rangers. "Lieutenant Wyatt, return to the legions at the Gate with Prince Conner's honor guard and offer General Brand any and all information you can about Ruatha. Draw him a map of the area around the Gate and assist him in any way he requires to make his legions ready for battle with the Reishi Army Regency."

"Understood, Lord Reishi," Lieutenant Wyatt said.

Conner briefed the commander of his honor guard and they continued north toward the Gate with the Rangers. Alexander turned east with his friends and Conner to skirt the city and head south toward Grafton Province. They each had a spare horse and plenty of supplies so they could travel fast and avoid stopping in any towns where they might be recognized. Alexander's plan depended on surprise.

Chapter 11

General Talia sat on his horse, looking out over the impromptu fortification. His legions had dug in across a wide swath of the valley not ten leagues from Kai'Gorn. After carefully scouting the entire area looking for the right conditions for his battlefield, he'd chosen this piece of ground because it was strewn with rocks and small boulders for miles in all directions. It was useless as farmland because years of wind had worn the topsoil away to bedrock and left a hard and barren field.

His men had worked tirelessly for the better part of a week to prepare the place to defend against an all-out assault by the Andalian Lancers. Talia knew that his first strategic objective was to eliminate the deadly threat posed by the formidable cavalry from Andalia. Once they were out of the way, the infantry defenders of Kai'Gorn would fall easily to his superior numbers.

Everything was in order. Most of his men were sleeping per his instructions. They had worked day and night to erect the berm of rock that would provide the last line of defense against the Lancers. General Fabian had taken five thousand heavy cavalry and was waiting for the signal to engage the enemy from their flank once the Lancers were fully committed to the attack. The infantry and archers all knew their jobs and were in place.

Five thousand light cavalry on loan from Kevin's legion of Rangers had gone to spring the trap. The battle would take place tomorrow. General Talia went over every detail of his plan again in his head and tested each part for flaws and weaknesses. Reports from multiple sources told him that there was just over a legion of Lancers in the area surrounding Kai'Gorn. He outnumbered them by a factor of five but their giant rhone steeds and their powerful magical lances made them a dangerous force. He knew his infantry wouldn't stand a chance against them in the open, so he'd taken every precaution and made every preparation to ensure that this would be a very one-sided battle.

All that remained was to wait and hope that the Rangers could goad the Lancers into a fight. Talia was confident in that part of his plan. The Andalians were known for their arrogance and quick tempers. No doubt, their sense of superiority stemmed from the power of their steeds and lances. But Talia knew that the Lancers were not effective within the walls of a city. Their favored battlefield was an open plain where they could bring the speed and weight of their steeds to bear. Talia had selected this location for that reason as much as any other. He wanted to provide them with a battlefield that would inspire confidence and prompt them to act without carefully evaluating the situation.

The Rangers had been harassing the enemy for the past three days, using hit and run tactics. For a brief charge, the rhone were faster than any horse, but their size limited their endurance; the light horses favored by the Rangers were easily able to outdistance them. Talia used this to his advantage. He instructed the Rangers to break into units of five hundred and attack relentlessly when and where they could. His purpose wasn't to cause great damage but to frustrate and anger the enemy while dropping breadcrumbs back to his prepared battlefield. He wanted the Lancers to learn of his encampment and decide to end the threat once and for all.

Wizard Rand was also a vital part of Talia's plan. Rand was an illusionist. His talent was rare and quite powerful when used creatively. It was Wizard Rand's magical calling that had led Talia to adopt this particular strategy. He knew better than most that deception is the most powerful weapon a general has at his disposal—the more convincing the ruse, the more deadly the result. His plan hinged on the wizard, and after seeing a few demonstrations of Wizard Rand's capability, Talia was quite certain that he would do his part.

When he saw one of the Ranger raiding parties returning in haste, his heart quickened. The time for battle was nearing. The report from the Rangers confirmed that the Lancers were massing north of Kai'Gorn. They would arrive by midmorning a day hence. Talia went over his plans again, scrutinizing every detail for flaws and weaknesses. He was a meticulous man who understood that victory often hinged on the most mundane parts of any plan.

He spent the rest of the day walking through his army and talking with the soldiers. Many had served under his command for years and knew his leadership style. He was as proud of them as they were loyal to him. Before he went to sleep that night, he went over his plans yet again just to make sure everything was in place. He had confidence in his soldiers and their commanders. Everyone knew their part and everyone knew the stakes. Everything within his power had been done, but he worried about those things outside of his power and those unforeseen events that always seemed to arise during battle.

The next morning, the stage was set. Everyone was in place. His commanders all reported ready and awaiting orders. General Talia sat on his horse atop the little hillock looking off into the distance where the enemy was stirring up a cloud of dust that left a brown smudge across the horizon. He surveyed the battlefield.

His forces were arrayed behind a berm of stones that stood eight feet tall and stretched for a mile or more in each direction. Rank after rank of men with shields and pikes were lined up facing the berm. Behind them was rank after rank of heavy infantry. And behind them all were a dozen ranks of archers with ample arrows for their task.

When a messenger brought word that the enemy was an hour away, General Talia ordered the first signal. A whistler arrow streaked into the air, sending out a shrill squeal that could be heard for miles.

Wizard Rand unleashed the spells he had been preparing all week. General Talia watched as the entire berm of stone vanished from sight, leaving a clear path between the advancing enemy and his troops. Rand's spells would hold for several hours.

The trap was set.

Talia schooled his emotions as he went over the details again. His part was done. He had laid the foundation for victory in this battle. Now all he could do was wait and set the different elements of his plan into motion when the time was right.

The enemy advanced until they were within a hundred yards. They stopped to form up into a giant front a thousand wide and ten deep. They were

disciplined and well ordered despite their arrogance . . . or perhaps because of it.
They knew that the enemy before them was no match for their superior mass
supported by the awesome power of their force lances.

What they saw on the battlefield was a wall of heavy shields forming an
interlocking line. Behind the shield line was a row of men with long pikes resting
on notches cut into the side of each shield. Behind them was row after row of
infantry followed by archers. Against a normal cavalry charge, the formation was
a good defense, but against the magic of a force lance charge, the wall of shields
would be shattered before the first Lancer reached the tip of a pike. They would
crash through the line and trample the infantry under hoof. Before the enemy
could regroup, the Lancers would be into the archers. By then, their lances would
be ready to discharge another deadly blast of magical force.

The Andalian Lancers began their charge. General Talia gave the order
and the second signal arrow streaked into the sky, putting his forces on notice that
the enemy was beginning their attack. General Fabian would start moving toward
the battlefield from the left flank and the Rangers would begin approaching the
Lancers from the right flank.

The thundering gallop of the giant rhone steeds was deafening even at
this distance. Talia understood why they were so feared. It was a terrible noise that
would have unnerved him if he hadn't made such meticulous preparations for this
battle.

The enemy came closer and the men on the battle line braced for the
attack that they would never feel. General Talia smiled at the theatre of it all. His
trap was about to be sprung. All across the battlefield, his soldiers had dug deep
pits in the stone. They had worn out hundreds of pick axes and chisels breaking
the rock so they could use it for the berm that was now hidden by Wizard Rand's
illusion. Each of the pits was covered with a few boards, then a piece of canvas
and a layer of dirt to make it look like the rest of the rocky plain.

The first Lancer crashed into a pit and was impaled on a number of very
sharp wooden spikes. Another fell and then another. They didn't let up on their
charge but pressed on with anger and determination. A tenth of their number fell
into the pit traps before the rest passed into the kill zone.

General Talia commanded the third signal arrow. The high-pitched squeal
could just be heard over the thunder of the advancing enemy. As one, the archers
released a volley. Thousands of arrows rose in a high arc floating over the infantry
and the invisible stone berm. They seemed to hang in the air for a moment, frozen
in time, before they came crashing down into the advancing Lancers. Their plate
armor and heavy shields defended most of them against the attack but a few dozen
more fell. Talia knew his archers would have little effect, but he also knew the
Lancers would be expecting an arrow volley. Deception so often played on
expectations.

More arrows rose into the air. The Lancers leaned into their charge as
they neared the line of soldiers—and then the trap was sprung. The first line of
Lancers crashed headlong into the invisible berm of stone. It flickered into view
now that contact had been made, but it was too late. The Lancers had too much
momentum. Rank after rank of the giant steeds hurtled into the barrier. The
thunderous crash reverberated through the air. Sounds of bones snapping and
lances shattering could be heard for miles. Men screamed in fear and wailed in

pain.

The next volley of arrows descended into a jumbled mass of fallen rhone and men and peppered the survivors with deadly effect. Another volley rose into the air before General Talia saw his heavy cavalry come over the small rise and charge along the outside edge of the stone berm toward the remains of the Andalian legion.

General Talia ordered the fourth signal. The last volley fell into the enemy with withering effect, leaving less than a quarter of the enemy Lancers still standing. Many were wounded and all were in disarray as the cavalry crashed into them from the flank. Those Lancers that met the cavalry on the leading edge of the attack fell quickly. The rest turned and ran away from the cavalry charge and straight into five thousand Rangers arrayed before them. Before they could react, the Rangers had loosed their first volley of arrows.

The Lancers lost unit cohesion and started to scatter. Some fell to the cavalry behind them while others were killed by the deadly accurate archery of the Rangers. Some few more turned and ran back through the field strewn with pit traps. Fewer than five hundred escaped the battle alive, but the Rangers gave chase without pause and harried them relentlessly until they had run down and killed every single Lancer.

The infantry poured over the berm wall and methodically killed all of the wounded Lancers who had survived the initial attack. General Talia would have preferred to take prisoners but Lord Alexander had been very clear: Kill them to a man. General Talia was a man who followed his orders.

By evening, the enemy bodies had been stripped of weapons and armor and piled into a giant funeral pyre. A few dozen of the giant rhone steeds had survived unscathed. They were taken and incorporated into the heavy cavalry commanded by General Fabian.

The force lances wouldn't work for General Talia's men. Wizard Rand surmised that they were tied to the oath given to the Andalian King and suggested that all of the force lances still intact should be shipped to Blackstone Keep for careful analysis by Mage Gamaliel.

The next morning they started their march toward Kai'Gorn. Talia sent a small contingent of soldiers north with the force lances and a message of his victory as the rest of his forces moved south.

Five days later his army of nearly five legions was arrayed around Kai'Gorn. The Rangers had tracked down and killed every last Lancer before returning to the main force. The immediate threat posed by Andalia was eliminated.

All that remained was to prevent them from using Kai'Gorn to land more of their fearsome cavalry. Talia was acutely aware that his victory over the Lancers would be difficult to replicate.

He waited with Wizard Rand and a squad of Rangers for the envoy from Kai'Gorn to approach. The three men carried the banner of the city and a flag of truce; they carried no weapons and didn't look like soldiers. Talia hoped they would surrender peacefully and allow him to take command of the city without bloodshed—but he doubted it.

They stopped a dozen paces away. The man in the center wore the emblem of Andalia on his tunic.

"I speak for the King of Andalia. He has claimed Kai'Gorn as a protectorate city. Your aggression here will not be tolerated. Further, Andalia serves the rightful Sovereign of the Seven Isles, Phane Reishi. Under his authority, I command you to withdraw your forces from the territory of Kai'Gorn."

General Talia regarded the man for a moment. He wondered if he might be a wizard but decided he was probably a noble who had been promised this city if he could hold it.

"I am General Talia and I speak for the King of Ruatha. He has commanded the immediate surrender of Kai'Gorn to his rule. You will open your gates and lay down your weapons. If you comply, you and your people will be treated according to the Old Law. If you resist, I will conquer your city by force."

"The people of Kai'Gorn do not wish to be governed by Ruatha and least of all by soldiers from Southport and Highlands Reach. You are not welcome here. Therefore, under the Old Law, you must leave."

General Talia smiled at his temerity. "You have brought forces hostile to the people of Ruatha to our shores and waged war against our rightful King. As such, you forfeit your right to life, liberty, or property. Surrender now and all will be forgiven."

"Your offer is rejected! If you attack our walls, you will pay a heavy price for your crime." With that, the three men turned and galloped off toward the city. Talia considered killing them on the spot but decided against it. He may need to speak to another envoy in the days to come and they would be very reluctant if he killed this one.

***

Kai'Gorn was well defended. Their walls were high and stout. Talia sent his soldiers in to probe their defenses and ascertain the range of their weapons. The city had heavy ballistae that were deadly out to a thousand feet and catapults that could hurl large stones or clay firepots almost two thousand feet past the walls.

Talia gathered the reports about the enemy brought to him from his army. He was a man who appreciated information and wanted as much detail as possible before he took action. He also understood the importance of a swift victory. The longer he waited to attack, the more likely it was that additional Lancers would arrive from Andalia.

After a day of surrounding the enemy, just out of range of their weapons, Talia decided he had enough information to formulate a plan. He'd lost a few men during the probing attacks and knew from the reports of those engagements that the soldiers within Kai'Gorn were well trained and dangerous.

He weighed the options and decided that half measures were not acceptable. His primary mission was to protect Ruatha from the Andalians. The port at Kai'Gorn had to be taken, and the sooner the better. Talia thought back to the instructions Alexander had given him. He decided to make an effort to take the city without fire even though he wasn't confident of his chances.

He ordered his soldiers to construct a battering ram. The next day, under cover of a magical fog conjured by Wizard Rand, a hundred soldiers approached the gate and made an attempt to break the giant reinforced doors. They defended against the arrows cast down from above with shields but then a hail of clay pots filled with oil rained down on them. Moments later they were peppered from above with flaming arrows. Those few soldiers that survived, retreated, leaving the battering ram ablaze behind them.

General Talia again considered his options and carefully weighed each. He decided that he didn't have the necessary heavy weaponry to breach the walls, nor did he have the magic necessary to gain access to the city. He didn't believe his men could scale the walls without massive losses. His probes had revealed a few passages that looked like they used to lead under the walls, but they had all been collapsed. Reluctantly, General Talia decided on fire.

Wizard Rand conjured his magical fog again and surrounded the entire city with the thick mist. Two thousand archers, each armed with a dozen flame arrows, approached to within a hundred feet of the walls.

When his men were in place, General Talia ordered the signal arrow.

Moments later, thousands of streaks of fire rose up out of the low fog, arced over the wall, and rained down into the city. Another volley followed another until the archers had loosed all of their flaming arrows, then they retreated back through the fog under a counterattack from the city walls.

Kai'Gorn opened up with their archers, ballistae, and catapults, sending a hail of deadly rain down on the retreating archers. The fog could shroud their location but offered no protection against a barrage of missiles. Unable to get out of range quickly enough, almost three hundred of Talia's men died, but the damage of the attack could be seen in the orange glow of flames that licked the sky over the walls of the city.

General Talia hadn't wanted to do it this way but he knew the longer he waited, the more dangerous the enemy would become. As the magical fog dissipated, he sat on his horse and watched the city of Kai'Gorn burn. Smoke billowed into the sky as the flames reached higher.

It wasn't long before the gates opened and a stream of people fled to escape the smoke and fire. General Talia ordered them disarmed and imprisoned in a camp not far from the city. He kept them under guard but treated their wounds and provided them with food and water. His soldiers were respectful but firm. They didn't treat anyone with cruelty, which seemed to come as a surprise to the refugees caught between Talia's advancing army and the tyranny of Kai'Gorn.

With the gates open, Kai'Gorn was vulnerable. Talia's forces stormed through and systematically worked to take the walls and fortifications surrounding the city without venturing into the city itself. They took and held the perimeter wall and maintained a cordon around the city to prevent any enemy soldiers from escaping. For three days the city burned and the people fled.

Small bands of soldiers tried to organize resistance against General Talia's forces. They were dispatched quickly and without difficulty. There was little organization left within the burning city and a great deal of panic. Once the fires died and the population had mostly fled the destruction, Talia's forces began moving into the city itself. They worked methodically to search out any enemy still present and any survivors who hadn't had the good sense to flee.

The place was in ruins. Over half of the wood buildings had burned to the ground and those that remained were scorched. General Talia walked through his conquest with a mixture of sadness and resolve. He understood war and knew the consequences as well as anyone, but he still had a heavy heart for the destruction he'd wrought. Most of the people living here were victims, first of Magistrate Cain's tyranny and then of the forces from Andalia. He knew that rule under Alexander would yield a much better life for those who survived but that didn't help the dead.

General Talia did his best to avoid harming the civilians but was ruthless with any soldier who didn't lay down arms and surrender. Some of the enemy went into hiding and tried to mount an insurgency but their numbers were few, and with the majority of the population contained in the massive refugee camp outside the city walls, the enemy soldiers were easy to find. By week's end, the city was secure and the docks and keep were under General Talia's control. Kai'Gorn had sustained heavy damage. The stone structures still stood and the docks had survived the fires, but nearly a third of the wooden buildings were lost and almost everything else was damaged to one degree or another.

Talia set about the work of rebuilding and invited the people to return to the homes that still stood. For those who were without shelter, he opened the barracks of the Kai'Gorn military while his troops camped outside the walls. After some semblance of order was reestablished, he started assembling crews for the ships still in the harbor. Many of the sailors were happy to have the opportunity to work, even if it meant crewing on warships.

Talia sent the half legion of Rangers north to Southport with word of his victory and of its cost. He requested that Kevin send lumber, nails, paint, and food south for the people of Kai'Gorn. He knew that the best way to create loyalty was to help these people rebuild their lives.

Once he knew how many of Kai'Gorn's population had survived, and once he had thoroughly scouted the surrounding area for any other threats, he sent two legions north under the command of General Fabian to report to Regent Alaric and seek further orders from General Valentine. Two legions would be more than enough men to hold Kai'Gorn and man the warships. Besides, every extra mouth to feed was an additional burden on the severely damaged economy of the local area.

General Talia stood on the battlements of the keep and looked south toward Andalia. He started making plans for moving his forces across the channel to the enemy lands in the distance. He didn't know if he would be called on to make such a voyage, but he was a general officer—he made plans for any possible course of action that might be required of him.

Chapter 12

Kevin stood on the battlements of Southport Keep, looking down on the docks below. The shipwright guild had just declared a strike. It had been two weeks since Alexander and Isabel had sailed away, and Kevin found himself preoccupied with his little sister. He knew Alexander would do everything in his power to protect her, but he was still worried about her.

The nightmare of trying to govern a city-state that didn't want to be governed was starting to take its toll on him. He idly wondered how things were going for Erik and Duane. He suspected Erik was dealing with some of the same problems he was facing in Southport. But Duane was in the field commanding a legion in pursuit of Elred Rake in the north; at least he had people who would actually follow his orders.

"We could hang a few of them," Lieutenant LaChance said. He was a big man, easily six and a half feet tall and weighing over two hundred and fifty pounds. His jaw was square, his shoulders were broad, and his ordinary brown hair was unruly and slightly longer than it should have been. Kevin's Second, Lieutenant Tanner was leading half of his legion in the south of Ruatha, fighting Kai'Gorn under the command of General Talia. LaChance was serving as his Second for the time being.

"The thought crossed my mind," Kevin said.

He'd spent the past two weeks skirmishing with the petty nobles about all manner of things. It seemed that every day they had some new complaint or dispute that required his urgent and immediate attention. Most of the issues they brought forward seemed like simple matters that could easily be resolved with a little compromise and common sense, but the petty nobles seemed to lack the ability for either.

Kevin was tired and frustrated. For the first week he had let the situation rule him. He tried to address every demand made by a city administrator or petty noble with fairness and justice, but he quickly realized they were playing a game with him and he didn't know the rules. His solution was to change the rules, a solution that proved most unpopular among those at court. Southport was a thoroughly corrupt place where the previous Regent had played one faction against another with favors and privileges in exchange for support and loyalty.

It was a place where merit and genuine value was scorned in favor of wealth granted by the Regent. At first it was totally perplexing to Kevin. He had spent his life in a place where things were most often exactly as they appeared, where a person's word was worthy of trust and where you could count on others to do the right thing given the chance.

Everything in the court of Southport was the opposite. It took a few days but Kevin soon discovered that every promise made to him by a courtier, administrator, or petty noble was nothing but fluff. When he attempted to hold them to anything, they denied, weaseled, and outright lied to avoid fulfilling their commitments. It was almost as if they resented him for reneging on some unspoken promise to them.

When he sat down with a couple of the city administrators and questioned them about the pathological dishonesty of the nobles and the courtiers, they stonewalled him at first. They hemmed and hawed, trying to avoid any concrete or substantive answers. Finally, Kevin lost his temper, threw the table over and drew his sword. The administrators very suddenly realized they were in a far different arena than the one they were accustomed to.

When Administrator Crandall explained Kevin's misunderstanding, it was all he could do to sheath his sword in its scabbard instead of the administrator. Apparently, everyone at court expected some type of bribe for everything they were asked to do. When Kevin hadn't taken them aside and offered a purse of gold or granted a special privilege, they thought he was taking advantage of them. In short, everybody in Southport who worked for the government expected some form of payoff before they were willing to do their job.

After some thought, he called the courtiers, administrators, and petty nobles in for a council meeting. They were all a little disconcerted by the full company of Rangers lining the walls of the council chamber. Kevin knew he wasn't going to make any friends but he decided he didn't care. The systemic corruption of the Southport government was the reason Isabel had been poisoned. Their willingness to compromise on any principle if the price was right was a problem that he had to address if he was going to live up to Alexander's trust.

He explained that anyone employed by the government of Southport who was found to have accepted a bribe would lose their job and face trial. If found guilty, they would lose all of their property except the shirt on their back and they would be put to work at hard labor for a period of one year to pay restitution for their crime.

They were stunned. A few chose to continue with their corrupt ways. Kevin was only too happy to make examples of them. They found themselves employed as scullions working to keep the floors of Southport Keep clean. After that, most of the city employees became very diligent about their work and were much more honest in their dealings. But now he found himself at odds with the trade guilds.

He had assessed the situation in the south of Ruatha and realized very quickly that General Talia would shut down the port at Kai'Gorn. When he did, the Andalians would look for another port to land their troops. That meant they would either come to Southport and attempt to take the city or they would bypass it and attempt to land at Northport. Either way, naval power would decide the day.

Kevin took inventory of the Southport treasury and found that he had ample gold at his disposal. The late Regent Landon had hoarded as much treasure as he could. Kevin intended to buy a navy with it. He thought the shipwright trade guild would be happy with the expanded shipyards he proposed but they saw it as an opportunity.

They demanded that their wages be doubled. When Kevin refused, they stopped working. He thought the example he'd made of the city workers would convince the people of Southport that he was serious. Apparently, he was wrong.

"Set up a meeting with the masters of the trade guilds," Kevin told his Second as he looked down at the idle docks.

"Right away," LaChance said before striding off to make the

arrangements.

A couple of hours later, Kevin sat at the head of the table as the guild masters entered the council room. There were almost a dozen of them. Each was well dressed and clearly ate well. It looked like it had been quite some time since any of them had actually plied his trade. Kevin waited patiently while they found their seats.

Once all were seated but before Kevin could speak, the master of the shipwright guild started making demands. "I'm Shipwright Guild Master Daley. We want three times our previous wage to build your navy for you. Take it or leave it." He was a sturdy man with grey stubble and stringy grey hair. At one time he had been powerful, with broad shoulders and a barrel chest, but now he was more portly than powerful. He punctuated his demand with a scowl.

Kevin schooled his demeanor. He'd learned that showing anger to these kinds of people would quickly turn them into simpering victims who demanded concessions for being put upon.

"Your wages are already twice that of the average worker in Southport," Kevin said calmly.

"Doesn't matter," Daley said defiantly. "We're the only ones who can build your ships for you. The way I hear it, you need those ships, so you'll meet our price." He put his index finger on the table for emphasis. "And I expect your answer right now or the price will go up to four times the going rate."

Kevin regarded him coolly and then looked to the rest of the guild masters. "Do the rest of you feel the same way?"

They nodded all around. A big man with a full beard of reddish-brown hair spoke next. "I'm Lumberjack Guild Master Garver. We all understand the urgency of the situation and we have to do what's best for those we represent. This is a rare opportunity for us to do better for our own."

"I see," Kevin said. "You do realize we're at war."

"Who cares," Daley said. "Doesn't matter if it's Landon, you, or Phane who rules us—everyone needs stuff built." He smiled like he was springing a trap. "Difference is, if Phane takes Southport, you and your Rangers will all be killed. We'll just have to renegotiate."

Kevin remained calm in spite of the twitch he felt in his sword arm. He turned to Administrator Crandall who sat in a chair along the wall. "What was that you told me about the trade guild charters?"

Crandall stood up, looking a bit nervous, but he answered with the smoothness of someone who lies for a living. "The trade guilds are granted charter by the Regent."

"And what does that charter entail?" Kevin asked. He saw the nervous looks of several of the guild masters at this line of questioning.

"The guild charter gives the guild the right to select who may work in a given trade, train workers in that trade, negotiate wages for guild members, and require dues from workers in that trade be paid to the trade guild for their services." Crandall spoke like he was reading from a book, without inflection or emotion.

"And you say that these charters are granted by the Regent?" Kevin asked calmly.

"Um, yes," Crandall said.

"So the Regent can revoke them," Kevin said.

"Well, um, yes, but there is no precedent for such a thing," Crandall said.

"I guess we'll just have to change that," Kevin said as he turned back to a table filled with now furious or terrified guild masters. He surveyed them calmly for a long moment. "What's it going to be? Will you do your work for the going rate or will I take your charters and dismantle your guilds?"

Daley stood up almost apoplectic. "You can't do that! We're the only ones who know how to build ships. Hire all the unskilled labor you like—without our expertise, your navy will sink. It's four times the going rate for you now!" Daley faced him as though trying to stare down his own reflection.

Kevin didn't flinch. "The shipwright guild's charter is hereby revoked. If you or any of your people interfere with the building of my navy, cause damage to property, or engage in any kind of violence, your actions will be met with swift justice."

Daley leaned in with a look of rage contorting his face as he screamed at Kevin, "You're going to regret this!" Then he stormed out of the council room.

"Have we settled the matter, gentlemen?" Kevin asked the remaining trade guild masters.

A few looked like they wanted to protest but they held their tongues. The anger was palpable as they filed out of the room.

Administrator Crandall cleared his throat. "I believe that was a mistake. They are liable to strike until you are removed as Regent—or worse."

"Are you suggesting that they would resort to violence?" Kevin asked.

"It's certainly within the realm of possibility," Crandall said. "Regent Landon took payment from each of them in exchange for letting them have control over the workers in their trade. They will resist such an abrupt change in the status quo."

"The sooner people in this city understand that the days of bribery and corruption are over, the better," Kevin said. "These people seem to need an example, so I intend to give them one."

Kevin instructed LaChance to increase patrols and place the Rangers and city guard on alert. He also doubled the number of Rangers guarding the docks and the shipyard. He hoped the shipwrights would come around and be willing to work whether they were represented by a guild or not, but he suspected there would be some trouble before that happened.

He wasn't disappointed. Early the next morning he was roused from his bed by the fire brigade's bells. By the time he made it to the keep wall overlooking the docks, the shipyard was on fire and there was a pitched battle between the Rangers and a mob of guild members.

The members of the fire brigade were doing their best to avoid the fighting and to put out the burning buildings, but the battle was hindering their efforts. Kevin saw at a glance that although his Rangers were easily outnumbered three to one, they were holding formation and standing their ground between the rioting mob and the remaining buildings that made up the shipyard.

Kevin thought about the duty of a regent for a moment. He thought about what Alexander had charged him with and his resolve hardened. The men rioting on the docks had resorted to violence because they didn't get their way. They were threatening the future of Southport and Ruatha. They had made a decision to violate the law. Choices had consequences.

LaChance trotted up beside Kevin with a squad of Rangers in tow. "Looks like they decided to make trouble instead of build ships," he said.

"Their loss," Kevin said with a mixture of sadness and anger. "Assemble three hundred Rangers on horseback and move into the shipyard. Arrest every single one of those men. Kill anyone who offers resistance."

"Understood," LaChance said before trotting off toward the barracks.

Kevin watched the battle unfold. He wanted to be in the middle of the fight leading his men, but he was the Regent, for the moment anyway, and that meant sending others to do the fighting.

The Rangers were well organized and disciplined. They formed a wall of shields and spears with half their force while the remaining force took positions atop the buildings and sent arrows into the rioters. The mob made several attempts to break through the Rangers' defenses but was repelled by a barrage of well-placed arrows at each attempt.

Crandall appeared beside Kevin. "Oh dear. You must bow to their demands to end the violence," he said with just a hint of panic.

Kevin turned a glare on the professional administrator. "Those men have chosen violence instead of reason. They will be met with the same." Kevin bored into him with an angry glare. "I will not be intimidated and I will not be blackmailed. I offered those men work at a good wage and they responded by setting the shipyard on fire. Now they will pay the consequences of their poor choices."

He turned back to look at the battle just as a column of Rangers on horseback came thundering down the docks. With precision timing, the front force of Rangers holding the rioters at bay opened a gap in their defenses just big enough for the charging column to drive through. They split the mob in half with their charge and broke the spirit of the rioters.

What had been an angry push to set fire to the rest of the docks was now a mad rush to escape the wrath of the Rangers. But the rioters soon found that the exits were all occupied by platoon-strength forces. Some of the rioters threw down their weapons and sought refuge along the walls of buildings out of the path of the mounted Rangers. Others tried to fight. They fell quickly.

The battle ended abruptly. Within minutes, the Rangers had the remaining rioters disarmed and standing on the docks with their hands on their heads. The Rangers that weren't needed to secure the prisoners went to the aid of the fire brigade and quickly extinguished the fires.

Half an hour later, Kevin stepped out onto the docks with a squad of Rangers. The remaining rioters were still lined up awaiting their fate. Kevin climbed up on a wagon and surveyed the bedraggled group of men. Some were crying, others wore looks of defiance.

LaChance stepped up beside Kevin and whispered, "Thirteen dead and twenty-seven injured. We don't have a count on the rioters yet."

Kevin nodded.

"You have all committed crimes against Southport and against Ruatha," Kevin said. He did his best to keep the seething anger out of his voice. "You have rioted and destroyed part of a shipyard that is vital to the defense of Ruatha against the armies of Phane. You have committed arson and you have murdered thirteen of my men!" Kevin glared at the now fearful line of men.

"By destroying the lives and property of others, you have violated the Old Law. Therefore, you have forfeited your rights to life, liberty, or property," Kevin said.

Guild Master Daley stepped out of the line with a look of belligerent rage. "You have no right to do any of this. We're the shipwrights! This shipyard is ours! All you had to do was pay us what we asked and none of this would have happened."

Kevin looked at the man for a moment before he made his decision. He vaulted over the side of the wagon and strode up to Daley, drawing his sword. The stout guild master jutted out his chin and faced Kevin in defiance.

"Did you incite this riot?" Kevin asked calmly, holding his sword casually at his side.

"Of course I did!" Daley said. "These men pay me to get them the best wages I can no matter what it takes. Now that you see our resolve, you'll pay what we ask." He looked so smug. The simpleton actually thought he'd won.

"I find you guilty of arson, murder, and treason," Kevin said loudly enough for the men nearby to hear. "I sentence you to death. Do you have any last words?"

A flash of fear transformed into rage before Daley took a step forward. "You wouldn't dare! I'm an important man in this town and I only did what I had to for my guild."

Kevin unceremoniously drove his sword into Daley's chest and through his heart. He looked the self-righteous little man in the eyes as his life faded.

"Cut off his head and put it in a bag," Kevin said. "Put the rest of these men in an unused barracks building under heavy guard while I figure out what to do with them."

By noon the prisoners were secured and Kevin had called a meeting of the rest of the guild masters. They were assembled and waiting for him to arrive. The walls of the council chamber were lined with armed Rangers.

Administrator Crandall had gone silent and wore a look of fear as if the whole world he understood had somehow morphed into something horribly outside the realm of his comprehension.

Kevin stood outside the council room with the administrator. He was waiting for the tension in the room to rise. He wanted the rest of the guild masters to be afraid of him. They clearly didn't understand honor or duty or loyalty to a cause—but they understood fear quite well.

Kevin turned to Crandall. "It's really quite simple, Administrator Crandall. Obey the Old Law. No backroom deals, no special treatment, no bribes, no rioting when you don't get your way."

He left the man standing in the hallway pondering his new reality and strode into the council room carrying Daley's head in a bag. The stink of fear was palpable.

He casually dumped the head on the table, leaving a red stain where it landed and rolled to a stop. The eyes of the guild masters widened and the room fell deathly silent.

"Daley chose to riot and burn the shipyard because he didn't get his way," Kevin said calmly. "I killed him for his crimes. For those of you who consider the punishment excessive, hear me now. He committed arson, murder, and treason. The penalty for these crimes is death. You will go back to your guilds and tell them that they will work for the going rate. The alternative is the immediate dissolution of your guild charter. You will each be held personally responsible for violence by members of your guilds.

"Tomorrow we will begin building a navy to serve Southport and Ruatha. I have a treasury full of gold that I intend to spend building defenses for the people of this territory. If you and your guild members wish to work and be paid, there will be no shortage of things to do. Your guild members can all do very well over the coming months. I suggest you tell them to go to work and take advantage of my desire to build a navy as quickly as possible. This is an opportunity for those who want to contribute their skill and labor to this community. For those who don't want to work, tell them to stay out of the way. The docks and shipyard are vital to our defense. Any attack against them will be treated as an act of war."

**

A few days later, Kevin stood on the keep battlements looking down on the docks and shipyard. The guild masters had all decided to make the best of the situation. There were no more disturbances. The guilds had opened their doors and taken in new apprentices. The city was abuzz with a new sense of purpose. The shipyards had four berths, the beginnings of a fast-attack boat growing within each.

Kevin had assembled a number of ship captains, master shipwrights, and several military officers to design the new Zephyr-class fast-attack boat. The design was sleek and efficient. There were two masts with enough sail to offer good speed when the wind permitted as well as a bank of ten oars on each side. Its main weapon was a powerful heavy ballista mounted on the foredeck that could launch an oil-filled firepot over two thousand feet with surprising accuracy.

Kevin looked off toward the Reishi Isle, idly wondering about his sister, when he saw the silhouette of the Angellica on the horizon. The flagship of the Southport navy was returning to port. Maybe Captain Targa would have news of Alexander and Isabel. Kevin scanned the horizon before heading down to the docks. The telltale plume of dust rising from the road to the north caught his eye. Riders from New Ruatha were coming fast.

Chapter 13

The Ranger scout entered the command tent still coated with road grime. Duncan sat at the head of a table surrounded by military officers and a few wizards. Hanlon sat at his right. The conversation stopped abruptly when the young man entered the room. He came to a halt and delivered a crisp salute.

"Report," Duncan said.

"The enemy is returning to the Gate," the scout said. "Our infiltrators report that they have begun to build a fortification around the Gate itself and are moving the bulk of their force behind the Gate."

"Thank you, soldier," Duncan said. "Go get yourself something to eat and some sleep."

The man saluted again and left the command tent without a word.

"Looks like Alexander's plan is working," Hanlon said.

Duncan nodded. "I just wonder how long the ruse will hold them at the Gate. Should be good for at least a few more days."

"I wonder how he managed to dupe Phane into responding to a feint," Wizard Sark said. "Phane is no fool. I suspect he'll be furious when the Gate does not open three days hence and deliver Alexander into the waiting arms of the Reishi Army Regency."

"If three days is all we can count on, then we'll need to take advantage of it," Duncan said. "Begin the evacuation of New Ruatha to Headwater and Blackstone Keep. Send word to Northport to evacuate to Southport through the forest and over the water with every ship they have."

"General Valentine, shouldn't we consider dividing our forces to provide some defense for Headwater and Northport?" asked General Markos.

"No," Duncan said. "As it stands we have ten legions assembled here at New Ruatha, two from Warrenton, two from Buckwold, three from New Ruatha, one from Northport and two legions of Rangers from Glen Morillian. The enemy is ten legions strong. If we split our forces, they'll be able to easily overwhelm us on whichever front they choose to attack.

"We'll maintain our fortified position on the plains north of New Ruatha. If they want to fight, they'll have to engage us on our terms. If they do attack, Duane will bring his legion south and hit them from behind, supported by Erik and the legion stationed at Blackstone Keep. If they want to take Northport, it should be close to deserted by the time they get there and we'll be in a good position to exact heavy casualties with the Ranger cavalry. If they move for Headwater, we can head them off easily enough.

"I'm concerned that this is just the first wave. We've had no word of General Talia's campaign against Kai'Gorn. If another legion of Andalian Lancers makes landfall, the enemy will have a distinct advantage. And there's no way to know how many soldiers Phane still has on Karth. If he can get them here, we'll need all the men we can get."

"There's still the matter of the scourgling," Wizard Sark said. "Mage

Gamaliel is working on a containment vessel for the beast but he was not optimistic when last I spoke with him."

"I wish I had an answer for you, Wizard Sark," Duncan said. "That thing makes me nervous. I'm kind of surprised they haven't unleashed it on us already."

"I suspect they fear we would contain it," Sark said. "As long as it stays with their forces, they can prevent us from trapping it within a magic circle. However, I'm sure that they'll lead with it when they decide to attack."

"We still don't know what happened to the one hunting Alexander," Hanlon said. "Maybe he could offer us some advice."

Duncan nodded. "It's worth a try. Send a message to Blackstone Keep and have them put the question on Alexander's message board. Also, send word south to Kevin in Southport. He needs to know refugees are coming. Have him relay orders to General Talia to send whatever forces he can spare north through the forest."

"I'll dispatch riders right away," Hanlon said.

Chapter 14

Lacy Fellenden had never seen her father afraid before. He sat at the head of the table, wearing the long red robes with gold filigree that signified his station as the King of the territory of Fellenden. Once, long ago, the family of Fellenden had ruled over the entire island but that was before the Reishi War. Now the House of Fellenden was just the largest landholder on the island, with eleven other territories also holding significant lands.

Lacy had heard the rumors of the army that had appeared out of nowhere. The report of the scout rider confirmed it. An army bigger than all of the armies of all of the territories of Fellenden put together was headed for the city of Fellenden.

At hearing the report, her father's face had slowly lost color and then grown white. It looked like he'd aged ten years in a matter of minutes. He was already an old man, but she had never seen him look as old as he did at this moment.

He shook his head in denial. "Surely, your estimate must be mistaken. How could such a large army have suddenly appeared right in the heart of Fellenden?"

"They come from the direction of the Reishi Gate, Your Majesty," the scout said. "I can only surmise that the ancient enemy has returned."

"Why would they come here?" Prince Torin asked. "We pose no threat. The war ended two thousand years ago. Surely the Reishi do not still hold us responsible for opposing them so long ago."

The King of Fellenden wasn't listening. He sat shaking his head ever so slightly and staring at the table before him with a blank look in his bleary eyes. After a moment of silence, he looked up with a start, then looked around at his family and courtiers. His distant gaze found the court wizard.

"What say you, Wizard Saul?"

The wizard was an old man with long white hair and a neatly groomed white beard. He wore simple grey robes and carried a well-worn oak staff for a walking stick. Even with his advanced age there was still a look of keen intelligence in his slate-grey eyes.

"I know of no magic save the Reishi Gate that could account for the presence of this army," Wizard Saul said. "As for their purpose, I cannot guess except to say that they do not mean us well."

The King of Fellenden turned to a big burly man wearing armor. "General, can we defend the city?"

The general shook his head slowly. "No, we have only a single legion. They have ten. Perhaps with the aid of the rest of the territories, we could mount a defense but we haven't the time."

"What are we to do?" the King of Fellenden asked the ceiling. "We haven't faced a war for centuries. We've lived in peace for so long, we're ill prepared to fight."

"Perhaps, if we knew their intentions, we could negotiate a peace with them," Torin said.

"That is doubtful, Prince Torin," the general said. "With such a large army, they can dictate their terms and we will have no choice but to accept."

The door to the council chamber flew open and a breathless soldier burst in. "The enemy's envoy is at the gate," he said. "They're demanding to speak with you, Your Majesty."

The procession to the city wall seemed surreal. Lacy followed her father and a gaggle of courtiers and royal guard through the streets of Fellenden. The fear was palpable. People looked at the King but drew little strength from his haggard and distraught appearance. Lacy tried to look confident in spite of her terror.

She stood just over five and a half feet tall with strawberry-blond hair and deep-blue eyes. She was beautiful by all accounts and smart as well. Deep down, Lacy knew that she had never been challenged in her life. She'd always had everything she wanted handed to her without question. Her father doted on her and her brother protected her.

She did her best to play the part of a princess but somehow knew that she was just going through the motions. All her life it was taken for granted that she would marry the son of the ruler of one of the other territories and in that way solidify an alliance that would serve her family and her people.

Part of the fear she felt as she followed the procession through the streets of her home was the knowledge that she wasn't prepared for what was coming. She rationalized that no one could be prepared for a thing like this but knew even as she formed the thought that she was lying to herself.

They reached the gatehouse and climbed the steps to the top of the wall. The enemy envoy sat atop their horses below. They were big men dressed in armor and furs. Each carried an assortment of weapons that looked to be of mediocre craftsmanship but no less lethal for it. More telling was the well-used look of the weapons. These men were killers. And they liked it.

"What is your purpose here?" King Fellenden asked. His voice broke slightly.

The leader of the enemy envoy, a big man with a bald head and a long goatee braided in two spikes, smiled up at the row of courtiers lining the wall. His teeth were crooked and stained.

"Lord Zuhl demands your surrender," he said.

"Lord Zuhl?" Wizard Saul asked. "Is he in league with Prince Phane?"

"Never!" the soldier said and then spat on the ground. "The Reishi are an abomination that must be exterminated."

"We have done nothing to provoke Lord Zuhl," King Fellenden said. "Why does he invade our lands?"

The soldier smiled up at him with arrogant malice and shrugged. "Because he can. You will surrender and serve Lord Zuhl or you will be destroyed."

"If we surrender, what will become of my people and my city?" King Fellenden asked.

"Your people will submit to Lord Zuhl. In exchange, they will enjoy Lord Zuhl's protection from the coming scourge of the Reishi."

"I need time to confer with my council," King Fellenden said.

The soldier smiled knowingly. "There is one more condition. Send out your daughter as a gift for Lord Zuhl to prove your commitment to your new master."

Lacy felt a chill race up her spine like nothing she'd ever felt before. It was terrifying and strangely exhilarating at the same time. Everything came into sharp focus. There was no past, no worry about the future, just this one moment. Her father looked over at her with wild eyes for only a moment.

"Never!" he said. "My family must be guaranteed safety or there will be no surrender."

The soldier smiled like a cat with a mouse. "I was hoping you'd say that. But Lord Zuhl instructed me to give you a moment to reconsider. If you don't surrender, there will be no quarter given. Your walls will be breached, your city overrun, and your people killed, raped, and enslaved. There is nowhere to run or hide. The entire Isle of Fellenden has been claimed by Lord Zuhl. Surrender will only be offered this one time. If you refuse, your people will be conquered without mercy."

A little of the color returned to the King's face. He seemed to find his mettle in the face of the unspeakable demands. "If I surrender it's clear to me now that my people will be enslaved or worse. If we are to die, then we will die well. Tell Zuhl the answer is no!"

Lacy heard herself speaking but wasn't sure where the words were coming from. "Father, if my sacrifice will save our people, then I will surrender willingly."

Her whole life she had always wondered what sacrifice was. She had never experienced it herself. She didn't even know what she was offering but she knew with a growing sense of certainty that she would endure whatever might come for the chance to do something worthwhile.

"No, Child," her father said. "Your sacrifice wouldn't buy what they promise."

The soldier said something to the others with him and they laughed as they turned their horses away from the gate.

"He's right," Wizard Saul said. "They made their demands hoping they would be refused. This enemy wants bloodshed."

"I fear they will have it," the general said.

Word spread quickly through the streets of Fellenden. Even before Lacy had returned to the palace with her father and his entourage, there was the stirring of panic within the populace.

Not ten minutes after they returned to the King's council chamber, a soldier burst in. "Your Majesty, the gates are breached!" the young man said with a quaver of fear in his voice. "A beast of magic is rampaging within the city walls and the enemy cavalry comes."

The King of Fellenden looked at his son and his daughter, all that was left of the line of Fellenden, and his resolve hardened. He was an old man. His life was behind him, but he had married late in life and his children were just barely adults.

"General, muster what defense you can. Raise the alarm and warn the people of the city to flee to the surrounding towns and territories. We cannot hope to defend against this enemy, so we must do what we can to preserve the lives of our people. Use your forces to provide the people with the time they need to survive the onslaught.

"Torin, send riders to the other territories with warning of the enemy at our gates. You ride with them. Organize the forces of the other territories into an army under our banner. Do not fight the enemy on their terms. Use your knowledge of our lands to kill them when and where you can without battle. We cannot win in an outright fight so don't give them one.

"Lacy, take Wizard Saul and go to Ithilian. King Abel has long been our friend. Beg him for any assistance he can offer. I saved his life once when he was a boy. Remind him of that if necessary."

Lacy shook her head in denial but King Fellenden stepped up and drew his son and daughter away from the others in the room. "Lacy, I'm entrusting you with the legacy of the line of Fellenden," he said as he pressed an ancient key into her hand. "Take this key to the family crypt in the south and find the tomb of Carlyle Fellenden. He ruled during the last years of the Reishi War. Within his sarcophagus is a small box. Take it with you to Ithilian and deliver it to Lord Abel's court wizard. Do not open it, Lacy. The wizards will know what to do with it. It cannot be allowed to fall into Zuhl's hands."

"Father, what will you do?" Lacy asked.

He smiled sadly at his daughter. "I will do everything I can to preserve our people. Now off, both of you and know that I love you." He held his son and daughter each in turn with his eyes and then turned to an aid. "Bring my sword and armor."

Torin hugged Lacy quickly. "Be safe and listen to Wizard Saul. He's wise. I love you," he said and then dashed off toward the stables.

Lacy could hardly believe how quickly things were happening. Just last week she was trying on yet another new dress and fussing about the stitching. Now her whole world was coming undone.

"Lacy, we have to go quickly," Wizard Saul said. "Go to your room and change into your riding clothes, pack your saddlebags, and get your knife. I'll meet you at the stables."

Lacy nodded. It took her a moment to realize that she hadn't moved and then she was running. Her fear propelled her through the stone corridors of her home and up the stairs to her elaborate rooms. She ripped off her light-blue dress and quickly changed into riding clothes. She shoved an extra set of clothes into her saddlebags, crammed a heavy blanket into the other side, and grabbed her little-used waterskin and long knife.

She'd learned how to fight with a knife when she was younger, but it had seemed like such an academic exercise. Now she was striving to revive those lessons as she strapped the blade to her waist. She slipped a smaller knife into her boot and hoisted her saddlebags onto her shoulder.

She looked at her rooms one last time before she left. The light pastels and elaborate decoration seemed jarringly frivolous. She snorted with derision at what she'd made of her life and vowed that she would live up to the duty her father had assigned her. She tried not to think about him as she made her way to the stables. In the back of her mind she knew with terrible certainty that she would never see him again.

Soldiers were running and servants were scurrying about in near panic. Lacy tried not to let their fear infect her. The whole keep suddenly shook from a blow that rang the stone walls like a bell. She tried to swallow past a lump of fear in her throat. As she bounded down the stairs and into the courtyard, the main gate shuddered under another mighty blow from something that could not be of this world. She froze and watched splinters from the giant gates flutter to the ground. Everything seemed to be moving in slow motion. The gate reverberated with the force of another attack, sending more splinters falling to the gatehouse floor. Soldiers poured into the courtyard prepared to meet whatever may come, but Lacy could see the fear in their eyes. Even the more experienced among the palace guard were afraid—or worse, they had a look of terrible resolve mixed with certainty that their time in this world was short.

"Lacy!" bellowed Wizard Saul from the stables.

She tried to pull her attention away from the impending doom that was trying to shatter the palace gate but couldn't. The gate shuddered again and the mighty Iron Oak bar that held it shut against the assault started to crack.

Lacy snapped out of her trance and raced to the stables. Wizard Saul took her saddlebags and flopped them over the rump of her horse. He wasted no time strapping them down and helping her into the saddle. The horse was skittish and snorted with fear at the commotion out in the courtyard. Wizard Saul whispered something to the big animal and the beast calmed almost immediately.

He mounted his horse and took up his staff. "Follow me, Lacy. Do not get separated from me. My magic can get us out of the city but you must do as I say without question."

She nodded tightly. The courtyard gates gave way with a thunderous crash. Wizard Saul led her cautiously into the courtyard just as the beast pushed through the ruins of the gate.

It stood twelve feet tall and looked like it was made of dark stone. It had broad shoulders and long powerful arms that ended in hammer-like stumps the size of a keg of ale. It walked on two legs but had no head or neck and only a single large eye in the middle of its chest. Lacy was stunned by how unnatural the beast looked. It was a thing that belonged in a nightmare.

The soldiers attacked with arrows and spears but the beast's skin was as hard as stone. It waded into the gathering sea of men, swinging its mighty fists in great arcs. The sound of bones breaking could be heard every time it made contact. A man in full armor flew through the air and landed with a sickening thud, never to move again.

Outside the gates, there was chaos. The people of the city were running every which way. Wizard Saul started chanting in an old language. Lacy could only watch the carnage unfold before her. The wizard finished his spell and turned to her.

"You must remain absolutely silent," he said before he took her reins and gently led the horses from the courtyard past the flailing demon and the growing field of human wreckage. The beast didn't seem to notice them and the soldiers either didn't see them or were too preoccupied to care.

Once they reached the streets, Lacy caught a glimpse of the army headed for her city. Thousands of men on horseback galloped across the plains in the distance. With the gates smashed by the demon, there would be little to stop them.

Wizard Saul stopped their horses and allowed a group of friendly soldiers to race by on horseback. They didn't seem to notice Lacy or the old wizard. Once they passed, Wizard Saul started moving again. He was taking her toward the south gates where they could escape the city before the enemy horde arrived.

They moved slowly and cautiously through the streets of Fellenden. The people were fleeing with what they could carry, and the streets were clogged. Saul guided her down the lesser traveled passageways between buildings to avoid the panicked crowds. When they did encounter people, Saul stopped and remained very still and quiet. Lacy watched one person after the next look right at her and go about their business as if they hadn't seen her.

As they neared the south gate, there was a loud cracking noise off in the distance. Lacy turned just in time to watch the central tower of the keep topple over and crash with thunderous noise. She felt the reverberations of her home's death throes and swallowed hard to stifle a sob when the throng of people streaming through the gate started screaming in panic.

They parted like water as a platoon of enemy soldiers pushed their way into the city. They wielded all manner of weapons, from spears to battle-axes, great swords to menacing-looking flails. The people who were trying to flee through the gate scattered before the onslaught.

Enemy soldiers hacked and slashed at anyone near enough to reach. Men, women, and even children fell to their indiscriminate assault. Lacy looked on with a mixture of shock and morbid curiosity. In the back of her mind, she wondered how she'd managed to live for eighteen years without ever even knowing that men like these existed. She had been so sheltered and protected all her life that she'd never actually seen anyone die before. Now there were broken bodies crumpled in lurid pools of crimson lying all around.

The slaughter lasted only a few minutes before the remaining civilians fled the open area around the gate. The soldiers didn't pursue but instead took up positions to prevent anyone from escaping through the gate, keeping the people inside the city so they could be enslaved or murdered more easily.

Wizard Saul looked at Lacy and gestured for silence. The men surveyed the scene of the battle with the intensity of trained hunters but they didn't see Lacy or the wizard.

Saul looked deep in thought. Lacy realized that they were trapped and her fear started to push its way through her shock. Saul reached out and touched her on the forehead with his index finger. She heard his voice clear as day, yet his mouth remained closed.

"When I attack those men, we must use the confusion to escape the city," Saul said in her mind. "Once outside the walls, run south with all possible speed. I'll be right behind you."

Lacy nodded with wide eyes. She wasn't sure it was wise to attack thirty armed men but she also knew that Wizard Saul was smarter and more experienced than she was. All she could do was trust his guidance.

Twenty of the men had formed a line in front of the gate, while the other ten dismounted and entered the gatehouse to close the portcullis and bar the gate.

Wizard Saul whispered the words of his spell for several minutes. Lacy started to wonder if he would attack before the gate was closed and their only escape cut off. He raised his staff and spoke the final word with firm authority.

At the sound of his voice, the soldiers all turned and looked directly at the two of them as if they'd just appeared out of nowhere. Before they could react, the tip of Wizard Saul's staff glowed bright amber and a wave of light pulsed out toward the soldiers. As it passed through them, they froze in place. A shimmering field of amber surrounded each soldier and their mounts, immobilizing them completely.

"Hurry, the spell won't last for long," Wizard Saul said, and they were off at a gallop.

They raced through the gate and out onto the fields surrounding the city of Fellenden. People were fleeing in every direction. Those on foot were not even a mile from the city as Lacy and Saul raced past. She looked back and saw a squad of soldiers in pursuit. They didn't seem interested in the civilians. It was clear from their course that they were coming for Lacy and the wizard.

Saul reined in his horse and slowed to a stop. "Lacy, I'm going to cast another concealing spell. We must be quiet and walk our horses slowly or they will see through the magic."

Lacy nodded and the wizard began casting his spell. They moved away slowly and quietly as the enemy soldiers charged past.

By nightfall they'd made it into the mountains southwest of Fellenden city. Lacy could see smoke rising in the distance. She quietly cried herself to sleep in the dark of night, clutching the key her father had given her. Her safe, perfect little world was gone. In its place was a world of fear and death. Lacy wasn't sure she knew how to live in such a world.

Chapter 15

Isabel and Wren stood on the observation platform overlooking the flight deck where Abigail was training with her wyvern. The beast had grown quickly and taken to wing less than a week after hatching. Abigail had been spending most of her time with Knight Raja learning about her wyvern and the code of the Sky Knights.

Today would be her first flight. It was a simple introduction to riding a flying steed. Abigail and Raja were to make a single loop around the fortress island and return to the flight deck. When they disappeared over the edge of the flight deck a moment after launch, Isabel stopped breathing. She had to remind herself to take a breath as she waited for Abigail to return.

She closed her eyes and tipped her head back. Slyder was floating high over the island. Through his eyes, she could see Abigail soaring in a wide arc that would bring her full circle around the island and back to the flight deck. She looked a little unsteady and her wyvern didn't fly with the same grace as Knight Raja's, but she was managing to stay in the air. At this point that was all that mattered. Isabel stayed with Slyder until Abigail was nearing the flight deck for her landing.

"Here they come," Isabel said to Wren.

The wide-eyed waif of a girl was nearly as excited as Isabel. She had become a fixture of their lives in the fortress island. Her assigned duty was to serve them and maintain their quarters but she had become much more than that.

She was their friend.

She shared meals with them and spent any free time she had tagging along behind them. Her curiosity was innocent and somewhat naïve but she had become more comfortable asking questions. She was always eager to hear any stories they had to tell of life outside the fortress island and yearned for the opportunity to see more of the world.

Abigail came into view out over the ocean. Her wyvern was flying unsteadily and they were coming in too high. She overcorrected at the last moment and they landed hard, her wyvern skidding to a stop on his belly. Abigail looked a little rattled by the experience but she shook it off quickly and was off her steed a moment later hoisting the hindquarter of a calf from the feed cart for him. He struggled for a minute to get to his feet but eagerly took the snack just as Raja landed gently nearby.

A throng of wyvern handlers swarmed the beasts, removing their saddles and tack while the riders fed their steeds. Once the wyverns were led off toward the stables, Raja and Mistress Bianca took Abigail aside to critique her first flight. Even at this distance, Isabel could see that Abigail wasn't happy with her landing but the more experienced Sky Knights didn't seem too concerned about it.

A horn sounded from the watchtower on the side of the landing platform signaling that another wyvern was inbound. Isabel watched as two more wyverns floated into the landing bay and touched down gracefully.

Her heart started beating a little faster when she realized that one of the riders was Magda. The triumvir had been away from the fortress island for several days. Isabel suspected that she'd been looking for Alexander. The triumvir dismounted and fed her wyvern while handlers removed its tack and saddle. She gave her steed a pat on the side of the jaw and strode purposefully from the landing bay.

Abigail and Isabel shared a look.

Isabel hurried back to her quarters with Wren in tow. She wanted to speak to Magda but knew that she would have to wait for the triumvirate to summon her. She wanted to be easy to find when the summons came.

Abigail arrived a few minutes later.

"How was it?" Isabel asked with a smile.

"It was the most exhilarating thing I've ever done," Abigail said with giddy happiness. "I've always loved to ride but this is beyond anything I've ever even dreamed of. I was pretty embarrassed by my landing, but Flight Commander Bianca said it was common for the first flight to end with a hard landing. Did you see Magda return?"

Isabel nodded with a frown. "I'd love to know what she's been up to. I'm pretty sure it has something to do with Alexander."

"Me, too," Abigail said. "Hopefully, they'll summon us so we can get some answers."

Almost as if on cue there was a knock at the door. Wren answered it and a Sky Knight entered.

"The triumvirate has summoned you both," he said. "Please come with me."

Isabel schooled her nervousness as they walked through the corridors toward the triumvirs' hall. The giant room was empty except for the three women who had been their hosts and jailers for the past several weeks. Two chairs were waiting for them before the triumvirs' bench. Isabel figured they used the grandeur of the room to lend credence to their authority. She understood well enough the power of appearances. She and Abigail took their seats without a word and the guard excused himself, leaving them alone with the three women.

Magda and Cassandra wore expressions of caution but Gabriella was clearly angry.

Isabel reminded herself that they may still be in danger. The reality of the situation brought her focus to a razor's edge.

"Thank you for joining us here today," Magda said. "I trust your stay with us has been comfortable."

This was new. Magda was usually very direct. Isabel wondered if the acceptance of Abigail into the Sky Knights had somehow changed their standing on the island or if there was more to it than that.

"It has," Isabel said, "after the initial unpleasantness, anyway."

Gabriella's mood seemed to darken perceptibly. Isabel reminded herself to tread lightly.

"I've just come from the Isle of Ithilian," Magda said.

Isabel's heart started pounding in her chest. Alexander was on Ithilian but the triumvirate didn't know she was aware of that. She still hadn't revealed the existence of Slyder to them and didn't intend to, since he offered her access to information that she desperately needed.

"I've spoken to Alexander," Magda continued.

Isabel had to remind herself to breathe.

"I delivered an offer of exchange to him—your lives for the Sovereign Stone." Magda's eyes bored into Isabel. "He refused."

The statement fell like a sentence. Abigail tensed as if preparing to spring into motion. Isabel calmed the hammering in her chest and willed steadiness into her voice.

"Have you summoned us here to murder us then?" she asked coolly.

"By all rights we should kill them," Gabriella said heatedly to the other two triumvirs. "The Stone must be placed in our care. We should make good on our threat and then take it from him by whatever means necessary."

"We've already had this discussion, Gabriella," Magda said with a tinge of ire in her voice. "You have been heard and the decision has been made."

Gabriella glared at the other two triumvirs and then at Isabel.

"Isabel, your husband made a compelling argument," Magda said. "The antidote provided by Mage Gamaliel will be administered this afternoon. Once you have completely recovered from the effects of your poisoning, you have a decision to make."

Isabel frowned. She could only imagine what Alexander had said to Magda to convince her to change her position.

Before Isabel could respond or Magda could continue, Gabriella interrupted. "Your husband was willing to sacrifice you for his own power. Doesn't that bother you?" Her tone had changed abruptly. She no longer sounded angry but was almost sickeningly sweet.

"Not in the least," Isabel said. "I'm proud of him for his courage and his resolve to preserve the future no matter the cost to himself."

Gabriella scowled. Exactly the response Isabel was hoping for. She understood Alexander's heart better than any and knew that the decision to risk her life was made from necessity rather than lust for power.

"Am I to assume that you have made an agreement with Alexander?" Isabel asked.

"Yes, but there are conditions that must be met," Magda said. "The Sovereign Stone has bonded to him and he has sat in council with the previous Reishi Sovereigns. The General Commander of the Reishi Protectorate has recognized him as the Sovereign, as has the King of Ithilian.

"In the time of the Reishi Empire, only a witch was permitted to marry the Lord Reishi. His mate must be capable of standing with him over the course of his reign. Only a witch has the strength and longevity to do so."

Isabel felt a tingle of dread wash over every square inch of her body. The implications of Magda's words terrified her.

"We offered to provide him with a suitable wife, but he refused," Magda said.

Isabel again reminded herself to breathe.

"I would make you the same offer," Magda said. "Renounce your vows to Alexander and allow him to choose an accomplished witch from the Reishi Coven as his wife."

Her green eyes flashed and she bolted to her feet. "Never! He is my husband and he will be my husband for every day that I draw breath. What's more, he would never accept such a thing."

Magda smiled slightly. "No, I don't suppose he would. In fact, he reached for his sword when I suggested it to him. That leaves you with only one choice." She placed two vials on the bench before her. "You must endure the mana fast and become ordained as a witch of the Reishi Coven if you are to be the Lady Reishi."

Isabel was stunned speechless. She had never even considered becoming a witch and would have never imagined that she might have the opportunity, let alone the obligation. Magda looked at her with expectation and maybe even hope, Cassandra wore an expression of skepticism, and Gabriella sneered with open contempt.

Magda continued, "In times past, the fast took forty days and was performed at a secluded and secret location on the Reishi Isle where there is a naturally high concentration of Wizard's Dust in the water. However, Alexander has provided us with enough Wizard's Dust for each of you to undergo the fast, as well as a gift of enough for another of our conclave to be initiated."

Isabel and Abigail looked at each other and then back at the triumvirate. The decision was so simple. Isabel knew it was a risk but she also knew that she would do whatever she had to do to be with Alexander.

"When can I begin the fast?" Isabel asked.

"Are you sure about this?" Abigail said.

Isabel looked over at her sister and nodded confidently.

Gabriella snorted.

"If you're certain, then you may begin training for the fast as soon as you recover from the poison," Magda said. "Normally, we train apprentice witches for many years prior to the fast but in your case I suspect you will not be willing to wait that long."

"The sooner I complete the fast the sooner I can return to my husband," Isabel said. "Provide me with the training that I require and let me take the fast."

Gabriella chuckled derisively. "Your arrogance will be the death of you."

Isabel had had enough of the third triumvir. "Why do you hate us so much?" she asked.

Gabriella fumed for a moment before she burst out with a shout, "Because your husband killed my husband!"

Isabel was shocked. It could only have happened during the wyvern attack off the coast of the Reishi Isle. She felt deflated as she imagined how she would feel if Alexander had been killed.

"I'm sorry for your loss," she said quietly and sincerely.

Magda cleared her throat.

Gabriella struggled to hold back her tears.

"Abigail, will you take the mana fast?" Magda asked.

"Not yet," Abigail said. "I still have a lot to learn about my wyvern. I should concentrate on that before I take on another challenge."

Magda smiled. "That is wise. I will hold the vial of Wizard's Dust for you until you are ready. Alexander asked that I deliver a message of love to you both. And he gave me this necklace for you, Isabel, as proof that I had indeed spoken to him."

Isabel smiled radiantly at the medallion of Glen Morillian. It had been a family heirloom for generations. She thought she'd lost it forever when the wyverns snatched her off the surf surrounding the Reishi Isle.

***

They returned to their quarters with a renewed feeling of hope and optimism. Isabel was a bit worried about the mana fast. She remembered the screams she heard coming from the tower when Alexander had undertaken the trials and hoped that she had the strength to survive. Alexander would never forgive himself if she died during a mana fast that he made possible.

Wren was waiting for them with dinner when they arrived. She didn't ask any questions but Isabel could see the curiosity burning within her deep-blue eyes.

"It seems that Magda has gone to see Alexander," Isabel said. "He convinced her to administer the cure for my poison. The healer should stop by this evening. I only hope that the magic Mage Gamaliel gave them works."

"I'm sure it will," Abigail said. "He knows how important you are to Alexander. He would have sent the most powerful magic he could." Abigail sat down at the table with a sigh. "I'm glad to hear that Alexander is well. I've been worried about him."

"Me, too," Isabel said. "I can't wait to see him."

"I'm still not sure how I feel about the whole Reishi bloodline thing," Abigail said. "It doesn't seem possible that we could be related to Phane."

"I know, but it has opened up a few opportunities," Isabel said. "Do you remember how Commander P'Tal fought? He was terrifying. And now he's protecting Alexander."

"That seems strange to me, too," Abigail said. "How do you change allegiances just like that?"

Isabel shook her head slowly. "I don't think he did. I think he was loyal to the Reishi all along, and now that Alexander has bonded with the Stone, Commander P'Tal has found his true master."

"I hope you're right," Abigail said. "It does make me feel better to have him watching over Alexander instead of hunting him." She chuckled at a sudden thought. "Can you imagine how mad Phane must have been when he learned that Alexander bonded with the Stone?"

Isabel whistled. "I feel sorry for anyone nearby."

Wren served dinner as she listened to their conversation with rapt attention. She was always eager to learn more about the workings of the world around her and she had become emotionally attached to her two charges.

Abigail gave Isabel an appraising look. "Are you sure about the mana fast? You don't have any training with magic."

Isabel shrugged. "What choice do I have? I won't forsake Alexander and I would be able to help him more if I had magic of my own."

Wren's eyes widened. "You're going to take the witch trials?" she whispered with awe.

Isabel nodded somberly. "It would seem so. The triumvirate thinks that only a witch can be married to the Reishi Sovereign, so they won't let me return to Alexander unless I survive the mana fast."

"Is it dangerous?"

Isabel nodded again. "I'm told that it's very dangerous, but it's the only way I can be with my husband, so I'm going through with it no matter the risk."

There was a knock at the door. Wren admitted three witches. The first carried a small box of carved bone on a wooden tray. The other two carried bags of healing supplies.

"I am Mistress Lita, the chief healer for the fortress island, the Reishi Coven, and the Sky Knights. These are my attendants. Mistress Magda has instructed me to administer the magic sent by the Ruathan Guild Mage. Before we begin, I have a few questions to help me ensure the most favorable result."

"All right," Isabel said. "Please, come in and sit down."

They seated themselves around the low table in the middle of the sitting room and Wren brought a kettle of hot tea.

"I'm told that you were poisoned," Lita said. "Was magic administered to slow or stop the effects of the poison?"

"Yes," Isabel said. "Master Alabrand, an alchemist, gave me a healing draught, then the next day he gave me another made with fairy dust under the guidance of a fairy named Chloe."

Mistress Lita blinked and then frowned. "I thought the fairies were creatures of story and legend. Perhaps there is a more plausible explanation."

Isabel leaned forward to emphasize her point. "I was married in the Valley of the Fairy Queen. They are real. Chloe is my husband's familiar. She guided Master Alabrand in the making of the healing draught that has stayed the poison within me for the past several weeks. However, the power of the magic is failing."

Mistress Lita's eyes widened and she cleared her throat. "Very well. Mistress Magda told me to accept your word and so I will. I do not fully understand the magic of this item," she gestured to the small, ornately carved bone box, "but I have been assured that it was provided by the Guild Mage of New Ruatha as a cure for your condition. Do you know of this mage?"

Isabel nodded. "He's a friend."

"I'm always wary of using magic that is beyond my understanding," Lita said. "Perhaps we should explore other treatments first."

"Do you have any healing magic more potent than fairy dust?" Isabel asked.

Lita shook her head slowly.

"Do you have power that exceeds that of a master alchemist?"

Again Lita shook her head.

"Very well then, how do we proceed?" Isabel asked.

Lita looked at her for a long moment as if searching for another argument that might prove persuasive before she nodded.

"First, you must ingest a healing draught. Then you must read the word on this piece of parchment aloud three times. Finally, you must break the seal on the box and open it. Once these conditions are met, the magic will be released and rid you of your poison. I must caution you, there may be other effects that are not known. This magic appears to be very old and there is no way of knowing what its true purpose is."

"I understand the risks," Isabel said. "Mage Gamaliel wouldn't have sent an item that would harm me. Proceed."

Lita placed the tray with the box before Isabel, handed her a wax-sealed piece of parchment, then placed a vial of syrupy-looking liquid on the tray.

"Open the healing draught," Lita said. "Once you drink it, you will begin to feel drowsy. You must speak the word on the parchment three times and open the box before you succumb to the sleep of the potion. We will remain in attendance until you wake."

Isabel took a deep breath and shared a look with Abigail.

"I'll be right here," Abigail said.

"So will I," Wren whispered.

Isabel opened the healing potion and quaffed it. She quickly took the parchment and broke the wax seal. She felt a little tingle of magic dance over her skin. For a moment the word was unreadable—the language it was written in was long dead. But a second later it shimmered and Isabel could read it and pronounce it clearly.

"Desiderates," she said deliberately. Isabel wondered what the word meant. "Desiderates," she said again. It almost sounded like a name. "Desiderates," she said one final time.

All eyes were on her as she broke the wire seal on the carved-bone box. She was starting to feel the effects of the healing draught as she lifted the lid and gently tipped it back. She blinked at the contents of the little box. It looked like liquid light swirling around under its own volition. She had only seen a light so pure one time before, during the birth of the fairy Sara, Chloe's daughter by Alexander. The light of that experience had been so pure and radiant that it rivaled the darkness of the netherworld for sheer intensity.

She was looking into the box as the drowsiness from the healing draught threatened to overcome her when the light started to swirl as if it had awakened. It abruptly flowed up out of the box and expanded into a glowing cloud of shapeless, undulating light, floating before her over the table.

Just as suddenly, it flowed into her and she fell back against the couch from the intensity of it. Everything around her was engulfed in bright white light as pure as true love. She felt like she lost consciousness for a moment before she awoke. Scintillating white clouds floated all around.

A man in white with long hair and a beard stepped out of the cloud and smiled at her.

"My name is Mage Desiderates. You have invoked my final spell."

"Where am I?" Isabel asked a bit warily. The place was so unlike any she had ever experienced that she was starting to wonder if she'd passed into the realm of light.

"You are within your own mind," Desiderates said. "Do you not understand the nature of the spell you have invoked?"

"Not really," Isabel said. "I've been poisoned. The Guild Mage sent a carved-bone box along with a piece of parchment. His instructions were to drink a healing draught, read the word on the parchment three times, and then open the box. The magic was supposed to cure me of the poison that threatens to kill me."

"I see. Perhaps if I knew more I could suggest the proper course of action. May I search your mind for the information I need?" Desiderates asked.

"I don't understand," Isabel said.

He nodded sagely. "When it became apparent that I was dying, I chose to cast a final spell in the hopes that I could still be of assistance to those who served the light. I was once an arch mage of great power. I spent many years studying magic, always seeking to expand the realm of possibility. Quite honestly, I'm delighted to see that my final spell was indeed my greatest accomplishment.

"You see, rather than die and allow my essence to pass from the world of time and substance into the realm of light, I chose to harness the power of my soul and my connection to the firmament within the constructed magic of the box. When you read my name aloud three times and opened the box, you activated the spell. I am here to provide you with that which you need most before I pass from this world."

Isabel blinked in surprise. She stared at the old man for several moments before she remembered to close her mouth. "I've never even heard of such magic. How could this be possible?"

He smiled somewhat smugly but with good nature. "As I said, I was a very powerful wizard. There were those who doubted me, to be sure, but I never doubted myself. And here we are." He chuckled. "I would very much like to point out my success to a few of my contemporaries, but alas, I suspect that they are all long dead. Time didn't intrude into the vessel that I have occupied but I sense that many years have passed since I walked the Seven Isles."

Isabel wasn't sure what to do. This was so far outside the realm of her expectation that she feared she might miss an opportunity if she simply asked him to heal her poisoning.

"What are the limits of your power?" she asked.

"For our purposes, only the boundaries established by my conscience," Desiderates said. "I can do nearly anything you need but I would caution you, once my magic is expended, I will fade into nothingness, so it would be wise to choose carefully."

Isabel frowned. "What do you mean fade into nothingness? Won't you pass into the light?"

"That is unlikely," Desiderates said. "I have no passage through which to travel to the realm of light."

"So you did this knowing that you would forfeit your soul?" Isabel asked with a bit of alarm.

"Indeed, child, I did just that," Desiderates said with a gentle smile.

"But why? Why would you do such a thing? Your soul is forever. You can't just throw it away." Isabel was becoming more distraught the more she understood the cost of undoing her poisoning.

"Be calm, child," Desiderates said gently. "You bear no guilt in this matter. I have done this freely, in part to be of greater service to the light, in part to expand the possibilities of magic, and in part to win a wager." He smiled with satisfaction at the third point.

Isabel looked at him with bewilderment. She started to wonder if all that time trapped in a box had driven Desiderates insane.

"I was once challenged to create a wish spell. I took the bet and lost but never stopped trying to achieve this greatest of magical accomplishments. At the end of my life I realized what must be done and the cost to myself of doing such a thing. I lived for four hundred and thirty-seven years during the reigns of Sovereign Constantine and Sovereign Darius. I spent my whole life in the pursuit of magical knowledge. I counted both Constantine and Darius as my friends and they both consulted me on matters of magic. In fact, it was Constantine that bet me I couldn't accomplish my goal. I have lived well and for all of my years, desire for greater accomplishment was the driving force of my life.

"I paid the price that was necessary to succeed and I am glad to have paid that price. I do wish I could tell Constantine though. He would appreciate both the cost I paid and the result I have achieved." He chuckled to himself almost as if he was laughing at an inside joke.

"Enough of that," Desiderates said with a warm smile. "You have need and I can help you. You say you were poisoned. That is a simple matter so perhaps I should look into your memories and thoughts so that I might suggest the best course of action."

Isabel was suddenly slightly wary. "How do I know I can trust you?" she asked.

He smiled with a shrug. "You don't, but then the time to consider that was before you opened the box. I have no wish to harm you. In fact, being that this is my greatest accomplishment, I intend to serve you as well as possible."

"All right," Isabel said. "You can look into my mind."

Desiderates closed his eyes and tipped his head back slightly. He was silent for several moments before he opened his eyes with a deep breath and a sigh.

"I'm saddened to see that the Reishi fell into darkness. When I knew them, they were honorable to a fault. It would seem that much has transpired in the many centuries since I passed from the world of life. However, I am somewhat excited that you are the Lady Reishi. Perhaps I could ask a favor."

Isabel blinked in confusion. "Sure, if I can do it."

"Please ask your husband to tell Constantine that I won our bet," Desiderates said with a satisfied smile. "It would mean a great deal to me."

Isabel laughed out loud. "You really are a bit crazy, aren't you? I'll make sure he gets the message."

"Thank you. Now, eliminating the poison is easily done. You already have the proper magic flowing through your veins."

"The healing draught," Isabel said.

"Exactly, it was unnecessary but helpful nonetheless. My power is substantial but not infinite. The presence of healing magic within you will make it much easier to eliminate the poison, but there is much more that I can do to assist you."

Isabel frowned in sudden thought. When she looked up, her piercing green eyes were on fire with an idea.

"Can you kill Phane?" she asked intently.

Desiderates smiled sadly and nodded. "I can, but I hope you would not ask that of me."

"He's trying to enslave the world," Isabel said. "What could be more important than stopping him?"

"That depends on whom you ask," he said. "If I gave Alexander the choice to kill both you and Phane or the choice to preserve both you and Phane, which would he choose?"

Isabel frowned with frustration. She knew the answer without question.

"He'd choose to preserve us both."

"Choosing life is always a better option than choosing death," Desiderates said. "If I kill Phane, I won't have the power I need to save you. Also, for my own selfish reasons, I ask that you not command that of me. I would not have my final act be one of killing."

Isabel sighed. "He's so dangerous. We have to stop him."

"And you will, but not this way," Desiderates said. "Besides, Alexander needs you. I have seen the bond between you within the lens of your memories. Your love is profound. Do not throw that away lightly."

"I'm not throwing it away," Isabel said. "But, if Phane was dead, then Alexander wouldn't be in danger anymore."

"You're wrong, child. There is always danger for one who wears the Sovereign Stone. It's part of the job, especially for one who wears it in the spirit with which it was created. A champion of the Old Law will always have the evil and the ambitious seeking his downfall. Killing Phane won't stop that, but it would destroy Alexander's heart and cripple his soul. He would be only a shell of himself with the weight of the world bearing down on him. Please, trust my wisdom on this matter and allow me to help you so that you can return to your husband. He needs you more than he needs anything else."

"All right," Isabel said reluctantly. "What else do you suggest?"

"You are wearing a necklace of great power. Greater power than even you know. It was made to be worn by a high witch and it confers not only the power to speak with animals but the power to control them as well. I can infuse this power into you permanently. The necklace will cease to be enchanted but the power will no longer be limited. Animals will obey you."

Isabel was surprised again. She knew the power of the necklace Mage Gamaliel had given to her, but she had no idea of its potential. Then a thought struck her like lightning.

"Would I be able to control wyverns?" she asked in a rush.

Desiderates smiled knowingly and nodded slowly. "Indeed you would, but there is yet more that I can do for you. You are quite unique. You have within you passageways to both the realm of light and the netherworld. The ability to assert greater control over those conduits will be useful to you, especially after you undergo the mana fast."

"Wait, how do you know about that?" Isabel asked.

He smiled. "I looked into your mind. I've seen your whole life and understand your duty and the challenges that you face quite well.

"Presently, access to the light and the dark exists only within your subconscious mind, no doubt a natural defense mechanism. I can bring those portals forth and give you control over when and how you choose to access them. Given the nature of your enemy, this capability may prove invaluable in the future.

"And there is one other thing. Since you have a gateway to the realm of light within your mind, you may be able to help me pass from this world into the light after all."

Isabel nodded. "Of course. Just tell me what to do."

"Once I release my magic, you will wake. Find the portal into the realm of light within your mind and will it to open. I will attempt to flow through. If I'm right, you may help me cheat death yet again."

Isabel gave him a warm smile and hugged him. "Thank you, Desiderates. You've saved me in more ways than you know."

"You are most welcome, child, and remember to send word to Constantine that I won our bet," Desiderates said with a smile as he raised his arms. He lost form and became a bright light. The light expanded to encompass all of Isabel's awareness, filling her entire being.

She woke up in bed and the reality of the spell hit her like a thunderbolt. Abigail was sleeping in a chair nearby. Wren was curled up on a mat in the corner. One of Lita's attendants was sitting at a small table watching for any sign from Isabel. She sprang to her feet and left the room the moment Isabel opened her eyes.

Isabel suddenly remembered the passageway to the realm of light. She found it easily and willed it to open. A radiant, life-giving light poured out into her mind and filled her with hope and purpose.

She heard Desiderates say, "Thank you," as he passed from the world of time and substance into the realm of light.

When Isabel blinked the light away, she was surrounded by people and she was suddenly famished.

"Are you all right?" Abigail asked with a mixture of grogginess and worry.

"I'm good," Isabel said. "The magic worked. The poison is gone."

Abigail smiled with relief. "You've been out for two days."

"Two days?" Isabel said. "How can that be? It only seemed like a few minutes."

"After that light went into you, we couldn't wake you up, so we moved you to your bed and we've been watching over you ever since," Abigail said, taking her hand.

Wren appeared on the other side of the bed. "Are you hungry? I have soup on the fire."

Isabel nodded emphatically. "I'm starving. Soup would be wonderful."

Wren hurried off and Lita took her place at Isabel's side.

"Can you tell me what happened?" she asked.

Isabel shrugged. "Not really. I remember a bright light all around me. I floated there for a while and then I woke up here. It didn't seem like it took all that long, maybe a few minutes."

"I've never seen magic like it before," Lita said. "I'm very curious to learn how it works. If you remember anything else about the experience, please tell me."

"Of course," Isabel said.

"I'm going to cast a spell over you now to determine if the poison is indeed gone," Lita said. "It is a simple spell and it won't hurt at all."

Isabel nodded.

Lita held her hands over Isabel and chanted softly for several moments. There was no outward sign of magic but when Lita stopped chanting, she smiled at Isabel warmly.

"There's no trace of the poison," Lita said.

Wren came in with a tray and stopped tentatively.

Isabel saw her and sat up. "Thank you, Mistress Lita," she said. "What

I'd really like right now is something to eat."

"Of course, we'll leave you alone," Lita said. "I recommend that you rest for the remainder of the day and through the night. I'll check on you in the morning to make certain there were no unforeseen effects from the magic."

Isabel ate her soup while Abigail and Wren watched. She felt a little awkward eating alone but they insisted that they'd already eaten. Isabel thought about the strange experience with the spirit of the long-dead wizard Desiderates. She'd seen magic before but nothing even close to the power she had just experienced. She pondered the possibilities while she ate. After she finished her second bowl, she sat back against her pillows and sighed contentedly. Even though she'd slept for the past two days, she realized she was still tired. When she looked at Abigail and Wren, it was apparent that both women were exhausted.

"Both of you look tired," Isabel said. "Why don't you go get some sleep? I'm going to take a nap." She closed her eyes before they left the room.

She woke with the light of the next morning. A cacophony of fierce thoughts and powerful feelings were coursing through her mind. At first she was alarmed but then she realized that she was hearing the thoughts of the wyverns. She reached up and found that her necklace was missing, yet she could still hear the sounds of the powerful animals that formed the basis of military power for the Sky Knights.

With a little effort she focused her mind and closed off the thoughts that were running rampant through her consciousness. It was a strange thing to hear the instinctual feelings of so many animals in her mind at once. She found that she could easily shut them out once she figured out how to control her newfound power.

Next, she reached out with her mind and found a single wyvern, making a connection with the animal easily. It was in the launch bay preparing to depart on patrol. It was excited and eager to be in the air. Isabel was surprised to discover how much the creatures loved to fly. As it launched she felt a kind of exhilaration and soaring freedom that she'd never felt before. She tried to look through the wyvern's eyes but was unable to. It was different than her connection with Slyder. She could sense feelings and instincts but wasn't able to access the beast's senses. She gently introduced her mind to him. At first she felt a sense of alarm from the wyvern, as if something wasn't right, but within a few moments it seemed to accept her and even respond to her thoughts.

"Are you hungry," Wren asked from the doorway.

Isabel severed the connection to the wyvern and looked up with a smile. "I'm starving, what's for breakfast?"

"I have eggs, potatoes, and biscuits, but I can have the kitchen prepare whatever you'd like," Wren said.

"No, that sounds wonderful," Isabel said. "I'll be out in a few minutes." Wren hurried off and Isabel got up and got dressed. She found her animal-charm necklace on the table beside her bed and put it on for appearance's sake. She had no intention of revealing her new ability to the Reishi Coven.

Breakfast was wonderful. Isabel ate two helpings before she sat back and sighed with contentment.

"Thank you, Wren. I think my stomach is trying to make up for lost time."

"I can get more if you want," Wren said.

Isabel shook her head, "That was plenty." She looked over at Abigail and smiled. "So, have you named your wyvern yet?"

Abigail frowned and shook her head. "I've been trying to come up with a good name for him, but so far I'm not happy with anything I've thought of."

"I always thought Kallistos would be a good name for a wyvern," Wren said.

Abigail considered it for a moment and nodded. "It's better than anything I've thought of. Kallistos. Huh, I think I like it. Knight Raja has been pressuring me to choose a name. He says the sooner I choose one, the sooner my wyvern can learn it and the sooner he'll respond when I call him."

"How's the training going?" Isabel asked.

Abigail shrugged a bit sheepishly. "I've been here with you as much as possible, between feedings anyway."

"Well, I'm fine now. You need to get back to your wyvern," Isabel said.

"You're sure you're all right?" Abigail asked.

"I'm certain," Isabel said. "In fact, I'm going to ask to start training for the trials as soon as possible. I know it's supposed to take years, but I don't have that long. Alexander's probably preparing to lead an army through the Gate from Ithilian to Ruatha. I want to be ready to help him when he does."

"If I know my brother, he's probably going to move sooner rather than later," Abigail said.

"Exactly my point," Isabel said. "We have to be ready to join him as soon as possible. He's not going to wait for us and I'm sure he could use our help."

"Wren, have you been sleeping here the past two days?" Isabel asked.

Wren shrugged. "Of course, I wanted to be here when you woke."

Isabel smiled fondly at the waifish young woman. "Thank you, but I'm fine now. You should go spend some time at home so your parents don't get worried about you."

"I sent word to them," Wren said. "They won't be worried."

"Maybe not, but I bet they'd like to see you now and then," Isabel said. "Besides, I'm going to go poke my nose into the coven's business. It would probably be best if you weren't with me when I do."

Wren's eyes widened a bit. "Please be careful," she said. "My mom always says it's a bad idea to cross a witch."

"I'll bet. Go on home. I'll see you at lunchtime," Isabel said.

Chapter 16

Wren left Isabel and Abigail alone. When Abigail got up to leave for her Sky Knight training, Isabel motioned for her to follow her out onto the balcony.

"The box did much more than cure my poison," Isabel said in a low whisper. "It was incredible. I'll tell you all about it later, but for now you should know that I can hear the wyverns and even control them. The magic in that box was amazingly powerful. It took the magic of my necklace, magnified it and infused it into my consciousness."

Abigail blinked in surprise. "This changes everything. With the wyverns, we could leave right now."

"I know," Isabel said, "but I think we should take advantage of the opportunities we have here. You still need to learn how to ride better, not to mention how to fight from the air, and I think I'll be able to help Alexander much more after I've taken the mana fast."

Abigail nodded slowly. "All right, but we have to make sure the coven doesn't find out about your power until we're ready to use it."

"I agree completely," Isabel said. "As fond as I am of Wren, I didn't want to risk telling her. I don't think she would intentionally betray us but she's young and naïve. There's no telling what she might let slip."

Abigail smiled. "That's probably wise. I'm off to ride," she said as she headed for the door.

"Enjoy yourself," Isabel said. "I'm going to see about the mana fast."

During their stay in the fortress island Isabel had familiarized herself with the layout fairly well. There were still a few areas where she got turned around but she always found her way eventually. Today was no different. She made her way to the triumvirate's audience chamber and found the hall that led to the working chambers for each of the triumvirs.

The passage was guarded by two big Sky Knights. They stopped her before she could enter the hall. "What's your business here?"

"I've come to speak with Magda," Isabel said simply.

The Sky Knight frowned disapprovingly. "*Mistress* Magda has not requested your presence."

"No, but I'd like to speak with her nonetheless," Isabel said.

"That's not how it works. The triumvirs are not to be disturbed. When she summons you, then you may speak to her, not before."

"I see," Isabel said as she peered around the big man and down the hall, which ran straight for fifty feet and had three doors, one on each wall and one at the end.

"Which doorway leads to Magda's chambers?" she asked.

He regarded her suspiciously for a moment. "Why do you want to know?"

Isabel shrugged innocently. "Just curious," she said.

"If I tell you, will you leave quietly?"

Isabel smiled brightly. "Of course."

"The door at the end of the hall is Mistress Magda's, the door to the right is Mistress Cassandra's, and the door to the left is Mistress Gabriella's," he said with a hint of exasperation.

"Thank you," Isabel said and started to turn when the door at the end of the hall opened. Mistress Lita stepped out and closed the door. When she looked up, she smiled brightly and waved at Isabel.

"Isabel, I was just coming to find you," Lita said. "Mistress Magda would like to speak with you."

The guard rolled his eyes when Isabel smiled with satisfaction and walked past him.

Magda's outer chamber was more an office than a sitting room or entry hall. The walls were richly polished walnut panels and the floor was covered with a large finely crafted carpet. Free-standing brass lamps were positioned at even intervals around the edge of the room. Two medium-sized oak desks faced the door with a woman seated at each. Both were reviewing documents when Isabel entered with Lita. One looked up with mild surprise before motioning them through the large door behind the desks.

Lita smiled her thanks and opened the door without hesitation. Isabel trailed behind her into a slightly larger square room. There was a large desk that looked like it had been carved from a giant piece of driftwood and then stained and polished to a shine. It was positioned to face away from the far left corner of the room. Opposite the door was a set of windows that opened out onto a small balcony. A small round table and two cushioned chairs occupied the far right corner, and a large stone hearth filled the wall to the right. Four comfortable-looking chairs faced the fireplace in a semicircle. On the left was a low table with couches on two sides and plush chairs on either end. Magda sat in one of the chairs, holding a cup of tea. She smiled at Isabel and motioned for her to sit.

"Thank you, Lita," Magda said. "Would you excuse us, please? I have some things to discuss with Isabel."

"Of course, Mistress," Lita said with an understanding smile as she left the room and closed the door behind her.

Isabel took a seat on the couch to Magda's left. Magda poured her a cup of tea as she sat down.

"Cream or honey?" she asked.

"Both, please," Isabel said. She took the tea with a smile.

"Lita tells me that you have recovered fully from the poison, although she is uncertain as to how," Magda said. "In any case, I'm glad to hear that the magic provided by Mage Gamaliel has served its purpose."

Isabel nodded her agreement. "Me, too," she said. "I knew the Guild Mage would do all he could to help me, but I wasn't sure it would be enough. I'm relieved that it was."

"I've given some thought to your training for the mana fast and decided that I will instruct you personally," Magda said. "If you are to survive, you will require very rigorous preparation. I must warn you, Isabel, this will not be easy. Most who attempt the trials have spent many years in preparation. I must help you accomplish a great deal before you will be capable of success and even then the outcome is not guaranteed."

"I understand," Isabel said. "I remember when Alexander took the mana fast. He had so little training. Wizard Kallentera recommended that he train more thoroughly. I also tried to convince him to wait, but he went ahead with it over my objections. That was one of the most frightening and difficult weeks of my life. All I could do was wait for him. I think I understand now what he knew then. Opportunities often come along only once. If you don't seize them, you may not get another chance."

"That is very true," Magda said. "If you're certain, then we shall begin."

"I'm certain," Isabel said. "I miss my husband. He needs me and I need him. Our people need both of us. The sooner I meet your conditions, the sooner I can stand with Alexander against the enemy."

"Very well," Magda said. "We will spend this morning talking about magic. A basic understanding of the nature of the firmament and how we interact with it will provide you with a solid foundation for your studies and help you fully comprehend the reasons for the exercises I will assign.

"Magic is the ability to impose your will on the firmament and thereby produce effects in the world of time and substance. The firmament is the source of reality. It underlies the world we see around us and creates the present moment. It is the source of creation. And it *is* a creation, because every moment is created by the firmament. We experience only the one moment of the present. The past is only memory and the future only possibility. The firmament is like a wave. We exist only on the crest of the wave as it flows through time.

"Left to its own devices, the firmament will create the next moment very much like the previous moment according to its own rules. Objects move or not according to the state they were in and the energy they possessed in the previous moment. People act with volition, but they too are governed by the rules of time and substance.

"Magic allows those rules to be broken. What is impossible according to nature is well within reach for one who can bend and shape the firmament. The process for manipulating the firmament is essentially a simple one. First, you must see the outcome you desire with perfect clarity in your mind's eye. Second, you must establish a connection to the firmament. Third, you must send your vision of the coming moments into the firmament with an uncompromising desire to see it become reality.

"In truth, everyone has a limited capacity for magic. Many people who have never taken the mana fast perform magic every day, although with far less dramatic effect. The child who wishes for a toy or a pet with such intensity that it becomes real to her within her own mind and then she acquires, through chance or accident, the toy or pet she desires is just one example. There are countless others. All life is connected to the firmament because all life is infused with Wizard's Dust to some degree.

"It is literally the stuff of life. Without it we would not exist. Consciousness and thought are made possible by the presence of Wizard's Dust within our bodies. It is the thing that links us to the firmament. In nature, it's very difficult for a person to accumulate a sufficient concentration of Wizard's Dust to make a deliberate connection to the firmament with his or her conscious mind. That is where the mana fast comes in.

"By consuming refined Wizard's Dust, we develop the ability to create a deliberate and conscious connection to the firmament. The small magic I spoke of a moment ago is accomplished through an unconscious connection to the firmament. Real magic depends on a conscious, deliberate connection.

"That is where the firmament becomes dangerous. It is a limitless, unimaginably vast ocean of potential. Within the firmament, anything is possible. When we make a connection to the firmament, we risk losing ourselves in the ocean of infinite possibility. It's almost as if the firmament craves our input, as if it wants us to use it to create. In exchange for our input, the firmament offers a feeling of joyous rapture unlike anything you will ever experience. Limitless creative power at your disposal is enough to overwhelm the senses of most people. Training is necessary to develop the ability to overcome the urge to blindly throw yourself into it.

"Wizards accomplish this through a rigorous mental training program that results in the ability to concentrate and focus their minds with great intensity and with great emotional detachment. This concentration is their defense against the firmament. Once a wizard has made contact with the firmament, he shuts out all distractions and focuses his entire mind and will on the vision of his desired outcome. As a wizard grows with experience, he's able to focus even more intensely until he reaches the rank of mage. Mages can open themselves to the firmament fully without fear of losing themselves in the ocean of creative potential. Less experienced wizards must carefully control the degree of their connection to the firmament in order to protect themselves from the full seductive power of the rapture.

"The rapture plays on emotion. Wizards learn to shut out emotion and rely on reason almost exclusively when they're casting a spell. This approach doesn't work nearly as well for women. The first attempts at creating female wizards ended badly. For many years it was forbidden for women to undergo the mana fast because those who survived eventually succumbed to the rapture and lost their minds in the firmament.

"Balthazar Reishi's youngest daughter secretly defied him and underwent the trials. She was a wise and passionate woman who devised a solution to the problem. Rather than viewing a woman's emotional nature as a weakness, she saw it as a strength. Kendra Reishi was the first true witch.

"She found that she could establish a connection to the firmament and withstand the rapture if she evoked a powerful emotion within herself before she established the connection. The more powerful the emotion, the more fully she was able to connect with the firmament. Through the use of deliberate emotion, she created a distraction that was sufficient to offset the pull of the rapture. To this day, witches use the discoveries she made to wield magic.

"The way a witch interacts with the firmament creates some advantages and some disadvantages. Since our connection to the firmament is based on emotion rather than concentration, we can establish a greater connection to the firmament much faster than a wizard. As a result, witches can wield great power relatively quickly. However, since emotion is not sustainable in the same way as mental discipline, witches cannot rise past the level of high witch, the equivalent of a mage.

"An arch mage is connected to the firmament at all times. Only their long years of training allows them to maintain the state of mental discipline necessary to defend against the rapture. Strong emotion cannot be sustained in the same way, so a witch who undergoes the mage's fast will eventually succumb to the rapture and lose her mind to the firmament.

"One mental skill that is common to both wizards and witches is visualization. The ability to see the outcome you desire is essential to success with magic. Your first exercises are designed to teach you this skill. It is essential that you practice diligently and intensely to train your mind to create visual images on command. You will start with the mundane and progress to the extraordinary.

"Use any ordinary item as the object of your practice. Look intently at the item and make note of every detail. Focus on it until you are confident that you have a clear picture of it in your memory. Close your eyes and create an image of the item within your mind's eye. Work with one item until you can call a perfect, clear vision of it at will.

"Once you've mastered visualizing the item, begin to work on seeing it quickly yet in clear detail. When you can call a perfect vision of the item instantly, then work on holding the vision in your mind without distraction. Meditate on it for as long as you can. When you can see it clearly for several minutes, then you can select another item to practice with.

"This exercise may sound simple, but it will develop a necessary set of skills. After sufficient practice, you'll be able to call forth intense, vivid, and clear images within your mind's eye. When you begin casting spells, you will use this skill to create visions of the effects you desire. Those visions will form the basis of your spells.

"The second exercise is one of emotional control. I want you to think back to a time when you felt intense anger. Take your time and find an event in your past that enraged you. Relive the event in minute detail. Evoke the anger you felt. Let it fill you. Feel it with every bit of the intensity that you felt when it happened. When you are in the height of this intense anger, pinch your right earlobe until you feel pain. Take a few minutes to clear your head and do the exercise again. Clear your mind and distract yourself with some other activity, then pinch your right earlobe until you feel pain. The intense anger should return quite suddenly.

"Once you can evoke the feeling of anger on command, practice nursing it and keeping it alive within you for several minutes. If it starts to wane, pinch your earlobe again to bring back the intensity.

"Now do the entire exercise again, except this time recall a feeling of deep love and pinch your left earlobe. Follow the same procedure to learn how to evoke the feeling and then focus on it and maintain it with intensity for several minutes.

"Once you can call forth a quick and intense feeling of both love and anger, then practice alternating between the two feelings. Emotional control is essential to a witch. This exercise can be unpleasant but it will teach you to master your emotions and harness them to your purposes.

"Finally, once you can call forth a powerful emotion at will and sustain it, then you will practice sustaining the emotion while seeing the items you worked with during your visualization exercise. You must be able to sustain an intense emotion at the same time that you are clearly and vividly visualizing an object, and you must be able to do both for several minutes at a time.

"Once you can do this, you'll be ready for the trials. I know you're anxious to begin, but don't underestimate the importance of these skills. They will serve you every single time you cast a spell, so be diligent and be thorough. It's better to err on the side of preparation than to undergo the trials with a poorly trained mind. Do you have any questions?"

Isabel stared blankly for several moments. Magda had covered so much that Isabel's mind felt full. She'd learned about magic mainly from listening to conversations between Alexander and other wizards. This was the first time anyone had explained it to her so directly and completely.

"That's a lot to process," Isabel said. "I'll probably have questions later but right now I need to think about everything you've taught me, and I'd like to get started on the exercises you gave me."

Magda smiled. "The information I've just given you is usually spaced out over a year for acolytes of the coven. We find that slow exposure to these ideas leading to greater and greater understanding is a more effective method of teaching. In your case, I believe you are sufficiently motivated that the slow approach is not necessary. Think about the things I've told you. Practice your exercises, starting with visualization. Come back tomorrow and we'll talk further. If you like, you're welcome to sit in with the other acolytes in the training hall. Head Mistress Theresa is very knowledgeable, and she has a number of suitable items to use for visualization practice. It's also sometimes helpful to discuss your practice with others who are going through the training because they see the process from a far different perspective than those who have already been through the trials."

"Thank you, Magda," Isabel said. "I look forward to talking with you tomorrow. I'm sure I'll have some questions by then."

Isabel returned to her quarters and sat down to think about everything Magda had told her about magic. She knew that the nature of a person's connection to the firmament was unique. Alexander was proof of that. She wondered how her magic would manifest. Then she thought about the trials. She remembered the screams she heard from Alexander when he was locked in the tower for his mana fast. Now that she was training for the trials, she faced the very real possibility that she wouldn't survive—she pushed the thought from her mind just as quickly. Alexander had given Magda the Wizard's Dust for her mana fast. If she died, he would blame himself. She vowed to herself then and there that she would survive the mana fast no matter what.

With a growing sense of purpose, she focused on a tea cup. She observed every detail of it, made note of the fine porcelain, the worn gold rim, the chip in the base, and the pattern of the design on the side. Other thoughts tried to intrude into her mind but she dismissed them and returned to her observation of the tea cup. When she had looked at it from every angle and considered every detail, she closed her eyes and sat back in her chair.

She quickly discovered how difficult it was to create clear, vivid images in her mind's eye. She practiced for a couple of hours until Abigail and Wren returned together. Wren was carrying a serving tray with their lunch in covered containers. Abigail was dressed in her riding armor, its buckles and straps rustling with each step.

"I see the witches didn't turn you into a frog," Abigail said with a teasing smile.

Isabel chuckled. "No, in fact, I had a long talk with Magda. She explained the difference between wizards and witches. I'd never given it much thought before but a lot of what she told me filled in a few gaps in my very limited understanding of magic."

"Did she say how long until you're ready for the trials?" Abigail asked.

"Just that it was up to me," Isabel replied. "She gave me a couple of exercises for training my mind. I'm supposed to practice them every day until they're second nature."

"Have you tried them yet?" Abigail asked.

Isabel nodded. "I was just working on one a few minutes ago. It's a lot harder than it sounds. All I'm supposed to do is visualize an object in clear detail. Magda said the ability to see an image in my mind is important for casting spells."

"Just make sure you're ready," Abigail said. "I want to get back to Alexander as much as you do but the mana fast is dangerous. Don't rush it."

"I won't," Isabel said. "Besides, you need some time to train with Kallistos before we can leave."

Abigail smiled at the mention of her wyvern.

"You should see him," she said. "He's growing so fast. He's already big enough to fly for extended periods of time. Knight Raja said I can start aerial combat training tomorrow."

"Wow, that was quick," Isabel said. "Are you sure Kallistos is ready? He isn't very old."

Abigail nodded as she smiled her thanks at Wren who was dishing lunch for the three of them. "Knight Raja says that wyverns grow very rapidly during the first month of life and usually reach full size within six months. It takes them a few years to fully mature but they can join the Sky Knights after only a month or two."

"Are you ready?" Isabel asked.

"I think so," Abigail said. "I've pretty much gotten over my fear of heights. The first few times were tough but now I can't wait for the next flight."

After they ate lunch, Abigail went back to the aerie and her wyvern while Isabel spent the rest of the day working on her visualization exercise until her mind was exhausted.

***

The next several days passed quickly. Isabel focused intensely on her mental exercises. Occasionally thoughts of Alexander would intrude into her mind and distract her from her practice. She learned quickly how to refocus her mind and quiet all of the little thoughts that so routinely occupied her mind. When she became tired or frustrated with her progress, she thought of Alexander and reminded herself that she would only be able to return to him once she had survived the mana fast.

Abigail trained hard every day. The Sky Knights were skilled warriors and they had high standards for members of their elite order. Abigail poured herself into her training and drove herself harder than was expected. There were several other young riders training with her but none as driven to master the Sky

Knights' trade. She quickly outpaced them and won the respect of many of the training cadre.

When they started weapons drills, Abigail began to struggle. The javelin was the preferred weapon of the Sky Knights because it was heavy enough to penetrate armor when thrown from above and it could be thrown with one hand, leaving the other free to hold onto the wyvern's reins. There was little danger of falling off in flight because the armor of a Sky Knight had a series of buckles and straps that connected to the saddle. Guiding the wyvern was the problem—the reins were as important on a wyvern as they were on a horse.

Abigail worked hard to master the javelin, but her slender frame simply didn't have the strength to throw one with nearly the range or accuracy of the other Sky Knights. After a particularly frustrating practice session where she missed her target in all ten of her attack runs, some of the other trainees began to tease her. Knight Raja silenced them but not before they added salt to the wound of her failure.

Raja pulled her aside after the morning training session. "You need to work on the javelin, Abigail. You have to be able to hit your target. Otherwise, you're just floating around above the battlefield."

"Let me try with my bow," Abigail said. "If I can't make it work, I'll double my efforts on the javelin."

"The bow is a difficult weapon to use while riding on the back of a wyvern," Raja said. "The javelin is a much better weapon once you learn how to use it."

"Let me try," Abigail said.

Knight Raja took a deep breath and nodded reluctantly. "Very well, you have the afternoon to prove that you can make your bow work. If you can't, then you'll focus on the javelin until you master it."

Abigail smiled, "Agreed."

They broke training for lunch. Abigail found Isabel and Wren when she returned to her quarters. It was a warm day with clear skies and a gentle breeze blowing across the ocean below. The big doors to the balcony were open to let in the sea air.

"Hi," Isabel said as she entered. "How'd the javelin training go?"

"Not well," she replied with a frown as she headed for her bedchamber. She emerged again a few moments later with her bow and quiver. "Knight Raja has agreed to let me try my bow. I hope I can make it work or I'm going to be doing javelin drills for the next several weeks."

"I'm sure you'll do fine," Isabel said. "I've seen you shoot from horseback. I don't know more than a handful of seasoned Rangers who can shoot as well as you do and none of them could match your bow."

"I hope you're right," Abigail said. "I just can't seem to throw a javelin with any accuracy at all." She sat down to the lunch of thick seafood chowder, crusty bread, and green salad that Wren was setting out for them.

Wren had been a waif of a girl when they arrived but she'd started to gain a little weight since she'd been eating with Isabel and Abigail at every meal. She looked healthier and happier. Her face wasn't as gaunt and she had better color. Isabel had grown very fond of the young woman and sometimes found herself wondering what would become of her once she and Abigail returned to Alexander.

They talked of little things while they ate. The chowder was filling and well seasoned. Once they were finished eating, Abigail strapped on her quiver.

"Mind if we come and watch?" Isabel asked.

Wren's eyes grew bigger and she smiled with excitement. She wasn't normally allowed on top of the plateau when the Sky Knights were training.

"Sure, maybe you'll bring me some luck," Abigail said.

Isabel could see the skepticism worn by the trainers as Abigail approached with her bow. She had tied it to her wrist with a lanyard to ensure that it wouldn't fall from her grasp in flight and she strode toward them like she had something to prove.

Isabel and Wren found an out-of-the-way place to watch the Sky Knights make their training runs against bales of hay stood on end, simulating human targets. A number of them had been set out, some in formations and others alone.

Knight Raja had Abigail shoot a number of targets from the ground first. He pointed to three targets set at about fifty yards—a good shot for a javelin but short for a bow. Abigail smiled with confidence and drove an arrow through each in turn with ease. Before Knight Raja could say another word, she sent an arrow at the farthest target and hit it with a clean shot.

He smiled at her skill and ordered her to mount Kallistos and make ten runs with the other trainees. A few minutes later, half a dozen wyverns were floating above the plateau in a wide orbit. They took turns making their attack runs, breaking off from the circling formation and diving toward the simulated enemies. Most of the new riders did fairly well with the javelin. They hit their targets about two of every three runs they made.

Abigail didn't follow the same attack pattern. Instead she floated high and slow over the field of targets. Several days before, the trainees had learned how to coax their wyverns into a slow glide. Given the right wind conditions, they could almost hover. Today was perfect. The gentle breeze provided just enough lift to float without too much forward motion.

Abigail loosed her first arrow and found a target. If she'd been shooting at an enemy, he'd be dead for sure. Her second arrow found its mark as well. She released three more arrows in her attack run before rejoining the circle formation of the other riders to let them have a turn at the targets. All of her arrows were direct hits.

Isabel saw the Sky Knight trainers look at each other with surprise at Abigail's proficiency with a bow.

Her next attack run was a repeat of the first, only this time she emptied her entire quiver, each arrow finding its mark with precision. She fired ten arrows in rapid succession and didn't miss a one.

"She's amazing," Wren whispered.

Isabel chuckled, nodding her agreement. "Abigail's a natural with a bow. I've been shooting all my life and I can't match her, especially with that bow of hers."

Wren frowned in confusion. "Is her bow special?"

Isabel smiled and nodded without explanation.

Abigail landed and the Sky Knight trainers converged on her. They offered congratulations and praise for a moment until Flight Commander Bianca approached. She had been watching from the shadows of a nearby tree. Isabel wondered why she hadn't noticed the woman.

The breeze carried their conversation to Isabel and Wren as they watched.

"Impressive," Mistress Bianca said, "but your bow is spelled. Are you as capable with an ordinary weapon?"

The crowd gathered around Abigail fell silent at the implied challenge. She didn't hesitate. "No, but I'm better than I would be with a javelin and probably deadlier than most Sky Knights."

"Bold words," Mistress Bianca said with a little grin. "Perhaps you'd like to prove your skills in a challenge."

"What did you have in mind?" Abigail asked.

"I'm sure we could find a suitable bow for you to use," Mistress Bianca said. "Let's see if you can repeat your performance."

Abigail shrugged. "Fine by me."

Mistress Bianca sent a Sky Knight to the armory to get a bow while Abigail went to where Isabel and Wren were watching. She handed her bow to Isabel. "Keep an eye on this for me."

"Of course," Isabel said, taking the finely crafted composite bow from her. "That was pretty good. Looks like it comes as easily for you as shooting from the back of a horse."

Abigail nodded. "It took a moment to get comfortable shooting down rather than away from my mount but it didn't take too long to figure it out. I knew I'd have to come in slower and higher to get a steady aim. Seemed to work out pretty well. I hope they bring me a decent bow to work with on the next run."

"I'm sure you'll do just fine," Isabel said.

Not too much later Abigail was again in the air floating high and slow over the simulated battlefield. She came in a bit lower this time to compensate for the less powerful bow but was able to get seven arrows off with deadly accuracy in her first attack run. The other trainees could only attack with a single javelin per run and didn't have the accuracy that she did. After three runs, her quiver was empty and she had hit for every shot except two. She landed with sunlight shining off her silvery blond hair, smiling brightly.

Mistress Bianca and Knight Raja approached as she dismounted.

"Well done," Knight Raja said with a proud smile.

"Indeed," Mistress Bianca said. "I'm convinced that the bow is a better weapon for you, but I still expect you to master the javelin over time. You may continue with your training regimen without any remedial instruction."

Abigail smiled with triumph. "Thank you. I'll work on the javelin but when I ride into battle, I'll be using my bow."

Bianca nodded with a smile. "I have no doubt, and I wouldn't expect anything else, but since a bow can be dropped, you must have effective weapons in reserve."

"That makes sense," Abigail said, nodding to her Flight Commander.

Isabel spent the rest of the afternoon practicing her visualization exercises while Abigail and the other trainees practiced aerial maneuvers, formation flying, and sequential attack runs. Even though Abigail had proven herself with her bow, she was not allowed to use it for training. Knight Raja said she was good enough with it that she didn't need any more practice so he sent her up with javelins.

***

The days drifted by quickly. Abigail spent every hour of daylight training with her wyvern and the Sky Knights. Her skills and confidence grew with each passing day.

Kallistos also grew. He was big enough to start hunting, which led to the next phase of her training—aerial attack with her wyvern as the weapon. Either with the tail or with talons, a wyvern could inflict withering damage with a single pass. Abigail remembered all too well the day she'd been abducted and how deadly the tail strike of a wyvern could be. She practiced diligently, learning the nuances of mounted flight.

Some days she lost all thoughts of anything else except for mastering the exercise of the moment. When she was in a steep dive making a run at a target, her intensity of focus was so complete that nothing else existed except for her target, Kallistos, and the wind. In those moments, nothing else mattered. She felt more alive than ever before.

Isabel spent her days in seclusion, practicing her mental exercises. A few times she returned to Magda to seek clarification on some concept or other but mostly she sat quietly with her eyes closed. An observer would think she was resting or even napping but she went to bed each night mentally exhausted. She focused on her training with intensity and drive. Each time she felt too tired to continue, she thought of Alexander and her mental endurance was restored.

After she felt confident in her ability to visualize an image at will, she moved to the practice of invoking powerful emotions. The practice of deliberately creating intense emotion proved to be even more exhausting and considerably more difficult.

She searched her memory for a moment of intense anger and found it. When Truss abducted her, she had been furious. Before Magda had instructed her to use past memories to create intense emotion, she had avoided thinking about that incident because it was so unpleasant but now she found that she was capable of drawing up a feeling of intense righteous anger almost on command. Her problem came when she tried to dismiss the feeling. It seemed so justified in the face of what had been done to her that it felt almost like a betrayal of something important to let it go.

After several attempts she became frustrated and decided to seek help. The anger came easily but she needed a technique for getting rid of it. As she strode through the halls of the fortress island, she tried to let go of her dark mood but was still angry when she arrived at the hall leading to the triumvirs' chambers. The guards stopped her. Isabel had to restrain her urge to lash out at them.

"I need to see Magda," she snapped.

"*Mistress* Magda is not accepting visitors today," the guard said.

"I'm not a visitor, I'm a student," Isabel replied with a bit too much intensity.

"Be that as it may, you will have to come back tomorrow," the guard said pointedly as the other rested his hand on the hilt of his sheathed sword.

Isabel glared at him for a moment before she turned on her heel and stormed off. She walked aimlessly for a while trying to take her mind off the memory of Truss binding her hands and loading her into a box. She wanted to strangle the little weasel.

After an hour of stewing over the past, a thought suddenly occurred to her. Magda had suggested that she could seek guidance from Head Mistress Theresa in the training hall. After asking directions, she found herself standing in the entry hall of the big room watching a small class of young women learn the history of Kendra Reishi and how her discoveries had led to the practice of witchcraft.

A young woman approached and spoke quietly. "Can I help you?"

Isabel schooled her tone. She didn't want to take her manufactured anger out on this young woman. "I'd like to speak with Head Mistress Theresa, please."

"Of course, she's teaching a class at the moment but she should be finished soon. You're welcome to wait if you like," she said, motioning to a set of comfortable chairs in the entry hall.

"Thank you," Isabel said as she headed for a chair. She sat and closed her eyes. Instead of her exercises she thought about Alexander and the relatively brief time they'd spent together. They had known each other for only a few months but she felt a deeper connection to him than she had ever felt with anyone in her life. When Theresa approached, Isabel discovered that she was no longer angry.

"I'm Head Mistress Theresa. How can I help you?"

Isabel stood with a smile. "I'm Isabel. Mistress Magda said I could ask you for guidance if I was struggling with some aspect of my exercises."

"Ah, yes, of course," Theresa said. "Please come with me so we may speak in private." She led Isabel into a small room filled with a large desk and shelves that lined the walls. Books, scrolls, and papers lay haphazardly on every surface. Theresa took a stack of books from a chair and motioned for Isabel to sit as she closed the door and settled in behind her desk.

"How can I help you?" she asked with a pleasant smile.

Isabel took a deep breath and ordered her thoughts. "I've been practicing an exercise for emotional control using anger as my focus. I can make the anger come easily enough but then I can't seem to make it go away."

"Ah, yes, that is a common problem with young acolytes and one that is easily remedied," Theresa said. "When you are feeling angry, simply see yourself from a different point of view. See yourself from the position of a disinterested observer and your anger will subside."

Isabel frowned. The advice seemed so simple but she decided to give it a try. If it didn't work, she could always go talk to Magda tomorrow.

She thanked Mistress Theresa and returned to her quarters. When she once again called forth the anger, it came quickly and intensely. She tried to shift her perspective to that of an observer and found it difficult to accomplish, but with a little effort she succeeded. The anger evaporated almost magically.

With work and practice, she gained greater control of her ability to dismiss her anger until she was able to bring it forth with a vengeance and then banish it with equal quickness and control.

Next she worked on love. She found this practice to be much more pleasant. She chose her wedding as the memory she used to invoke a feeling of powerful love. It came to her easily but inevitably led to a feeling of sadness because she was separated from Alexander. That feeling proved to be even more difficult to banish because it was so much more important to her, but with time and effort she gained the ability to create feelings of love or anger at will and then detach from those feelings with a thought.

The days passed and her mental control grew. She started mixing the two by calling forth an intense emotion and then seeing an image in her mind's eye. The balancing act was daunting at first. She found that she was so focused on seeing the object that she forgot to be mad. Or she would invoke a feeling of love and was so distracted by her feelings for Alexander and her desire to see him again that she couldn't focus on the object she wanted to see. It took time and determined effort before she felt ready for the trials.

She resisted the urge to request the trials prematurely. Instead, she spent a few days walking the halls of the fortress island while practicing her twin mental exercises. She needed to be certain of her ability to control her thoughts and feelings. Once the trials began, there would be no turning back and failure was death. She didn't want to die and she simply would not subject Alexander to a life of believing that he had sent her to her death because he had provided the means for her to take the mana fast.

When she was certain, she brought it up at dinner with Abigail and Wren.

"I think I'm ready for the trials. I'm going to go see Magda tomorrow."

"Are you sure?" Abigail asked. "It might be better to take a few days to think about it."

"I've been thinking about it for the past three days," Isabel said. "I've mastered the exercises that Magda gave me. She said that once I could do both with control, I would be ready."

Abigail took a deep breath and let it out slowly. "If you're sure, but don't rush into this, Isabel. The mana fast is dangerous. You remember the screams we heard from the tower when Alexander went through it. Even if you're ready, it's not going to be easy."

Isabel nodded somberly. "I know and I'm not too proud to admit that I'm a bit scared, but the sooner I get through it, the sooner we can get back to Alexander."

"I know," Abigail whispered, "I miss him, too. And there's no telling what kind of trouble he's gotten himself into by now."

Isabel grinned. "How soon will you be done with your training?"

"Not long," Abigail said, "maybe a week. Knight Raja has already told me I'm ready but he believes in being thorough. Truth is, I'm ready to go as soon as you are."

Wren looked at the table and a tear slipped down her cheek and into her dinner. "I'm going to miss both of you."

Isabel smiled fondly at the young woman and took her hand. She looked up only after Isabel gave her a gentle squeeze. "I've been thinking about that. How would you like to come to Ruatha? It's more dangerous than here because of the war, but I'm sure we could find work for you in Blackstone Keep."

Wren's eyes grew wide and she nodded with disbelieving excitement. "I've always wanted to see more of the Seven Isles. I'd love to come to Ruatha with you." Then she stopped suddenly. "What about my family? I can't leave them behind and I have duties here."

"There's more than enough room for your family and I'm sure the fortress island will manage without you," Isabel said.

"The owner of this Blackstone Keep would really welcome me into his home?" Wren asked with a little touch of awe. "It sounds like such an important place."

Isabel and Abigail chuckled gently. "Wren, I'm the Queen of Ruatha. Blackstone Keep belongs to my husband. I guarantee that you're welcome there."

Her eyes went wide and then she looked at the table again. "I'm sorry, sometimes I forget you're so important."

"Nonsense," Isabel said with a hint of sternness in her voice. "You are my friend. Titles and kingdoms mean nothing when compared to love and friendship. I only mentioned my title to prove that you are welcome at Blackstone Keep."

"You two have been so good to me," Wren said softly. "I never thought I would have such good friends in my whole life. Thank you for everything."

"You're welcome, Wren," Isabel said. "You've made us feel at home here despite the fact that we were brought here against our will. It may take some time to make the arrangements to get you moved to Ruatha, but I promise that as soon as it's safe, we'll help you get there."

Wren left giddy with excitement. She couldn't wait to tell her parents.

"I'm glad you did that," Abigail said. "I've grown fond of her. I wasn't looking forward to saying goodbye."

"Me, neither," Isabel said. "I'm sure we can find a place for her at the Keep."

Abigail nodded. "I actually have an idea about that. Remember when we first got here and we asked Wren what she wanted to do?"

Isabel nodded with a knowing smile. "She said she wanted to sing. I've caught her singing under her breath a few times and she has a beautiful voice."

"I bet Jack could find her a place in the Bards Guild," Abigail said. "He told me once that he's always on the lookout for talented singers or storytellers."

"You know, I bet you're right," Isabel said with a smile. "Let's not tell her about that for now. She's already excited enough about the idea of moving to Ruatha. I don't want to get her hopes up too much. Besides we do have a few more pressing concerns at the moment."

"Agreed," Abigail said. "But it would be nice to make her happy if we can."

Chapter 17

The next morning Isabel went to the triumvirs' working chambers. She took a deep breath to steady her nerves as she stopped before the two big men guarding the hall.

"I'm here to see Mistress Magda," she said simply.

This time they didn't object or question her. Instead they stepped aside and nodded for her to proceed.

The two women in the entry hall invited her to sit and wait while Magda finished with her current appointment.

Isabel was nervous as she waited. To dispel her anxiety, she started working through the visualization exercise she had learned by calling up all of the objects she'd worked with over the past several days. They sprang into her mind with vivid detail on command and remained in her mind's eye for as long as she chose to focus on them.

She was concentrating so hard that she didn't hear the woman behind the desk tell her that Magda was ready to see her. When the woman touched Isabel on the shoulder, she snapped out of her trance with a start.

Magda was waiting in her sitting room when Isabel entered. She smiled warmly. "How can I help you?"

"I'm ready," she said simply.

"Are you certain?" Magda asked.

Isabel nodded gravely. "I've mastered the exercises you gave me and I feel a greater degree of control over my mind and feelings than I've ever had before. I'm ready."

"Very well," Magda said as she stood. She placed a hand on Isabel's forehead and closed her eyes while she murmured something under her breath. When she opened her eyes, she fixed Isabel with a firm look and nodded slowly. "I believe you are as ready as you can be given the short time you've been preparing."

"When can I take the trials?" Isabel asked.

"We will begin tomorrow," Magda said. "Take the rest of the day and walk in the gardens or take a nap but don't practice your exercises anymore until after the mana fast is over. You need to rest your mind. Eat a good dinner tonight and go to bed early. Come to my quarters first thing in the morning and I will accompany you to the chamber where your trials will take place. You will spend the next seven days locked away for your mana fast. Talk to Abigail tonight so she knows what to expect."

"I will," Isabel said. "Thank you."

Magda gave her a serious look. "Don't thank me yet. You have yet to survive the mana fast. The trials are difficult and intense, and this next week will be very challenging."

"I understand," Isabel said before she left with a firm sense of resolve. This was the path she must walk to return to Alexander and her people. She would do what was necessary, come what may.

She wandered up to the plateau and watched a squad of six wyverns float past. They were still guarding the Reishi Isle even though the Sovereign Stone was no longer there. Isabel wondered about the leadership of this very powerful enclave of soldiers and witches. They seemed so engrained in their ways that they couldn't see the senselessness of continuing to do as they'd always done even though the world had changed before their very eyes.

No matter, she thought. They would either join Alexander or remain here. Either way, Isabel would be free to return to her husband in just over a week, provided that the coven lived up to their promises. She decided to dismiss the possibility of treachery for the time being. Magda had been forthcoming and helpful, Cassandra was noncommittal yet willing to listen to reason, only Gabriella was stubbornly opposed to Isabel leaving, and her feelings were the result of grief over her dead husband—killed by Alexander's hand. Isabel couldn't fault her for her feelings on that score, for now at least. Although, there would come a time when Gabriella would have to choose a side. Isabel decided not to worry about that either.

The day was clear and warm, even with the gentle ocean breeze blowing over the top of the fortress island. She found a bench made of driftwood under a tree and sat down to enjoy the peace and beauty of one of the well-tended flower gardens. It was midspring and the flowers were in bloom. The groundskeepers prided themselves on the careful arrangements of their flowering plants. They staggered them so there was always something in bloom during the spring and summer months. The variety of flowers and colors was delightful.

Isabel sat for a while and simply enjoyed the breeze in her hair and the sun on her face. She relaxed and let her mind wander. It wasn't long before she was thinking about Alexander. He was so far away. She wanted to see him before the mana fast if only to hear him reassure her that she was ready.

She heard a rustle above and looked up to see Slyder peering down at her from a branch in the tree. She smiled at him and gently made contact with his mind. He was restless and wanted to return to the forest. The ocean was unfamiliar to him and he made it clear that he didn't like it here. Isabel reassured her friend that they would be returning to land soon enough. She also tried to communicate the danger and necessity of the mana fast, but try as she might, the bird simply couldn't understand. To Slyder, danger was something to run away from or confront. Finally, she tried to impress on him the need to remain hidden from the witches and the wyverns while she underwent the fast, even if he could feel her distress. That confused him even more and he gave a sharp shriek and took to wing. Isabel let him go and decided to explore her bond with other animals.

She saw a smaller bird and reached out to it with her mind. It was a much more nervous consciousness than Slyder's. Isabel could sense the constant state of alertness that the tiny little creature lived with and imagined that it must be exhausting. She gently commanded the bird to come to her. For a brief moment she felt a slight resistance and then the colorful little bird was sitting on her shoulder with its head darting all about. Isabel released it and the bird fluttered off to a branch in a nearby tree and chattered at her for a moment before flying off deeper into the garden.

Two wyverns glided by overhead, casting their shadows down onto the plateau. Isabel reached out to one of them and found a much more alert and fearsome mind. It was the mind of a predator that had little fear of anything. Most creatures were its prey and those few that could best a wyvern could usually be avoided. She rode along with the beast for a few moments to get familiar with his thought process and stream of consciousness. Mostly, the giant animal was responding to the guidance of its rider. Isabel decided to test her newfound power and commanded the wyvern to bank right. Not a moment passed before the aerial hunter pulled sharply to the right. The rider grabbed the reins and pulled his mount back into formation slightly behind the right wing of the lead wyvern.

She waited patiently for the next pair to float by and entered the minds of both animals at once. Her connection seemed more tenuous and less certain but when she commanded, they both dove for the deck until their riders regained control a moment later. Isabel relinquished her hold on the beasts almost at once to prevent injury to the animals or to their riders.

She sat back and thought about the power she had at her disposal through the gifts Desiderates had given her. Mage Gamaliel was a sneaky old wizard for sending such a powerful solution to the poison that had almost killed her. She resolved to use that power to bring the full force of the Reishi Coven and the Sky Knights to the aid of Alexander and Ruatha whether the triumvirate liked it or not.

With that thought, she made her way back to her quarters. Wren was waiting with lunch. Abigail arrived not long after.

"Well, how'd it go?" Abigail asked before she'd even closed the door behind her.

"I'm going to start the trials tomorrow," Isabel said. "Magda said it will take a week and I'll be isolated for the duration."

"Pretty much like Alexander was during his fast," Abigail said, nodding. "Are you sure you're ready? I know you're as anxious to get back as I am but you won't do anyone any good if you get yourself killed."

"Your concern is touching," Isabel said.

"You know what I mean," Abigail replied as she took her seat at the table.

Isabel nodded with a gentle smile for her sister. They had become close friends over the past weeks. Isabel valued Abigail's insight and opinion but more than that she trusted her.

"I'm ready," Isabel said firmly. "I'm sure it won't be easy but I'm also sure that I'll succeed. I have to."

"Funny how necessity can drive us to accomplish things we'd never even try if we had a choice," Abigail said.

Isabel spent the rest of the afternoon mentally preparing for her trials. She didn't work on her exercises but instead focused on her reasons for taking such a risk. When faced with the alternatives, the path she was walking was the only way. Alexander needed her and she needed him and not just for the war against Phane. Once the Seven Isles were free, there would be other challenges. Alexander was the Sovereign and he needed a wife who could stand with him. Only a witch could be everything she needed to be for him. The trials were the only way.

She woke early the next morning and dressed deliberately. Breakfast with Abigail and Wren was quiet. They spoke of little things and avoided talk of the dangers Isabel would be facing. Isabel hugged them both before leaving to begin her mana fast.

Magda was waiting for her when she arrived.

Isabel felt unusually nervous. She was normally confident when facing a challenge but this was different—so much depended on her success.

"Good morning, Isabel. Do you have any questions before we begin?"

Isabel shook her head slowly.

"Just so we're clear, this is dangerous and difficult. There is no pressure if you wish to continue your practice and build on your skills before you undergo the trials."

"I understand," Isabel said. "I'm ready now."

"Very well, come with me," Magda said as she retrieved a small box from a locked cabinet.

Magda led her through a twisting maze of corridors that wound deeper into the bowels of the fortress island than Isabel had ever been. There were a number of doors that were locked and spelled to prevent entrance to anyone but authorized members of the coven. They arrived at a nondescript door that opened to a circular room with a magic circle inlaid in the floor. It was a simple stone room carved from the rock of the island. The ceiling was high and the walls were bare. There was a low bed with a thin feather mattress in the center. Two neatly folded blankets and a pillow rested on the foot of the bed. A cistern filled with water sat next to the bed and a single oil lamp rested on a small table nearby.

A single ray of sunlight stabbed through the dim light of the lamp from a slit in one wall, brilliantly illuminating a spot on the opposite wall.

Magda placed the box on the table and opened it carefully. Within were seven heavy glass vials filled with liquid that was glowing slightly with a pure white light. Each vial was fitted into a red felt-lined indentation designed to hold it in place.

"You must drink one vial each day for the next seven days," Magda said. "Use the position of the sunlight to mark time. Do you understand?"

"Yes," Isabel said.

"Once the trials begin, you will be on your own," Magda said. "If you fail to drink all of the vials, you will die. If you drink more than one per day, you will die. If you succumb to the pain, fear, or despair, you will die. The firmament has no consciousness of its own but it seems to crave the input of the conscious mind. It is believed that this is the reason for the difficulty of the trials. People are more apt to act rashly to escape unpleasant feelings, so the firmament induces the worst emotions possible with great intensity in order to motivate you to release your hold on your own identity and surrender your will to the firmament. If you let go, you will die.

"You must face each of the trials directly and endure. You must maintain a hold on your identity and your will in order to survive. Once you can face the unmitigated torment of each trial, the firmament will give up and move on to the next trial. Remember, everything you are about to experience is both very real and completely imaginary at the same time. Real in the sense that you will experience the feelings with great intensity and unreal in the sense that the feelings are fabricated and artificial—but your psyche won't know that. You must not let the intensity of the experience fool you into believing that the experience is real. You must maintain a firm grasp on the truth that this is a test of your will that is taking place within your mind and nowhere else.

"If you are ready, I will activate the magic circle and seal you into this room for the next week. Once you drink the contents of the first vial, the trials will begin at a time and in a way that is completely unpredictable, except that they will take seven days to complete. Some people report the trials beginning within minutes of drinking the first vial. At least one witch I know said that her trials all happened on the final day of the mana fast.

"On the morning of the eighth day, I will return to release the magic circle. Until then, no magic or substance will be able to pass into or out of the circle. Occasionally, uncontrolled magical energies of great power are released during the mana fast. The circle is here to ensure that you cause no harm to those around you as well as to ensure that you finish the fast.

"Use your emotions to your advantage. Focus on your love for Alexander and use that love to remain grounded in reality."

Isabel nodded and sat down on the edge of the little bed.

"Are you certain that you're ready?" Magda asked. "Once you drink the first vial, there is no going back. You'll either survive the trials or you will die."

Isabel looked over to the spot of sunlight on the wall. It fell on the fourth stone up from the floor. She marked the position in her mind and took the first of the seven vials. She looked briefly at the magical elixir, at the way it glowed with the kind of light she had seen when she witnessed the birth of the fairy Sara within her own mind. With a smile of love for Alexander and a firm sense of resolve, she uncorked the vial and drank the sweet-tasting liquid.

Magda nodded with a mixture of approval and concern before she stepped out of the circle and spoke a few words under her breath. The circle pulsed with light and the air shimmered briefly.

"The trials have begun," Magda said. "May the Maker of the world watch over you and deliver you through the ordeal you face." She held Isabel with her eyes for a moment before she left the room. Isabel heard the bolt on the outside of the door slam into place and then the sound of Magda's footsteps echoing in the corridor as she walked away. Then there was only silence.

She sat cross-legged on the bed and closed her eyes.

The onslaught was so sudden and so intense that she nearly cast herself into the firmament without even thinking of the consequences. An instant after she closed her eyes, she found herself standing in the small room within her mind that Alexander had helped her construct, looking through what used to be a secure doorway leading to the netherworld. Only now, where the door used to be, there was a gaping hole in the imaginary wall leading to a place of inky blackness, endless emptiness, and palpable malice.

Isabel stared into the netherworld with breathless terror, and the darkness stared back. She was paralyzed with fear. Overcome with cold dread.

She had opened the doorway to the netherworld and unleashed the shades. They had come forth into the world of time and substance with the singular goal of finding and opening the Nether Gate. Creatures of the dark would pour forth and consume the world of life, ending all hope, not just for the people of the Seven Isles but for every creature everywhere.

Isabel had doomed them all.

She felt the rush of fear come in waves that threatened to overwhelm her sanity. Guilt crushed in on her. She cowered away from the consequences of her actions. It was the most horrible thing she had ever felt. She had to escape it. But before she could release her hold on her will, she became dimly aware of a quiet place of calm deep within her psyche.

She focused on that place and found herself wondering how Alexander could have possibly endured such terror. The shock of the revelation hit her like a lightning bolt. In an instant, she realized that she had allowed the intensity of the trials to overwhelm her reason and drive out her sense of reality. Alexander had gone through the trials. He had endured. She could too.

Facing her fear of the darkness before her, she withdrew into that place of calm and reason, but the fear followed her. She vaguely remembered Alexander explaining how he had taken refuge within that place of calm in his mind and how the fear and pain couldn't exist there. For her it still did. She couldn't find a refuge. She felt trapped in her own mind with a beast of unspeakable evil and cold malevolence. It chased her until she was frantic and exhausted. Then the darkness was all around her. The sensation was familiar. She had fallen into the darkness of the netherworld. The coldness and emptiness threatened to tear her soul apart—she couldn't find the strength or the resolve to resist the overwhelming pull of the void.

What had been terror only a moment ago spiked into wild panic. She felt the tug of countless formless manifestations of evil pulling at the edges of her soul, trying to unravel the very essence of her being. The abstract fear of unleashing the darkness into the world transformed into a visceral, hopeless horror of being lost to the endless torment of the netherworld.

She felt trapped and alone without any place of refuge. Her fear only fueled the hunger of the darkness and drew the lifeless beings that lived there to her failing light. Her desperation ignited a spark of anger within her that she seized and nurtured into a full-blown rage, but that only seemed to feed the creatures in the dark. They took strength from the negativity of the anger she had deliberately flooded herself with and renewed their attack with a vengeance.

Isabel frantically focused on the exercise she had learned for dispelling anger. She stepped outside of herself and looked at the events transpiring within her mind from the perspective of a disinterested observer. Almost as quickly as she had given her anger life, she snuffed it out and extinguished the passion of it, leaving her vulnerable to the cold, life-leeching darkness of the netherworld. The fear threatened to overwhelm her sanity and she considered letting go—but only for a moment.

Thoughts of Alexander filled her mind and she saw the path to salvation. She focused on him and her love for him. The light of her soul grew bright and drove the creatures circling in the darkness far enough away for her to gain greater control of her mind and her reason. She could still feel the fear but it was less important in the face of her love for Alexander. She renewed her efforts to focus on the light of her love and regained some sense of her circumstances. The panic receded into manageable terror.

When she realized she didn't know the way out of the darkness, the panic threatened at the edges of her consciousness again, but again she pushed it back. In that moment of relative calm, she understood what she had to do. She reached deep into her mind and found the pathway that led to the realm of light, the portal that had opened within her mind when Sara was born.

With an effort of will and her newly gained powers of visualization, she threw open the passageway to the realm of light. A ray of pure white light the color of life stabbed through the darkness and showed her the way back into her own mind and the world of time and substance. The creatures swirling in the darkness shrieked with fury at the intrusion of the Maker's light into their realm, but they cowered from it in spite of their hatred for it.

Isabel willed her soul through the darkness toward the source of the light until she found herself back in her own mind. She opened her eyes and gasped for breath as she stood and looked around frantically. She was standing next to the bed in the chamber of trials. The sun had moved down the wall and several feet across the floor.

Isabel had passed the trial of fear.

She had no way of knowing whether she had actually passed into the netherworld or if it had all been an illusion created within her mind by the firmament, and she didn't really care. She was through the first of three trials and the mana fast had only just begun.

For the next three days she struggled with isolation and hunger. The second day was the worst. She paced for hours trying to take her mind off food, but the grumbling of her empty stomach always brought her back to her hunger.

She drank the Wizard's Dust-infused water at the correct time each day and waited for the next of the trials to manifest.

She tried to keep her mind busy with her visualization and emotional-control exercises. When she tired of that, she replayed the experience of the trial of fear over in her mind in an effort to learn what she could from it. Her connections to the netherworld and the realm of light led her to speculate about the nature of the world she lived in and how it interacted with the higher and lower planes. When she tired of speculating about things she could not prove, she thought about Alexander. He always brought her back to a place of clarity and purpose. Thinking of him centered her and gave her hope for the future, not just for herself but for the entire Seven Isles.

She drifted off to sleep on the third night of her trials thinking about her husband. Without waking, she found herself floating as a disembodied point of awareness over a battlefield. Alexander was surrounded by an army of enormous proportions. He fought fiercely and with reckless abandon but there were just too many enemy soldiers. One by one she watched her friends die trying to save Alexander. Anatoly fell first. He stepped in front of a volley of enemy arrows and took several long shafts in the chest. He slumped to his knees with blood bubbling from his mouth. Alexander cried out. Isabel could see his horror at losing his mentor, but he was forced to defend himself against another surge of enemy soldiers.

Isabel felt a growing sense of hopelessness begin to build within her as she floated above the fray. Lucky rushed to help Anatoly when a big enemy soldier broke through the cordon of loyal protectors surrounding Alexander and ran Lucky through with a spear. Isabel heard Alexander sob even as he renewed his drive into the enemy.

She saw the frantic and desperate struggle in Alexander's movements as he tried in vain to overcome impossible odds. From where Isabel floated over the field she could see the enemy horde stretch off to the horizon. Alexander was fighting a hopeless battle. He would strike down hundreds, maybe even thousands of the enemy with the Sword of Kings—but, in the end, he would fall.

She felt a lump growing in her soul. A feeling of loss and despair began to build. She imagined a world without Alexander and quailed from the prospect.

Still the enemy came.

Jack flickered into view as he stabbed a soldier coming up behind Alexander and then fell just as quickly from the crossbow bolt of another soldier. Isabel could see the wild loss and desperate need in Alexander's eyes. She struggled to reach out to him, to enter the battle at his side, if only to die in the struggle with him. But she had no power. She was a helpless observer without form or substance.

One by one his protectors died trying to save him. Nameless soldiers sworn to the Old Law mounted a valiant struggle to preserve their King, but hack by thrust they were felled in a growing ring of carnage.

And still the enemy came.

Isabel watched as the last of the soldiers loyal to her husband died, leaving him to fend for himself against impossible numbers. He fought on with renewed fury. All was lost but he didn't give in. He fought on. An arrow found his left arm, rendering it useless, but still Alexander lashed out at the enemy soldiers. The ground was slick with bloody mud and the air was thick with the stench of death.

Then Isabel noticed Phane off in the distance, standing on a rock to get a better view of Alexander's death. He wore a smile of triumph. Isabel felt the despair threaten to claim her. Only moments later, Alexander was driven to his knee by an arrow through his leg. He struggled in vain to regain his footing but his leg was too badly injured to bear his weight. Even on his knees, Alexander killed three more soldiers before a big man with a blunt mace stepped up behind him and clubbed him in the back of the head.

The wet thud was sickening. Isabel felt an overwhelming flood of loss fill her to overflowing as she watched her best reason for living die right before her eyes. Her sanity threatened to dissolve under the onslaught of loss that filled her with despair.

Somewhere in the back of her mind, she knew this was a test. But the things she had witnessed were too real and too vibrant to be denied. Alexander was gone. Her love had been killed.

She floated for a time and watched the enemy mutilate his dead body for their amusement while the despair overcame her and pushed everything else out of her awareness until there was only loss.

Then time sped up and she saw Phane standing before the Nether Gate chanting a spell. She almost didn't care anymore until she saw the Gate come alive and the darkness of the netherworld slowly spill out into the world of time and substance.

Phane panicked and fled—the creatures he had unleashed were beyond even his power to control. They ran him down and devoured him, leaving the world naked before the onslaught of the darkness. And still Isabel was powerless to act, trapped in a place of helpless observation. She watched as the world died.

The darkness devoured and consumed everything good in all of the Seven

Isles and left only broken, twisted, and corrupted remains. The whole of the world descended into a pit of torment and despair until even the sun itself began to dim.

Isabel felt lost and helpless as the despair threatened to consume her. She could feel nothing but the hollow ache of loss until she simply wanted to cease to exist. Deep within her psyche, a part of her revolted at the spark of hope she felt at the thought of her own dissolution. Somewhere, she knew this was the test of despair. But she no longer cared. She just wanted the endless loss to end. She was ready to let go and release her will into the firmament just to make it stop.

But she couldn't let go. Alexander would want her to keep fighting no matter what. He'd done just that. Even when all of his allies had fallen, he had fought on. When he was alone, surrounded by a horde of enemy soldiers, he struggled with his last breath for the cause he had vowed to protect. She could do no less.

She struggled to find a place within herself where the despair couldn't find her. But there was nowhere to hide. The feelings of loss were so real and so pervasive that she couldn't escape them. With an effort of sheer will, she focused on her memory of her wedding. At first it seemed distant and unreal but the more she focused on it, the more tangible the feelings became until she reached a tipping point and the love she had for Alexander filled her and drove out the despair.

She woke with a start. It was just after dawn. The spot of sunlight was high on the wall and the room was chill with the morning air. She sat up on her bed and breathed deeply, trying to gain some composure and reconnect with reality. She shuddered when she thought of the terrible images of Alexander's death. She remembered how much she'd worried for him when he had undertaken the trials. If she'd known what he was actually facing, she would have done nearly anything to protect him from the horrors he had endured.

The fourth, fifth, and sixth days of the trials passed quietly. Her hunger had faded and she learned to accept the solitude. She spent the days meditating and practicing her exercises, drinking another vial each day at the appointed time and waiting with trepidation for the trial of pain to begin.

On the morning of the seventh day, she had just swallowed the seventh and final vial when a stabbing pain shot through her stomach like a spear had been driven into her. The pain was so intense, it froze her in place. She couldn't breathe or even scream. With a shudder she toppled off the bed and landed hard against the cold stone floor. The pain flowed into her from the center of her gut and spread out like tentacles of molten agony. They bored into her and ignited her nerves everywhere they went. Just when she thought the pain couldn't be any worse, another jolt of agony would pulse through her.

She gasped for breath and screamed with an effort of wild panic. As her scream trailed off, she realized she had made a potentially fatal mistake. She was out of breath and the wracking torment was so great that she couldn't draw another. She closed her eyes and focused on her lungs, commanding them to fill with air but the convulsions shuddering through her prevented her from inhaling. She struggled as the world started to go dark. Her lungs burned with their searing need for air but still she couldn't make them work.

As her consciousness faded, she made one final effort to draw breath and managed to gasp a small gulp of air. It wasn't nearly enough but it did stave off the darkness of unconsciousness and oblivion for a few more moments. Each small gulp of air was a struggle. She didn't know how long she lay there on the cold stone floor struggling to breathe. Each little bit of air took a monumental effort but didn't lessen the pain.

She began to feel exhausted from the convulsions of agony that tore through her body and her psyche. She had spent so much of her energy trying to take the next breath that she had failed to remember that each trial must be faced and endured. She felt her grip on her identity start to loosen as the pain worked to pry her will to live away from her soul. Darkness closed in around her and her consciousness faded.

Some time later, she found herself floating in the small room looking down at her corpse.

Isabel was dead.

Chapter 18

Alexander scanned the horizon. It was evening of the third day since they'd separated from Conner's honor guard and headed south toward Bradfield Province, which was adjacent to Grafton. They were being followed. Alexander had noticed their pursuers earlier in the day and was becoming concerned that his ruse might not work. Much hung in the balance. His father was defending against an invading army and needed all the time he could get to prepare his defenses and evacuate New Ruatha and Northport before either city was overrun by the Reishi Army Regency. The life of Abel's daughter was also at stake. She was being held prisoner in Grafton Province by Phane's agents. If they learned that Abel had no intention of negotiating with them, they might kill her.

The men following him could only be enemy spies. Abel had no reason to send men after him. They had agreed on their course of action, and Alexander trusted the King of Ithilian. He'd looked at his colors and found him to be a good and honest man. More than that, Abel knew that Alexander's mission would succeed only if kept secret. He wouldn't risk exposing their plan. Too much depended on secrecy.

The men following them had to be enemy. The only questions Alexander had were who sent them and why. Cassius was the only player on Ithilian that he was aware of who might have dispatched them. But Alexander wasn't about to rule out the possibility of other forces at work. He'd learned through bitter experience that there was often more to a given situation than met the eye—even eyes as penetrating as his.

From his vantage point on the little hillock, he could just make out the smudge of color in the distance that gave away the enemy's position. They were easily a league behind and didn't look like they were trying to close the distance. That concerned him even more. If they were hunters, they would be making best speed to close with them but they were deliberately keeping their distance.

Their purpose was apparently more strategic, so it stood to reason that they were working with others who had unknown resources at their disposal. Alexander knew as well as anyone that magic could be used to communicate across great distances in the blink of an eye. If they warned the enemy in Grafton, Alexander might arrive to find the princess dead and a trap waiting for him.

Yet again, he wished that Isabel was with him. She would be able to tell him more about the enemy. And he missed her terribly. As he rode through the fertile and well-cared-for countryside of Ithilian, he'd been trying, unsuccessfully, to keep his worry for her and his sister to a manageable level. Both were more than capable of taking care of themselves but they were also in a dangerous place, surrounded by potential enemies. Add to that the fact that Isabel was going to undergo the mana fast and Alexander felt yet another thrill of fear in the pit of his gut. He refocused his attention on the enemy following them and tried to decide if there was anything he could, or should, do about it.

Anatoly nudged his big mare alongside Alexander but remained silent.

"They're still there," Alexander said. "I just wish I knew what they're planning."

"It's a good bet they're planning trouble," Anatoly said. "Maybe we should circle around at night and catch them off guard. If we take one of them alive, we might learn something."

Alexander nodded, "Maybe, but I'm concerned they might have some means of getting a message to Grafton before we get there. Speed seems like our best plan for the moment."

"If they can send a message, they probably have already," Anatoly mused. "We may be walking into a trap."

"I know, but what else can we do?" Alexander said. "Abel's daughter is in danger and I gave him my word that I'd do everything I could to save her. Not to mention that Phane is landing more forces by the day in Grafton. Our chances in the long run will be much better if Ithilian is spared the disruption of all-out war. Next winter Ruatha is going to need food and it's a good bet that we won't have a very productive harvest this year. We have to stop the enemy before any more make landfall, and we can't do that as long as Grafton is run by people sympathetic to Phane."

Anatoly nodded silently.

***

After dinner that evening, Alexander drew a magic circle in the dirt and sat cross-legged in the protection of the magical barrier. He closed his eyes and quieted his mind. The process of reaching the firmament was becoming familiar, even routine. After a few minutes of meditation, he reached the state of empty-mindedness that led to the source of creation and then he was floating on the endless ocean of potential.

He brought his awareness into focus just above his campground. Anatoly was sharpening his axe, Boaberous was already snoring, as was Lucky. Jack was writing in his little notebook by the light of the fire and Jataan was standing, hands clasped easily behind his back, just outside of the firelight. Alexander turned his attention to the enemy in the distance and brought his point of focus high into the sky with impossible speed. In moments, he was hovering thousands of feet overhead looking down on Ithilian. He could see the mountains to the distant west and the coastline to the east but he focused on the dim smudge of color almost three leagues from his camp. With a flick of his mind, he was there looking at the enemy.

There were three men, half a dozen dogs and as many horses. He could tell at a glance that one of the men was a wizard. The other two looked experienced and formidable, and their colors revealed a corrupt character. These men were for sale.

Mercenaries.

One was clearly the master of the tracking dogs that were, no doubt, responsible for the unerring path they were taking in pursuit of Alexander and his companions. The other man wasn't a wizard but there was a slight aura of magic around him that was hard to see, let alone understand. It almost reminded Alexander of the slightly brighter colors that Isabel had because of Slyder, but different.

Alexander floated there for several minutes but didn't hear the men discuss their mission or even talk to one another at all. They were busy with the mundane tasks of making dinner and setting up camp. Timing really was everything, he thought to himself.

He faded back into the firmament and returned to his body, then joined Anatoly by the fire.

"Learn anything?" Anatoly asked after a few minutes of silence.

"There are three of them. One's a wizard, the second has some kind of magic that I don't understand, and the third is a tracker with a pack of dogs. Other than that, nothing."

"That's something," Anatoly mused. "Maybe that Lucky has something in that bag of his to throw off the dogs."

Alexander nodded, considering the suggestion. "I'll ask him in the morning. No sense waking him now."

Both looked over at the rotund alchemist as he snored gently.

"They don't seem like they're trying to catch up with us," Alexander said. "Even with the wizard and their dogs, they would probably have a pretty bad day if they did, so I'm wondering what they're up to."

"Hard to say, but I bet they're up to no good," Anatoly said softly as he stared into the crackling fire. "With a wizard, they can probably send a message ahead of us or maybe even to Phane. We'd do well to keep our eyes open."

The next morning, Lucky listened to Alexander describe the enemy and a smile grew across his face. He rummaged around in his bag for a moment and produced a little metal canister of reddish powder.

"This is powdered hot pepper. I usually use it for seasoning the stew but it'll disable the tracking dogs' sense of smell for several hours with one whiff." Lucky carefully sprinkled the finely ground powder around the camp. "There, that ought to do it. At the very least, it will slow them down, and it may give us the chance to lose them altogether."

They rode hard all day. Alexander wanted to take advantage of the distraction that Lucky had left for the trackers.

Ithilian was a beautiful country, lush and green. The farmlands were well tended and fertile with rich dark soil and ample water for crops. The herds they passed were healthy and fat. Alexander enjoyed the ride in spite of the feeling of being pursued. They were taking care to avoid towns if at all possible. Chances were, no one would recognize Alexander, but Conner was another matter. He was the crown prince and his armor bore the Crest of Ithilian. He would be recognized and Alexander wanted the greatest chance of surprise that he could get.

That evening Alexander looked in on the trackers again and saw that they were a good four leagues behind and moving through the dark to make up ground. Lucky's powdered hot pepper had slowed them down but they were still on the trail. Alexander considered doubling back and confronting them but decided the time lost wouldn't be worth the information they might gain.

***

Several days later they crested a rise on the gently rolling hills of Ithilian and saw Bradfield Township. It was a thriving port city nestled into a little cove on the southern point of Bradfield Province. From their vantage point they could see the masts and sails of several merchant ships anchored in the deep waters of the cove and a few smaller ships moored at the docks in the port proper.

"What are the chances of hiring a boat without anyone figuring out who you are?" Alexander asked Conner.

"Better if I'm not part of the negotiations," Conner said. "Once we're on the water it won't matter much if the crew learns who I am."

Alexander nodded. "Jack, you think you can come up with a convincing story to explain why we're going to Grafton Island?"

"Of course," Jack said with a shrug. "We're on our way to visit my dying grandfather. I only hope we're not too late. The letter said he was very ill, so we simply must hurry. Naturally, I've brought some family friends to sit with him in his final hours and a few house guards to protect us on our voyage."

Alexander chuckled as he nodded. "Sounds good. I'd like Anatoly to go with you to secure the boat while the rest of us stay out of sight until we're ready to board. The sooner we're on the water, the better I'll feel."

"I'd agree with you if I liked being on the water," Anatoly grumbled. "There's just something unnatural about the ground moving under your feet."

"Indeed," Jataan said quietly.

Boaberous grunted in agreement.

Alexander tucked the Sovereign Stone under his tunic and pulled his cloak around the hilt of the Thinblade. Conner threw a nondescript cloak over his armor before they headed into the port city. The place was bustling. Carts of goods were moving to and from the port. People were busy. Trade flowed into and out of Ithilian through this thriving little city. The buildings were well built and clean. The streets were paved with carefully cut flagstones and were wide enough to accommodate the influx of merchants during the busy summer months and the harvest of early autumn.

As they moved through the streets of Bradfield, Alexander had the nagging sense that he was being watched, but he couldn't identify the source . . . even with his all around sight. He reminded himself that those watching might be using magic to spy on him but he couldn't decide if his worry was genuinely warranted or simply paranoia. He'd spent so much of the past several months being hunted that he'd come to expect danger at every turn.

They made their way to a horse trader and sold their horses without much trouble. The man wanted to haggle, but Alexander wasn't too worried about the price he got. More than anything he wanted to make sure the animals were treated well. Transporting them across water was more trouble than it was worth, and once they reached Grafton Island they would be traveling through the mountains over terrain that horses couldn't manage anyway.

Next they went to the port. Anatoly and Jack went to the docks while Alexander and the rest of the party went into the small market square adjacent to the port. There was a wide variety of merchants set up in stalls or wagons all around the edge of the square. Most of the goods being offered were fresh off the boats from all around the Seven Isles. Alexander cautiously moved through the crowd, pretending to check the wares of a few merchants while carefully keeping watch on the people milling about. He couldn't shake the feeling that he was being watched and didn't want to be caught off guard.

With his all around sight, he caught a man looking at them from across the square but the man disappeared between two wagons before Alexander could focus on him.

"Did you see him?" he asked Chloe without speaking.

"Yes, he looks like he recognized you," she answered in his mind.

"Can you see what he's up to?" he asked her.

"Of course," she said silently.

Chloe had been invisible since they came close to the city. Alexander didn't want the attention a fairy would draw.

"We're being watched," he whispered.

"Where?" Jataan asked.

Alexander motioned with his head. "I saw a man watching us but he slipped out of the square before I could get a closer look at him."

Jataan gave Boaberous a look and the giant started making his way through the crowd. Jataan scanned the area with renewed caution. He was calm but Alexander could see his colors flare slightly at the potential of a fight.

The crossbow bolt came from a space between two wagons not far from where the man had slipped out of the square. Alexander caught the motion of it with his all around sight but it was coming so fast that all he could do was turn toward it so it would hit his armor instead of his shoulder.

Jataan moved with impossible speed. In the space between the blink of an eye, Alexander saw his colors flare brightly as he darted in front of the bolt and caught it with his left hand as his right came up with a knife. Before he could throw the knife at the would-be assassin, Boaberous looped a length of rope around the man's neck and dragged him back out of the square.

Alexander scanned the crowd but no one had even noticed the attack and he saw no other signs of danger. They made their way out of the square and found Boaberous between a line of wagons and the backs of several buildings that formed the boundary of the market square. He had the man tied up, sitting with his back to a wall. Alexander sent Lucky and Conner to watch for Jack and Anatoly.

The assassin's eyes went wide when he saw Jataan.

"Commander P'Tal, I don't understand," he said with a look of disbelief.

"Hello, Ezra. Are you alone or are there others working with you?" Jataan asked.

"Prince Phane sent me with the advance party from Karth. I just got word from a team of trackers that the pretender was headed for Grafton through Bradfield," Ezra said. "I'm working alone and acting on Prince Phane's standing order to take any opportunity to kill the pretender."

Alexander stepped up next to Jataan and regarded the man for a moment. "Care to explain?" he asked.

"Lord Reishi, this is Ezra," Jataan said. "He's an operative of the Reishi Protectorate."

"I don't understand," Ezra said. "Why are you with the pretender, Commander P'Tal?"

"Ezra, this is Lord Reishi," Jataan said. "He has bonded with the Sovereign Stone. Phane is the real pretender."

Alexander took the Sovereign Stone from under his shirt and let the man take a good look at it. "Where does your allegiance lie?" he asked pointedly.

Ezra looked at the Stone with surprise and slowly shook his head. "How can this be? Prince Phane is the only remaining Reishi."

"Apparently not," Alexander said. "Now, answer my question."

Ezra blinked several times before he answered. "I serve the Reishi."

"I'm afraid you'll have to be more specific," Alexander said.

"Ezra, will you swear loyalty to Lord Reishi, the bearer of the Sovereign Stone and rightful Sovereign of the Seven Isles or will I have to kill you?" Jataan asked impassively.

Ezra went slightly white and then he nodded. "I swear loyalty to Lord Reishi."

Alexander watched his colors carefully. He was telling the truth. "Very well, cut him loose."

Boaberous hauled him to his feet and untied him.

"Tell me everything you know about Phane's forces here on Ithilian," Alexander commanded.

Ezra cleared his throat and gave a quick look at Jataan before he spoke. "There is just under a legion of Reishi Army Regency regulars in Grafton Province with the remaining troops en route and due to arrive within the month. General Gord is commanding the force and he has three wizards assigned to him. One of the three has been tracking you from Ithilian city and reporting back to General Gord on your progress. I received word this morning that you would arrive here today. There is at least a company of infiltrators in Bradfield laying the groundwork for invasion from Grafton. They're probably aware of your arrival as well, although I doubt they've located you yet or they would have attacked already."

"Are there any other members of the Protectorate here?" Jataan asked.

"Yes, I'm aware of two," Ezra said. "One is a merchant and the other is a ship captain that transports goods between Ithilian and Tyr."

"Is Princess Evelyn still alive?" Alexander asked.

"To the best of my knowledge, she is," Ezra said. "Prince Phane commanded that she be kept alive to use as leverage against the House of Ithilian."

"At least there's that," Alexander said. "What can you tell me about General Gord?"

"I've never met him," Ezra said. "He's a senior general of the Reishi Army Regency and apparently well respected by his peers and his soldiers. He's reputed to be an able strategist."

"What kind of ships does he have at his disposal?" Alexander asked.

"He has a small fleet of troop transports that are busy moving soldiers from Karth and he's commandeered the patrol ships out of Grafton."

"Sounds like we need a new plan," Alexander said. "If this General Gord knows we're coming, he'll probably have his patrol boats waiting for us in the strait."

Lucky walked from between two wagons, followed by Conner, Jack, and Anatoly.

"What's this?" Anatoly asked warily.

"This is Ezra," Alexander said. "He's Reishi Protectorate."

"Where'd he come from?" Anatoly said.

"Actually, he found us," Alexander said. "He just tried to kill me."

Anatoly frowned. "Why's he still in one piece?"

Alexander shrugged. "Turns out he didn't know I had the Sovereign Stone. Now that he does, he's pledged his allegiance to me. He was just telling us that the enemy knows we're coming."

"I see," Anatoly said, "and you believe him?"

Alexander looked over at the big man-at-arms and nodded.

"In that case we should probably reconsider our travel arrangements," Jack suggested. "I didn't really trust the captain we hired to ferry us there anyway."

"I'm starting to think it was a mistake to let those trackers follow us," Alexander said. "Maybe we should start with them. If we can blind the enemy to our movements, it'll be a lot easier to get where we're going."

"That doesn't get us to the island," Conner said. "As soon as Phane realizes we intend to move against Grafton, he'll kill Evelyn."

"Perhaps, but since they think they know where we're going, we might be able to use that against them," Alexander said. He turned to Ezra. "What do you know about the merchant traffic between the island and the mainland?"

"Not very much, I'm afraid. Vessels still come and go but I don't know any more than that."

Alexander nodded in thought.

Conner started to say something but Jack silenced him with a hand on his arm.

Alexander made his decision. "Ezra, spread the word to any Reishi Protectorate operatives you know that I am the Reishi Sovereign and that Phane is the pretender. Strike his forces whenever and wherever possible. Hit him where he's weak and avoid him where he's strong. Fight from the shadows and avoid confrontation."

"By your command, Lord Reishi," Ezra said as he saluted, fist to heart.

"Jack, let's go see that ferryboat captain," Alexander said. "I think we'll be needing his services after all."

They emerged from behind the wagons into the market square and Ezra melted into the crowd. Jack led the way to the docks through the milling throngs of people. Alexander was vigilant. He knew the enemy was nearby and they were probably looking for him. He still hadn't worked out how to get to Grafton Island but he was certain that the direct route was not an option. A ferry against patrol boats armed with ranged weapons was a recipe for disaster.

The shops near the market square gave way to warehouse buildings as they neared the docks. Alexander could hear the seagulls and smell the salt air mixed with the odor of fish as they walked down the narrow road.

A single man with a sword stepped out from around the corner ahead of them with a smile and fixed Alexander with the look of a predator.

"Surrender to me and I'll let your friends go," he said.

Alexander stopped in his tracks. Behind them a wagon that had been parked in a cross alley was pushed across the road, blocking their retreat. Alexander reached out with his all around sight and saw a large number of men waiting in the alleys on either side of the road ahead and a smaller contingent behind them in the alley where the wagon had been parked. When he looked closer, he was relieved to see that they were armed with swords rather than crossbows.

"Anatoly, Boaberous, move that wagon back where it came from," Alexander said just loud enough for them to hear. "There are half a dozen men in the alley behind it."

"I was hoping you'd refuse," the enemy commander said as he started to advance.

Thirty men poured out from the alleys into the road in front of them and fanned out around their commander.

Alexander drew the Thinblade. Jataan produced a knife from somewhere and Conner drew his sword. Jack tossed up his hood and flickered out of sight as Lucky backed off toward the wagon, rummaging through his bag.

As the enemy neared, Jataan darted in with impossible speed and drove his knife through the lead soldier's breastplate and into his heart. He snatched the dying man's sword from his hand and pushed him into the path of the next two soldiers. They stumbled, trying to get over their fallen comrade as Jataan cut their throats with lightning quickness.

Alexander met the next enemy with a flick of the Thinblade, cutting his sword off just past the hilt. The blade clattered to the ground as Alexander slashed the man cleanly in half across the torso. The man just behind him faltered at the sudden carnage. Alexander took his head with another flick of the Thinblade.

Side by side, Alexander and Jataan met the enemy charge. They gave ground in measured paces, mostly to avoid becoming entangled in the fallen bodies. Each new enemy met the uncompromising sharpness of the Thinblade or the inhuman speed of the only living battle mage. Within a minute, the enemy force was reduced by half.

"We're clear!" shouted Anatoly.

Alexander glanced back to the wagon with his all round sight even as he met the next enemy, cleaving his shield in half along with the man's forearm.

"Fall back," Alexander commanded.

Jack, Lucky, and Conner slipped past the wagon into the alley. Alexander and Jataan hastened their retreat as a javelin darted between them and killed the nearest soldier. They reached the wagon as Boaberous hurled another javelin. Once they were all into the alley, Anatoly and Boaberous pulled the wagon in behind them to block the advancing enemy, then Alexander sliced the wheels, causing the heavily laden wagon to collapse under its own weight.

They fled down the alley and found another route to the docks. Moving quickly through the warehouses, they reached the docks within a few minutes. Jack pointed out the little ferryboat they had hired. As they approached, Alexander could see the surprise on the captain's face. He had sold them out. Alexander didn't need his second sight to tell him about this man—he was an opportunist and a liar.

Thinblade still in hand, Alexander boarded the little ferryboat and marched straight up to the captain.

"You told the Reishi Army Regency where to find us, didn't you?" he asked calmly as he leveled the Thinblade at the terrified captain.

"They said they'd pay if I told them when someone tried to hire me to take them to Grafton Island," the captain said.

"Very well, you sold me out. Your life is forfeit. But I'm willing to sell it back to you if you're interested." Alexander said.

The captain's eyes widened. A few of his crew, mostly oarsmen, stood up like they were going to come to their captain's aid but when they saw Anatoly and Boaberous eyeing them, they sat back down.

"Whatever you want, just don't kill me," the captain pleaded.

"Good. Cast off. Take us across the inlet to Grafton Province mainland. Make landfall as close to the port as you can without being seen," Alexander said as he wiped the blood off his sword.

The captain nodded but stood stock-still like he wasn't sure what to do next.

"Go!" Alexander said firmly.

The ferry captain sprang into action, yelling orders at his men. Within moments they were moving out onto the water.

They weren't fifty feet from the dock when two dozen men led by the enemy commander came running up to the water's edge.

"Jataan, can you kill him from here?" Alexander asked quietly.

"Of course," Jataan said.

"Do it," Alexander said.

Jataan nodded to Boaberous.

The giant drew a javelin smoothly from the oversized quiver on his back and hurled it with surprising force. It flew true across fifty feet of water and buried into the enemy commander's chest. He slumped to his knees and then toppled into the water.

"Nice shot," Anatoly said.

Boaberous grunted.

***

The trip across the inlet was quick. They left Bradfield at midday and arrived on the shores of Grafton Province just after dark. The captain drove his rowing crew mercilessly, coaxing every bit of speed he could from the well-muscled men. Despite his character flaws, the ferry captain did know his trade. He expertly maneuvered his boat through the shallows and made landfall gently and quietly.

Before Alexander stepped off the little boat, he fixed the captain with his glittering golden eyes. "Speak of this trip to no one. If I discover you've sold me to my enemies again, I will find you and claim your life in payment."

The captain didn't say a word but nodded his understanding. Alexander could see from the fear in his colors that he would keep quiet, for a while anyway.

They moved through the darkness along the coastline toward the ports. It was several miles and slow going but much safer than venturing inland and chancing an encounter with an enemy patrol. Grafton was a fair-sized city about as big as Southport. When they reached the city itself, they found several small fishing docks and private boat moorings lining the water's edge. They moved carefully, keeping watch for anyone who might see them. Most of the townspeople were sleeping, so Alexander and his men had little trouble until they reached the wall of Grafton Keep sometime in the middle of the night. The keep extended to the water's edge, blocking their path. They would either have to go through Grafton or swim around the keep walls in order to get to the docks and the merchant ships preparing to sail for the island and ports beyond.

Chapter 19

"Let's rest here for a few minutes," Alexander said quietly.

He found a flat space in the sand and carefully drew a magic circle. Lucky produced some jerky from his bag and passed it around to the others while Alexander sat cross-legged in his circle and closed his eyes. He was tired from the long day's travel. At first he felt like he could simply fall asleep sitting up, but he cleared his mind and brought his focus to the task at hand. It took him longer than usual to slip free of his body and enter the firmament but he eventually found his way there.

He didn't waste any time listening to the song of creation but instead focused on his location and coalesced his awareness above his body. From there he floated up over the keep and took in the lay of the land. He saw the port and picked out a number of ships that might be headed for Grafton Island. The keep had several small doors that opened onto the docks while the outer wall extended to surround the entire port. Trade was Grafton's lifeblood. It was clear that the people who had established this city wanted to protect their livelihood.

Alexander turned his focus to the keep itself and moved within the walls of the large stone building. It was made of granite blocks and had clearly stood for many centuries. It wasn't fancy but it was well armed and well positioned to defend the port. Several towers lined the wall facing the sea. Each housed a large catapult on its flat, crenellated top. The tops of the walls provided ample cover for archers and there were several smaller positions along the seawall armed with heavy ballistae. The walls facing the city were smaller but still well armed. The main gate was closed and the guard tower was manned and well lit with oil lamps.

Alexander searched through the keep for the Governor and General Gord. He found a set of well-appointed living quarters high in the main building. The Governor had offered the general a suite of rooms that looked like it was reserved for honored guests. The entire floor was accessible through a single heavy oak door that led to a guard room manned by six men who were awake and alert. Adjacent to the guard room was a barracks with another six men sleeping in their bunks. The door leading from the guard room was barred from the other side and opened to a staircase leading up to the central hall of the Governor's floor. The hall ran down the center of the entire level and had two doors on either side that led to each set of living quarters and a third door at the end of the hall that led to a well-furnished covered terrace overlooking the ocean. There were four guards standing watch in the hall, two at each door.

The Governor was sleeping with his wife. Otherwise his chambers were empty. The general slept with a young woman. Another room was occupied as well on the other end of the general's suite. Alexander examined the man's colors and discovered that he was not one of the wizards assigned to General Gord's forces.

He withdrew from the floor and traced a path into the lower levels of the keep, sending his awareness into each room in turn until he found what he sought.

The wizard sat in a comfortable chair reading an old book by the light of two bright lamps. The room looked like a study. Alexander wasn't too surprised to find the wizard awake. He examined the man's colors and decided that he was a master wizard, although he couldn't discern his calling. He did notice that there were a few spells surrounding the wizard but he couldn't determine the purpose of the magic. Alexander remembered Mason Kallentera telling him that he often cast spells on himself designed to last for the day and provide him with magical insight and protection.

He withdrew from the wizard's study and descended lower into the bowels of the keep. After several minutes of searching he found a passage that led along the outer wall where he and his friends were resting. He pushed through the wall and found that it was easily four feet thick and made from large blocks of carefully cut granite.

Finally, Alexander slipped back into the firmament and thought of Evelyn. His awareness came into being in the central tower room of the keep on the south point of Grafton Island. She was locked in her chamber and sleeping soundly. Satisfied, Alexander returned to his body and opened his eyes.

"I'm glad you're back, My Love," Chloe said in his mind. "There was a dark spirit in the aether circling you, trying to get through your defenses. I was worried."

"I'm sorry I worried you, Little One," Alexander said without speaking.

He remembered the horror of the last time a dark spirit had taken advantage of his absence and used his body to kill two Rangers. He was glad to have proof positive that a magic circle could keep spirits from the darkness at bay while he used his clairvoyance.

Alexander stood and stepped out of his circle.

"What did you learn?" Lucky asked, handing him the bag of jerky.

"General Gord is here with one of his wizards," Alexander said. "It doesn't look like they're expecting us, and I know where they are in the keep. We might as well take the opportunity to strike at the enemy while we have the chance."

"I don't understand," Conner said. "How can you know where the general is?"

Alexander smiled with a shrug. "Magic. I looked inside the keep and found where they're sleeping. If we're quick, we can hit them before they know what happened and leave the entire province and the enemy army without leadership. The confusion should buy us the time we need to commandeer a ship and make our way to the island."

Conner blinked a few times and shook his head. "I won't pretend to understand how you can know these things, but I'll take your word for it. How do you plan to get into the keep?"

Alexander drew the Thinblade and carefully pushed into the wall of the keep at an angle. He made three cuts in the stone.

"Anatoly, I need you to hold this block of stone in place and then let it down quietly when it breaks free."

The big man-at-arms stepped up to the section of wall and held it while Alexander made the last cut. Anatoly carefully lowered a large piece of stone the shape of a pyramid to the ground. It took several minutes for Alexander and

Anatoly to remove sections of the stone wall until there was an opening big enough for even Boaberous to crawl through.

The passageway they entered was dark and dank. Water dripped from the ceiling to form little pools on the floor before it could drain between the cracks.

"I've seen my father use the Thinblade in battle only twice," Conner said. "I knew it was powerful but I had no idea until today what it's truly capable of."

Alexander nodded knowingly.

"What's the plan?" Anatoly asked quietly.

"We go to the wizard first," Alexander said. "Once he's dead, we'll make our way to the Governor's quarters and kill him and the general, then out to the docks and onto one of those merchant ships. I'd like to avoid a pitched battle if possible and be gone before anyone knows what happened."

Conner looked a little uncomfortable with the plan. He started to voice his concern but stopped himself.

"Say what you have to say," Alexander said.

"I don't feel right killing people in their sleep," Conner said. "Taking a life in battle is one thing, but this feels more like assassination."

Alexander nodded. "That's because it *is* assassination. These people have come to your home and abducted your sister. They've landed an invasion force and are planning to make war on your people. They've forfeited their right to live under the Old Law. We are at war with them and it doesn't matter how they die so long as they do. Make no mistake, Conner, there is no glory in war. It's ugly and sad, nothing more. Our duty is to end this conflict as quickly as possible by killing those who started it. How we kill them doesn't matter."

Conner frowned and nodded. "I've spent my life studying warfare. I've read a hundred books about battles of the past. The writers of those books all try to romanticize it and make it seem so noble and honorable. I never thought it would be like this."

"Remember the truth of it, Conner," Alexander said. "One day you will wield the Thinblade of Ithilian and the decision to go to war for your people will be yours. Remember for every day that you draw breath that war is the ugliest thing humanity ever invented. Avoid it if you can, but not at the cost of the lives and liberty of the people you're sworn to protect. If you must wage war, be ruthless and without mercy for those who brought war into your home."

Anatoly nodded silently.

Jack was taking notes in his head again.

They moved quietly through the lower halls of the keep. It was dark and quiet. No one came down into the bowels of the keep if they could help it. Alexander kept his vial of night-wisp dust partially covered to limit the amount of light it produced. After several flights of stairs and a few wrong turns, they came to a level of the keep with oil lamps burning in their wall sconces. They redoubled their caution.

Alexander led the way with his companions following in single file. They rounded a corner into a hall leading to the wizard's study and Alexander stopped. He motioned to the door two dozen feet down the hall and carefully drew the Thinblade. Everyone else followed suit and armed themselves. Jack tossed up his hood and flickered out of sight. Lucky produced a shatter vial filled with a pinkish-looking liquid from his bag.

They slowly crept up to the door. Just a few steps away, Alexander felt the tingle of magic race over his skin. He knew instinctively that the wizard had been alerted to their presence so he closed the last few steps quickly and sliced vertically through the door even as his second sight registered the faint aura of magic surrounding the heavy oak door. A moment later the door detonated outward toward Alexander, spreading a shock wave of magical energy racing both directions down the passageway.

Alexander was blown across the hall into the far wall. He fell to the floor with a thud and couldn't move. It was as if his body simply couldn't hear his mind. He tried to move, tried to regain his feet but he couldn't make his arms and legs respond. With his all around sight, he saw the wizard standing in his study facing the open doorway with a look of recognition and happy surprise. Alexander shifted his sight to his friends and found them all standing stone-still where they'd been when the door detonated, all except Jack who hadn't yet rounded the corner into the passage.

"I must say, I didn't expect this," the wizard said. "Prince Phane said you were unpredictable and resourceful but I never imagined you'd come to kill me. It's almost flattering. I'm sure he'll be most pleased when I present him your head." He sauntered confidently out into the hallway and his smile broadened when he saw Jataan standing frozen in place.

"Ah, General Commander Jataan P'Tal, Prince Phane was most unhappy with your betrayal. I'm quite sure you will die badly, but then I am equally certain that I will be handsomely rewarded for delivering you to face justice for your crimes.

"What's that? Oh, that's right, you can't speak," he said chuckling. "I'm rather proud of this spell, although I never imagined it would ensnare such valuable prey. I can't tell you how long I worked on it to get just the right effect. Sadly, the first few attempts killed my test subjects, but their sacrifice was more than worth it. You are much more valuable alive than dead. I'm quite sure Prince Phane will enjoy your, um, interrogation," he chortled.

"Don't fret now, the effects of the spell will keep you paralyzed for an hour or so," he said as he strolled down the hall. "More than enough time for me to summon a platoon of soldiers and slap you in chains."

Chapter 20

Isabel's soul slipped free of her body to defend against the dissolution of existence that she would have faced had she become lost in the firmament. The world around her looked strangely translucent, as if the walls and objects had less substance than before. With a sudden shock she realized that her soul was in the aether, the place that separated the world of time and substance from the netherworld and the realm of light.

She looked down at her lifeless body. It couldn't end this way. She couldn't die. Not because she loved her own life, though she did, but because there were others who would suffer if she died. She couldn't let that happen.

A passage opened to the realm of light and she felt a strange tug toward it. It was gentle and reassuring, beckoning her to a place of safety.

Then she thought of Alexander and pulled back with an effort of will. She couldn't be dead. It wasn't acceptable. There had to be another way.

Isabel frantically reached out to the light and drew it to her. To her amazement, it obeyed. A cloud of white light floated to her disembodied soul and enveloped her with its power. She focused on her body and moved her soul and the light back to her lifeless self.

A moment passed and then there was darkness. She gasped as the pain slammed back into her. She was back in her body, pain coursing through her. This time she was more determined than ever. She called forth the anger she had worked so hard to nurture and control. It came with an effort at first but the more she focused on it, the greater it grew until she was able to sit up out of sheer spite.

She took another breath and opened her eyes. The pain ebbed briefly before it slammed back into her with renewed intensity, but she met it with growing fury. She focused on her anger, fed it until it overshadowed the pain.

With a fierce battle cry, she gained her feet and steadied herself. She drew another breath and closed her eyes. Focusing on her fury, she embraced the pain and laughed at it, mocked it, challenged it to do its worst. It had already killed her—what more could it do?

After several hours of facing the pain and smothering it with her deliberate rage, it succumbed to her will and faded away, leaving her exhausted and elated at the same time. She collapsed onto the bed and fell into a deep and dreamless sleep.

As she began to wake the next morning, just before she was fully conscious, she saw the ocean of potential spread out before her, beckoning with its infinite possibility. It called to her with promises of rapture but she was wary of it and responded with sudden, all-encompassing love for Alexander. Her feelings overwhelmed the promise of rapture offered by the firmament and she woke with a connection to the source of creation intact and under her control.

Magda opened the door an hour later to find Isabel sitting cross-legged on her bed. With a word, Magda dispelled the magic circle and stepped up to Isabel, placing a hand on her forehead and muttering under her breath.

"You have succeeded," she said with a guarded smile. "You will be ordained into the Reishi Coven tomorrow." Magda's expression turned deadly serious, sending a flutter of nervousness through Isabel. "I have grave news. Abigail has been injured."

Isabel shot to her feet. "How?" she demanded urgently.

"She fell from her wyvern into the ocean," Magda said. "Kallistos retrieved her from the water before she could be pulled under by the weight of her saddle and brought her to safety but she has not yet regained consciousness. It's been three days."

"Wait. Her saddle came free of Kallistos and she fell with it?" Isabel asked with a hint of anger.

"I'm afraid so," Magda said. "Her saddle straps were cut so they would give under the stress of flight. Someone tried to kill her."

"Who?" Isabel asked with deadly calm. Her blood ran cold and she restrained the fury that was building within her.

"The handler responsible for her saddle killed himself before we were able to question him," Magda said. "We don't know if he was working alone or with someone else."

"Why would he want to kill Abigail?" Isabel asked. "Did he have any connection to any of the Sky Knights that fell in the battle that brought us here?"

"No. We've been unable to find any connection," Magda said. "I assure you that our investigation is ongoing."

"Take me to Abigail," Isabel commanded.

Magda nodded and led her out of the room. Isabel's mind raced as she walked through the halls of the fortress island. She kept coming back to Gabriella. There was no one else, except maybe Warrick.

Abigail was asleep in her bed, breathing deeply. If not for the lurid purple and yellow bruising all across her face and shoulders, she would have looked almost peaceful.

When Isabel entered, Mistress Lita stood from the chair at the side of the bed. Wren stirred from the chair in the corner of the room. When she saw Isabel, she started crying anew and rushed into her arms.

"I've been so worried about both of you," Wren said through a sob. "Are you all right? Did you survive the mana fast?"

"I'm fine, Wren, save your worry for Abigail."

The waifish girl looked up with a smile of relief even though her eyes were red and swollen from crying.

Isabel looked at her sister and a lump started to form in her throat. She swallowed hard and took a seat at the side of the bed. She looked up at Lita questioningly.

"She had several broken bones and significant bruising when Kallistos brought her to the hangar. Knight Raja said that her saddle came loose and she fell into the ocean from several hundred feet. We have mended her bones and are administering additional treatments to heal her bruising. She has not regained consciousness since she was injured." Lita looked down at her sadly. "Isabel, she may never wake up. Such trauma can be fatal even if healing is administered."

"Is there nothing else you can do?" Isabel asked.

"We have done all that is within our power," Lita said. "All we can do now is wait and hope."

"There may be something I can do," Isabel said.

Magda frowned with concern. "What exactly did you have in mind?"

"I'm not sure yet," Isabel said as she placed her hand on Abigail's stomach and summoned feelings of love for her sister. She worked her feelings into a great intensity and then opened a connection to the firmament. The rapture called to her and tugged at her will, but the love she was feeling offset the draw of limitless possibility. She opened the portal to the realm of light and formed an image in her mind of the light of life flowing into her and through her hand into Abigail. With focused will and a clear image of the outcome she desired, as well as the mechanism for creating that outcome, Isabel released her vision into the firmament and commanded the firmament to obey.

Intense white light of radiant purity flowed from her hand into Abigail. Magda and Lita both gasped at what they were witnessing but Isabel ignored them, focusing on sending love and light into her sister. Several moments passed before the spell ran its course. After a few moments, Abigail opened her eyes and murmured something unintelligible.

"Hush, you're safe," Isabel said. "You've been injured, but you're going to be all right."

Abigail looked over at Isabel and gave her a small smile before closing her eyes and drifting off to sleep.

"Isabel, come with me," Magda said with a slight edge to her voice. "Lita will look after Abigail."

Isabel gave Abigail's hand a gentle squeeze and left the room behind the triumvir.

"Explain how you did that," Magda demanded bluntly.

Isabel shrugged. "I called on the light from the realm of light to heal her."

"How is that possible? The realm of light is only accessible from the aether," Magda said.

Isabel shook her head. "When Alexander was bonded with Chloe, I surrendered my body to her so that she could spend a night with him. It was the price the Fairy Queen demanded in exchange for her consent to the bonding. The next morning a fairy named Sara was born of Alexander and Chloe's union. She came into this world from the realm of light through a portal within my mind. I discovered during the mana fast that that portal still exists. I can call on the light if need be. In fact, it saved me from the trial of pain." Isabel left out her experience with Desiderates. She still wasn't ready to reveal her ability to control the wyverns.

Magda stood with her mouth agape and shook her head in disbelief. "What you are saying is beyond anything I have ever heard of and I am well versed in the magic of light. If this is so, then you are already a far more powerful witch than many of our coven."

"Then I will be well suited to stand with my husband," Isabel said with satisfaction.

Magda actually laughed. "Indeed you will. Be cautious with your newfound power, Isabel. Go slowly and learn well before using your magic. It's dangerous, especially for one who has so recently made a connection with the firmament."

"I'll be careful, but not at Abigail's expense," Isabel said. "If I have the power to help her heal, then I will use it."

"Very well, but remember, normal healing is always better than magical healing even if it's much slower. Go and tend to your sister. I'll come for you in the morning to introduce you to the coven and ordain you as a Reishi Witch."

After Magda left, Isabel went out onto the balcony to reflect on all that had transpired in the past week. It was clear from Abigail's injury that the fortress island was still a dangerous place. She needed to make plans to get to Alexander as soon as Abigail was ready to travel.

Slyder floated up to the balcony and landed on the railing. The bird gave her a reproving look. She hadn't made contact with him for a week. She touched his mind as she stroked under his chin and reassured him that all was well. He leaned into her affections and she took solace in his unquestioning loyalty.

Abigail woke several hours later, with Isabel at her bedside and Wren still curled up in a chair in the corner of the room.

"What happened?" Abigail asked.

"You fell from Kallistos," Isabel said gently. "He pulled you out of the ocean before you could drown but you got beat up pretty good. You've been out for three days."

"I remember falling and then nothing but cold and darkness," Abigail said. "How could I have fallen? My armor was strapped into my saddle."

"Your straps were cut," Isabel said.

Abigail tried to sit up but Isabel stopped her gently with a hand on her shoulder. "The handler responsible for your saddle has committed suicide. Magda said they are investigating. One way or another, we'll find out who did this."

Abigail's eyes suddenly opened wider and she looked at Isabel intently. "Is the mana fast over? Are you a witch?"

Isabel smiled wearily and nodded. "It's over. I survived. And I have to say, if I had any idea what was involved, I never would have let Alexander go through with it, let alone do it myself."

"That bad?" Abigail asked.

"More difficult than I ever imagined," Isabel said quietly. "I actually died for a few minutes."

Abigail, Wren, and Lita all looked at her with shock and alarm.

"Are you sure?" Lita asked. "I remember my trials and it felt like I was dying."

Isabel nodded humbly. "I was floating in the aether over my body. I could see that I wasn't breathing and then a passageway to the realm of light opened and tried to draw me in."

Lita's eyes went wide. "How can that be? You should have been unable to resist the pull of the light."

Isabel shrugged. "I drew the light to me and used it to revive my body. I'm not really sure how, but it worked and I was able to finish the trial of pain."

"Is that how you were able to heal Abigail?" Lita asked. "I've been a healer for many years and I used all of my power to help her, yet I failed to revive her."

Isabel nodded with a loving smile for her sister. "I called on the same light to heal her. I'm just glad it worked, even if I don't quite understand it yet."

Abigail gave her hand a squeeze and smiled her thanks. "So I guess that means we can get out of here as soon as I'm ready to fly."

"Magda said I'll be ordained into the coven tomorrow," Isabel said. "Once I'm recognized as a Reishi Witch, we can return to Alexander."

Abigail leaned back against her pillow and closed her eyes. "Thank the Maker, there's no telling what kind of trouble he's gotten himself into by now."

Isabel chuckled softly. "You get some rest. You still have a lot of healing to do before you'll be ready to fly."

Abigail nodded and her breathing became deep and rhythmic as she drifted off to sleep.

Lita insisted on staying with Abigail through the night just in case there were any problems. Wren wanted to stay as well, but Isabel told her to go home and sleep in her own bed. She left begrudgingly.

The next morning, Wren was in the sitting room of their suite when Isabel emerged from her bedchamber. She poured her a cup of hot tea without a word. Isabel smiled at the young woman as she sat down in front of the steaming cup.

Not long after dawn, Isabel heard Lita protesting from within Abigail's chamber. Before Isabel could reach the door, Abigail emerged, still looking bruised and battered but on her feet in spite of Lita's obvious disapproval.

"I'll be fine," Abigail said. "I can't stay in bed forever. The sooner I'm up and on my feet, the sooner I'll get my strength back."

"I wish you would take it easy," Lita said. "You're still weak and your bones are not fully mended."

"I agree with Lita," Isabel said.

"Me too," Wren whispered.

Abigail looked around like everyone was conspiring against her. "I'm fine," she said. "I just want to sit down and have breakfast like a real person instead of spending my day in bed like an invalid."

Slowly and carefully she made her way to the table with the aid of Lita's arm and sat down heavily with a grimace.

"Just don't overdo it," Isabel said. "If you push too hard, you'll injure yourself again and we'll be here that much longer."

"I know, I'll be careful. Now, tell me about the mana fast," Abigail said.

They spent the next hour talking about their experiences over the past week. Wren went and got them breakfast and then sat listening to their accounts with rapt attention while they ate. Not long after breakfast, there was a knock at the door.

Wren opened it to admit Magda.

"How are you feeling?" she asked Abigail.

"Much better, thank you," Abigail said. "I should be ready to ride within the week."

"Perhaps, but I would suggest you allow yourself more time to heal before you get back on Kallistos."

"You and everyone else," Abigail said. "I'm not as fragile as I look."

"I have no doubt," Magda said. "That fall would have killed most people. You are lucky to be alive."

"So I've heard," Abigail said as her mood darkened. "Any idea who tried to kill me?"

"Not yet," Magda said, "but the investigation isn't complete."

"Any chance they'll try again?" Isabel asked.

"Possibly," Magda said, "which is one reason I've asked Lita to remain here."

"Good enough," Isabel said.

"Isabel, the others are ready," Magda said.

***

She led Isabel to the plateau and the circular amphitheatre in the center where the witches cast the spells that required the combined power of many. Isabel remembered seeing the place through Slyder's eyes when she first learned that Alexander was on Ithilian.

They wove through the throng of women who had all come to witness the ordination of a new witch of the Reishi Coven. At the lowest point was a broad pedestal surrounded by a seven-foot-wide circular walkway. From there, stone rings of increasingly larger diameter stepped up toward the plateau surface above. Each ring was occupied by progressive ranks of witches, with those of the highest rank standing on the lowest step and those of the lowest rank standing on the top ring of stone.

Cassandra and Gabriella stood next to the pedestal as Magda led Isabel to the center of the assembly. Cassandra wore an unreadable and noncommittal look, but Gabriella was openly contemptuous.

"Step up onto the pedestal," Magda commanded.

Isabel complied without a word.

The three triumvirs joined hands in a circle around the pedestal and around Isabel. The crowd fell silent.

"Today, we ordain a new member of the Reishi Coven," Magda said in a clear voice. "Isabel Reishi has survived the mana fast. From this day forth she is a sister of the Reishi Coven. So mote it be."

There was a cheer from the assembled women. Isabel felt an outpouring of love and acceptance from her new sisters as they smiled and clapped for her. Through the din of it, there was one voice of discord. Gabriella was laughing with forced glee. The clamor of the women all around died down but Gabriella continued to laugh. Isabel caught the look of concern on Magda's face and felt a tingle of dread race up her spine.

"Ladies, please hear me," Gabriella said.

The noise died down and the women of the coven gave her their attention.

With a menacing smile, Gabriella turned to Isabel and gave her a murderous look. In that moment Isabel knew that she was responsible for the sabotage of Abigail's saddle. Her blood ran cold and rage began to boil quietly within her soul. Gabriella would pay for her crimes, one way or another.

"I challenge Lady Reishi to single combat," Gabriella said as if she was springing a trap.

The whole coven erupted into turmoil. Magda and Cassandra looked at Gabriella with alarm.

"Quiet!" Magda commanded. Silence came quickly. "You have no right to challenge Isabel. The challenge is only for the station of triumvir. It's never been used for any other purpose."

"Oh, but you're wrong, Sister," Gabriella said calmly. "Coven law clearly states that any member of the coven may challenge another for station or title. I challenge Isabel for her title as Lady Reishi."

"What?" Isabel said with shock and alarm. "Alexander would never have you."

Gabriella shrugged. "That is his choice, but I will have my vengeance." There was a hint of madness glittering in her wild eyes.

Silence fell on the assembly as the magnitude of the situation sank in. Magda turned to Gabriella with a look of terrible resolve.

"If you choose to challenge Isabel, then I choose to fight in her stead," Magda said with a steel edge to her voice.

Gabriella's eyes flared with rage. "We've been sisters for more than a hundred years and you would choose this pretender over me?"

"If I must," Magda said firmly.

"So be it," Gabriella shot back.

"No," Isabel said. "Gabriella has challenged me. I will stand against her and for the same reason. She is behind the attempted murder of my sister Abigail. I will have my vengeance for her treachery."

Magda and Cassandra both looked alarmed. Gabriella laughed out loud and the rest of the assembly stood in stunned silence.

"You are newly ordained," Cassandra said, ignoring the charge of attempted murder. "Gabriella has been a witch for five times longer than you have been alive. Consider your choice here very carefully. You are well within your rights to choose a champion to fight on your behalf."

"What are the rules of the challenge?" Isabel asked.

Gabriella chuckled.

"There are none," Cassandra said. "You may bring any power or weapon at your disposal to the battlefield. The challenge ends with the death or surrender of one and the victory of the other."

"So be it," Isabel said with a clear voice. "I accept the challenge."

Chapter 21

General Gord's wizard started to turn the corner at the end of the hall and looked over at Alexander and his companions with smug satisfaction that suddenly turned to shocked horror as Jack flickered into view and stabbed him in the heart with his dagger. The wizard tried to say something with his last breath but all he could manage was a gurgle. Jack let him down quietly and rushed to Alexander.

He gently rolled him onto his back. "Can you speak?" he asked quietly.

Alexander was paralyzed but he could still talk to Chloe in his mind.

She buzzed into existence in a ball of light and hovered in front of Jack. "He's under the effects of the spell but otherwise he's not seriously injured," she said. "He says you should keep watch and wait for the spell to wear off."

Jack nodded. "That was too close. One more step and I would have been around the corner and in the area of the spell's effect along with the rest of you."

Jack and Chloe kept watch for the better part of an hour before the spell wore off. Fortunately, it was the middle of the night and they were in the lower parts of the keep, so no one came down the hall while Jack nervously waited for his companions to regain the ability to move. Control of their bodies returned to them gradually, starting with a twitch here and a jerk there. Once the spell broke, they were able to regain full control within a few minutes by working their muscles and stretching to restore full range of motion.

"Well done, Master Colton," Anatoly said. "You might have to work yourself into one of your stories if you keep it up."

Jack shook his head solemnly. "A bard is supposed to be a chronicler of events, not a participant."

"Don't be so humble, Jack," Lucky said. "You saved us all, and not for the first time, I might add."

"Be that as it may, my deeds have no place in my songs and stories," Jack said. "My role in history is in the telling of it."

"Either way, I'm glad you're with us, Jack," Alexander said.

"Your gratitude is all the recognition I could hope for," he said with a formal bow.

They dragged the wizard into his little study, snuffed out the lamps, and propped the pieces of the door into the doorframe as best they could. After cleaning the bloodstain on the floor and dimming the lamps in the hall, it was hard to tell from a cursory inspection that anything had happened at all.

Alexander led them up through the keep toward the Governor's living quarters. They nearly encountered a few servants going about their tasks in the night but were able to avoid them without a confrontation. They moved slowly through the cold stone passageways taking great care to remain silent and leave no trace of their presence.

Alexander stopped before rounding a corner and closed his eyes to focus his all around sight. He saw two men standing outside the guard room that stood between the Governor's quarters and the rest of the keep. His biggest concern was avoiding an alarm. He almost reconsidered the attack but then he remembered a lesson from his father about battle: More often than not, victory goes to the bold. Those who strike when they have the opportunity, succeed, while those who hesitate and wait for perfect circumstances lose the chance to act and are forced to meet the enemy on their terms.

Alexander was tired of facing the enemy on their terms. He had a chance to strike a blow and he meant to make it a good one.

He unslung his bow, then turned to his companions and signed that there were two guards about forty feet away. He pointed to Boaberous and motioned like he was throwing a javelin. The giant nodded. They moved as one, gliding out from behind the corner and loosing their respective weapons at nearly the same time. Both guards turned when they saw the movement but were silenced a moment later without so much as a groan.

Alexander placed his hand on the door, sending his all around sight into the room. The door was barred from the other side and there were six men sitting around a table playing cards. He signed that there were six men and then drew the Thinblade. Carefully and quietly he slipped the Thinblade between the door and frame, then drew down through the bar and lock. The door opened noiselessly as he rushed into the room followed closely by Jataan and Anatoly. The six men were caught completely by surprise. Within seconds they were surrounded, still sitting at the table holding their cards. Jack and Lucky dragged the dead guards into the room from the hallway and then Jack refitted the bar to close the door behind them while Lucky went to the small barracks room off to the side of the guard room.

"Remain silent and keep your hands on the table," Alexander said quietly. "If you resist or raise the alarm, I'll kill you all."

The six men nodded nervously.

Lucky returned from the room filled with sleeping guards. "They won't wake for several hours."

"My friend here is going to give you something to put you to sleep," Alexander said. "Cooperate and you'll wake up in a few hours alive and well. Do you understand?"

All six of the guards looked at one another, then nodded. Lucky blew a small amount of powder into each man's face in turn. Within seconds they fell unconscious and slumped over on the table.

Alexander put his hand on the door leading to the Governor's quarters and sent his all around sight to the other side. Two sleepy-looking guards stood on the landing at the base of a long staircase leading up to the level above.

"Two guards on the other side of the door," Alexander said.

Anatoly stood by the wall nearest the door hinges, Jataan stood directly in front of the door with his knife in hand, and Alexander stood just to the side of the door so he could cut the bar and bolt in one stroke.

He sliced downward through the edge of the door and Anatoly pushed the door open. Jataan was through it like a blur. He cut the throat of the guard to the left of the door, spun and lashed out at the guard to the right, cutting his throat as well in one clean slice. Both slumped to the floor in shocked surprise but neither was able to make a sound.

Alexander was momentarily sickened by the sudden violence and death but he steeled himself to his task. The enemy had brought war to the Seven Isles and it fell to him to make war against them in return.

"The reason you are worthy of the Sovereign Stone is because it hurts you when you kill, even when it's necessary," Chloe said silently in his mind.

"Thank you, Little One," Alexander replied without speaking, "but, honestly, I wish I could have just been a rancher."

"Perhaps someday, if you succeed against Phane, you will be," she thought to him.

Alexander smiled at the thought for only a moment before he brought himself back to the present and the two warm corpses lying in pools of their own blood. The staircase leading to the next level was long with a landing about halfway to the top. Alexander knew there were probably four guards in the hall above. They would be the most difficult to eliminate silently, although it was doubtful that they would be able to do more than alert the Governor and General Gord.

They crept up the stairs with Alexander in the lead. As they neared the top, he sent his all around sight down the hall and saw the four men standing on either side of the hall beside each of the two doors facing each other. They were about forty feet from the top of the stairs. He communicated the enemy numbers and distance with hand signs and motioned for Anatoly, Boaberous, and Conner to take the Governor's chambers. He knew from experience that Jataan would follow him without question or command.

On his signal, they raced up the remaining stairs and charged down the hallway with weapons drawn. The guard who saw them first turned and looked at them with unbelieving surprise for a moment before he tried to shout a warning. A moment later, he fell back with a knife buried to the hilt in his eye socket. Jataan slipped his second knife free as he closed the distance.

The three remaining guards turned as one, raising their spears and shouting a warning. Alexander and Jataan reached them a moment later. Alexander slashed the haft of the middle guard's spear and stepped into the space it created as he stabbed forward into the guard on his left, driving the Thinblade through his breastplate and into his heart. Jataan trapped the spear of the soldier on the right and slipped inside his guard, stabbing him in the throat with precision and blinding speed, then slipped past and rolled behind him in a fluid motion, bringing his blade around and neatly cutting the throat of the center guard from behind. The battle lasted only seconds.

Alexander slashed down through the bar and bolt of the Governor's door, then turned to the guest quarters where General Gord was quartered, cut through the door and kicked it open.

He entered a well-appointed and lavishly furnished main room with Jataan right behind him. Two men emerged almost simultaneously from different doors. The one on the right was armed with a sword and wore a pair of unlaced boots and a hastily strapped on breastplate over a nightshirt. The one from the left was armed with a short sword and wore a chainmail shirt.

The one in chainmail attacked Jataan without hesitation, apparently thinking he was an easy foe armed with only a knife. Jataan slipped past the sword thrust and sliced the inside of his upper arm to the bone. The short sword clattered to the floor and the man stumbled to his knees, staring at the battle mage in disbelief. He struggled to regain his feet as his life's blood drained away, then he slumped over and rolled onto his side, groaning softly.

General Gord assessed the situation quickly and lowered his blade slightly as he faced Alexander. He was a big man with a barrel chest and greying hair. A scar stood out on his left cheek from a wound sustained long ago.

"You must be the pretender Phane wants dead so badly," Gord said. "It seems you have me at a disadvantage." He had the demeanor of an old soldier who'd always known he would die on the end of a blade.

Alexander looked closely at the man's colors and saw an opportunist who was comfortable killing for the power it gave him. He knew in a second that Gord was not to be trusted or underestimated.

He felt slightly sick to his stomach as he advanced. General Gord was no match for Alexander. His death would be more an execution than a fight, but then he was the commander of the enemy forces that had taken Grafton by bribery and were preparing to invade Ithilian.

Gord's eyes grew wider as he saw the look of resolve settle on Alexander's face. "I'll give you the girl. I'll tell you Phane's plan," he said as he took a step back. "I'll turn on Phane and swear loyalty to you. My men will follow me."

Alexander might have been persuaded by his offers if he couldn't see the flare of dishonesty in his colors as the doomed general tried to bargain for his life. The instant Alexander reached striking range, General Gord thrust with surprising speed but Alexander was ready for the attack. He spun to his left avoiding the blade and brought the Thinblade around in a high arc, slicing cleanly through General Gord's neck. He remained standing for a just moment with his head still in place before a line of blood began to show around his neck and then he crumpled, his head toppling off his body and rolling several feet across the floor to stop at the feet of the Governor of Grafton.

The Governor fell to his knees with a sob, "Please don't kill me. I didn't have any choice. They threatened to kill me if I didn't help them. I don't want to die."

Alexander felt the heaviness of his burden once again. The Governor was lying. His colors were as dishonest as a thief's.

For a moment, Alexander wished he hadn't decided to come here. Killing in battle was one thing. Executing a defenseless man was quite another. It turned his stomach, but he knew his duty demanded it. Some people were just too dangerous to be permitted to live. Allowing them to survive was tantamount to passing sentence on all of their future victims.

Alexander turned to the Governor's wife and sighed with resignation. "Are you part of his plan to betray Ithilian?"

Her face went white and she shook her head without saying a word. Alexander examined her colors and saw that she was telling the truth.

"Do you share power with him?" he asked next.

Again she shook her head.

Alexander nodded. "Anatoly, take her to the other room and tie her up, please. Jack, see if there's a woman in the general's sleeping quarters and bring her here." He turned to Conner. "The Governor has betrayed your House, he's thrown his lot in with Phane, and he's an accomplice to the abduction of your sister."

The Governor interrupted, "No! I'm innocent. I'm a victim here as much as anyone. I've been a hostage in my own home."

"Enough!" Alexander said. "You're lying. You've made your choice and it's time for you to face the consequences of your decisions. Having power does not make you immune from justice. Desire for power does not exempt you from the duty to respect the lives and liberty of others. The Old Law is clear."

Jack brought a terrified young woman into the main room. She was trying unsuccessfully to keep from sobbing at the sight of death all around her.

"Why were you in General Gord's bed?" Alexander asked her.

"My madam sent me," she said. "The Governor requested a girl for one of his guests."

Alexander nodded. "Jack, take her in the other room and tie her up with the Governor's wife."

Jack nodded and they left.

Alexander turned back to Conner. "He's yours to kill if you wish."

Conner blinked and nodded. The Governor sobbed. Conner raised his sword over the kneeling man and held it high in the air for a long moment before lowering it with a look of tortured anguish.

"I know he deserves to die," Conner said, shaking his head. A tear slipped from his eye as he looked up at Alexander. "I just can't bring myself to kill him."

Alexander smiled sadly. "You're a good man, Conner. Killing's not supposed to be easy, killing like this least of all. Unfortunately, sometimes the alternative is worse. If we let him live, he'll continue to give safe harbor to enemies of Ithilian and the Old Law. Eventually, they'll make war on the innocent people of Ithilian."

"No, I won't," the Governor said. "I'm innocent. You can't kill me without a trial. The law of Ithilian is clear. I'm entitled to defend myself before an impartial jury."

Alexander regarded the self-centered little man for a moment.

"Did you make an alliance with Phane?" he asked.

"No," the Governor lied. Alexander was watching his colors closely.

"Did you assist in the abduction of Princess Evelyn?"

"No," he lied again.

"Are you working with the soldiers of Phane's army to help them gain a foothold on Ithilian in preparation for an invasion?"

"No," he lied yet again.

"You've lied with every breath since my friends brought you into this room," Alexander said. "What's more, I can tell when you lie to me."

The Governor's eyes went wide and his face became suddenly very pale.

Alexander took the Sovereign Stone from under his armor and let it fall against his tunic. "This is the heaviest burden I've ever had to carry." The Governor's eyes grew wider still with recognition of the Stone. "The most important duty this Stone confers upon me is the obligation to defend the Old Law. The things I have to do to live up to that responsibility often turn my stomach but they must be done. In this case, I claim your life as punishment for making war on Ithilian and for abducting Princess Evelyn."

The Governor shook his head violently. "No! You can't kill me. I don't want to die. I'm the Governor of Grafton. I deserve consideration for my rank and station."

Alexander shook his head slowly. "No, you don't. If anything, your rank and station only add to your guilt. You have a duty to uphold the Old Law, not deliberately betray it."

"Lord Reishi," Jataan said, "I will execute him, if you wish."

"No, Jataan, this is my duty and I intend to live up to it." He paused for a moment as a thought occurred to him. "Sometimes I wonder if the worst crime evil people ever commit is forcing good people to kill them in defense of life and liberty."

Alexander took a deep breath and let it out with a sigh, then turned back to the Governor. The self-important little man started to protest but stopped suddenly when Alexander took his head off with a flick of the Thinblade.

"We're done here," he said quietly. "Let's go find a ship." With that he turned and left the room.

They were halfway down the stairs leading to the guard room on the level below when someone pounded on the door. The guards in the room remained unconsciousness as Alexander raced to the door and sent his all around sight through to the other side. He saw six soldiers wearing the markings of the Reishi Army Regency. The sergeant in command of the squad sent one of his men to raise the alarm.

"Looks like getting out might be complicated," Alexander said. "There are five soldiers outside this door and more on the way. We're going to have to move fast. We kill the five as quickly as possible and then get to the docks. I know the fastest route from here but we'll probably run into some resistance. Fight through and keep moving." Alexander drew the Thinblade. "Jack, get the bar on the door."

"Lord Reishi, allow us to meet the enemy first," Jataan said, motioning to Boaberous.

Anatoly stepped up next to them with his axe and nodded his agreement. "You've been in the front of the battle far too much lately for my liking."

Alexander started to protest but Lucky put a hand on his shoulder and gently turned him away from the door and the enemy waiting beyond. "Your duty is to rally the Seven Isles against Phane, not to fight a squad of soldiers who are no match for your protectors. Let them do their job so that you can do yours."

With an effort of will, Alexander nodded and stepped back. Anatoly nodded to Jack who lifted the bar and pulled the door open. Boaberous thrust his hammer into a surprised-looking squad sergeant's stomach and sent him flying into the far wall of the hallway. The giant swept into the remaining soldiers followed closely by Jataan and Anatoly, each fighting with their own style.

Anatoly killed with measured efficiency and the cool, calm precision of an experienced soldier. Boaberous fought with focused rage, bludgeoning his enemies with his giant war hammer fueled by his bulk and ferocious strength. Jataan fought with impossible speed and deadly accuracy coupled with calm detachment. The five guards didn't stand a chance. They fell with surprising quickness but even as the last hit the ground, Alexander could hear the footfalls of more soldiers coming. Then a bell began to toll. The alarm had been raised.

They raced down the hall with Boaberous in the lead followed by Alexander directing him at each turn. After only a couple of minutes of fleeing through the keep, they rounded a corner and encountered two soldiers coming toward them. Boaberous charged them and hit the first man in the side of the head with his hammer, crushing his skull and driving him into the second man. They both crashed to the floor. Boaberous didn't stop or turn to finish them but instead resumed his place on point and let Jataan kill the remaining soldier. They worked well together, each anticipating the actions of the other with unerring accuracy.

Alexander led them through a large door and into a wide, high-ceilinged hall. He pointed to the door that led to the docks and Boaberous headed for the exit without hesitation, in spite of the fifty soldiers on the other side of the hall that were assembling to respond to the alarm. When they saw Alexander and his companions, they immediately gave chase.

Five men was one thing, but fifty was something else altogether. An engagement could very easily cost the lives of one or more of his friends and it simply wasn't worth it. Alexander had accomplished his purpose in raiding the keep. All that was left to do was escape.

"Run!" he commanded.

They fled through the halls with near recklessness. The few soldiers they encountered were totally unprepared for the three hundred and fifty pounds of Boaberous hurtling through the halls of the keep. He smashed into them and sent them sprawling without a second look. The thunderous sound of boots behind them only served to spur them on.

"There. That door opens to the port," Alexander said.

Boaberous lifted the bar and opened the door carefully to see if there were more enemy soldiers beyond, but the dock was clear. Fifty soldiers rounded the corner behind them and charged. Alexander turned to face them, reasoning that they would be far more manageable in a confined space than outside, but Lucky had a better idea. He threw a glass jar into their path, which shattered on impact and scattered a handful of small pinkish crystals onto the floor. For a moment, nothing happened.

The soldiers drew closer.

"What was that supposed to do?" Anatoly asked as he readied his axe.

Lucky smiled. "You'll see."

As the soldiers neared, the crystals began to grow impossibly fast. Within only a few breaths time, they grew into a mass of beautiful light-pink crystals that completely filled the hallway from floor to ceiling and from wall to wall for a good ten feet. Several soldiers were caught up in the rapid growth of the magical crystals and died badly.

"That should hold them for a while," Lucky said with a nod of satisfaction.

"Huh, not bad," Anatoly said with a grin for his old friend.

They fled out onto the docks in the darkness of early morning. Several vessels of different types were moored in the slips lining the waterfront of Grafton Harbor. Most looked like ocean-going merchant ships. A few were passenger ferries. And still fewer looked like patrol boats used by the Grafton navy to maintain control of the waters around the province. They were fast-looking, narrow little ships with three masts and several sails as well as a bank of oars on each side. The bow of each was armed with a heavy ballista and the prow culminated in a barbed battering ram.

Alexander scanned the walls of the keep and saw lamps flickering to life as the enemy soldiers responded to the alarm. It was only a matter of time before the wall facing the port was lined with archers. He tapped Boaberous on the shoulder and pointed at the nearest patrol boat. The giant nodded and started toward the small ship. They moved quickly and quietly through the shadows of the early morning and out onto the dock running alongside the warship. It was tied off with two heavy ropes, and the gangplank was deployed, allowing easy access to the decks.

A single guard stood on the dock watching Alexander and his companions approach. Alexander saw his colors flare with fear when he realized that the people approaching him in the darkness were the reason for the alarm. But he was too late.

Boaberous grabbed him by one arm and flung him into the water before racing to the top of the gangplank. Anatoly chopped the rear mooring rope with a single stroke of his axe, while Alexander raced ahead to cut the fore rope. Within a minute they were aboard the little ship. The one man standing watch on the ship was tossed overboard and the gangplank was pushed off the deck, clattering loudly onto the dock below.

Alexander opened the door to the deck below and found the sleepy eyes of a man with a captain's coat hastily thrown on over his nightshirt. He leveled the Thinblade at the man and bore into him with his glittering gold-flecked eyes.

"Are you the captain of this ship?" Alexander asked.

The man looked at the Thinblade for a moment before he nodded, swallowing hard.

"Is your crew on board?"

He nodded again without a word.

"Good, wake them and make best speed for Grafton Island," Alexander commanded. "I have no wish to harm you or your men but I will if necessary. Do you understand?"

"Yes," the captain said, nodding quickly.

Alexander could see from his colors that he was afraid but also courageous enough to make good decisions in spite of his fear.

"My large friend here will accompany you during our trip," Alexander said motioning to Boaberous. "If you or your men attempt to resist, he'll kill you first." He raised the Thinblade so the captain could get a good look at the ancient Sword of Kings. "Let me be clear, you and your men do not have the ability to overpower us. If you try, you will all die. If you do as you're told, we will get off your ship at Grafton Island and you will not be harmed. Do we have an understanding?"

He blinked a few times as he looked around at the faces surrounding him and nodded. "We do."

"Good, get us under way with all possible speed," Alexander said, then turned to Anatoly. "Take a look at the ballista and get it ready for a fight."

Anatoly nodded and headed off to the large siege weapon mounted on the bow deck of the little warship.

The captain went below decks shouting orders interspersed with profanity. Within a few minutes the ship was alive and moving. Most of the crew were rowers with a few deckhands to man the sails. Since the air was relatively calm so near to the shore, the captain kept his deck clear, ordered the row master to give him best speed, and sent his first mate to man the wheel and guide the ship out of the bay.

Shouts came from the docks as the soldiers realized that the enemy was escaping, followed by a volley of arrows that fell well short.

Alexander watched from the aft deck as the keep and port came alive. A warning fire was lit on a high tower overlooking the bay and the three remaining patrol boats in port took on soldiers and began moving to give chase.

For the moment, he was powerless to act. There was nothing he could do now but wait and see if the enemy ships would close within weapons' range before they made it to Grafton Island.

As they left the safe harbor of the bay, the wind picked up and the captain came to Alexander with Boaberous following behind.

"The wind would give us more speed but I'll need my deckhands to manage the sails," the captain said without emotion.

"Do what you need to do, Captain. Just get us to Grafton Island as quickly as possible," Alexander said.

"There are patrol boats watching for any ships headed to the island," he said. "They have orders to stop and board every vessel for inspection."

Alexander nodded. "I expected as much. How many patrol boats can we expect?"

"At least three, plus the three that are pursuing us," the captain said. He was calm and matter-of-fact in spite of the fear that Alexander could see so clearly in his colors.

"What will they do when we don't stop for them?"

"They'll attack with fire pots launched with ballistae," the captain responded.

"Head straight for the closest patrol ship in our way," Alexander said. "We'll hit them first. Hopefully the others won't be able to close within range before we make landfall."

The captain hesitated.

"Speak your mind, Captain," Alexander said.

"I . . . those ships are commanded by my friends," he said. "I don't want to hurt them."

Alexander nodded with genuine sadness. "I understand, Captain. In truth, I don't want to hurt them either but I will if I have to."

"If you don't want to hurt them, then why are you doing this?" he asked.

"Grafton has declared war against Ithilian and taken sides with Prince Phane," Alexander said. "The Governor helped Phane's people abduct Princess Evelyn and is allowing an army from Karth to use Grafton as a staging ground for an all-out invasion of the rest of Ithilian. I intend to stop them—and your friends are in the way."

The captain shook his head. "I don't know about any of that and neither do they," he said, pointing out into the darkness toward the patrol boats that waited in the distance. "We're just doing our jobs."

"In doing your job, you are committing treason against Ithilian and waging war against the Seven Isles and the Old Law," Alexander said. "Doing a job that requires you to betray basic morality is not an excuse worthy of consideration. By defending Grafton, you are aiding those who would wage unprovoked war against innocent people and abduct others for the purpose of using their lives as leverage against their loved ones."

"None of that is our doing," he said with indignation. "We have to feed our families so we do as we're told. Otherwise, we'd lose our jobs and others would take our places. You can't blame us for what the Governor does."

"No, I can't," Alexander said. "I can only blame you for what you do. You and others like you are the means through which the Governor wielded his power. Without people like you who blindly follow his commands, he would be powerless. Obedience to authority does not absolve you of guilt if your actions are immoral. We must all choose when faced with a moral dilemma. How you choose reveals your nature and your character."

"And what about you?" the captain spat back, growing more angry by the moment. "You've hijacked my ship at the point of a blade. What gives you the right? How are you any different from the Governor?"

Jataan stepped up. "Lord Reishi has no need to explain himself to you. His word is law."

"Lord Reishi?" the captain said as his face went slightly pale.

"It's all right, Jataan. His question is valid, so I'll answer it," Alexander said. "I'm acting in response to provocation. I did not start this war. I did not ask for this power. I did not bring enemy soldiers into a peaceful nation. I did not abduct an innocent woman from her home and ransom her back to her family. This war was brought to my doorstep. My family was attacked, my brother was killed, my home was burned to the ground, my nation was invaded and my enemies have tried to kill me time and time again. My actions are in response to aggression against me and other innocent people. If I wish to survive, I must destroy those who are making war against me and mine. They cannot be reasoned with, they cannot be bargained with, and they cannot be permitted to continue to live. They lust for power over the lives of others and will stop at nothing until they impose their will on every life in the Seven Isles. Their actions have condemned them to death. They have murdered innocent people, abducted innocent people, and stolen from innocent people. They have violated the Old Law and as such, they have forfeited their right to life, liberty, or property. Taking your ship is not a violation of the Old Law because you serve the enemy that has made war against me. Your rights under the Old Law are forfeit."

The captain swallowed hard. "Are you going to kill me?"

"Not if you do as I tell you," Alexander said. "I'm not bloodthirsty. I don't want to kill but I won't hesitate either. For the moment, you represent no threat to me. Killing you wouldn't further my cause. However, if the day should come that I face you on the battlefield, I will kill you without a second thought."

The man in the crow's nest called out and pointed into the gradually brightening dawn.

Alexander and his friends went to the foredeck.

Anatoly was standing on the bow, looking out across the water at the patrol ship on the horizon. "The ballista is loaded with a fire pot and ready to fire. I've set the range at maximum and checked the sights. It's in good order. We should be able to hit them within a few minutes."

"Lord Reishi, I believe I can hit them from here," Jataan said.

Alexander and Anatoly frowned in unison.

"How? Anatoly asked. "The ballista can't shoot that far."

"Not on its own," Jataan said, "but my magic will add considerably to its range."

Anatoly shrugged and looked over at Alexander. "I guess it couldn't hurt. We have plenty of ammunition and it won't take long to reload."

"Give it a shot," Alexander said.

Jataan nodded and went to the firing controls of the big siege weapon. He made a few adjustments and nodded to Anatoly to light the fuse on the fire pot. When Anatoly gave the signal, Jataan checked his aim and fired the weapon. The clay pot filled with lamp oil sailed through the air in an impossible arc propelled more by the magic of the battle mage than the power of the ballista. It hit the deck of the patrol boat and shattered in a spray of fire.

"Nice shot," Anatoly said grudgingly.

The sails went up in flames quickly. Within minutes, the boat was listing and the crew was abandoning ship. Alexander watched their desperate struggle to save themselves as his ship sailed past. The remaining two patrol boats in the blockade and the three that launched from the port in pursuit were well out of attack range.

Grafton Island grew on the horizon as the light of day grew brighter.

Alexander suddenly realized he was tired. They hadn't slept for the entire night, and the rest of the day would be spent running into the interior of Grafton Island in an attempt to elude whatever soldiers made landfall from the ships behind them.

He thought about Isabel and wondered what she was doing in that moment. He hoped the mana fast was successful and worried that it wasn't. He told himself that his worry was irrational, Isabel was strong, she would survive and emerge stronger, but he still worried. More than anything he just wanted her with him. Her presence made everything better, calmed his nerves and soothed his soul. He missed her terribly.

"She will return to you, My Love," Chloe said in his mind.

"You sound so certain, Little One. How can you be sure?" he said without speaking.

"I have seen her mind and her soul. She is strong and she loves you just as much as you love her," Chloe said. "You will be together again."

"Thank you, Little One."

Chapter 22

They had sailed for several hours through the morning and into midafternoon when the captain came back to Alexander.

"Where should I make port?" he asked. "There are adequate ports at the northernmost settlement and one around the west side of the island. The one to the east is farther and would take longer because the winds shift out on the open ocean and we would have to rely on the oars."

Alexander scanned the island looming up before them. "We aren't going to a port. There will be soldiers waiting for us. Run aground there," Alexander said, pointing to a sandy beach in a little cove a few miles from the northern port town.

"But, we'll be stuck," the captain complained. "I'll never get my ship off that beach."

"Captain, your ship is a thing," Alexander said. "I am trying to save the lives of innocent people. Do as I tell you or you'll find yourself swimming to shore."

The captain grudgingly followed his orders in spite of his crew's protests. Less than an hour later, they ran aground in the shallow waters on the northern shore of Grafton Island. The water was only four feet deep, but Alexander still took the longboat from the ship, mostly to prevent the captain and his crew from getting to shore quickly enough to warn the enemy forces stationed on the island. It was a quick ride to the beach.

The road that circled the island was about a quarter mile from the shore. They approached it with caution but it was empty so they crossed quickly and headed due south into the interior of the mountainous island. As they gained altitude, Alexander stopped to check on the progress of his pursuers whenever a clear view presented itself. They were closing fast but it appeared that they weren't willing to run aground. Several vessels were heading for the port a mile or so east along the northern coast while one remained anchored in the little cove near the ship Alexander had commandeered. He estimated that they were at least three hours behind, plenty of time to lose them in the rugged wilderness of the island.

By dark they were well away from the coastline and into the foothills of the mountain that loomed up from the center of the island. They made camp and Lucky prepared a hearty stew over a little campfire.

Alexander could tell that Conner was nervous about something but he waited for the young prince to speak up rather than ask him about it. After dinner was eaten and their bedrolls were laid out under the clear sky, Conner cleared his throat and took a deep breath.

"Legend has it that this mountain is haunted," he said quietly. "I don't know how much is true and how much is a story, but we should be cautious."

"Caution is always wise," Alexander said. "As I understand it, there are ganglings in these mountains, possibly dragons as well. There might also be a creature called a revenant. They're supposed to be strong and fast. And winged, so they may strike from above. Malachi Reishi created them by mating a virgin witch with a demon. He said they heal very quickly from injuries and that the only sure way to kill one is to cut off its head. Hopefully, we won't encounter anything, but we should be careful nonetheless."

"I figure it'll take a couple of days to reach the keep," Anatoly said. "Might go faster if we stay in the foothills and skirt around the mountain rather than trying to go over it."

"The enemy soldiers are more likely to find us if we stay closer to the road," Alexander said.

"Soldiers are much easier to contend with than the creatures you spoke of, Lord Reishi," Jataan said. "I would recommend the course Master Grace has suggested."

"I agree," Lucky said. "Ganglings are dangerous in the mountains, especially if they ambush us from higher ground."

Alexander nodded. "All right, we'll avoid the mountains and stay to the foothills."

They woke early the next morning and began the long walk around the mountainous island to Lighthouse Keep on the southern bluff. The forest was thick and travel was slow, but the density of the foliage in the early months of summer offered ample cover from the enemy patrols that frequented the road not a mile away.

Several times during the day, the group stopped and hid to avoid soldiers that made sweeps into the forest near the road. Alexander preferred to avoid a confrontation, more to protect their position than out of fear of the outcome. He had become confident in his deadliness with the Thinblade, and Jataan had proven to be a formidable ally. He still didn't really like the little battle mage but he had to admit that his assistance was helpful, and it was certainly preferable to having the man as an enemy.

At nightfall they made a quiet and dark camp, ate a cold dinner, and laid out their bedrolls. Alexander thought about Isabel as he drifted off to sleep. He worried for her safety and wondered what she was doing but mostly he missed her. Her presence had a way of calming and centering him like nothing else. She made him feel like he was exactly where he was supposed to be.

He woke with a start. Jack was kneeling beside him, shaking his shoulder gently. He motioned for silence in the dim light of the stars and the half moon overhead, then pointed into the forest. Alexander sat up quietly, checking the Thinblade at his side, and looked to where Jack was pointing. In the flickering moonlight, he thought he saw the silhouette of a man standing several dozen feet outside their camp, except the man had no colors. Alexander pulled on his boots and drew the Thinblade. Anatoly came awake from the stirring in the camp and fluidly rolled to his feet with his war axe in hand. Alexander motioned for silence and began to advance on the man's position.

The silhouette didn't move or react as Alexander approached. The trees swayed from a gentle breeze, throwing shadows and moonlight across the forest floor. Then the man suddenly disappeared. Alexander froze, scanning the forest with his magical sight. There was nothing out of place, no evidence of any threat.

"Did you see anything, Little One," he asked Chloe in his mind.

"No, My Love. What was there?" she responded silently.

"I'm not sure."

He went to the place where the man had been standing and carefully searched the forest floor for any sign of his presence but found none. It was as if they had seen a ghost, except Alexander had seen ghosts before and they didn't look like this.

Jataan came up silently through the darkness. "Is there a threat, Lord Reishi?" he whispered.

"I'm not sure," Alexander said. "There was a man standing here watching us but he didn't have any colors."

"Have you ever seen a person that didn't have colors before?" Anatoly asked.

"Never," Alexander said. "A living aura is produced by a person's life force. Whatever was out here in the trees wasn't alive and it didn't leave any sign at all. No footprints, nothing."

"Maybe there's more to the stories of haunting in these mountains than we thought," Jack said.

The rest of the night offered little rest. Alexander slept fitfully and dreamt of shadows in the dark. He came awake several times with his heart hammering in his chest. By morning he was both relieved to see the dawn and tired from the restless night. After they ate their cold breakfast, Alexander described what he'd seen. Jack and Anatoly added a few details as well.

Lucky frowned in thought as he chewed a bite of biscuit with jam and then shook his head. "If it was alive it would have been visible to your second sight. If it was actually there, it would have left some trace of its coming and going, not to mention Chloe would have seen it as well. I'm not sure what we're dealing with, but I don't believe it's a man."

"Could it have been the effects of a spell?" Jack asked.

"Possibly, but I suspect Alexander would have been able to see some trace of the spell's aura," Lucky said.

"If anyone sees anything out of the ordinary, speak up," Alexander said. "There's no telling what's out there. It could be the revenant we were warned about or it could be something else. Let's make sure it doesn't take us by surprise, whatever it is."

They moved cautiously throughout the day. Several times they heard the sounds of galloping horses in the distance as patrols rode by on the road. They continued on slowly, listening for any hint of enemy in the forest around them.

About midafternoon, they came to a little clearing with a small spring bubbling out of the ground and running off through the thick, mossy meadow into the forest. Standing near the little pool of crystal-clear water was a man dressed in charcoal-grey robes. He was old with long white hair and steel grey eyes. He stood leaning on a staff and was looking at the spot where Alexander stepped from the forest as if he were waiting for him to arrive. He locked eyes with Alexander for a moment and then smiled ever so slightly.

"Anatoly?" Alexander said.

"I see him," Anatoly responded.

"I don't," Chloe said as she buzzed into a ball of light and became visible.

"I see him as well," Lucky said.

Alexander nodded. He stepped out into the meadow and said, "Hello."

The man flickered and vanished from sight as if he'd never been there.

Alexander froze in place and scanned the forest. There was nothing out of the ordinary, just thick foliage surrounding the entire meadow with a few large rocks here and there.

He went to the place where the man had been standing and examined the ground for any trace of his presence but found none.

"Chloe, we saw him standing right here," Alexander said.

"I saw nothing," Chloe said. "Did you see his colors?"

Alexander shook his head absentmindedly. "No," he said. Then he looked up at Lucky. "Any thoughts?"

"This is most puzzling," Lucky said, shaking his head. "Clearly, there's more at work here than we understand. Whatever it is, it hasn't posed a threat so far, but that doesn't mean that it can't or won't. I suggest an abundance of caution."

"Some of the stories of these mountains tell of seeing things in the forest," Conner said, "and others tell of deadly creatures that roam the night. Most of the people who live here don't venture into the forest or the mountains after dark and the few who have and returned, speak of seeing many strange things."

A shadow passed over them and all eyes went to the sky. Alexander felt a tickle of fear when he recognized the silhouette of a wyvern gliding toward the mountain peaks in the distance. A closer look told him that it was very real with vibrant colors and that it had an elk clutched in its talons. Alexander breathed a little easier as the beast drifted away from them. It had its meal and probably wouldn't be hunting for the rest of the day.

"Obviously, there are several very real dangers in these mountains," Alexander said.

Camp that evening was cold and dark again. They were taking every precaution to avoid the soldiers still searching for them as well as the other threats the wilds of the mountainous island had to offer. Alexander felt like he had just drifted off to sleep when he woke to a terrifying scream.

He rolled to his feet with the Thinblade in hand just as everyone else in the camp came awake and rose to meet the threat. Lucky had been standing watch. He pulled a vial of light from his bag and raised it high just as a creature from out of a nightmare landed in the middle of the camp.

It stood seven feet tall and was proportioned like a man with arms and legs but that was where the similarities ended. It had charcoal-black leathery skin stretched tight over its muscular frame, long lanky arms that ended in clawed hands, fangs protruding from its mouth, and a crown of black horns. Its eyes glowed red and it had giant black batlike wings.

Alexander tried to make sense of the creature's colors. They were a mixture of the vibrant colors of a wizard and the inky blackness of a demon. Then the thing screamed again, seemingly in response to the light cast by the vial of night-wisp dust that Lucky held in the air.

It was a shriek of madness so penetrating that Alexander stood almost paralyzed with irrational fear. The terror flooded into him and filled him with cold stark panic. He struggled to move but couldn't even flinch away from the terrible creature. He could see with his all around sight that his friends were all in a similar state of frozen panic. With an act of will, he fled into the place in his consciousness where the witness lived, where emotion had no hold and cold reason reigned supreme. In that instant, the spell was broken, the fear subsided, and he stepped forward to face the monster.

It swept its wings forward, propelling itself backward over Jataan, who stood stock-still behind it, and landed outside the field of light.

Alexander didn't hesitate for even a second. He pulled his vial of night-wisp dust from his pouch and held it high to cast the captured light of the sun at the dark creature. With a powerful stroke of its black wings and a shriek of frustration, it took to the air. His friends broke through the spell of terror that gripped them as the creature fled from the light.

"That was unsettling," Jack said, still trembling from the unnatural fear conjured by the creature's scream.

Boaberous grunted.

"What was that thing?" Anatoly asked.

"I'm pretty sure that was a revenant," Alexander said.

"I haven't felt fear like that since the trials," Jataan said. "I must beg your forgiveness, Lord Reishi. I'm ashamed to admit that I was overcome with terror and unable to move."

"I'm pretty sure that was a result of the revenant's magic," Alexander said. "Don't worry about it, I felt the same way."

"How did you break the spell?" Lucky asked. "I struggled to break the grip of the fear but was unable to move."

"During the mana fast, I discovered a place in my mind where emotion has no power. From there I was able to face the trials and overcome them. When I felt the fear caused by the revenant's scream, I retreated into that place and the spell broke."

Jataan and Lucky nodded in unison.

"The stillness," Jataan said. "I remember it from my trials. When the trial of fear came upon me, I was lost to it for a long time until I found that place within where everything was still and calm. Only after I found it was I able to face the fear."

"I recall a similar experience," Lucky said. "The detachment of that place enabled me to face the trials and succeed. I'll keep that in mind if we encounter that thing again."

"The good news is, it really didn't like the light," Jack said. "Unfortunately, I suspect that any soldiers nearby have marked our position."

"Probably, but I doubt they'll risk moving through the night, especially after hearing that thing scream," Anatoly said. "Still, we should probably double up the watch and have a vial of light ready just in case."

The rest of the night was spent in a state of half sleep and half wariness. No one wanted to be caught asleep if the revenant came back. About an hour before dawn, they heard the beast scream off in the distance followed by the screams of men. Everyone was up and ready in an instant.

After a tense moment of waiting and straining to hear any sign of a threat, Boaberous chuckled.

"Sounds like our pursuers have met the revenant," Jataan said.

"At least they didn't get a good night's sleep either," Anatoly said. "It'll be dawn soon. We might as well strike camp and get an early start."

"Yeah, I doubt I could get back to sleep if I tried," Alexander said.

They risked a fire for a hot breakfast of porridge and a cup of tea as the light of day grew brighter. After the encounter with the revenant, the thought of facing a squad of soldiers was almost refreshing. The enemy was dangerous but also a known quantity. Alexander understood how to fight them and knew the limits of the danger they represented. The revenant and the man in the forest were both still a mystery and the unknown nature of their capabilities only served to heighten the threat they represented.

They made better time as the forest thinned and became more rocky and mountainous. The southern tip of the island was a high bluff that jutted up out of the ocean and then grew steeply into the mountain that dominated the center of the island.

While walking through a boulder field at the base of a high cliff, the enemy ambushed them. In the back of his mind Alexander chided himself for not anticipating the attack, since they had revealed their position with the light they cast in the night and with the smoke of their cook fire. Given a known position and a known destination, it was a simple matter for the enemy to guess at their route.

When Alexander and his men entered the small clearing with the cliff face on one side and dozens of twenty-foot boulders on the other, they heard a battle cry and suddenly a platoon of Reishi Army Regency soldiers poured out from their hiding places behind the boulders and surrounded them. They were armored with the signature breastplates of the Regency, emblazoned with the letter R over the heart, and they were armed with short spears, large round shields, and short swords at their belts. They fanned out around Alexander and his friends but didn't attack immediately.

The commander of the platoon stepped out from the semicircle of his men and bowed formally to Alexander.

"Prince Phane extends his congratulations and an offer of truce," he said. "Surrender the Sovereign Stone and bow before the rightful Sovereign of the Seven Isles, and you, your family, and your friends will be allowed to live. You will rule Ruatha in his name and live as a king. This is the last time he will make such a generous offer."

"That's what he said the last time he made me the very same offer," Alexander said, shaking his head. "Do you even know who you serve?"

"I serve the rightful Reishi Sovereign," he said.

"Lord Reishi is the rightful Sovereign," Jataan said. "He has bonded with the Stone and taken counsel from the sovereigns of old. Prince Phane is a pretender. You serve the wrong master."

The commander smiled with a shrug. "Yet it would seem that we have you in our grasp. You are outnumbered five to one and I can see that two of your number are ill-equipped to fight."

"Your numbers are insufficient," Jataan said calmly.

"Don't be a fool, Lord Alexander," the commander said. "Accept the offer and we will escort you as a royal guard to Lighthouse Keep where you can await the arrival of Prince Phane, pledge your loyalty to him, and end this destructive war."

For what it was worth, Alexander could see from the man's colors that he believed what he said. Phane was nothing if not a skilled liar.

Alexander shrugged off his bow and pack, then calmly drew the Thinblade with a smile. "Let me make you an offer, Lieutenant. Stand down and leave us to our task. I have no wish to harm you or your men but if you don't accept my generous offer, I will kill you all."

The lieutenant forced a laugh but his eyes never left the Thinblade. "You're hopelessly outnumbered. We have you surrounded. Don't be a fool. You can't possibly win."

"You're wrong," Alexander said. "You're the one who's at a disadvantage. Withdraw or die." His words hung in the air as the lieutenant weighed the wisdom of carrying out his orders. The power of his loyalty to a fraudulent authority won out.

"Take them," he commanded.

Not a second later a knife drove through the lieutenant's breastplate and into his heart. He stared in shock at the sudden pain as he slumped to his knees and fell dead on the ground in front of his platoon. Jataan calmly drew his second knife and stepped forward to meet the attack.

Jack flickered out of view as Lucky tossed a jar filled with amber-colored liquid at the soldiers on the left side of the semicircle. It shattered against the shield of a soldier and splashed the liquid everywhere for ten feet. For a moment nothing happened, then the liquid transformed into a thick amber-colored fog that grew quickly and surrounded eight of the soldiers. A moment later, it solidified into hard, clear stone the color and translucency of amber, entombing all eight of the soldiers.

Boaberous swept into the other side of the semicircle with his giant war hammer, hitting the fourth man in from the end of the half ring. The man's shield buckled and he went flying into the other three men, sending them all to the ground.

Anatoly sidestepped a spear thrust and hooked his axe blade over the top of the man's shield, pulled him forward then quickly reversed the direction of his war axe to drive the top spike into the man's eye socket.

Conner parried a spear thrust and lunged into an enemy's shield, sending him backward off balance, and then thrust into the ribs of the next man, killing him in one stroke. The soldier on the other side thrust hard and drove into Conner's backplate with enough force to penetrate an inch or so. Conner cried out and went to a knee. The soldier stiffened as Jack knifed him in the back.

Jataan waited until the man facing him attacked and then moved like a blur, slipping past his spear and behind him as he spun and drove his knife into the man's neck, severing his spine and dropping him like a sack of beans. He let go of his knife and drew the soldier's short sword as the man fell. The next man turned to bring his shield up but Jataan squatted low and sliced the inside of the man's leg with clean precision, cutting to the bone and spilling bright red blood in spurts as the man fell screaming.

Alexander lopped the tip off the spear of the man lunging at him, then brought the Thinblade up through his shield and arm, stepped in and cleaved the man from shoulder to hip. He took a step to his right and brought his sword across in an arc and took the next man's head with a stroke. Another soldier thrust into him from behind. The spear hit hard in the middle of his back but didn't penetrate his dragon-scale chain armor. The force of the blow sent Alexander stumbling forward into the attack of another soldier. Wildly, he flung the Thinblade up through the enemy's shield and cleaved his arm off above the wrist. Still stumbling forward, he caught his balance as he thrust into the wounded enemy's heart.

The remaining soldiers fell back, attempting to regroup and present a front of interlocking shields, but Alexander pressed the attack, lopping spears in half and cleaving through shields with every stroke.

Anatoly took measured strides into the enemy, attacking with efficiency and practiced technique. He faced each one with calm calculation, taking his shot when it presented itself and never missing once he committed to his attack.

Boaberous fought with bursts of rage and fits of fury, smashing his opponents with the blunt force of his giant war hammer powered by his bulk and strength.

Conner regained his feet and managed to dispatch another of the enemy soldiers in spite of his wound. The man tried to knock him off balance with his shield but when he stepped into Conner's guard, Conner stabbed him in the foot, caught the bottom of the shield with the cross guard of his sword, lifted the man's shield up, and drove the point of his blade into his midsection.

Jataan moved through the enemy with bursts of inhuman speed. He wielded the sword he'd taken from his first opponent with the same exacting precision and speed that he wielded his knives. In the moment of the attack he would find a point of weakness and strike with ruinous effect, and then he would almost saunter through the carnage and the enemy surrounding him until he found his next opponent.

The battle didn't last long. Alexander took a cut on his left shoulder and was bruised from the spear thrust to his back, Anatoly was battered and bruised from a few close-quarters' engagements, and Conner suffered a wound from the spear thrust that pierced his armor, but otherwise they came through the engagement without serious injury. The enemy fell so quickly that the two soldiers still standing suddenly realized they were all that was left and turned and ran. Boaberous dispatched them one after the other with two rapidly cast javelins.

Alexander sat down on a rock. "Everyone all right?" he asked.

Conner was the only one with any serious injury.

The broken bodies of dozens of men lay scattered all around. None had escaped.

Lucky treated Conner with healing salve and they took an hour to rest so the magical ointment could do its work.

It was a little unsettling having the eight men encased in magical amber looking at them with fear and shock.

"How long will they stay like that?" Jack asked as he studied the enemy soldiers frozen in time.

"The amber will gradually dissipate over the next week or so," Lucky said. "But they're already dead from suffocation."

Jataan selected a sword from among the fallen soldiers and took a scabbard and belt as well. He retrieved his knives and strapped on his new weapon.

"I thought you preferred your knives," Anatoly said.

"I do, but decapitating a revenant will be much easier with a sword."

"I suppose so," Anatoly said, as he cleaned the blood off the blade of his war axe.

***

It took longer than Alexander would have liked, but eventually they arrived at the bluff where the keep stood, late in the afternoon of their third day on the island. From their vantage point in the trees about a mile away, they could see that the road was busy with squad-sized patrols of soldiers and that the walls of the keep were well manned and well armed. Getting inside would take some effort.

Chapter 23

"I hope Evelyn is still alive," Conner said quietly. "By now, they surely know we're coming for her."

"I'll take a look in a few minutes, but I can't see why Phane would kill her," Alexander said. "She's no threat to him and as long as she's alive and under his control, he can use her for leverage against your father. Phane may be a monster, but he's not stupid. He'll keep her alive until he has what he wants or she's of no further use to him."

"I concur with Lord Reishi," Jataan said. "Prince Phane is very shrewd. Killing her would gain him nothing. Holding her gives him options."

"I hope you're right," Conner said. "My sister doesn't deserve this. She can be difficult at times but she's never hurt anyone."

"We'll get her back, Conner," Alexander said. He withdrew back into the forest and found a small open space to draw a magic circle.

He found the firmament easily and brought his awareness into focus over his meditating body. With impossible speed he moved to the keep and into the tower where Evelyn was being held. She was pacing back and forth across the room, wearing an expression that was a mixture of boredom and indignation. He moved through the door and saw four guards standing in the hall just outside her chamber. Next he searched for the wizard. He found him busy studying an old book in a workroom on the other side of the keep. Alexander spent the next few minutes exploring the interior of the keep. He floated through rooms and hallways looking at the layout of the place and at the defenses.

There were easily a thousand Reishi Army Regency soldiers stationed there with scores manning the walls and towers. They were barracked in the main building and had even set up cots in the banquet hall to accommodate the large number of troops. Alexander picked the place in the wall where he planned to enter and carefully traced his route to the base of the central tower. Once he was satisfied with his reconnaissance, he returned to his body.

He stood and stretched, then joined his friends who were sitting nearby talking quietly. He sat down and described the layout of the keep and the nature of the defenses. After he explained his plan, they laid out their bedrolls and got some rest in the late afternoon. At dark they rose, ate a quick meal, and struck camp.

The keep was well lit with oil lamps lining the battlements. Men stood guard at close intervals along the top of the walls, and patrols moved frequently from one battlement to the next. Clearly, the occupants of the keep were expecting an attack. Alexander only hoped they wouldn't be imaginative enough to guess at his tactics.

He led Jataan and Jack through the darkness to the place where he intended to enter. The enemy soldiers had lowered the portcullis and closed the gates, securing the fortress from most conventional attacks. They seemed hesitant to venture from the keep at night, no doubt because of the encounter with the revenant the night before.

When Alexander reached his destination, he went to work cutting chunks out of the wall with the Thinblade. After several minutes he'd opened a hole large enough for the three of them to crawl through. The corridor beyond was dark and little used. They slipped inside and made their way to a door leading to the courtyard.

The keep was essentially a thick outer wall with battlements, interior corridors, and towers surrounding an inner yard where the main building and central tower were built. It was very old but well constructed and still solid.

Alexander stopped at the door and sent his all around sight through to the other side. From his clairvoyant scouting he knew that the door opened to a narrow space in the yard not ten feet from the base of the tower, which formed the rear portion of the main building. Two guards stood at the door leading from the yard to the tower. Alexander knew the guards were no match for him and Jataan but he also knew it would only take a second for them to call out an alarm and bring far too many soldiers for the two of them to face with any hope of survival.

He withdrew back into the dark corridor and whispered to Jataan and Jack, "There are two guards ten feet from the door. We have to silence them before they can raise the alarm. Jack, you pull the door open quickly and quietly, Jataan you go first and I'll be right behind you. As soon as they're down, we drag them into this corridor and out of sight."

The plan was sound. Jack smoothly drew the door open. Jataan shot through with frightening speed, a knife in each hand. He closed with the two men before they understood what was happening and drove the point of each knife into the windpipe of each man simultaneously. Alexander caught one before he fell and carried him into the dark corridor. Jataan was right behind him with the other, and Jack quietly closed the door again.

Alexander reached out with his all around sight for any sign of other guards but saw none. They slipped across to the tower door. Alexander quietly slid the Thinblade through the edge of the door to cut the bolt, then sent his sight through into the room beyond. It was a round room easily forty feet across with three doors leading out, one to the main building of the keep and the other two out into the courtyard. A single staircase led up the outer edge of the room to the next level of the tower above. The thing that stopped Alexander cold was the twenty soldiers barracked in the room. They appeared to be sleeping and the room was dark, but it was impossible to tell if any of them might actually be awake.

Alexander remembered his dad's admonition about war: No plan ever survives contact with the enemy. It was proving to be maddeningly true. When Alexander had done his magical reconnaissance, the room at the base of the tower had been empty, but that was in the late afternoon when these soldiers had probably been searching Grafton Island for him.

He knew that the longer they were inside the keep, the more likely it was that they would be discovered. He'd planned to have Anatoly create a distraction so they could escape the keep once they had the princess, but he quickly decided that the distraction was more useful now. Hopefully, if the alarm was raised, the soldiers within the tower room would go to meet the threat.

"Little One, I need you to go to Anatoly and tell him that the plan has changed," Alexander said to Chloe without speaking.

"Are you sure, My Love?" Chloe asked silently. "The enemy are many.

You are at risk if they discover you."

"I know, but we've come too far now," Alexander said silently. "If we withdraw, they'll discover the hole in the wall and our chance will be lost. Tell Anatoly to attack now, then move to the rendezvous point and try to draw as many soldiers after him as possible."

"As you wish, My Love, but I don't like you putting yourself in such danger," Chloe said in his mind.

Alexander motioned for Jataan and Jack to follow him back into the corridor and quietly closed the door. "There's a platoon of soldiers in the room at the base of the tower. I've sent Chloe to tell Anatoly to make his attack now and draw the enemy away. Hopefully, the soldiers in the tower room will respond to the diversion and leave us a clear path to the princess."

They waited quietly for the commotion to begin. Not a minute later, Chloe was back but still not visible.

"Anatoly will begin his attack in a moment," she said silently in Alexander's mind.

"Thank you, Little One," Alexander replied without speaking.

A minute or two later the alarm bell began to toll. The shouting of soldiers could be heard from all around the keep. Alexander sent his sight through the door and watched as most of the soldiers in the tower room strapped on armor and boots before pouring out into the courtyard and racing for the gates.

"There are four men left in the tower," Alexander whispered. "We'll kill them quickly and move up the stairs. Don't leave any soldiers behind us and keep moving."

Jataan and Jack nodded.

They entered the room and the guards shouted for help but the keep was already in such a state of commotion that their alarm went unnoticed. Alexander and Jataan made short work of the startled soldiers as Jack headed up the stairs. When Alexander and Jataan reached the second level, they found two guards dead from Jack's knife.

They made their way up through the seven circular rooms of the tower. Most of the rooms looked like they'd been converted into workrooms for the wizard that led this contingent of soldiers for Phane. All were empty of soldiers except for the next to the last room from the top, which was manned by six men in armor who were alert and waiting for an attack. When Alexander peeked up the staircase, two men fired crossbows at him. The first bolt struck dead center in his chest. The impact was painful but it didn't penetrate his armor shirt. The second bolt caught him in the outside of his left shoulder and drove clean through the muscle. He cried out involuntarily in pain as he stepped back from the staircase and out of harm's way.

Jataan moved to the base of the stairs and stood defiantly. Two more guards loosed their crossbows, but he moved in a blur and avoided the deadly projectiles.

Jack went to Alexander. "This is going to hurt," he said, looking him in the eye before pulling the bolt through his arm. Alexander withdrew into the place in his mind where the witness lived to avoid passing out from the intense pain. Jack quickly bound the wound and made a makeshift sling to immobilize his arm.

Jataan dodged the remaining two crossbow bolts, then darted up the stairs.

By the time Jack and Alexander made it to the level above, the six guards were scattered about in moaning heaps of human carnage with their lifeblood draining away in pools of red. Jataan stood calmly waiting for Alexander and Jack.

There was a single door leading to the main room where Evelyn was imprisoned. Alexander sent his sight through and saw Princess Evelyn standing in the middle of the room, looking at the door and straining to hear any indication of what was happening beyond it.

When he opened the door, she was still standing in the middle of the room with her fists planted on her hips. She was petite with black hair and her father's slate-grey eyes. She gave Alexander a look of pure contempt that morphed into a combination of caution and curiosity when she saw the dead soldiers behind him. He scrutinized her colors for a moment. She had an intense aura that was full of life and energy. There was no magic present but her colors were clear and bright. Alexander sensed the self-centeredness of youth. She looked about eighteen years old.

"Who are you?" she demanded.

"My name is Alexander. I'm here to rescue you," he said.

She huffed with exasperation. "Well, it's about time," she said as she retrieved her riding boots from beneath the bed and sat down to strap them on. She wore a simple dress and didn't take the time to change into anything more appropriate. With her boots on, she stripped the blanket off the bed, rolled it up quickly and tied a sash from another dress hanging in the armoire around it so she could sling it across her back.

"All right, I'm ready," she said impatiently as if she'd been waiting on Alexander. "How many men do you have with you?"

"Two with me and four more outside the keep," Alexander said.

"That's it?" she said indignantly. "All I'm worth is seven men?"

Jataan started to say something, but Alexander silenced him with a shake of his head. Jack chuckled at her brashness.

"Do you want to go home or not?" Alexander said with a hard look.

She frowned and huffed again as she motioned for him to lead the way.

They made it to the base of the tower without encountering any resistance, but as they descended the final flight of stairs a squad of ten soldiers came into the room with weapons drawn. The sergeant ordered his men to attack.

Jataan lunged into the advancing enemy.

Jack flickered out of sight.

Alexander waited for the first soldier to reach him before he attacked. His shoulder hurt terribly and it was distracting him from moving more fluidly, so he chose simple attacks that relied on the power of the Thinblade.

As he killed one soldier, another managed to step in and smash into his wounded shoulder with his shield. Jack killed the soldier in the next second but not before Alexander went down hard. The fall coupled with the renewed pain of his wound stunned him for a moment.

One of the enemy soldiers tried to take advantage of his distracted state and stab him in the head with a spear, but Alexander managed to roll to the side and swipe across his ankles with the Thinblade, toppling the man in a screaming heap.

The battle ended as quickly as it had begun. Most of the enemy soldiers sustained deep slashes across vital arteries in their arms and legs from Jataan's knife. The ones who were not dead yet soon would be.

Evelyn looked at the sudden carnage with shock that slowly transformed into righteous satisfaction. She went to the nearest dying soldier and removed the belt that held his knife and sword and strapped it on over her dress.

Jack helped Alexander to his feet. His shoulder throbbed but he shoved the pain aside and shook the stunned feeling from his head as he sheathed the Thinblade and drew one of Lucky's shatter vials from his belt pouch. He kicked the double doors open to the large adjoining room in the center of the main building and threw the vial in a high arc that brought it crashing down onto the central table. The orange-red liquid fire splattered across the table and onto the carpet, igniting everything it touched.

Alexander turned to lead the way out when Evelyn stopped and faced him with suspicion.

"Who are you and why do you have my father's sword?" she demanded.

"I told you, my name is Alexander," he said. "As for the Thinblade, this one is mine. Now let's go. We don't have much time before the enemy comes back to fight the fire."

"I'm not going anywhere with you until I know you aren't the enemy," Evelyn said stubbornly.

Jack interceded. "Princess Evelyn, your brother is waiting for us outside the walls of the keep. Please come with us and all will be explained."

She looked around at the carnage and the growing glow of fire coming from the other room and nodded grudgingly.

They left the tower and retraced their path to the hole in the outer wall without encountering any more resistance. The bulk of the enemy soldiers were outside the walls of the keep pursuing the rest of Alexander's companions.

As they crawled out of the keep, the air changed. It became charged and filled with power. Alexander looked up and saw the clouds start to spiral above the keep. Then he saw the colors of magic within them and he knew it was time to go.

They moved quickly but quietly through the night toward the rendezvous point where his friends were waiting. As they got closer, they heard the sounds of battle. They entered the little clearing and saw a platoon of thirty men surrounding Alexander's friends. Anatoly had positioned his group with their backs to a large boulder and was fending off the enemy as best he could. He was bloody from a gash in his leg and another on his shoulder. Lucky was on one knee behind them, ministering to Conner who was down with a belly wound. Boaberous was cut in several places but still fought with bursts of deadly rage. The enemy surrounding them had barred their escape and was wearing them down with cautious attacks designed more to draw them out and waste their energy than to kill them outright.

Alexander didn't hesitate. He drew the Thinblade and swept into the enemy from behind in spite of the pain from his wounded shoulder. He killed three before they even knew what was happening.

Jataan knifed four men in the back in rapid succession before the platoon realized they were under attack from behind.

Jack flickered out of sight and found the leader of the enemy soldiers. He cut the man's throat before he could issue any orders, leaving the rest of the men uncertain and in disarray.

Evelyn, seeing her injured brother, drew her sword and ran a soldier through with a scream of rage and fear.

The sudden onslaught from behind gave Anatoly and Boaberous the opportunity to strike out at the distracted enemy. They drove through the cluster of men before them and felled six with a furious assault. The remaining men turned and tried to run. A few made it into the forest but most died trying to escape the sudden attack.

Evelyn raced to her brother's side. "Conner, please tell me you're all right."

"I'll be fine," he said through gritted teeth.

Lucky had stopped the bleeding and bandaged the stab wound in his belly, but Conner was clearly hurting.

Alexander quickly assessed the situation. He could feel the air around him becoming charged with magic. The sky above was darkening with unnatural clouds and the enemy would soon return in greater numbers.

"Can everyone move?" he asked urgently.

"Everyone but Conner," Lucky said as he stood. He had an angry-looking bruise on his face.

Alexander winced at seeing his old tutor's injury. Lucky was as gentle as they came, even if his magic was deadly. Seeing him hurt made Alexander's stomach squirm.

"Anatoly, Boaberous, go find a couple of saplings and make a stretcher," Alexander said. "We can't stay here, they'll be back in force soon and the wizard in that keep is conjuring something." As if to punctuate his statement, a bolt of lightning shot down from the gathering storm clouds and struck a tree not a hundred feet away with a deafening crack that nearly knocked them all from their feet.

"Chloe, let me know when the enemy gets close," Alexander said aloud.

She buzzed into a ball of light, emerging from the aether and flew in an orbit around his head once before darting off above the trees to watch for approaching soldiers.

Evelyn gasped, "What was that?" she asked in stunned amazement.

"Not what. Who. That was Chloe. She's a fairy and she's my familiar," Alexander said.

Anatoly and Boaberous returned in short order with two saplings about eight feet long, each stripped of branches. They laid out two blankets one atop the other and then rolled the saplings up from either edge to make a stretcher. Within a few minutes they had secured Conner and were traveling through the forest by the light of night-wisp dust. Alexander didn't want to give away their position, but he felt it was more important to get some distance from the enemy.

It started to rain, lightly at first, then more heavily until it came in great torrents. The air sizzled with the power of the wizard's spell. Lightning flickered across the sky and great peals of thunder shook the ground beneath them. A bolt of lightning struck nearby and knocked them to the ground. The concussion was so great that Alexander lay stunned for several long moments as he struggled to regain his senses. Another bolt struck a tree several hundred feet from their position and shattered it into splinters in a terrifying explosion that sent deadly shards of wood flying in every direction.

Alexander realized the wizard was using the light of the night-wisp dust to target their position, so he doused the light and changed direction to evade the deadly lightning being called down from the angry clouds overhead. The strikes came more frequently but not as accurately. Trees exploded in the distance. The rain was making it difficult to move with any speed through the pitch-black forest. Alexander could see the colors of the trees all around and was able to lead his companions along a path that avoided the most difficult terrain, but it was still very slow going.

Through it all they heard shouts in the distance as enemy soldiers followed them through the forest and into the higher reaches of the mountains. As they gained distance from the keep, the severity of the magically conjured storm began to wane and the frequency of the random lightning strikes diminished.

Alexander and his friends were exhausted and soaking wet. Conner was bleeding through his bandages. Yet the enemy could still be heard pursuing them through the night.

Then Alexander heard the shriek of the revenant from above. In spite of the thrill of terror that shot through him, he knew they would be saved by the beast. He withdrew his vial of night-wisp dust again and raised the light high into the air. He heard the revenant shriek again as it moved off toward the pursuing soldiers. Alexander looked around in the forest for some form of shelter but saw nothing suitable. They kept moving, although much more quickly now that they were once again traveling with the aid of light.

In the distance, the revenant shrieked again, followed by the screams of men in the dark. Alexander smiled grimly. Sometimes the best tactic was introducing one enemy to another.

They pressed on for another hour through the night. The rain of the unnatural storm subsided completely as they moved out of the range of the wizard's power. When they found a small cave formed by three large boulders piled on top of each other, they stopped to rest and heal.

Alexander decided that warmth was more important than revealing their position, so he started gathering wood for a fire.

Anatoly joined him without a word.

Lucky helped Conner sit up and put a pack behind him to rest against.

"Drink this," he said, holding up a vial of clear-looking liquid.

Evelyn stopped him. "What are you giving my brother?" she demanded.

Lucky sat back, weary from the battle and exhausted from traveling through the forest at night in the rain. He was bruised and beaten up himself and in no mood for an argument.

"Don't be difficult, Evelyn," Conner said as he took the vial and downed the contents.

"The draught will make you sleep," Lucky said. "When you wake, your wound should be mostly healed. Given the severity, it may take a few days for it to heal completely."

Conner nodded and motioned for his sister to help him lie back down. Soon he was breathing deeply and evenly.

Alexander and Anatoly returned from the darkness and stacked the wood they'd gathered, then began stacking stones in a circle for a fire.

"You said you would answer my questions," Evelyn said.

Alexander gave her a look that stopped her from saying another word. "I will, but not tonight. For now, go help Jack gather some more firewood."

She looked surprised to be told what to do but then looked over at her brother and seemed to make up her mind. With a huff, she got up and stomped off into the woods with Jack trailing behind her wearing a mischievous grin.

Lucky tended to the multiple injuries sustained by nearly everyone and then they went to sleep. Jataan stood watch in the night with a vial of night-wisp dust in his pocket just in case the revenant came back. Since they had only four hours or so before dawn, Jack split the watch with the battle mage so each of them could get a couple of hours of sleep. They rose at dawn and broke camp quickly. The enemy soldiers weren't nearly far enough away and Alexander didn't want them to get any closer.

Conner had awakened with a groan but he was able to get to his feet and even heft his pack. Most of their minor injuries were healed by Lucky's magical salve. Alexander's shoulder still ached, and he could see that the gash in Anatoly's leg gave him some stiffness.

They ate a simple breakfast as they walked in the early dawn.

"Now will someone answer my questions?" Evelyn asked with exasperation.

"Don't be difficult, Evelyn," Conner said to his sister. "This is Alexander Reishi, the Sovereign of the Seven Isles, and he just saved your life. Say thank you and be nice to the man."

"But, how can that be? He has a Thinblade but he says it's not father's. Yet I thought his was the only one that survived the Reishi War. Also, I thought Phane was the only Reishi still alive in the Seven Isles and he was the one who ordered that I be abducted."

Conner answered his sister's questions as they walked through the forest. With every answer, she asked a series of new questions. Alexander walked ahead and listened to the exchange to keep his mind off the threats they faced. In some ways Evelyn reminded him of Abigail. They were both inquisitive and unafraid to ask questions although Abigail was a bit more tactful. He felt a sudden pang of loneliness. His sister was his best friend and he missed her. He trusted that she was alive and well but that did nothing to fill the void created by her absence.

Chloe was keeping watch for Alexander from the safety of the aether. From there she could see everything that transpired in the world of time and substance but she wasn't vulnerable to detection or harm. She reported that two hundred men armed with bows and swords were about an hour behind and force-marching through the forest. Alexander wasn't worried about the swords, but the bows had him concerned. A large number of men armed with bows was more than they were able to defeat. Without adequate cover, they would be cut down in the first volley. Alexander stepped up the pace even as the terrain became steeper and more treacherous.

Evelyn came up beside him breathing heavily from the exertion but not complaining about the pace. "My brother explained who you are and what's going on," she said. "I just wanted to thank you for coming to save me. I know I wasn't very polite to you and I'm sorry for that."

Alexander chuckled. "Think nothing of it, Evelyn. You've been through an ordeal that would put anyone in a foul mood."

"If I may ask, where are we going?" she said.

Alexander hesitated for a moment, trying to decide how much to reveal to her before he spoke. "There's a ruined keep in the mountains. We're headed there."

"Those ruins are supposed to be haunted," Evelyn said cautiously. "Are you sure that's the best way to go?"

"I don't know about best, but it's where we're going," Alexander replied. "We have two hundred men armed with bows about an hour behind us. We need someplace with cover and the high ground to face them or we're all dead. Those ruins are our only hope, and if they are haunted, that might actually be helpful. Those soldiers have probably never seen a ghost before—but I have."

She was silent for a while as she thought over what he'd said. "Why did you come to rescue me? I mean, you obviously have more important things to be doing than trying to save one person. From what Conner tells me, your home of Ruatha is at war and you're way out here with just a handful of men. I don't understand."

Alexander let her ramble until he was sure she was finished before he tried to answer. "As long as Phane had you under his thumb, your father couldn't commit his troops to help fight my enemies. I need his help, so I did the one thing for him that he needed more than anything else: I protected his family."

"So what, I'm just a piece on a board to you?" She seemed agitated that Alexander had motives other than simply rescuing her.

He looked at her with a sidelong glance and shook his head. "You're not a piece on a board to me. You're an innocent young woman who was being held for leverage against her father. In answer to your real question, yes, I do have multiple reasons for being here."

"Like what?" she shot back.

Alexander smiled to himself. Despite her recent abduction and imprisonment, she was still feisty.

He thought about his answer for a moment as he moved through the thinning forest of the mountain lowlands. "As you've said, my homeland has been invaded. But I don't have enough soldiers to defeat the enemy's army. As long as Phane had you, your father was powerless to act. With you safe, your father is free to throw his lot in with me and help me defeat the invading army on Ruatha. Second, Phane was building an army here in Grafton. I don't want him to gain a foothold here because war here would destroy much of your food crops. Famine would follow. Thousands would die. Finally, there's something I need on this island. Coming to get you provided a logical pretense for my enemies that prevented them from seeing my true intent."

She frowned, furrowing her brow deeply as she processed what he said. "What are you here to find?" she asked with genuine curiosity.

He could see Conner perk up with curiosity as well. Alexander had been careful to avoid the subject of the adept wizard's keep for fear that Phane might be listening. Now that they were so close, he knew the Reishi Arch Mage wouldn't be able to interfere.

"I'm not actually sure," Alexander said, "but I know that it's important and I hope it will help me fight Phane."

Before Evelyn could ask another question, Chloe buzzed into existence in a bright ball of light. "There's danger ahead, My Love. Ganglings are lying in wait on the ridge above the ravine we must pass through to reach the ruins."

"That complicates things," Alexander muttered to himself. "How many did you see?"

"I counted five," Chloe said. "Each has a big pile of rocks."

"Five ganglings with the high ground and ample weapons," Anatoly said as he shook his head. "Might be time to rethink our path."

"I concur with Master Grace," Jataan said. "Given the superiority of their position, they are too dangerous to engage."

Alexander nodded, then turned to Lucky. "I don't suppose you have anything in that bag of yours that might get us through the ravine without them seeing us."

"I'm afraid not. I don't have another potion of fog and even that would only conceal us. The ganglings might still get lucky with one of their rocks."

Jack cocked his head and smiled. "Just exactly how big is that bag of yours on the inside?"

Lucky blinked and then frowned for a moment before he smiled broadly. "It's quite large actually. It certainly has more space than I've had a chance to fill up. I think your plan might just work."

"What plan?" Evelyn asked with the frustration of someone who didn't like to be kept in the dark.

Lucky sat down and started emptying the items from his magical bag. A minute or two later, he had a large pile of stuff: his bedroll, rations, waterskins, oil flasks, and stacks of vials, bags, pouches, small boxes, canisters, jars, and metal tubes. Some containers were full while others were awaiting the next ingredient that Lucky might find in his travels. He tipped the empty bag upside down and smiled as he handed it to Jack.

"I would suggest Lieutenant Grudge go first," Lucky said. "If he can fit, then everyone else will be easy."

Boaberous frowned in confusion. Jack set the bag out on the ground and opened it up. It was a remarkable sight—the interior was several times bigger than the exterior. Grudge looked to Jataan, who nodded toward the bag. The giant shrugged and carefully lowered himself inside. He nearly fit with only his head protruding from the opening.

Jack smiled to himself as he took his cloak off and handed it to Alexander, hoisted the bag's strap over his shoulder and then threw his cloak over himself and his bagful of Boaberous.

"I shall return," Jack said with a flourish as he tossed his hood up and flickered out of sight.

They didn't have to wait too long before Alexander saw Jack's colors moving toward them in the forest. He flickered into view and startled several of the others with a smile of mischief.

One by one, he ferried everyone past the threat of the ganglings to a safe spot under the cover of a large rock overhang. Anatoly went last, right after all of Lucky's belongings. Jack and Anatoly were able to hear the enemy soldiers coming through the forest less than a mile away during their trip through the narrow mountain ravine.

As Lucky was packing his things carefully back into his magical bag, they heard the shouts of soldiers in the distance behind them as the ganglings sprang their ambush.

"Time to move," Alexander said as he motioned for Boaberous to take point. The giant nodded and proceeded into the rocky foothills ahead. The sounds of battle behind them faded as they moved higher into the mountains.

Not an hour later, Boaberous stopped suddenly and pointed toward a rocky outcropping across a ravine. Alexander saw a man standing on a rock looking in their direction. He had no living aura.

"He seems to be everywhere we go," Anatoly said as he stepped up next to Alexander.

Alexander nodded, "Except he's not really there."

A moment later the mysterious man turned to shadowy smoke and blew away on the gentle breeze. Alexander puzzled over him. He hadn't posed a threat . . . yet. He didn't have the colors of a living being but that didn't mean he couldn't be dangerous.

"Keep an eye out for him," he said.

Chapter 24

They continued into the mountains toward the ruined keep. The very real threat of the enemy soldiers was not too far behind them. They needed the cover of the keep if they were going to have any chance against the numbers they faced, but Alexander was eager to get there for his own reasons. He nurtured the hope that the ancient ruins contained answers about his magical calling that would help him master his wizardry and give him the power to face Phane with at least some chance of victory.

They rounded a corner and caught the first glimpse of the ruins. The ancient keep had been built on a rocky outcropping jutting out of the side of the mountain. There were steep cliffs on three sides and a broken and treacherous road that wound up a series of switchbacks on the side facing the mountain. The walls were crumbling in several places and the main tower had collapsed, leaving a line of scattered stone at the base of the cliff wall that had long since grown over with moss and lichen. The place was dark and foreboding, but Alexander felt more certain than ever that answers about his calling would be found within.

The old man in grey robes was standing on a broken wall. When they stopped to peer up at the keep, they saw him abruptly change into a form that looked almost like a dragon except it was made of smoky black shadow. It glided down toward them with frightening speed and raised its giant black talons to strike.

Boaberous threw a javelin. Evelyn screamed. Jack flickered out of sight. Alexander stood defiantly and watched the deadly looking apparition come for him. He could see that it had no colors, no life, and no magic. His normal vision told him it was a creature of terrifying size and power with otherworldly qualities, but his second sight told him it wasn't really there.

"Do you see that, Little One?" he asked Chloe without speaking.

"No, My Love," she said silently in his mind. "I see nothing."

It roared in preparation for its attack and everyone scattered, except Alexander. He stood and faced it, willing his fear into check. In the last moment, Jataan darted back into the path of the creature and pulled Alexander to the ground. Just before it would have reached them, the shadowy dragon dissipated and faded into nothingness.

Anatoly picked Alexander up and set him on his feet. "What were you thinking?" he said harshly. "That thing would've killed you!"

Alexander looked Anatoly in the eye and slowly shook his head. "It wasn't even there," he said. "Whatever it was, it never had any substance."

"And you thought you'd prove it by letting it tear you to pieces?" Anatoly asked. "How many times have I told you to err on the side of caution? Did you learn nothing training alongside your brother?"

"I learned to use my mind and rely on reason," Alexander said gently yet firmly. "That's exactly what I'm doing. That thing didn't have any colors and Chloe couldn't even see it. It was an illusion."

"Maybe," Anatoly said, "or maybe it was some form of magic you've never encountered before."

Alexander shrugged. "Whatever it was, it disappeared before it struck, but I understand your concern. I probably shouldn't have tested it with my life."

Anatoly harrumphed, then walked several steps away toward the ruins and stopped, looking up at the crumbling structure.

"It looked plenty real to me," Evelyn said, still visibly shaken. "Maybe it lives in the ruins and doesn't want to be bothered."

"Our course is set," Alexander said as he stared at the dark and foreboding keep. "We make our stand in those ruins or the enemy will run us to ground and pick us apart."

"Evelyn may have a point," Conner said. "We know what's chasing us. If we pick our battlefield, someplace narrow and confined, we might stand a chance against them. Whatever's haunting those ruins could be far more dangerous than a company of soldiers."

"What if the wizard's with them?" Alexander asked, without looking away from the keep that he'd pinned his hopes on.

Before anyone could answer, an arrow struck him in the back and broke against his dragon-scale shirt. He stumbled forward from the force of the impact. Everyone whirled to see the commander of the enemy soldiers standing on a rock, well out of normal bow range, nocking another arrow. Soldiers were moving around the rock and up the ravine about eight hundred feet away. Alexander looked down at the broken arrow and saw the fading colors of a magical aura.

"Move," he commanded.

No one questioned his order. Boaberous took point and headed for the base of the road that led to the ruins. The path was strewn with rocks and scree which made it treacherous and difficult to navigate quickly. Alexander nearly fell but caught his balance. Lucky stepped on a rock and turned his ankle. He cried out as he went down. Anatoly picked him up and helped him up the path as Jataan brought up the rear.

The soldiers in the distance had the scent of their prey and were closing the distance quickly. When Alexander glanced back, he saw a flood of men washing through the ravine toward them. There were many more than two hundred.

The road leading up to the keep was cut into the steep rock face of the butte that formed the foundation of the ancient fortress. It switched back and forth eight or ten times before it reached the gatehouse high above. The first four legs of the road were easily passable in spite of the many boulders and rocks in the way but the turn leading to the fifth switchback was crumbled and broken, leaving only a craggy rock face some twenty feet from the lower section of road to the one above.

Alexander looked down and was relieved to see that the enemy soldiers hadn't yet reached the base of the cliff. They still had time.

"What now!" Evelyn said. "I told you this was a bad idea."

"Don't be difficult, Evelyn," Conner said.

Alexander ignored them as he tried to formulate a plan. They might be able to climb the rock face but it would be slow going. He wasn't sure if they had enough time to reach the relative safety of the higher sections of road before the soldiers were within bow range.

"If I may, does anyone have a rope?" Jack asked.

Anatoly nodded as he unslung his pack. After only a moment of digging, he produced a neatly coiled length of sturdy rope and handed it to Jack.

"Excellent," Jack said as slung it across his shoulder. "I won't be a minute."

With that, Jack started to climb up the rock face. He seemed to know instinctively where to put his hands and feet and found purchase where there didn't appear to be any. He moved methodically and steadily toward the top without a slip or a misstep. Once on top, he secured the rope around a large stone, easily heavy enough to support even Boaberous, and tossed the line down to the road below.

Alexander smiled with mischief at Evelyn as he took the end of the rope and climbed easily to the top. With a little assistance for Lucky and Evelyn, they all made it up the rock wall before the first of the soldiers reached the base of the road.

Alexander looked up and found a point on the ruined wall above where they would have a clear view and pointed it out to Anatoly.

"We can hold them off from there, provided they don't find another way up."

Anatoly nodded his skeptical approval of the plan. "And provided there isn't anything up there that doesn't want houseguests."

"There is that," Alexander said. "Truth is, I figure the revenant probably lives here."

He didn't wait to see the look of consternation that Anatoly gave him as he headed up the road toward the gatehouse. There were a few places that were broken and falling away but there was enough of a path to make it through without the need of a rope.

The gatehouse was little more than a pile of rubble framed by the four corners of the ancient structure that were still partially intact. Alexander carefully picked his way over the mound of old stones into the courtyard of the ruined keep. In its glory it would have been a modest yet very secure fortress. The walls once stood a good ten feet above the level of the courtyard. They had been wide and sturdy with a six-foot walkway along the top. Now they were crumbling and broken with only a few sections rising to the height they once stood.

Once, the manor house had proudly occupied the center of the two-hundred-foot-wide sanctuary. Now it was only a shadow of its former splendor. The ceiling had collapsed, crushing most of the third and second floors under its weight. The outer walls were still relatively intact but they were buckling in places and the mortar was long eroded away by the weather. The main doors leading into the entry hall were gone, long ago fallen from their hinges and rotted into dust. The main tower that had once risen from the right rear corner of the building had collapsed and fallen down to the base of the cliffs below. The smaller tower that formed the left rear corner still stood, although it leaned slightly toward the outer wall as if it might topple at any moment.

Anatoly and Jataan came up beside Alexander and appraised the dilapidated structure.

"I'm going to take a look at our defenses," Anatoly said after a few moments. Jataan nodded to Boaberous who dutifully followed after Anatoly. Jack helped Lucky sit down on a nearby rock, and Conner stopped to look at the ruin with his sister.

"Now what?" Evelyn asked. "We're trapped up here."

Alexander chuckled without turning. "You were right when you said she could be difficult, Conner. She reminds me of Abigail when she was younger. In answer to your question, Princess Evelyn, we defend against the enemy.

"Lucky, we have some time. You'd better tend to your ankle. Conner, take your sister and go help Anatoly," Alexander commanded.

Evelyn started to protest but Conner forestalled her with a hard look. She frowned and stomped off after her brother.

"She's quite a handful," Lucky said as he started unlacing his boot.

Alexander nodded, smiling. "Makes me miss Abigail," he said quietly to himself.

Lucky and Jack nodded their agreement in unison.

Alexander took a deep breath and sighed. "There's more to this keep than a defensible position. When I asked the sovereigns about my calling, they told me that I'm an adept. Apparently there have only been two before me. One of them used to live here."

Lucky stopped applying healing salve to his twisted ankle and looked up. "And you hope to learn something about your calling in these ruins?"

Alexander nodded as he sat down on a rock. "The sovereigns suggested that this was the best chance I had to learn something useful."

"You were wise to keep your true intent to yourself," Jataan said. "Had Phane discovered your purpose, he would have been waiting here when you arrived."

"I just hope there's something in these ruins that can help me," Alexander said. "The sovereigns said that an adept's power is great but only within the limited confines of a small number of magical abilities."

"That explains a great deal," Lucky said.

"Hopefully there's something in there," Alexander said pointing toward the ruins, "that will explain more. We have a few hours of daylight left. Jataan and I are going to take a quick look around inside. Jack, I'd like you to stay with Lucky while the healing salve does its work. When Anatoly comes back, let him know where we went."

Jack nodded as he sat down on his pack. "Be careful. There's no telling what's taken up residence in there."

Alexander smiled as he drew the Thinblade and headed for the ruins with his vial of night-wisp dust in hand. Jataan followed a step behind and to his left.

The entry hall was still largely intact except for several holes in the vaulted ceilings where debris from the collapse of the building had broken through and littered the floor. He surveyed the large room, looking for exits. Three doorways led out, one on each wall but the doors were rotted away.

Alexander picked the doorway to the right and started for it when he saw the footprint in the hard-packed dirt of the floor. He knelt to examine it and knew in an instant that it wasn't made by a man. He raised the night-wisp dust higher to cast his light farther and went to the door with caution.

The place was cold and quiet, the air still and dank. It reminded

Alexander of a tomb. They quickly searched the small series of rooms to the right of the main hall and discovered that they'd once been a dining hall and kitchen with a number of pantries, storage rooms, and servants' quarters.

The rooms to the left of the main hall were the remains of a library and a study. Alexander's heart sank when he realized that the wizard's collection of books had long since rotted to dust. He searched carefully but discovered nothing of any use or value. Everything in the place had succumbed to time and the elements.

They returned to the main room and carefully approached the door opposite the entrance to the ruins. It led to a sitting room and a large master bedchamber. The skeleton of a staircase led up to the floors above but Alexander judged that the ancient wood was so rotten and aged that it wouldn't hold. The furniture that had once filled the sitting room was nothing more than moldering stains on the stone floor.

The bedchamber was the same, bereft of anything of value. Except, the closet had so rotted away that a section of the stone wall was exposed, revealing a hidden passage. Alexander searched the floor near the hidden door and discovered several more footprints—also not made by a man. He carefully and methodically probed the wall until he found the stone he was looking for. It pushed in on a swivel and revealed a small lever.

Alexander pulled the lever and a section of the stone wall swung open. When he raised his light to peer inside the passageway, he thought he saw a shadow move in the darkness. The portal opened to a stone landing that had once led to a wooden staircase. The wood had long ago turned to dust, leaving a drop of ten feet or so to the level below. When he held his night-wisp dust out to cast light into the hole in the floor, the shadows moved again.

Then he heard a scream. The intensity of the piercing wail reverberated around the little room and seemed to penetrate into the depths of his psyche in waves. Fear washed over him, momentarily freezing him in place before he could flee into the safety of that place in his mind where fear couldn't reach.

It was the revenant and it wasn't happy about being disturbed. Fortunately, the light of the night-wisp dust kept the dark creature at bay while Alexander and Jataan struggled to overcome the fear induced by its unnatural scream. Alexander stepped back and closed the door to the secret passage. Jataan broke free of the grip of fear a moment later.

When they returned to the entry hall, Anatoly and Boaberous burst in with weapons at the ready.

"We'll talk outside," Alexander said as he headed for the exit. Once outside, he looked up to the sky to gauge the hours of light they had left. It was late afternoon, only a few hours from dusk.

"Was that what it sounded like?" Anatoly asked.

Alexander nodded, still thinking about his next move.

"That might be a problem, considering the enemy below has several hundred soldiers and they're making preparations to attack," Anatoly said.

"How are the defenses?" Alexander asked.

"Good enough for now," Anatoly said. "The only way up is the road and we can defend it easily by tossing stones down on them. Trouble is, we can't get out of here and we're going to run out of food and water sooner or later."

"The wizard will be here long before that happens," Alexander said. "Once he starts calling lightning down on us, we won't stand a chance."

Jack and Lucky came up to the group.

"Was that a revenant we heard?" Jack asked.

Alexander nodded, "The revenant lives in the rooms beneath the keep. When night falls, it'll come out to feed and defend its lair. Fortunately, the night-wisp dust seems to keep it at bay, which means it'll wreak havoc on the soldiers below rather than attack us. If we can just make it until dark, the Regency soldiers will have more than enough to worry about."

Without warning, a dozen corpses rose straight up out of the ground surrounding them. They looked like men who'd been dead for months, with rotting flesh and broken bodies, some with terrible wounds that left bone exposed. The dozen animated corpses started shambling toward the six of them, groaning as they closed in around them.

Alexander was startled at first, but when he saw that the creatures had no colors, he relaxed and waited even as his friends drew weapons and prepared to meet the attack.

Boaberous was the first to strike. He brought his hammer down on one of the zombies with a blow that crushed the dead man into a broken heap on the ground. Anatoly brought his axe down in a diagonal strike, cutting another in half. Jataan drew his sword and decapitated another followed by taking the leg of the next.

Alexander watched and waited. He knew the zombies weren't real but he had no way of proving his certainty to his friends, especially since the creatures seemed to fall from the onslaught of attacks being leveled at them.

"What are they fighting?" Chloe asked without speaking.

"Illusions," Alexander replied to her silently.

"Why aren't you fighting?" Anatoly shouted as he felled another of the slow-moving animated corpses.

"Because they're not real," Alexander said. As he spoke, the zombies turned to black smoke and evaporated in seconds, leaving no trace of their existence.

"I'm getting really tired of that," Anatoly growled.

Before they could finish their discussion, Evelyn came running up. "The soldiers are coming!"

She didn't stop or wait for a response, but turned and ran back to help her brother. They all followed her to the section of wall that stood over the broken switchback.

The enemy was advancing up the road with shields raised. There were easily a hundred men with many more formed up below, well out of range of any stone they might throw. The soldiers' plan seemed simple enough. The unit advancing up the road would try to enter the keep while the unit at the base of the road would provide cover fire with their bows.

Alexander heard the commander of the archers order the first volley. "Duck!" he yelled.

They took cover to avoid the hundred arrows rising toward them. Many struck the base of the wall while others overshot and arced over the broken wall, falling into the courtyard.

Everyone took up a stone and went to the edge, where they saw three soldiers trying to climb to the top. They tossed their stones and the three men fell into the soldiers below. Another volley of arrows lifted toward them from the archers and they took cover again. Arrows clattered against what remained of the face of the wall and whizzed past over their heads.

They tossed another volley of stones into the soldiers on the road, knocking two over the edge and wounding several more. More arrows rose up to meet them, but this time only half of the archers fired. They took cover again, but when they went back to the edge of the wall to throw more stones, another volley of arrows nearly caught them in the open. They dropped back quickly and managed to avoid being hit but they weren't able to keep some of the soldiers from climbing to the top of the wall and securing ropes so the rest could follow more quickly.

"Can you hit those archers with a rock from here?" Alexander asked Anatoly.

He grinned as he found a stone half the size of a man's head. He moved down the wall to get a better vantage point. Powered by the magic of his belt, Anatoly heaved the stone into the ranks of the archers far below. Alexander watched the stone sail through the air. It was a powerful throw that he could never match. It hit an archer and the lightly armored man crumbled.

"Little One, can you see what's happening below without putting yourself in danger?" Alexander asked Chloe in his mind.

"Of course, My Love, I can see everything around me in the world of time and substance when I'm in the aether."

"Good." Alexander sent his sight to her and looked through her eyes. He sat down and focused on orienting himself to his new point of view.

"Anatoly, I want you to focus on the archers. Keep moving so they don't know where you're going to be next. Everyone else, start throwing stones over the edge and listen to my guidance for direction and distance. Chloe is going to spot for us."

With their new plan in place, they threw a steady stream of stones over the edge of the wall without getting close enough to the edge to risk being shot with an arrow. Alexander called out distance and direction corrections and they followed his instructions diligently.

Anatoly moved from place to place along the wall, taking shots at the archers. Each stone he cast killed another archer, while each volley the archers loosed depleted their supply of arrows.

The battle lasted only ten minutes before the soldiers withdrew. They suffered many casualties under the steady stream of rocks cast down on them. Each stone was deadly from such a height and, with Alexander's guidance, accurate enough to prevent all but a handful of soldiers from reaching the crumbled gatehouse. Those few who did met Jataan and died quickly.

The remaining enemy soldiers assembled not too far from the keep but well out of normal bow range and began making camp. Alexander and Jataan appraised the situation from atop the wall while Anatoly prepared stacks of stones in a few strategic locations and the rest of Alexander's friends gathered arrows that had fallen in the courtyard.

"Lord Reishi, I can reach them from here if you permit me to use your bow," Jataan said.

"You can really shoot that far?" Alexander asked.

"Quite accurately."

Alexander chuckled, "Good, but let them get settled in first."

This time it was Jataan's turn to chuckle.

They gave the enemy time to pitch their tents and start cooking dinner before Jataan took Alexander's bow and tested the string. He nodded his approval then nocked an arrow. They'd gathered over a hundred of the enemy's arrows that were still flight worthy and set them out on the wall closest to the enemy encampment. Jataan drew, took aim and loosed his first arrow. What followed left Alexander and his companions speechless. Jataan loosed five arrows before the first hit its mark. He drew and fired so quickly that it was hard to believe he could be taking aim, yet every arrow dropped another enemy soldier. Within moments the camp below was in disarray. After twenty men lay dead, the rest were in a panic, scattering into the surrounding rocks to find cover from the sudden onslaught. Once the enemy had all taken refuge, Jataan stopped.

"Huh," Anatoly said, shaking his head in wonder.

"Well done, Commander P'Tal," Alexander said. "Keep an eye on them until dark. If they give you an opportunity, take a shot but don't stay here past sundown. We're going to make preparations for tonight."

Jataan nodded and stood his post.

Without a word, Boaberous took Jataan's place as Alexander's shadow.

Alexander picked a place in the middle of the ruined keep's courtyard and placed a stone.

"Clear a space twenty feet from this point in every direction," Alexander said. "We're going to make a magic circle to help protect us against the revenant."

Lucky, Jack, and Anatoly nodded and started working to clear the debris and stones from the area. Conner and Evelyn looked dubious.

"Do you really think that will work?" Evelyn asked.

"I honestly don't know," Alexander said, "but it might and I'm willing to try anything to get an edge."

"I'm afraid," Evelyn said in a small voice. She was no longer being difficult. Her façade had failed. After all she'd been through, she could no longer mask the strain of it behind a brave face.

Alexander stopped clearing stones and stood to face the young princess. "I am too," he said. "There's no shame in being afraid, especially given what we're up against. The only real question is, how will you face your fear?"

"I don't know," she said with a slight tremor in her voice. "This is all so much bigger than me. I feel powerless to do anything about it."

"All we can do is all we can do," Alexander said. "Courage isn't about power, it's about making good decisions in spite of our fear."

"I've heard stories about the revenant," Evelyn said. "Some say it can't be killed."

"Those stories are wrong," Alexander said. "It's hard to kill, but it will die if we cut its head off."

"How can you know that?" she asked with a little more vigor. She was working through her fear and her contrarian nature was shining through.

"The Sovereign Stone lets me talk to the previous Reishi Sovereigns. The

Sixth Sovereign, Malachi Reishi, created the first revenant. He told me how to kill it."

"We faced one on our way to rescue you," Conner said. "It didn't like the vial of light that Alexander has in his pocket. I think we'll be safe enough if we stay in the light."

"That's part two of my plan," Alexander said. "We'll set out our night-wisp dust on three stones so the light overlaps. When the revenant comes out, we'll all stand ready and see what it does. If it attacks into the light and past the circle, then we'll kill it."

He started drawing a giant magical circle that would be big enough to enclose all of them for the night. He worked carefully to ensure that the grooves he cut into the packed dirt of the courtyard were well defined and faithfully represented the image of the magic circle he'd learned from the Reishi Sovereigns.

After several minutes of work, they had a space forty feet in diameter that was cleared of all debris and completely enclosed in the circle. Alexander directed the construction of three pillars of stone three feet tall and flat on top, then placed his vial of night-wisp dust on top of one of them. Jack placed his vial on top of another and Lucky placed his vial on the third. The light cast by the night-wisp dust filled the entire circle with bright, warm light.

Before dusk fell, Jataan returned to the rest of them and handed Alexander his bow. "The soldiers have retreated out of my range and are remaking their camp. Also, I believe the wizard has arrived with more troops."

Alexander looked up and appraised the clear sky above. The sun had fallen past the horizon but the stars hadn't yet started to show through the deep blue. It would be a cold night, especially without a fire. The ruins were bereft of any wood and they hadn't packed any with them. He fought to keep his fatigue from overwhelming him. None of them had slept the previous night and the day had been spent fleeing from the enemy. Everyone was exhausted, but between the soldiers below and the revenant within, there would be little rest for anyone.

"Keep an eye on the weather," Alexander said. "I'm more worried about the wizard's magic than anything else. We've done all we can to protect against the revenant, and the soldiers won't be able to get enough men up here in the dark to pose any real threat so long as we stay alert."

He stopped and looked at his friends. They were all worried and weary but he also saw resolve. He decided it was time to reveal the rest of his plan, the part he knew they would like the least. He took a deep breath and plunged in.

"Once the revenant comes out to feed on the soldiers below, we'll find its lair and seal it from inside so it can't get back in."

"Won't that make it mad?" Evelyn asked.

"I hope so," Alexander said. "I want it to spend the entire night terrorizing the enemy soldiers. Maybe we'll even get lucky and it'll kill the wizard. Whatever else happens, we need to get inside this mountain. I believe there's information about my magic that could prove to be the deciding factor in this entire war. As it stands, I can't beat Phane, and without a greater understanding of my magic, that will never change. This place is the best chance I have of discovering how to use my powers to their fullest extent. Of more immediate concern is the wizard and the army encamped around us. We're vulnerable to the wizard's magic out in the open, but inside the mountain, his magic can't reach us. As for the army, we can't hold them off forever. When they come, I would much prefer to face them in a confined space rather than out in the open."

"How do you plan to get out once we're sealed in?" Conner asked.

"We can always cut our way out," Alexander said. "There's also every possibility that we'll find a secret passage leading out of the ruins. Wizards are nothing if not cautious."

"It's starting," Jack said, pointing to the sky.

The stars were just starting to shine through the fading blue but they were being occluded by dark and angry clouds forming far too quickly overhead. Darkness fell rapidly as the light of day faded and the clouds grew into a swirling vortex above them. The temperature fell several degrees and the wind started to blow.

Alexander knew his plan depended on timing. He needed the revenant to come out of its lair before the wizard could start calling lightning down on them. From their experience with the wizard's power the night before, it was clear that he could easily kill them all if they remained out in the open and stationary. But they didn't dare venture into the lair of the revenant while the creature remained within.

When Alexander heard the shrill scream come from the ruins, the fear it evoked mingled with the thrill of his plan taking form. He was hoping beyond hope that the answers to his many questions would be found in the chambers and passages below the keep.

The terrifying creature stepped out of the door of the manor and screamed again. The sudden fear was primal. It engulfed Alexander, freezing him to the spot where he stood. He withdrew quickly into the safety of that corner of his mind where emotion was distant and powerless, slowly regaining control over his body.

His companions were also frozen with the unnatural fear created by the revenant's scream. Jataan broke through the fear first, followed a moment later by Lucky. Everyone else remained paralyzed. The rain was just starting and the wind was blowing. Flickers of lightning danced through the swirling vortex of black clouds high overhead, but the light of the night-wisp dust was clear and bright.

Then something happened that Alexander hadn't counted on. A second and then a third revenant stepped out of the ruins and screamed in unison. The sound was deafening and palpable. It penetrated through Alexander and found its way into the depths of his psyche, awakening a basic and instinctual terror. For a long moment, he couldn't overcome it. He felt panic well up within and threaten to drive him mad.

When Evelyn screamed and ran from the protection of the light, Alexander's fear-induced paralysis broke. She sprinted toward the crumbled gatehouse, fleeing from the revenants in blind panic. Two of the three revenants launched into the night sky, while the third and largest slowly advanced toward Alexander's paralyzed companions.

Alexander spun and dashed toward Evelyn. She'd lost all reason in the face of the magically induced fear and was headed for the edge of the ruins. He ran with all the speed he could muster, closing the distance to her before she reached the mound of rubble that used to be the gatehouse. With one hand he grabbed her arm and turned her toward him and away from the cliff's edge. When she wheeled around to face him, Alexander saw nothing but terror in her eyes. There was no rational thought, no reason, only the most basic need to escape danger. She looked up past him and screamed again.

The revenant landed in the middle of Alexander's back, pushing him on top of Evelyn. The beast's clawed hands pinned him to the ground and crushed the air from his lungs. He struggled to draw breath as it sank its fangs into the left side of his neck.

He felt a sharp pain at first that stunned him anew but the pain quickly turned to a numbing coldness as he felt the strength of his will sapped from him. The numbing coldness spread quickly from the wound as the revenant drained first his strength and then his life force itself.

The second beast landed nearby, yanked Evelyn from under Alexander and clamped its fangs into the side of her neck. She tried to scream but only managed a helpless whimper.

Alexander struggled to resist but his energy was waning. His arms and legs felt too heavy to lift. The numbing fatigue and penetrating coldness threatened to overwhelm him. Just as he was about to surrender, he felt a thin line of hope as Chloe linked herself to him and fed his life force with her own. Her love for him sustained him and gave him the strength he needed to renew his struggle against the beast.

He jerked free and rolled to face the creature, sending the revenant toppling off him. With a great effort he gained his knees and then staggered to his feet. Through his weariness, he assessed the situation with his all around sight. He was so tired and drained that he had to remind himself to care about the outcome.

Evelyn was collapsed on the ground like a discarded rag doll, the revenant clamped onto her neck. The beast feeding on her was oblivious to everything transpiring around it as it fed. The one that had bitten Alexander was drawing itself up to scream again. Somewhere in the distant fog of his mind, he knew he wouldn't have the strength to resist the fear of its scream in his weakened state. He staggered in an effort to remain standing.

Within the circle of light, Jataan and Lucky broke free of the paralyzing effects of the revenants' screams. Jataan sprinted toward Alexander with magical speed. Lucky rummaged around in his bag.

The third revenant launched itself into the air, spiraling into the sky.

Then the world exploded. A bolt of argent-white lightning stabbed down from the swirling clouds overhead and struck the remains of the tower on the left rear corner of the ruins. The lightning dazzled Alexander, leaving him blinded and stunned. The revenant that had bitten him screamed in pain at the sudden onslaught of brightness and launched itself into the sky. The one feeding on Evelyn fell back, simpering and mewling from the pain of the light.

The tower exploded as the thunder of the lightning strike reached them. The ground shook. The force of the explosion sent Alexander onto his back, gasping for breath once again. Evelyn lay helpless and pale where the revenant had left her. His companions still in the grip of the revenants' screams tumbled to the ground as the spell was broken.

Jataan managed to keep his feet and his wits even in the face of the sudden detonation. He darted between them with such speed that Alexander only caught a blur before the battle mage cleanly decapitated the revenant that had fed on Evelyn. In unison, the other two screamed again from somewhere in the darkness of the magically tortured sky. The world lit up again as another bolt of lightning struck the ruins on the right rear corner and shattered part of the building into rubble.

Jataan stood, sword in hand, and watched the sky for any sign of a threat as Anatoly and Boaberous charged up to the site of the brief battle.

"Take them to the light," Jataan commanded.

Anatoly didn't miss a beat; he scooped Alexander up and tossed him over his shoulder, then turned and ran for the light flooding the magic circle. Boaberous carried Evelyn. Jataan followed. They lay them both down and moved away to stand guard while Lucky went to work on their wounds. He slathered healing salve on Alexander's neck, then did the same for Evelyn, handing Conner a bandage before he returned to Alexander to bind his wound. Evelyn woke with a start and tried to struggle with her brother for a moment before she realized who he was. Then she collapsed into his arms and wept.

Alexander schooled his mind and conserved his strength. He kept his eyes closed but assessed the scene with his all around sight. They had succeeded in drawing out the revenants. All that was left was to get into the dungeons beneath the ruins. Then they would have the time they needed to recover their strength while the enemy faced the revenants.

He reached up and grabbed Lucky's robe to pull him closer. "Into the ruins," he whispered with a great effort.

The revenant had sapped so much of his strength that he felt unconsciousness claiming him in spite of his struggle to remain awake. As he slipped into darkness, the world shook again in a brilliant white flash.

Chapter 25

Lacy held her breath. They'd been fleeing south for the past week with soldiers always just behind them. Wizard Saul had used his magic to deceive their pursuers several times, buying them precious hours to gain distance from them. The week had been terrifying and exhausting. And now that she was so close to the Fellenden family crypt, the enemy had caught up with them.

She and the wizard crouched behind a moss-covered rock at the edge of the forested area surrounding the entrance to the crypt, the location of which had been chosen at the end of the Reishi War. It had been built overlooking the battlefield where Carlyle Fellenden had died defending the Old Law against the ambitions of Malachi Reishi and his armies. In the intervening centuries, the family had expanded the crypt to accommodate the kings of Fellenden that had died since.

It was built mostly within the stone of the rocky hilltop, the only entrance being a simple but solid stone archway and heavy door. Lacy felt in her pocket for the key and took small comfort that her father's last request was still within her reach.

She and Wizard Saul had been riding hard until Lacy's horse came up lame not a league from the crypt. They just made it on foot before the platoon of soldiers chasing them arrived on their heels.

Now they were trapped. The thirty men on horseback had immediately separated into squads of six. No doubt, they knew Lacy and Wizard Saul were on foot. The only place to hide was in the woods that covered most of the butte, giving the soldiers a limited area to search. It was only a matter of time.

Six of the soldiers were milling around the entrance of the crypt, looking for some sign that their quarry was nearby. Sounds of the other soldiers could be heard off in the distance as they searched. Lacy didn't know what to do. She had followed the lead of Wizard Saul for the entire week as he worked with magic and cunning to preserve them. Now there was nowhere left to escape, and she still had to get into the crypt before she could make her way to Ithilian.

She was exhausted, bruised, and sore. In her whole life she'd never exerted herself like she had over the past week. Before her life had been turned on its head, she was prone to losing her temper when she didn't get her way but now that the stakes were real, she found there was no time for her emotions. She had to think clearly and make good decisions or she would die, and badly.

Oddly, she found that she was stronger than she would have ever imagined. Once the initial fear had worn off and the pain of loss had settled on her, she discovered that she was angry. Not the simple petty anger at her dress being hemmed wrong but a righteous anger that fueled her and drove her to accomplish things she would have never thought possible. The people of Fellenden had done nothing to warrant the atrocities that were being inflicted on them. She was angry that they were being made to suffer, she was angry that her family had been torn asunder, but mostly she was angry that she was powerless to stop what was happening.

Over the course of the week, an idea had begun to take shape in her mind and then take root in her soul. If she survived this ordeal, she would do whatever was necessary to gain the power to protect her people.

Power had always seemed like such an abstract thing. Her father had power. People did as he told them but he never used his power for anything great or sweeping. Mostly, he concentrated on the mundane things that made life in the city possible: the supply of food, the removal of waste and garbage, the flow of water to the people and the fields. He paid attention to the army, but not a lot. He was far more likely to put great effort into negotiating with neighboring territories to avoid conflict.

The past week had taught Lacy that there was a whole different dimension to power. It could be used to destroy or it could be used to protect the innocent from those who would destroy them.

On one occasion, three days into their journey, a scout had located them. He tried to flee to tell his superiors where Lacy and Wizard Saul could be found, but Saul killed the man with a spell. It wasn't fancy or flashy, but it was effective—Wizard Saul caused the man's horse to lose control and throw him. The scout broke his neck when he fell. Saul didn't blink at what he'd done. Instead, he searched the man's belongings and took a good knife, some food, and two waterskins, along with a pouch of silver coins.

Lacy stood watching Saul search the freshly dead man with a growing sense of horror. When she confronted the wizard, he just shrugged and said that war was ugly. She thought a lot about that as they rode. By the time they reached the crypt, Lacy had promised herself that she would learn how to fight so that she could defend her people—she just had to survive first.

The six men fanned out in the area around the crypt entrance. Then one started coming straight for them.

Wizard Saul touched Lacy on the back of the head and she heard his words in her mind even though he didn't speak aloud.

"Remember your training, let it guide your hand. When the opportunity presents itself, open the crypt. I'll be right behind you."

She processed what he had said even as he started whispering words of power. At first, she couldn't imagine that he would attack six armed soldiers . . . but he was a wizard. When she thought about it for a moment, the fear of battle subsided and the anger she'd been nursing rose to the surface. These men had come to her homeland and killed her people. They were trying to kill her. She drew her knife.

Wizard Saul stood abruptly. The soldier that had been heading toward them stopped for an instant and then called out to his companions. The other five men turned as one and pulled their horses around. Saul planted his staff in the ground and spoke the final word of his incantation. The tip of his staff grew bright with a yellowish light. The light arced from the tip and hit the first man squarely in the chest. The crackling yellow fire maintained an arc from Saul's staff to the first soldier, then leapt to the next nearest soldier and then to another and finally to a fourth. The spell ran its course in the span of a few seconds, leaving four men dead with holes the size of a grapefruit burned through the center of their chests.

The remaining two soldiers called out for help as they charged. Lacy waited until their horses had enough momentum to make changing course difficult and then darted for the crypt. One of the soldiers pulled his horse around wide and tried to lash out at her, but he was too slow. The other soldier headed straight for Saul who was softly muttering words of a long-dead language. The soldier's horse reared and threw him to the ground before he reached the wizard.

Lacy fumbled for the key to the crypt as she raced for the door. She could hear the hoof beats of the horse as it came around and headed for her. The shouts of other soldiers in the distance frightened her and made her rush and she dropped the key.

"Watch out!" Saul called to her.

Lacy turned to see the soldier quickly dismounting and heading straight for her. His face was scarred and pockmarked. His teeth were yellow and crooked. His hair was stringy and greasy. And the look in his eye told her in a glance that he would have his way with her before he killed her.

She faced him in a low stance with her knife drawn and waited for his attack. He grinned as he stopped just out of range of her blade and sneered at her. Suddenly, he looked behind her and smiled. Lacy whirled to see if another man was coming, then realized her mistake in the same moment. There was nothing behind her but the door to the crypt. When she turned back to face her attacker, he grabbed her wrist with one hand and slapped her hard with the other. She was dazed for a moment while he wrenched her knife free and shoved her into the door.

When Saul called out a challenge to the soldier, the man spun to face him. Saul had just killed the man on the ground and was speaking words of power forcefully as he advanced toward the soldier threatening Lacy. But the soldier had a knife in hand. As he flipped it around and drew back to throw it at Saul, Lacy drove her boot knife into his back. He stiffened in surprise but couldn't even muster a scream. She twisted the blade the way she'd been taught so long ago and the man slumped forward off her blade to his knees.

"Well done, Lacy," Saul said. "Now open the crypt, quickly."

For a moment, she stood mesmerized by the spectacle of death caused by her hand, but her trance broke when she heard the shouts of soldiers approaching. She snatched up the key and thrust it into the lock. A tingle of magic raced over her body as she turned the key and heard a muffled click. The door swung open to reveal inky darkness beyond. Saul led two horses into the darkness without a word and motioned for her to follow. Once inside, he quickly shut the door to the crypt and spoke a few words of power in the darkness. A faint magical light leapt from the tip of his staff and traced around the outline of the door, then faded. He held up his staff and the tip glowed brightly, revealing the entrance to the family crypt of Fellenden.

Lacy had never been here before but she had heard of it in stories about her ancestors. The antechamber was about twenty feet square with a high arched ceiling and a single door on the wall opposite the entrance.

Saul whispered a few words and touched each horse in turn. They calmed and stood quiet and still. He motioned for silence and led Lacy to the door. Once they were through and the door was closed, Saul breathed a sigh of relief.

"When they discover two of their horses missing, they will assume we have taken them and fled. Hopefully, they will attempt to pick up our trail and leave this place while we search the crypt for the correct tomb."

"Won't they try to search the crypt?" Lacy asked.

"They may try, but I've spelled the door. Without a wizard's help, they won't be able to open it. Come, it's been many years since I was here last, but I believe I know the way."

"What's in this box and why is it so important?" Lacy asked as she trailed behind the wizard in the dark.

"The legend says that the last Reishi Sovereign created an item of such power and malice that it could bring darkness to the entire Seven Isles. To ensure he retained control over the device, he created a number of keys. One of those keys was stolen by the Rebel Mage during the war and given to the House of Fellenden for safekeeping. It was placed in this crypt and has remained here, hidden from the world and from magical detection, for all this time. It cannot be allowed to fall into Zuhl's hands. If he discovers it and learns of its power, he may be able to use it to his ends."

"What is this item? Could we use it against them?" Lacy asked.

Saul stopped and turned to face the princess. He held her with a very stern look for a long moment before he answered. "No, the legend says that Malachi Reishi's greatest and most terrible creation would mean the doom of the world. As for what it is precisely, we don't know. The Rebel Mage was careful to ensure that its true nature remained a secret."

He gripped her shoulders and looked her straight in the eye. "The greatest duty of your entire bloodline is to prevent this key from falling into the wrong hands. Do that and you will preserve the world."

Lacy swallowed hard then nodded. Her father had entrusted her with this task. She would honor him by living up to his trust.

Wizard Saul turned and resumed the winding path through the ancient tombs in search of the oldest sarcophagus in the crypt.

They found it after an hour of searching. The sarcophagus was made of marble and carved with an intricate scene of Carlyle Fellenden's final battle. With a great effort, they pried the heavy lid loose and slid it open. The bones had long ago turned to dust, leaving nothing but a small box resting just beneath where Carlyle's feet would have been. It was black as night and had no markings, hinges, or keyholes anywhere on its surface. Lacy lifted it from the tomb and inspected it carefully. Her curiosity burned to look inside but she didn't know how to open it, even if her father hadn't forbade her from doing so. She wrapped it in a piece of cloth and put it in her pack. Then they replaced the heavy lid of the sarcophagus and made their way to the antechamber where their stolen horses waited in a magically induced state of calm.

"Have something to eat and get some rest," Saul said. "We'll have to wait here at least for the rest of the day, so we might as well take advantage of the time and safety."

They stayed in the darkness of the antechamber until well past sundown before venturing forth. The woods were quiet when they opened the door and led their horses out. Lacy resealed the crypt with the ancestral key before mounting up.

They headed out into the night, moving quietly and carefully to avoid any soldiers who might have remained behind. The plains surrounding the butte were wild grasslands with no cover for miles. When they reached the base of the butte, a man was standing in the middle of the trail waiting for them. Saul stopped and searched the surrounding area for any sign of other enemies but saw none. Lacy wasn't sure what to make of the single soldier standing in the middle of the path— until he spoke. There was something about his voice that wasn't quite right, almost like he was being tortured from within.

"Give me the keystone and I will permit you to live, for now," he said with a hint of menace.

Saul started muttering words of power. The man began to advance toward them, not quickly, but like a man who has the advantage and knows it. Saul released his spell and a burst of invisible magical force caught the man in the chest and knocked him back ten feet, crushing his chest in the process. He was dead when he hit the ground.

What happened next threatened to overwhelm Lacy's sanity. A shadow rose up from the corpse and looked straight at her. Its eyes glowed with malice and it began sliding through the night toward them. Saul gasped with sudden realization of the enemy he faced and the cost of it gaining the treasure that Lacy carried.

"I won't be here to protect you anymore, Lacy," Wizard Saul said with a slight tremor in his voice. "You must go on alone now. The shade will take me and I can't stop it; I carry too much guilt from past deeds. If you see me again, run, I won't be myself. That thing," he pointed at the shade moving toward them, "will be in control of my body and my magic. No matter what happens, protect that box and know that I believe in you, as did your father."

With that, Saul drove his dagger into the neck of his horse and slipped off the dying beast to face the shade. As it reached him, he broke his staff and tossed the pieces aside. The shade flowed into him. They struggled against each other for several long seconds.

Lacy sat atop her horse, frozen with a mixture of curiosity and horror as she watched a beast beyond her imaginings destroy her protector.

When Saul looked up at her, she could see the eyes of the demon through his and the sound of his voice was somehow wrong when he spoke.

"Give me the keystone and you may live, for now," he said.

"What are you?" Lacy asked.

"I am Rankosi. Now give me the keystone!"

Lacy kicked her horse into a gallop and charged into the night away from the terrifying creature. The scream of rage that rose up behind her was not of this world.

Chapter 26

"You're going to do what?!" Abigail said.

"I'm going to fight Gabriella to the death," Isabel said firmly.

She was still angry at the turn of events. It was clear now who was behind the attempts on their lives during the time they'd been on the fortress island. If for that reason alone, Isabel was happy for the opportunity but there was much more at stake. Gabriella was a triumvir. If Isabel killed her in a challenge, she would take her place in the triumvirate. That would give her a voice in deciding the course of the Reishi Coven and the Sky Knights. They would make powerful allies and add to Alexander's army a capability that was difficult to match. She knew she was taking a terrible risk but it was well worth it, considering the potential gain if she succeeded—if she survived.

"She'll kill you," Abigail said as she started to get out of bed.

Isabel stopped her with a gentle hand on her shoulder. Abigail was still bruised and beaten up from her fall into the ocean. Her recovery was coming along better than anyone had any right to expect but she was still stiff and weak.

"No, she won't. I'm going to kill her," Isabel said with deadly seriousness.

"Isabel, I know you're angry. I am, too. That witch tried to kill me," Abigail said, "but think about what you're doing. She's a high witch. Her magic is beyond you. Don't do this."

"I have to. As long as Gabriella is alive, she'll keep trying to kill us both. Sooner or later, she'll succeed and then any chance we have of bringing the Reishi Coven and the Sky Knights into this war on our side will be lost. You know what Alexander will do if one of us dies here."

"Exactly my point," Abigail said. "Gabriella's dangerous. What makes you think you can beat her?"

Isabel smiled without humor and touched her necklace. She hadn't spoken to anyone except Abigail about the power Desiderates had given her and she wanted to be sure that no one found out about it until it was too late for Gabriella. Isabel's plan hinged on Gabriella coming to the battle on her wyvern, and she expected as much. The rules were clear. Any and all weapons were permitted. It only made sense that Gabriella would come to the battle with everything at her disposal.

"You're playing a very dangerous game," Abigail said. "I really wish you'd reconsider."

"There's too much to gain in one stroke," Isabel said. "If I defeat her, I will become a triumvir."

Abigail looked at her sharply. "Are you sure?"

Isabel nodded firmly.

"That certainly would change things," Abigail said. "Magda seems like she's willing to throw in with us already. With your voice on the triumvirate . . . still, are you sure you can beat her? If she kills you, all is lost. Alexander will destroy this place and everyone in it."

Isabel nodded seriously. "I know. That's why I have to win."

"Take my bow," Abigail said. "They said any weapon at your disposal, right? Well, it's at your disposal."

"I hadn't considered that," Isabel said, "but I doubt I'll be able to get to her with a normal weapon. She's bound to come prepared."

"Take it anyway," Abigail said. "Use it as a distraction or a ruse. She might think you're desperate if you come to the field with a sword and a bow. My father always said the most powerful weapon on any battlefield is deception."

"You have a point there," Isabel said, considering her strategy.

Until now she had allowed emotion to drive her, and she hadn't fully thought through her battle plan. Abigail's bow would certainly add to her capability, even though she knew she would never win the day with weapons. Magic would be the deciding factor in this battle. She just had to trust in her newfound power.

There was a knock at the door of the bedchamber and Lita peeked in. She stepped back and Magda entered, stood at the foot of the bed, and put her hands on her hips. She was angry.

"Gabriella will kill you, Isabel," Magda said. "She's a powerful, intelligent, and very devious witch with years of experience. Let me fight in your stead."

"Thank you, Magda, but I can't."

"Why not?" she demanded.

"Because there's much more at stake here than just my life," Isabel said. "If I defeat her, then I take her place on the triumvirate, is that not correct?"

Magda frowned deeply and nodded. "Yes. But she will kill you!"

"If you fought in my stead and she killed you, what then?"

"I doubt she would defeat me but I see your point," Magda said. "Still, there are other options."

"Perhaps, but none get me what I need most," Isabel said.

"And what is that?" Magda said.

"You and your Sky Knights to fight at my husband's side in this war," Isabel said firmly.

Magda blinked and then shook her head. "Your life is not the only one at stake. If you die here, I fear Alexander will destroy this island. My sisters don't believe he can but I'm not so sure."

"I wouldn't bet against him," Abigail said. "He doesn't make empty threats."

"You could run," Magda said. "I can get Kallistos to the launch bay and you can both ride out of here."

Isabel stood up with anger flashing in her green eyes. "No! There are people dying out there, right now! I need to help them. My husband is raising an army to make war against Phane and his followers but their numbers are too great. I need to bring an army to stand with him. The Reishi Coven and the Sky Knights will stand with us against Phane or I will die trying to make that happen."

They stared at each other for a long moment as if engaged in a battle of wills. A little smile slowly spread across Magda's face and she gestured to a chair. "May I sit?"

Isabel took a deep breath and let it out. "Of course."

Magda took the chair from the corner of the room and pulled it closer to the bed. "All my life, I've lived to protect the Seven Isles from the threat the Sovereign Stone represents. Our coven was created by Aliyeh Reishi to prevent her own son from using the Stone to harm the people of the Seven Isles the way her husband did. We never foresaw Alexander. We never imagined that the Stone would be recovered by someone loyal to the Old Law.

"There are many who believe that such power will eventually corrupt the one who wields it and if not him then his son or his grandson as the Reishi proved with Malachi. They argue that the Stone should be hidden away or destroyed to prevent it from bringing such darkness to the world ever again."

Isabel nodded, "I understand your concerns. In truth, there are precious few that I would entrust with such power and Alexander is first on that very short list. I've seen his soul and I know he is true to the Old Law. I can't speak for our children because they haven't been born yet, but I have to believe that we will do everything in our power to leave the world a legacy that is loyal to the Old Law.

"The Reishi reigned for two thousand years. For most of that time the Seven Isles enjoyed peace, prosperity, and stability like nothing seen before or since. Consider the state of the world the day before Phane awoke. There was open war on Karth, tyranny on Andalia, Ruatha was a disparate collection of territories with only a handful of them respecting the Old Law, Zuhl was in a constant state of border wars, Tyr was ruled more by pirates than anyone else. Only Fellenden and Ithilian enjoyed stability. The Old Law is meant to govern those who govern the people. Without someone with the moral character and strength to keep the kings and nobles in line, they will continue to run roughshod over the rights of ordinary people.

"The Reishi Empire ended badly, no question, but there was a period of eighteen hundred years where an average family could live in peace without fear that some noble would come and take everything they own, or worse. The Reishi recognized that those who desire power cannot be trusted with it, so they set themselves up as the defenders of the people against those who would rule. It wasn't perfect but it was far better than what we have now."

"And what of the future?" Magda asked. "What if you're successful and Alexander reconstitutes the Reishi Empire and brings the Seven Isles back under the rule of the Old Law? What happens when a sovereign comes along who follows the same path that Malachi Reishi did?"

"Those who love life and liberty as much as we do will face him and defeat him," Isabel said. "The Old Law cannot defend itself. It must have a champion. If the people of the Seven Isles become blind to the beauty, power, and simple rightness of the Old Law, then they will face the consequences of their failure. We can't protect them from themselves, we can only show them the truth and hope they have the wisdom to see it.

"But more importantly, you speak of possibilities and distant futures, let me ask you another what if. What if Phane kills Alexander and takes the Sovereign Stone, right now. What if, in the coming months, Phane conquers the Seven Isles? What then?

"All I am asking of you is that you fulfill your purpose—protect the Sovereign Stone by protecting the one who bears it. He's carrying a great and terrible burden, a burden that he doesn't want, a burden that has been thrust upon him without his consent.

"Many would kill to have the power that Alexander has amassed in such a short time, but I know his heart as well as any and I can tell you with certainty that he would give it all up right now if he thought the world would be safe and he could go back home and herd cattle. He doesn't want to be the Sovereign. What better qualification for such a terrible duty can there be?"

Abigail nodded her agreement. "She speaks the truth. My brother never wanted power, not even to be the head of Valentine Manor. He told me his dreams. They're simple and honorable. He just wants a plot of good land and a herd of cattle." Abigail paused for a moment as she collected her emotions. "He used to read about battles fought long ago. After we'd been running from Phane for a few weeks, after he'd killed men with his own blade, he told me that those stories were all lies. The glory, honor, and splendor of those stories were all wrong. He doesn't see any glory in killing, he sees only sadness."

The room fell silent for a moment before Abigail continued. "You know, he has his homestead picked out. He found a little hillock overlooking a meandering stream that runs through the northern part of our family estates. He knows right where he wants to build his house. He even took me there once and described what it would look like, where the barn and paddock would be, even which direction the porch would face.

"He never wanted power, but now that he has it, he can't escape it. He either wins or he dies and he knows it. If he fails, then everyone in the entire Seven Isles will lose. Please, help him!"

"You both make compelling arguments," Magda said. "For my part, I believe you. At least I believe that you believe what you say, but you are both very young and idealistic. I have lived for many years and I have watched power twist and warp the souls of good men and women until they were little more than a shadow of their former selves. Gabriella is a prime example. A century ago she would never have challenged you for something as petty as vengeance but a hundred years as a triumvir has altered her mind. She now believes that her station makes her desires more important than other people's lives.

"She challenged the previous triumvir, her own mother, mind you, because she had become corrupt and was working behind the backs of the coven to advance her own ambitions. Gabriella offered her mother quarter in that battle but her mother attacked even though she had been bested. Gabriella struck her down then spent a month locked in her chambers crying. She was inconsolable.

"When she took her place on the triumvirate, she was a voice of temperance, reason, and compassion. She agonized over the consequences of our decisions and thought through all of the ramifications that she could foresee before casting her vote for any course of action.

"Over the last century I've watched her lose touch with her sense of duty and cling to her own self-importance. She has come to see power and station as her due rather than a privilege or a duty.

"The Sovereign Stone is the ultimate symbol of power in all of the Seven Isles. How can you be certain that Alexander won't succumb to the temptation to use that power for his own selfish reasons?"

"I can only tell you what I know in my heart," Isabel said. "Alexander will reign with wisdom and temperance. He will stand against those who would wield power for the sake of wielding power and he will leave the people alone to live their lives.

"I can only offer one piece of objective evidence for my belief in him. Phane offered him the rule of Ruatha, safety for his friends and family, and assurances that war would not be fought on Ruatha if he would only bow before Phane and serve him. He made this offer well before Alexander recovered the Sovereign Stone. Alexander refused. If he wanted power, he could have had it."

Magda smiled gently. "Your belief in him has quelled many of my doubts, though I still fear the power that the Stone represents . . . in anyone's hands. Given the choices before me, I can only hope that Alexander lives up to your faith in him.

"That still leaves a profound challenge before you. Gabriella is skilled and powerful. She will offer no quarter or mercy. You are young and without training. How can you hope to defeat her?"

Isabel looked down as she composed her thoughts. She was still holding the secret of her connection to the wyverns close and couldn't risk Gabriella discovering her capability, but she needed to give Magda a credible explanation for her confidence in the coming battle.

"During our travels I've come into direct contact with both the realm of light and the netherworld. The experiences left permanent connections to both places within my mind. I discovered how to access the power of both the light and the dark during my mana fast. I used that connection to the light to heal Abigail. I'm hoping I can learn how to use those connections to fight Gabriella."

"You risk much on an untested ability," Magda said, "but perhaps I can help you prepare. As the one challenged, you have the right to set the date of the battle, within reason. It's quite common to choose a date a week or two away to give yourself time to put your affairs in order and to make preparations. Given the power you brought to bear when you healed your sister, it may be possible for you to learn a spell or two that will help you fight, although I'm not optimistic about your chances of success."

"I'm confident that, with your guidance, I will prevail," Isabel said. "I have to."

Wren burst into the bedchamber with a look of wild fear. She stopped short when she saw Magda but couldn't help herself. "Is it true? They say Mistress Gabriella has challenged you and you've accepted."

Isabel nodded and Wren burst into tears.

"She'll kill you," Wren said through a sob. "You have to run. Take Abigail and Kallistos and leave here. Go back to Alexander and forget this place. It's the only way you'll survive." She broke down sobbing and sank to her knees in front of Isabel. "Please don't die. You and Abigail are my best friends. I can't stand the thought of either of you dying," she said through her sobbing.

Isabel pulled Wren's head onto her lap and smoothed her wispy hair. "It's all right, Wren. I won't die, but I have to do this. It's the only way."

"I don't understand," she sniffed. "You were just ordained into the coven. How can Mistress Gabriella challenge you? Why would she do such a thing?"

"Gabriella's husband died when the Sky Knights attacked us on the Reishi Isle," Isabel said. "She wants revenge for her loss."

"But she's a triumvir, she's supposed to be above such things," Wren said, composing herself. "She has a duty to protect the Seven Isles." Wren turned to Magda. "Doesn't she know what it will do to Alexander if she kills Isabel?"

"I'm afraid she does, child," Magda said gently. "I fear she's counting on it. It was Alexander's blade that killed her husband's wyvern and led to his drowning. She wants him to feel the pain she lives with."

"But if Alexander's heart is broken, he won't have the will to fight Phane," Wren said. "How can Mistress Gabriella risk everyone's future over her own grief when she has sworn to protect the Seven Isles?"

Wren's fear was transforming into indignant anger. She stood up and faced Magda.

"How can you let this happen? All my life I've been told that I must do my duty for the greater good of the Seven Isles. I've never complained, even when I was treated wrongly by those of higher station, even when I learned that my own dreams would never be realized, I did my part because I believed in the duty of the Reishi Coven and the Sky Knights. Was it all a lie? Does this place exist to protect the Seven Isles or does it exist to feed the egos of those who rule here?"

Magda sat impassively as the waifish young serving girl railed at her. When she stopped, Magda raised one eyebrow. "Are you finished?" she asked calmly.

Wren shrank a little but held her ground.

"Child, I do not condone Gabriella's decision and I intend to help Isabel prepare for this challenge in every way that I can. Like you, I have suggested that she run, but she has stubbornly refused. As for your question about the purpose of this place, I believe we have a vital role to play in defending the Seven Isles, although I must admit that there are those who have come to value their station and privilege more than their duty."

"How is it that I can see the folly of Mistress Gabriella's decision when I'm just a serving girl and she can't when she's a triumvir?" Wren asked quietly.

Magda sighed. "Humility tends to see and accept moral clarity more readily than does power." She gave Isabel a pointed look.

Wren frowned. "If powerful people can't see what's right or wrong, then how can they be trusted with their power?"

"That, child, is the question at the heart of humanity's struggle," Magda said as she stood and looked at Isabel. "Think on what we've discussed. You have options until you set foot on the battlefield."

Magda left them alone and the room fell silent for several long moments before Wren sniffed away her tears and tried, unsuccessfully, to smooth her unruly hair back into place.

"Are you hungry?" she asked with a small voice.

"I am," Abigail said. "Some lunch would be wonderful, Wren."

"All right, I'll be back in a few minutes." She left quietly with her head down, clearly still preoccupied and filled with emotion.

"If I fall in this battle, you have to run, and quickly," Isabel said. "With me gone, Gabriella will move against you, so be ready to leave."

"First you tell me you're going to win and now you're telling me to be ready to run. Which is it?" Abigail said.

"We have to be ready for any outcome. I have every intention of killing her, but she may surprise me with something totally unexpected. Just be ready."

"Lita says I'll be able to ride in a week or so," Abigail said. "Either way, we won't be here too much longer."

"I'm going to make the best of the next two weeks and learn everything I can from Magda about witchcraft," Isabel said. "I suggest you focus on healing. Once we leave, there's no telling when we'll have a safe place to rest again."

"I wish I knew what Alexander was doing," Abigail said. "I can only assume he's raising an army on Ithilian and preparing to lead it through the Gate, but knowing when he plans to attack would be helpful."

"All we can do is be ready as soon as possible," Isabel said. "If we can win over the coven, we can send scouts to Ruatha and make contact with your father and the wizards. Alexander will try to coordinate his attack with them."

"I'm still worried about Gabriella," Abigail said. "You need to be really sure about this before you take such a risk. I suggest you take some of the time you have to make certain your plan will work."

After lunch Abigail went back to her bedchamber to rest while Isabel went out onto the balcony to practice her connection with the wyverns and other beasts. She started with the seagulls, reasoning that they were smaller and stupider so they would be easier to control.

Her first attempt to touch the mind of one of the seabirds was successful. Even though the thoughts and instincts were very different from Slyder's, she was able to gain control of the bird and soon had it flying to her command. After an hour or so of establishing control and then relinquishing it, she decided to focus on more than one bird at a time. Two were more difficult and five required a level of focus that she couldn't maintain for very long. She also discovered that she could only send a single command to all of the birds she was controlling at any one time. She couldn't make one bird dive and the other climb at the same time but she could make them all act together. She also discovered that the more she practiced, the easier it got to establish control and to maintain it even while focusing on other things.

She linked to a single bird and made it fly in a circle just below her balcony, then focused on creating a feeling of intense love and made a link to the firmament. The lure of the infinite was intense, especially with the distraction of her connection to the bird. Before she could form an image of her desired outcome, she felt like she was falling into the limitless possibility of the firmament and she broke off her connection in a sudden panic. She checked the position of the sun to assess how long she'd been attempting her spell and felt a sense of relief when she realized it had only been a few minutes.

She sat down and cleared her mind. One thing at a time, she told herself. With clear focus she reached out into the fortress island and found the mind of a wyvern. He was napping in the large cave that served as his home. His mind idly drifted on thoughts of the wind and the sky. Isabel moved into his mind and focused her will, infusing the beast with her presence. Once she felt firmly established in his mind, she commanded him to roar. A moment later she heard the faint echo of a wyvern's roar reverberate through the stone of the island. She sat back and smiled to herself with satisfaction, then just as quickly chided herself for congratulating herself too soon.

Gabriella was formidable and Isabel couldn't come up with a reliable way to test her battle plan that didn't completely violate her own sense of morality. She needed to know if she could command a wyvern to kill for her. What's more, she needed to know if she could command a wyvern to kill its own rider, but she had no idea how to test such a thing without killing someone who was completely innocent. She'd made wyverns change course while their riders struggled to correct their flight path but that was such a minor thing next to killing. From Abigail's description of her relationship with Kallistos, there was a very definite bond created between rider and wyvern. Isabel's life rested on knowing if her magical command of the beasts was greater than that bond.

With grim resolve she stood up and looked out over the ocean. Perhaps another kind of test would help her get closer to the answer she needed. She reached out and found a seagull. With a bit of a struggle she overcame her conscience and took command of the bird. She weighed the consequences of failure both for herself and for Alexander and hence the rest of the Seven Isles and made her terrible decision. She needed to know the truth of her power. The life of one bird was a small price to pay for that knowledge, even though she felt a pang of guilt for what she was about to do.

She commanded the bird into a fast and steep dive to gain speed and then turned the seagull into the side of the fortress island. She felt an instinctual resistance from the animal as it struggled to veer away from a fatal collision with the stone wall but she kept a firm grip on the creature's will. A moment later it crashed into the side of the fortress island and tumbled away, falling into the sea. Isabel felt her bond with the dead bird break and a heaviness settle on her soul.

She sat quietly for a long time, evaluating her own moral character. She'd just killed an innocent creature—the thought made her sick to her stomach. She decided she didn't like the demands that power placed on her but she had to admit her terrible experiment had proven the extent of her power, at least with more simple-minded creatures. But the nagging question still remained: Would it work with a wyvern?

Isabel called Slyder to her. A minute or so later her forest hawk landed on the balcony wall, then hopped onto her knee and looked at her curiously. She scratched under his chin and he happily leaned into her affections.

"Am I a terrible person, Slyder?"

Her hawk didn't answer.

After some soul-searching, Isabel renewed her efforts to connect with and control the wyverns. She worked diligently and carefully for the remainder of the afternoon. By the time Wren arrived with their dinner, Isabel was confident in her ability to make a connection with a wyvern quickly and equally confident in her control over the beast. She was very careful to ensure that she didn't cause the wyverns to do anything too much out of the ordinary for fear that the sudden odd behavior of the giant pseudo-dragons would draw attention from the witches and especially from Gabriella.

She practiced making contact with more than one wyvern but found that the level of concentration necessary increased dramatically with the number of creatures she tried to control. She could sense the presence of hundreds of wyverns in the fortress island and even make a passive connection with many of them all at once but that only gave her access to their very primal thoughts and instincts without giving her much control. She felt that with work and effort she could probably issue a single, very basic command to all of them at once but it would take a great deal of concentration.

***

The next day a guard came to their chambers just after breakfast with a summons from Magda.

Isabel went to her chambers and found the triumvir reading from a very old volume.

"Ah, Isabel, do you feel like learning a spell or two?" Magda asked with a smile.

"Absolutely," Isabel said. "I feel like I can touch the light or the darkness but beyond that, I'm not sure what to do with them."

Magda nodded knowingly. Spellcraft was as much about imagination and visualizing an outcome as it was about connecting with the firmament. Before a spell could be effective, the spell caster needed to know what they wanted to happen.

"You were able to heal Abigail with the light because giving life and healing is the natural power of light, however, it can also be used to kill," Magda said. "Focused light, projected at an enemy, can burn like fire. This spell is called light lance. It is very old and commonly understood among both wizards and witches alike; however, none before you had such a connection to the realm of light, so it's hard to predict how the spell will function for you.

"I suggest you learn how to cast the light-lance spell in its basic form before you attempt to cast it while you're connected to the realm of light. It's hard to say if the addition of your unique connection to the light will increase the power and deadliness of the spell or change the nature of the magic altogether."

"All right. Tell me what to do," Isabel said.

"Very good," Magda said as she handed Isabel the book she'd been reading. "I wrote this myself many years ago when I was learning to create new spells. At the time, I knew this spell already so it made an ideal subject for the practice of writing a spellbook.

"Take this to your quarters and study it carefully. Do the exercises provided and be thorough about your practice. When you've done a particular exercise until you're sick of it, you're halfway there. Go on to another exercise and then come back to those that you've practiced previously.

"Do not attempt to cast the spell until you've returned to me and we've had a chance to discuss your understanding of the material. This is important, Isabel. More witches and wizards have died from attempting to cast a spell that they didn't fully understand than from becoming lost in the firmament.

"Once you've mastered the contents of this book, come back and we'll talk it over. When I believe you're ready, I'll guide you through the casting process. If you're successful, then you'll practice the spell until you can bring forth the magic with ease even while being distracted.

"After you've mastered that, you may attempt the spell while linked to the realm of light. Honestly, I have no way of predicting the results of such a thing."

Isabel frowned a bit. "Doesn't Gabriella know this spell and how to counter it?"

"Of course," Magda said. "She's familiar with every commonly known spell within your ability to learn in such a short period of time, as well as the proven counters for each of them. As I've said, Gabriella is a powerful and dangerous witch. You will not learn any common spell in the next two weeks capable of defeating her.

"As for your connection to the light, perhaps it will lend great power to this spell or maybe it will simply transform it into a means of healing another at a distance, which would be a profound capability even if it's useless against Gabriella."

"How long does it normally take to learn this spell?" Isabel asked.

"Typically, two to four weeks," Magda said, "although that's for a novice training on a normal schedule. You'll probably master it in less time, provided you're diligent in your studies and practice."

Isabel nodded as she tried to frame her next question. "What do you know about the darkness?"

Magda looked at her for a moment before nodding to herself. "Please sit," she said, motioning to a comfortable chair.

"There is the darkness of the night and there is the darkness of the netherworld. Many witches and wizards commonly use spells that create or manipulate the darkness created by an absence of light. Such spells can be useful for obscuring the vision of others, hiding in the night, or creating fear, but they have no substance. What you speak of is necromancy. Calling on the forces of the netherworld is a dangerous game even if you aren't summoning a creature from the darkness into our world. There is always a price when dealing with the netherworld. I've been careful to avoid learning any magic related to the darkness for fear that I might be tempted to use it—and I would caution you to do the same.

"The stories say that Malachi Reishi started out dabbling in the magic of darkness to prolong the life of a beloved pet. Once he got a taste of the power it offered, he couldn't resist the urge to call on it more often, until finally, it consumed him and he lost touch with his essential humanity.

"Another word of caution. If you were to defeat Gabriella with necromancy, there would be many within the coven who would be very skeptical of your character and unwilling to trust you, myself included. Focus on the light, Isabel. Keep your connection to the netherworld closed."

Isabel swallowed hard. She knew that the netherworld was not the place she wanted to go for power but she was looking for any edge she could get in the coming fight. She realized that there were other considerations that she needed to explore, so she forged ahead.

"I can tell you from personal experience that the netherworld is a place of hate and suffering," Isabel said. "I have no desire to call on it if I can help it, and I will heed your advice with regard to this fight with Gabriella. However, in the past, I've faced creatures conjured from the darkness that were sent to kill Alexander. Is there a way to use my link with the netherworld to send those creatures back where they belong?"

Magda furrowed her brow in thought as she sat back in her chair, looking up at the ceiling. "That may be possible. There are those who've studied the netherworld who have developed spells to banish creatures summoned from there.

My understanding is that, if a passageway is created between the world of time and substance and the netherworld in proximity to a creature from the darkness, the creature is drawn into the portal because its presence here creates an imbalance. I've never had cause to learn a banishing spell, so my understanding of the process is limited. But I will do some research on the matter and offer what insight I can."

"Thank you, Magda. I'll study this and be back when I'm ready to proceed," Isabel said as she stood.

"I can see your resolve, Isabel, but I still wish you'd reconsider this challenge," Magda said. "Gabriella will kill you. You simply can't learn enough in the short time you have to change that."

Isabel smiled her thanks for the book. "I'll be back soon."

Chapter 27

She left Magda's quarters and made her way back through the fortress island. A few of the Sky Knights snickered at her when she passed them in the halls. Others gave her a look almost bordering on pity for her plight. It was obvious that word of the challenge had spread to every corner of the aerie and Gabriella was the clear favorite.

Isabel felt a little hint of doubt creep into her psyche but she shoved it aside with ruthless severity. She was Lady Reishi. She had a duty to her people and her husband. Risk to her life was secondary. She'd chosen her course, now she just had to prepare for the task at hand.

Abigail was sitting out on the balcony in the early summer sun when Isabel returned to their quarters. Wren smiled a little sheepishly and offered a pot of tea. Isabel returned the smile and nodded. The waifish serving girl had been even more reserved and timid since her outburst the previous day. It seemed that she was embarrassed for her display of emotion and for questioning the motives of the triumvirate so openly. For Isabel, the entire incident had only served to endear the young women to her further. In spite of her frail appearance, Wren had mettle when she chose to display it. The thought made Isabel smile.

She went out onto the balcony and sat down next to her sister. The bruising on Abigail's face and arms still made Isabel wince. If nothing else, Gabriella had to be brought to justice for her attempt on Abigail's life.

Abigail opened her eyes and smiled at Isabel when she heard her sit down. "If I didn't know better, I'd think all was right with the world," she said.

"It is a beautiful day," Isabel replied.

The sky was crystal clear and there was just enough breeze to take the edge off the heat of direct sunlight. From the balcony they could hear the calls of the seabirds and the gentle rhythm of the ocean crashing against the island wall far below.

Wren set two cups of steaming hot tea on the low table between the lounge chairs.

"Aren't you going to join us, Wren?" Isabel asked.

"If you'd like," she said quietly.

"Of course, get a cup of tea and come sit with us," Abigail said.

After several minutes of total silence from the young serving girl, Isabel and Abigail shared a look of concern.

"What's wrong, Wren?" Isabel said.

She hung her head. "It wasn't my place to question the triumvirate the way I did yesterday. I'm ashamed of how I acted and I apologize."

"Don't you dare," Isabel said. "You have nothing to apologize for. Gabriella *is* putting her own selfish interests ahead of her duty and the future of the Seven Isles. You were exactly right and you have every reason to feel disillusioned and betrayed after serving these people for so long only to discover that some of those you've served aren't worthy of your loyalty."

"I told my mother what happened," Wren said. "She was mortified by my behavior. She said I should apologize to everyone involved as soon as possible and try to make amends as best I could or I might find myself demoted to scullion, or worse."

"Your mother has lived here her whole life," Abigail said. "I have no doubt that she's looking out for you, but speaking just for myself, I wanted to stand up and cheer at what you said to Magda yesterday."

Wren smiled timidly. "Really?"

"Yes, really," Abigail said. "You spoke the truth with conviction and courage. I'm proud of you."

"Me, too," Isabel said. "I understand if you have to apologize to Magda to protect your family's place here but you certainly don't have to apologize to us. And honestly, I don't think Magda is worried about it at all."

"Thank you both," Wren said with a sigh of relief. "I feel much better. I was so worried after what my mother said that I could hardly sleep last night."

"So take a nap," Abigail said. "I'm going to."

"I couldn't," Wren said.

"Sure you could," Isabel said. "I'm just going to read for a while. I'll wake you if you sleep too long."

Isabel read the spellbook for the rest of the morning while Wren and Abigail slept. It was complex and detailed, explaining the nature of light and how it could be focused and directed into a concentrated beam capable of burning flesh from bone. After a very complete explanation of how light worked, it offered a summary of the process for casting the spell, then proceeded into specific exercises designed to guide the spell caster to develop the visual images necessary to manifest the spell's effects.

Isabel read it through completely by lunch, then read it again that afternoon. By midafternoon she started practicing the first of several exercises. It was tedious and repetitive but she stayed with it. When the boredom of one exercise threatened to overwhelm her, she went on to the next. By dark she had a firm grasp of the first two visualization exercises.

The next day she woke early and started her work. She focused ruthlessly on the task until her concentration broke, then moved on to another exercise. She worked until dark again and then for several hours by lamplight until she had mastered all of the exercises. When Isabel lay down to sleep, she was mentally exhausted but confident that she'd done all she could to master the lessons of the spellbook.

She arrived at Magda's chambers just after breakfast the following morning to begin the next part of her training. She knew from the book what to expect and was eager to begin. Hours of study had imparted an academic understanding of the process but she knew that nothing compared to experience. She needed to actually cast the spell in order to master it.

Magda opened the door and smiled warmly. "Come in. I assume you believe you're ready for the practice phase of the training process."

Isabel nodded firmly. "I've studied this book backwards and forwards. I'm ready to try casting the spell."

"Good. Come and sit with me," Magda said.

They sat talking for an hour. Magda quizzed her on every aspect of the spell from the abstract understanding of light and how it worked to the details and nuances of the visualization exercises. Isabel answered all of her questions with as much clarity and accuracy as she could muster. It was a rigorous and thorough examination of her studies that left Isabel with a new respect for the exacting requirements of spell casting.

The process of recounting her lessons served to reinforce the principles she'd learned and solidified her understanding so that, by the time Magda was satisfied with her new understanding, Isabel was confident that she'd mastered the lesson in its entirety.

"Very good, Isabel," Magda said. "You are a diligent student. Thoroughness and attention to detail will serve you well in your pursuit of the craft. Now it's time to put what you've learned into practice. Come with me."

Magda led her from her chambers deep into the bowels of the fortress island to a large, unfinished cavern. The ceiling was high and the walls were slick with condensation. The air was cold and still but the place looked like it had been visited recently. Magda lit a couple of lamps positioned on two pedestals. As the light in the chamber grew, Isabel saw what looked like an archery target on the far wall.

"This is a practice chamber," Magda said. "We come here to test our spells and hone our skills. We are very deep within the fortress and there is nothing nearby that can be hurt by a spell gone awry.

"Stand here and direct your spell at the target. Be very deliberate and take your time going through all of the steps in the casting process. It's vitally important that you master the process correctly before you work on the speed of your casting."

Isabel nodded and stepped up between the two pedestals. She was suddenly very nervous. Her confidence evaporated and she felt a wave of self-consciousness wash over her as all of the concepts she'd learned during the past two days became a jumble in her mind.

Magda smiled gently and put her hand on Isabel's shoulder. "It's common to be uncertain at this point. Take a deep breath and focus on performing one step at a time."

Isabel nodded tightly and deliberately released the tension she was feeling. She closed her eyes and focused on the emotion she needed to protect herself from the tug of the firmament. This was a spell used for battle so she called on her anger. It came easily. There were so many injustices that she could use to stoke the heat of her anger that the first step in the casting flowed naturally.

Next, she carefully formed an image of the outcome she wanted. In this case it was a focused beam of white-hot light. She saw it in her mind's eye streaking from her hand to the target with unerring accuracy. She saw the heat of the light burn into the stone itself and then she saw the light wink out of existence as quickly as it came forth.

With careful and deliberate focus, she touched the firmament. It felt like she was falling. In a sudden panic she closed the connection and shook her mind clear. She had focused so intently on the image of the outcome she wanted that she forgot to keep the anger alive at the same time. It was a delicate balancing act that required deep concentration.

When she glanced over at Magda, the triumvir smiled knowingly and nodded for her to try again. Isabel took a deep breath and again called the anger. Once the emotion was boiling within her, she formed the image in her mind but this time she kept a part of her focus on the rage slowly boiling in the pit of her stomach. With both her emotion and her image firmly in mind, she touched the firmament. It called to her but she was angry enough that the allure of the limitless possibility had no power to draw her in. She extended her hand and released her image into the firmament.

Isabel felt the surge of power flow into her as the nature of reality itself was bent to her will. Her outstretched hand glowed impossibly bright and a streak of light stabbed out and burned into the target at the exact spot she was aiming for. An instant later the cavern went dark as she severed her connection to the firmament.

She felt a surge of pride and satisfaction. The power she'd just unleashed would have burned a hole through a man at a hundred feet. No armor or shield would have protected her target from the intense heat of the magical light she'd just created.

"Well done," Magda said. "The spell can be produced with varying degrees of intensity depending on how fully you open your mind to the firmament. Of course, you must have sufficient emotion present to protect yourself from the pull of the firmament if you are to call forth the most powerful results.

"Do it again but this time spend more time on building your emotion so that you can make a more complete connection to the firmament."

Isabel nodded and began the process again. This time she nursed her anger until she was in a state of controlled rage. All of the sorrow and loss caused by those who would rule for the sake of their egos fueled her fury until it was a torrent within her soul. This time she mentally leaned into the firmament and dared it to tempt her. She mentally hurled her vision of the light into the firmament with force and anger. This time the spell was altogether different. Where the last time it had burned into the stone an inch or so, this time she bored a hole three feet deep into the side of the cavern wall. The brilliance of the light was so intense it left her dazzled for a moment after she released the spell. She felt drained by the experience as she let go of the anger she'd built up and she deliberately calmed herself.

"Impressive," Magda said. "There are few within our coven who could power a spell with such intensity. However, I would caution you. I know the frame of mind it takes to do what you've just done. The kind of wild, almost reckless link you made with the firmament. Don't attempt such a thing unless you've built your emotional state into one of unbridled passion and intensity or you risk losing yourself to the firmament.

"Now, do it again, but this time at half the power you just displayed."

Isabel ran through the process again but with greater control and less force, though still more than enough to kill a man or a beast. She could feel the strain of such intense emotion wearing on her, but Magda pressed her to continue practicing. With each casting, Isabel became more familiar with the nuances of the process and more comfortable calling on the firmament. She came to know how intense her emotional state needed to be for her to make a connection with the firmament.

After a dozen castings, Magda introduced another idea. "Now I want you to repeat this phrase," Magda said and then uttered a string of words from an ancient language.

Isabel repeated the words again and again until they were burned indelibly into her mind. Once she could say the words flawlessly, Magda proceeded to the last part of the lesson.

"You will associate these words with the casting of this spell by saying them as you call forth the magic. Doing so will create a bond between these words and the process of casting this spell. Once you've established this connection, the spell casting process will unfold naturally when you utter these words. They are not necessary for the spell to work but the technique of associating a set of words with a given spell has been proven to help make the casting process faster and more reliable."

Isabel added the last piece to the puzzle by casting the spell another dozen times. By the time she was done with her practice, the spell was becoming a single action rather than a series of steps. She started to feel exhausted from the emotional strain that the spell casting took on her. When Magda noticed her fatigue, she put a stop to her training session.

"You've had enough for today," Magda said. "You've made excellent progress but it's important that you not push yourself too hard with a new spell. When you become exhausted, it increases the risk of a mistake that could be catastrophic. Go have some lunch, take a nap and spend the rest of the afternoon resting your mind. Try not to think about what you've learned over the past few days. A period of time spent focusing on other things gives your mind time to fully integrate your new skills. Come back tomorrow morning and we'll continue your practice."

"Thank you, Magda," Isabel said sincerely. "I've learned so much in the past few days."

"You are very welcome, Isabel, but you must remember, this spell will not carry the day when you face Gabriella. I don't mean to nag but I'm still hoping you'll reconsider."

"I know you're concerned but this is something I have to do," Isabel said. "I'm confident that I'll survive her challenge and once I do, we can turn our focus to the real enemy of the Seven Isles."

"You're young and headstrong, Isabel, and while I admire your courage, I fear it will be the death of you."

"If I am to be Lady Reishi I can't shrink away from a challenge, even one as daunting as this. Power is as much about perception as it is about capability. If people see me as weak or cowardly, then I won't be able to support Alexander. He needs a wife who can live up to his commitment to the Old Law and stand with him in the face of any threat. If I run, Gabriella will make sure that everyone in the Seven Isles knows I'm not worthy of my place beside Alexander. I can't have that."

"Your reasoning is sound and your grasp of the nature of power is insightful but your opponent is beyond you," Magda said. "Perhaps, with training and experience, you would be a match for her, but right now you are simply out of your depth."

"I've only just learned my first spell," Isabel said. "Tomorrow, I hope to add the realm of light to my spell and see if I can bring something to the battlefield that Gabriella doesn't expect."

"Perhaps you can try that the day after tomorrow," Magda said. "You still have some work to do with the basic version of the spell. When I'm satisfied that you've mastered it, then I'll help you modify it to include your unique connection to the light.

"You must understand, the basic version of the light-lance spell is tried and tested. It's proven to work for countless witches in the past. Adding such a profound variation may prove more complex than either of us realizes and may essentially create an entirely new spell, one that has never been tested or attempted before. Such things are not to be undertaken lightly. Under other circumstances, I would insist that you wait and hone your skills as a witch by learning and practicing proven spells before attempting such a thing."

Isabel nodded. "All right, but I'm pretty sure I'm ready now and I don't have much time. What if I come back after lunch and we work on it some more today?"

"No, your mind needs time to rest and assimilate what you've learned," Magda said. "Spend the rest of today focused on something else. That is the most important thing you can do right now to master this spell."

Isabel made her way back to her quarters in a daze. She didn't remember the path she walked because her mind was reeling from the strain she'd placed on it. Wren was preparing a lunch of seafood stew and hard rolls with butter. The waifish young woman had actually gained a few pounds since Isabel and Abigail had arrived. She had been almost gaunt when they first met her but now her face was more filled out and her skin looked healthier. Wren had become a close friend and regularly shared meals with them, providing her with a much better diet than she ever got as a serving girl.

Isabel smiled hello and went to an overstuffed chair in the sitting area of their main room. Abigail was napping on the couch. Her lurid bruises had faded into a pale and sickly yellow all across her face, neck, and shoulders. Isabel felt a hint of anger at seeing her sister's injuries but it faded quickly. She was too emotionally exhausted to sustain any more anger after the morning spent deliberately invoking intense rage to protect her from the pull of the firmament. She sat down and closed her eyes. It seemed only a moment passed before Wren shook her shoulder gently.

"Isabel, you fell asleep. Are you hungry?"

Isabel blinked the sleep from her eyes and smiled up at Wren. "I'm starving."

After two helpings of stew, she recounted the events of the morning to Abigail and Wren. Both listened with rapt attention as she described the process of calling on the firmament to manifest magical effects in the world of time and substance. Wren was enchanted by the wonder of it all but Abigail was listening closely for another reason.

"It sounds like you can do some serious damage with that spell," Abigail said. "Do you think it'll be enough to kill Gabriella?"

Isabel shook her head. "No, Magda says she'll be able to defend against it, but I'm hoping to modify it into something she doesn't expect."

Wren looked down at the table and whispered, "My momma thinks you're doomed."

"Wren, look at me," Isabel said softly. "It's going to be all right. Gabriella is powerful so she'll be overconfident and I have something she doesn't. I'm serving a cause and a purpose that's bigger than just me. I have to believe that'll count for something."

"I wish there was something I could do to help you."

"There is . . . you can believe in me," Isabel said. "I'm going to win this fight even if no one thinks I can."

"I do believe in you, Isabel, but I'm also afraid for you," Wren said. "Mistress Gabriella is powerful. Even the Sky Knights are afraid of her."

"Thank you for being worried about me," Isabel said as she gave Wren's hand a squeeze. "Right now, I'm going to take a nap. This morning was exhausting."

She slept soundly for an hour, then woke and made herself a cup of tea before going out onto the balcony to practice her real secret weapon. She cleared her mind and reached out for the mind of a wyvern. This time she was searching for a specific creature among the hundreds living within the fortress island. At first it was a struggle to learn how to distinguish one wyvern's mind from another. It took linking with Abigail's Kallistos and finding the thread of connection to the beast's master to discover how to find the one wyvern she needed to control.

After more than an hour of painstaking effort, she found Gabriella's steed. He was an ancient beast named Asteroth easily twice the size of Kallistos. He had served as Gabriella's steed since she took her place on the triumvirate. Isabel gently slipped into his mind. He was napping lazily in his aerie. She didn't attempt to command or influence the beast but instead just made her presence known and maintained a link to develop a sense of familiarity with his mind so she could find him and link to him more easily in the future.

Her plan hinged on using Gabriella's wyvern against her. The surprise of such a sudden betrayal by her steed was the greatest weapon Isabel could bring to the battlefield. Spells and Abigail's magical bow were distractions meant to conceal her real plan. The only part she couldn't count on for certain was Gabriella coming to the field riding her steed. If she came alone, the fight might be very short and end badly, so Isabel started working on a way to ensure that Gabriella rode into battle against her.

She recalled Alexander speaking about his father's lessons on deception in war. How creating a false belief in the mind of the enemy was the most powerful weapon a soldier had. For her plan to work, if she was to survive the day, Isabel needed to deceive Gabriella into coming to the battlefield riding the instrument of her own doom.

As her plan began to take shape, she commanded Asteroth to roar. From deep in the bowels of the fortress island, a thunderous sound reverberated through the stone and sent the handlers to work calming and soothing the suddenly agitated wyvern. Isabel relaxed her focus and let go of her worries about her own troubles and thought about Alexander. She wondered what he was doing and hoped he was safe. She drifted off to sleep and woke with a start when Abigail shook her shoulder to wake her for dinner.

She spent the next morning with Magda in the practice room casting her light-lance spell over and over again. At first, Magda let her cast it a few times at her own speed, then demanded that she do it faster. Once she'd halved the time it took to produce the effect, Magda started adding distractions during her casting until finally she had Isabel running across the cavern while she tossed rocks at her.

The first attempts to cast the spell under such distracting conditions were total failures but after a few tries, she succeeded. Then after several more attempts, it was like something clicked. She thought back to when she was learning how to ride a horse. At first there was so much going on all at once that she got distracted—she was so busy focusing on one part of the task that she forgot other critical parts. But, after practicing for awhile, the whole thing became a skill that she could do without even thinking about it.

The light-lance spell had become the same thing. A simple action she could call forth in a few seconds with devastating effect, even while dodging rocks and running as fast as she could across the dimly lit cavern. By the time Magda called an end to their training session, Isabel was exhausted but she had to admit that her grasp of the spell had become complete. She could cast it at a moment's notice even while under attack. She returned to her chambers more confident of her success and eager to add the next part to her newfound capability.

The next day she would attempt to incorporate the power of the realm of light into the spell and see if it added any measurable effect to the result. Her hope was that she could defeat Gabriella's defenses with the addition of her unique connection to the light. That way she would have a backup plan in case her ability to control Gabriella's steed failed.

Despite her fatigue, Isabel had trouble sleeping that night. There were so many thoughts pressing in on her from all directions. Her worry for Alexander, her anger at Gabriella, and her concern for the people of Ruatha all conspired to keep her awake. Every time she pushed one worry from her mind, another would intrude to take its place.

She woke tired and agitated but resolved to clear her mind and press on with her plan. After a quick breakfast, she went to Magda's chambers and found the triumvir reading while sipping a cup of tea.

"Please sit with me for a few minutes before we begin," Magda said, motioning to a nearby chair.

"I've been doing some research into the realm of light and I've come to believe that what you seek to do can be accomplished. However, it will likely have a very different outcome than what you're hoping for."

"How so?" Isabel asked with a frown.

"The realm of light is the source of life energy. When you called upon it to heal Abigail, it was doing what it exists to do. Adding its power to a spell of destruction will probably negate the damage caused by the spell. Of course, it's impossible to know for certain without making the attempt, but I wanted you to be aware that your time may be better spent pursuing other spells."

"You said that no spell I can learn in the time I have available will win the day against Gabriella, so I must find something to give me the edge. My connection to the light and the darkness are the only places I can look for that power."

Magda nodded solemnly. "I know," she whispered.

"So how should I begin?" Isabel asked pointedly.

Magda smiled and sighed. "You must exercise your ability to connect to the light. Once you've developed that skill, you must incorporate it into the process of casting the spell, simultaneously drawing on the light while casting your will into the firmament. It will add a degree of complexity to the process that may take some time for you to master.

"The first step is to practice creating a connection to the light. Spend the morning working on that. Create a connection and then close it, over and over until it becomes second nature. You may use my meditation room. If you have any questions, I will be here studying the problem. Perhaps with further research I can help you create the spell you seek."

"Thank you, Magda," Isabel said as she stood.

She went to the little room Magda used to meditate. It was about ten feet square with a beautifully crafted crystal skylight that showered the room with soft illumination. The floor was bare stone with a seven-foot-diameter magic circle inlaid in gold in the center. In the center of the circle was a comfortable cushion. Otherwise the room was empty and bare.

Isabel sat on the cushion and closed her eyes. She relaxed and cleared her mind for a moment before she opened the portal to the realm of light left behind by the birth of the fairy Sara. Whatever Desiderates had done within her mind made the process a simple matter. The light filled her with a feeling of love and safety. She felt rejuvenated and her spirit was buoyed with hope beyond reason. Reluctantly, Isabel closed the link to the light. She felt almost deflated when the life-giving energy faded. After a few moments she realized that the fatigue she was feeling when she arrived at Magda's chambers was gone. She felt awake and alert. Her mind was clear and sharp.

She linked her mind to the realm of light again. The light was bright like the sun, clear and perfect, yet she could look directly at it in her mind's eye without any discomfort. She basked in the warmth of it for a few moments before she closed the connection. It came easily and quickly. She knew within a few minutes of her practice that she was ready to move forward, so she went back to Magda.

"Back already?" Magda asked.

Isabel nodded. "The light comes easily. I can link my mind to it at will with a simple thought and it fills me with warmth and hope. It's beautiful."

Magda nodded with a frown. "I was worried about that. I suspect you will find the next step much more difficult. You must call the anger and then connect with the light. I fear the contradiction will be difficult, if not impossible, to overcome."

Isabel blinked with the realization of what she was trying to do. "I see what you mean. I'll try, but I think you might be right."

She returned to the meditation room and sat down, thinking of Phane and all he'd done to harm the innocent people of the Seven Isles. A spark of anger ignited in the pit of her stomach. She nursed it and fed it with thoughts of injustice and the selfishness of evil until it grew into a formidable rage. With her anger firmly in place, she called to the light. The link came less easily but it came nonetheless. When the light washed into her, the anger she was holding onto with grim determination faded away like fog in sunlight. Hope flooded into her soul and filled her with purpose and faith. She closed the connection and tried again and again, but no matter how determined she was, she could not hold on to anger in the face of the light.

She returned to Magda and sat down, dejected. "I failed. The light and the anger can't coexist within my mind. No matter how hard I try, I simply can't resist the hope of the light."

Magda chuckled softly. "That's a good thing, child. The light shouldn't be resisted. Embrace it and accept it into your soul. We'll find another way."

A thought occurred to Isabel. "What about love? What if I use love to resist the firmament instead of anger?"

"That would set you up for another contradiction," Magda said. "During battle, it's very difficult to create a feeling of love. That's why we use anger for most of the combat-oriented spells we cast. For creative and healing magic, love is the best defense against the pull of the firmament."

"I think it might be easier for me because of the strong positive feeling evoked by my connection to the light. I'd like to try."

"Very well," Magda said. "You may have the capacity to fight with love in your heart. It's rare, but not unheard of."

When Isabel sat down in the meditation room and opened her link to the light, the intense feelings of love necessary to protect her mind from the pull of the firmament came easily and powerfully. She sat for a time simply basking in the glow of it.

She released the link and then created it again. It came quickly, easily, and intensely. Carefully, tentatively, she made a connection to the firmament. It was a juggling act within her mind to hold on to her feelings of love, maintain a mental link to the light, and touch the firmament all at once but she was successful with her first try, even if her connection to the firmament was limited and restrained.

After several hours of work creating the right conditions within her mind to cast the spell, she was ready to attempt it. She returned to Magda with much greater confidence.

"I think I'm ready to give it a try."

Magda raised an eyebrow. "Perhaps some more practice would be in order. This is a new variation on a spell and may produce unforeseen consequences."

"That's what I'm hoping for," Isabel said. "I'm sure I can cast it and I think the only way I can judge the wisdom of continuing to work on it is to attempt it."

"Fair enough. But have some lunch first," Magda said, gesturing to a covered platter. "You've been meditating for hours."

Isabel suddenly realized that it was the middle of the afternoon and she was starving. She ate quickly while she thought about the process of casting the spell. It was very similar to the common version but with the added twist of her unique connection to the realm of light and the usage of love rather than anger to defend against the pull of the firmament. She had no way of knowing what it might do and was eager to find out.

She didn't have long to wait. Soon enough she stood between the lanterns in the practice cavern and faced the target on the distant wall. Very deliberately, she began the process of casting her new spell. First, she called on the light. Then she used the flood of hope and faith she felt to cultivate a feeling of intense love. Once her distraction emotion was firmly in place, she opened a connection to the firmament, although she deliberately restrained the degree of connection she created. Caution was in order. Finally, she envisioned a beam of pure white light leaping from her outstretched hand and striking the target in the distance and she released her vision into the firmament.

Her hand briefly glowed with pure white light that streaked to the target with exacting precision but nothing happened to the stone on the far wall of the cavern. Isabel completed the spell, closing off her link to the light and her connection to the firmament, then frowned with disappointment.

"Nothing," she said, shaking her head.

"Not necessarily," Magda said with a look of deep concentration. "The spell fired. Although it didn't burn the stone, it might have some effect against another person or creature. The realm of light is a place of great creative power. It's very unlikely that you could harness that power in such a direct and concentrated way and yet create no actual effect on your target. Perhaps a different target would reveal something more."

"What did you have in mind?" Isabel asked.

"Long ago, the Reishi Coven developed a spell for just this purpose," Magda said. "It's a variation on a projection spell that's designed to allow a witch to discern the effects of a spell cast at her projection. Normally, a projection is capable of allowing a spell caster to see and hear in the surroundings of their projection as well as speak through their projected image. This version is much more advanced and requires some preparation. It will allow me to identify the specific effects of the spell as if it had been cast against me—without any risk of injury."

"You can do that?" Isabel asked excitedly.

"I can, but I need some time to prepare," Magda said. "I suggest you spend the next few hours practicing your new spell. Use the same process we went through with the basic version. You should always refine any combat spell down to a simple process that comes quickly and easily, even if you aren't quite sure how it will affect your enemies. While you practice, I'll review the advanced projection spell. We'll meet in my chambers after breakfast tomorrow."

Isabel spent the rest of the afternoon casting her spell. She refined the mental process until it came easily. After several hours of practice, she had a sudden thought that sent a thrill of fear up her spine. She felt wonderful from the repeated creation of loving emotions and her connections with the realm of light, so when she tried to cast the basic version of the spell that relied on anger, she couldn't create a strong enough sensation of anger to dare make a connection to the firmament.

After several failed attempts she sat down and focused on Phane and his war against the people of Ruatha. She envisioned all of the hardship, suffering, and despair that he was creating until her anger ignited. Carefully and methodically, she fed her anger until it boiled into rage. Once she had a firm grip on her anger, she cast the basic version of the spell. It came easily and quickly, burning several inches into the stone of the far wall.

The process of moving her emotions from love to anger was slow and difficult. Perhaps the other direction would be easier. She linked her mind to the realm of light and hope flooded into her. Her carefully nursed anger resisted for several moments but eventually washed away in the face of the creative light, leaving ample emotional space for her to create a feeling of love.

She made a mental note. Once she used the light to build a feeling of love, it was much more difficult to cultivate the anger necessary to cast the light-lance spell. While the battle wouldn't be won with the light lance, she might need to cast it nonetheless.

Chapter 28

The next morning in the practice chamber, Magda prepared her advanced projection spell. It took several minutes of concentration and chanting. Isabel watched with rapt attention as the triumvir completed the spell and produced an exact duplicate of herself on the other side of the chamber. Magda sat on the floor in a deep state of meditation while her projection walked over to the place in front of the target.

"Cast your version of the spell at me, Isabel," Magda's projection said. "Be quick, I can't maintain this spell for long."

Isabel called on the light and cast her spell. Light leapt from her hand and stabbed into the image of the triumvir. Love and hope filled Isabel as she released her hold on the firmament.

Magda gasped and her projected image flickered out of existence as her eyes fluttered open. She looked up at Isabel with an expression of serenity and pure contentment, then stood with a gentle smile.

"Child, you have created a spell of profound power even though it will cause no damage to a living creature. It filled me with feelings of hope, faith, and reverence for life. I believe it would dispel the anger a witch needs to cast combat spells as well as induce such intense positive emotion within a wizard that he would not be able to maintain the state of emotional detachment necessary to touch the firmament. A spell capable of disabling another's ability to cast spells is no small thing. As for those who cannot cast spells, I believe your spell would dampen their will to fight."

"It wasn't what I was expecting, but I'll take it," Isabel said. "Any idea how long the effect will last?"

"Not yet, child," Magda said. "I still feel the effects but I'll let you know as soon as I've had time to process the feelings more completely. Come. Walk with me to my chambers."

Magda maintained a wistful smile as they walked through the passageways of the fortress island, even humming to herself a few times. Isabel wondered at the power of her new spell. It had the potential to offer her another edge in the coming fight, but it wouldn't carry the day. Isabel still had a week before she was to meet Gabriella on the battlefield. She intended to make good use of that time.

Magda led her into her chambers and retrieved a book she had set aside on the little table next to her reading chair. She handed it to Isabel with a smile.

"Take this spellbook and study it well. It's a shield spell capable of defending against most physical weapons and some, though certainly not all, direct magical attacks. Take the next few days to master the principles involved with the casting and practice the exercises thoroughly. I will meditate on the effects of your spell and let you know what I learn when next we meet.

"On another matter, it's customary for the one who invents a spell to give it a name. Any thoughts about what you'd like to call your new spell?"

Isabel shrugged. "Maker's light sounds good."

Magda nodded with a smile. "Indeed it does. Study the shield spell and return when you're ready."

Isabel read the book and mastered the principles involved in creating a magical shield around herself. She practiced the exercises for three days until she was confident that she was ready to attempt casting the spell.

It was slightly different from the light-lance spell in that the shield was designed to be created and maintained for several minutes, while the light lance was almost instantaneous. The difference required a shift in her mindset when she released her vision into the firmament. Her vision had to incorporate an element of time in order to impart duration on the spell. Several of the exercises were designed to help her accomplish this.

During the days spent in study, she could see Abigail and Wren worry for her. The battle was quickly approaching, and while they were confident in her, they still feared for her survival. Isabel did her best to put on a brave face but she occasionally felt the nagging doubt of inexperience push in on her.

She decided it was time to begin putting her plan into place. Subtly and gently, she began to worry aloud about Gabriella bringing her wyvern to the battle. She expressed her concern only in the presence of Wren, displaying confidence against Gabriella but not if she came to the battlefield riding her steed. It didn't take long for her worry to transfer to Wren. The young waif of a serving girl was eager to see Isabel survive and began to grow concerned about Gabriella bringing her wyvern to the fight.

Isabel felt slightly guilty for using Wren in such a way but she also knew that a good deception had to play on the assumptions of others. Isabel felt certain that Wren would innocently express her concern to her mother, and her mother would ensure that the message was delivered through the circuitous route of gossip to Gabriella's ears. Planting the seed in this way, Isabel was hopeful that Gabriella would do exactly what she needed her to do: come to the battlefield riding Asteroth.

Abigail was healing quickly. Once she was strong enough to move about, she started walking in the gardens with Wren to build her strength and stretch her legs. The bruising on her face and shoulders faded and her color returned to normal. Isabel was grateful for her recovery. Abigail had become one of her best friends and the sight of her injuries made Isabel's stomach squirm.

After several days of careful study, Isabel went to Magda with the spellbook under her arm. She had grown accustomed to the looks she got from people in the halls. Some seemed to feel sorry for her, while others were openly gleeful at her coming demise. Occasionally she would let their doubt of her survival get to her but mostly she remained confident in her plan. She had abilities that Gabriella didn't know about. Isabel intended to exploit those abilities to secure her survival, and more importantly, her place as Lady Reishi.

She suspected that Alexander would be furious if he knew what she was facing. He would never accept that anyone could challenge her marriage to him, least of all for simple personal vengeance. As she knocked on Magda's door she hoped she was doing the right thing.

"Come in," Magda said from behind the door.

Isabel found the triumvir sitting in her reading chair sipping tea from a fine ceramic cup. She motioned for Isabel to sit and poured her a cup.

They talked for most of the morning as Magda questioned her about the shield spell. By the time Magda was satisfied with her understanding of the spell, Isabel was mentally tired from the thorough examination but she knew time was short and she needed to make the most of it, so she insisted that she attempt the casting.

She struggled for most of the afternoon to cast the spell. She failed over and over because she wasn't accustomed to creating a spell with a duration effect. It took several hours before she was able to create the shield and then it only lasted for a few moments before it winked out of existence. When Isabel began to become frustrated with her repeated failure, Magda stopped her.

"You've done enough for today, child. Think about how it felt when the shield worked. Your mindset was different during that casting than all of the others. Spend the evening thinking about that feeling and frame of mind. Return to me tomorrow and we'll continue with your practice.

"Also consider the emotion you choose to use with the spell. A shield can be cast with either love or anger. Both will work as your distraction emotion but you should choose carefully to ensure that you can cast the other spells you may need since it's often difficult to switch emotions quickly."

Isabel nodded and returned to her chambers dejected and exhausted. After a quiet dinner eaten amid worried looks from Abigail and Wren, Isabel retired to her room to meditate on the shield spell. She played the attempts to cast the spell over and over in her mind, looking for the difference between all of the failures and the one successful casting.

By bedtime she thought she'd discovered the difference. The one time she was successful she had envisioned motion occurring around her. The times she had failed, she had seen her surroundings as static. She drifted off to sleep wondering about the significance of the difference.

The next morning the concept seemed to spring full-blown into her mind the moment she woke. Motion could only happen within the context of time. Adding motion to her visualization communicated the concept of time to the firmament and therefore created a shield that had duration.

When she explained her conclusions to Magda, the triumvir smiled and nodded. "Well done, child. That concept is often difficult for novices to grasp and even more difficult to implement. Spend the rest of the day working on your visualization exercises, paying particular attention to the third exercise that focuses on your surroundings. Come back tomorrow and attempt the casting again."

Isabel was impatient to make the spell work but she reluctantly agreed. The day passed quickly. Abigail had regained enough strength that she was tending to Kallistos, so Wren spent the day watching Isabel meditate. At first it was a bit unsettling but Isabel chose to use the harmless distraction as an opportunity to hone her powers of concentration.

She returned to Magda the following day with renewed confidence. Her first attempt at casting the shield spell created a bubble of magical energy surrounding her at a range of about three feet that lasted for nearly a full minute.

By the end of the day she could cast the spell with greater ease, although not nearly as fast as the light lance, and she could maintain it for almost ten minutes.

The following day, Magda spent the morning launching attacks at Isabel to build her confidence in the shield. At first she flinched and ducked out of the way of the rocks that Magda hurled at her but once she saw how they bounced harmlessly off her shield, she became more confident in the magic. When Magda moved on to magical attacks, Isabel was again less sure of her ability to protect herself but she soon found that her shield spell protected against the light-lance spell, although Magda admitted she was not powering the spell at her full potential. Magda directed a variety of other spells at Isabel from magically hurling rocks at her with significant force to casting a gout of magical fire at her to directing a burst of magical force at her.

The second time Magda hurled the wave of magical force, it penetrated the shield and sent Isabel sprawling onto her back. She felt the shield spell collapse as the magic hit it and knew instinctively that, without the protection of the shield, the spell would have probably killed her.

"You've done enough for today," Magda said as she helped her to her feet. "I hit you harder that last time to show you what you can expect from Gabriella. She will not use the restraint I have shown today. With all of my attacks, I was careful and measured to ensure that I wouldn't overpower your shield. It will absorb the brunt of the first attack she throws at you but will probably collapse in the process. Her second attack will kill you.

"It's not too late to reconsider. I can fight in your stead or you can flee this place and be done with her challenge. Either way, you will survive. If you fight her, even with your Maker's light spell, she will most likely kill you."

"I've made up my mind," Isabel said firmly. "I'm going to face Gabriella and I'm going to kill her, even if no one believes I can."

"You certainly have the stubbornness of a witch," Magda said, shaking her head. "I've taught you all I can in the time we've had. The challenge will take place in a few days. Spend the time with Abigail and prepare as best you can. If you reconsider, I'll help you in any way that I can. If you choose to fight, I cannot intervene once the battle has begun."

"I understand. Thank you, Magda. You've given me a fighting chance. When this is over, I hope you'll forgive me for killing Gabriella."

Magda chuckled. "If I didn't know better, I'd suspect you're bringing something to the battlefield I'm not aware of."

Isabel schooled her face and calmed her emotions. She couldn't let anyone know that she could control the wyverns. Her survival depended on that one ability.

She shrugged. "Once I've disabled her spell casting with my Maker's light spell, I'll kill her with Abigail's bow or my sword. Without her magic, she's no match for me on the battlefield."

"Perhaps, but I must warn you, Gabriella is very cunning. She will come to the field with a plan and she has a wide variety of spells to draw on. Don't believe everything you see—she's very good at deception and illusion."

The remaining days before the challenge passed quickly. Isabel went over her plan again and again. She refined it and added contingency plans to compensate for Gabriella's actions. She sharpened her sword and practiced with Abigail's bow. She reviewed the three spells in her repertoire and very carefully practiced her control over the wyverns. When she was sick of preparing, she thought of Alexander and hoped he was safe. She longed to see him again but her only path lay through Gabriella. Defeat her or die. Those were her choices.

The morning of the challenge came and Isabel woke well rested and confident. She was tired of the anticipation and wanted the fight over with, one way or another.

Abigail and Wren were at the breakfast table when Isabel emerged from her room. Wren had laid out a large spread for breakfast. The possibility of it being her last meal wasn't lost on Isabel. She ate her fill, deliberately savoring every bite.

"You're sure about this," Abigail said as Wren cleared the dishes.

"I am. One way or another our stay here is coming to an end," Isabel said. "If Gabriella kills me, you need to leave as soon as possible. Go to Magda and ask for her help. Take Kallistos and Wren and go to Ithilian. Find Alexander and tell him that I love him."

"I thought you said you were sure about this," Abigail said with a frown.

Isabel shrugged. "Can't hurt to have a contingency plan."

The morning passed quickly and quietly. Isabel reviewed her strategy, her spells, her weapons, and her connection to the wyverns until she was sure of herself. In a prayer to the Maker, she said her goodbyes to Alexander and her family, then began nursing her anger as she strapped on her armor.

She focused on Gabriella, on her selfishness and desire for petty vengeance in the face of such a dangerous time for the people of the Seven Isles. She let the anger build into a coiled rage and held it in the pit of her stomach as she walked with Wren and Abigail to the top of the plateau. The witches and the Sky Knights were all assembled around the battlefield. The sun had reached the highest point in the sky on a clear and warm summer day. Under other circumstances it would have been a wonderful day for a stroll through the gardens.

Isabel gave Abigail and Wren a hug, checked her sword in its scabbard, and stepped onto the battlefield. She heard Slyder screech from overhead and felt a sense of comfort knowing her familiar was watching over her.

Gabriella arrived a few moments later, riding her giant wyvern Asteroth, and landed on the opposite end of the field. She gave a nod to Cassandra and Magda who stood on a platform at the center of one side of the battlefield.

In a clear and unwavering voice, Magda spoke to the assembled witches, Sky Knights, and trade class. "We have come to witness the challenge issued by Mistress Gabriella against Lady Reishi for her title. This contest will end only with the death or surrender of one and the victory of the other. The victor will claim the title of the vanquished. Mistress Gabriella, Lady Reishi, you have three minutes to make preparations. The battle will begin when the bell tolls."

Isabel reached out with her mind to make contact with Gabriella's steed. A thrill of alarm ran up her spine when she couldn't find the wyvern that was plainly standing before her. She looked across the battlefield. Gabriella was sitting atop her magnificent wyvern, watching her like a bug in a jar—but Isabel couldn't find Asteroth's mind. When she broadened her search, she was alarmed to find Gabriella's steed napping lazily in his aerie.

Things were not as they seemed. Not for the first time, Isabel wished she had Alexander's sight. He would know the truth of what she faced.

She tipped her head back and looked through Slyder's eyes at the field below. What she saw made her gasp. Gabriella stood off to the side of the field near the edge opposite the other two triumvirs and her steed wasn't even there. Gabriella was using the magic of illusion.

Isabel touched Asteroth's mind and called out to him, demanding that he come forth for battle. A roar reverberated through the stone of the fortress island. She only hoped he would arrive soon enough to make a difference. Her plan had backfired. Gabriella was showing her what she wanted to see. Deception indeed.

Isabel quickly cast the shield spell to give herself some measure of protection against Gabriella's first attack and then nocked an arrow. She faced the illusion and closed her eyes to link with Slyder. Through his eyes she could see the entire field as it really was. Gabriella's magic appeared to work on all of the assembled people yet not on Slyder, possibly because Isabel had never revealed that she had a familiar to anyone on the fortress island.

She waited, holding her breath, until the bell tolled. As the clear tone died out, Isabel loosed her arrow at Gabriella's true position. The triumvir dodged quickly and cried out in rage as the shaft sliced along her left shoulder.

The battle was joined and Isabel had drawn first blood. She felt the calm of the fight settle on her. All of her nervousness faded as her senses sharpened and her mind focused.

She opened her eyes to see the illusion of Gabriella and Asteroth fade while at the same time the real Gabriella came into sight. Isabel loosed another arrow but Gabriella raised a shield of her own that deflected the shaft.

She turned a murderous glare on Isabel even as she raised her hand and cast a spell. A wave of magical force crashed into Isabel's shield, collapsing the magically protective bubble and knocking Isabel flat on her back. She hit the ground hard and shook her head in a daze from the shock of the blow. She heard a wyvern roar from above, but Asteroth would be too late. Gabriella's next attack would finish her.

Isabel shook off the haze in her mind and tried to get up, only to find that the grass of the field had grown up and around her arms and legs, pinning her to the ground. From off in the distance, she heard the gloating laughter of Gabriella as the triumvir walked toward her prey.

Isabel felt a thrill of panic but pushed it away in favor of rage. She poured the fuel of fear into her anger and ripped her right arm free of the grass so she could hit Gabriella with a light-lance spell. It came easily and was fueled with greater rage and a stronger connection to the firmament than Isabel had ever managed before. The heat of battle mixed with the deliberate anger she'd been nursing protected her from the full and unrestrained connection she made with the firmament. The power of the spell should have been enough to sear the flesh from Gabriella's bones, but she stood leaning into her shield as the piercing heat of the light was absorbed or deflected away.

When the light was spent, Gabriella laughed. "Is that everything, girl? Do you have anything else you'd like to try?" She sauntered toward Isabel, still pinned to the ground by magically animated vegetation, with a grim and menacing grin.

Isabel touched Gabriella's steed with her mind. He was still a minute or two from arriving at the field after breaking free of his handler's attempts to restrain him and launching himself into the sky from the nearest bay.

Isabel thought of Alexander. She needed to see him again. If she could survive for just a minute more, she had a fighting chance. With thoughts of him, her anger broke. She linked to the light and hope flooded into her. She let it come and embraced the feeling of love that grew within her soul. When she felt as if she might burst from the overwhelming power of the emotion, she connected to the firmament and embraced it.

The love she felt was bigger than the draw of the firmament, even when she stared it straight in the face. She cast her shield spell using Slyder orbiting high overhead as her point of reference for motion. Her shield sprang to life just a moment before Gabriella cast a light-lance spell of her own. The brilliance of the light was dazzling but the heat of it never reached her. Her shield held.

Gabriella stopped and stared in disbelief. "How can this be?"

The triumvir raised her hand again, muttering an angry chant. An orb of blackness formed before her outstretched hand. Isabel heard a collective gasp from the onlookers as Gabriella released the dark magic. It hit Isabel's shield and seemed to drain the magic from it, until only a moment later, it sputtered out and vanished, leaving her vulnerable and still pinned to the ground.

She clung to the hope of the light and cast her last, best hope for survival. Her Maker's light spell stabbed out from her hand and hit Gabriella's shield, driving through it as if it wasn't even there. The light flooded into Gabriella and a strange expression ghosted across her face, as if she was remembering something vitally important that she had forgotten long ago.

Gabriella raised her hand and tried to cast another spell at Isabel but stopped with a look of sudden concern just as a shadow was cast across her from behind. She turned to see Asteroth, her faithful steed, land within striking distance. Gabriella faltered at the sight. She had been bonded to Asteroth for nearly a hundred years. He was loyal to her and yet he stood poised to strike.

Isabel shouted the command into Asteroth's mind, "Kill her!"

The wyvern didn't hesitate. His bone-bladed tail whipped over his head and drove through Gabriella's shield and into her chest, cutting her in half with a single strike. She toppled over with a stricken look of shock, terror, and surprise.

The grass abruptly released its hold on Isabel and she struggled to her feet even as Asteroth tipped his head back and roared with the realization of what he'd just done. His bond was broken and he was feeling lost and alone. Isabel reached into his mind and imposed her will on him once again, this time to comfort the beast and to win his loyalty. She imprinted herself on him and assumed Gabriella's place as his rider.

When she stood and patted Asteroth's giant jaw, the assembled crowd fell deathly silent. When she mounted her new steed, the Sky Knights collectively dropped to one knee.

Isabel faced the two remaining triumvirs from atop Asteroth. "Gabriella is dead. I claim the title of triumvir and I confirm my right to the title of Lady Reishi."

To punctuate her proclamation she touched the minds of every wyvern in the fortress island and issued a single command: Roar!

Chapter 29

Alexander's eyes flickered open. He was in a stone room with no windows but ample light. He felt cold, not like the cold of exposure but deeper, in his bones. Chloe flitted up over his face and smiled at him with a mixture of worry and relief before she buzzed off to find Lucky.

The earth shook and a rumble reverberated through the stone of the floor. Lucky came to his side a moment later, along with Jack.

"Lie still, Alexander. You've been out for about an hour," Lucky said. "How do you feel?"

"Cold . . . and empty," Alexander said as his hand went to the bandaged wound on his neck. "What's happened?"

"We retreated into the underground chambers beneath the ruins," Jack said. "That wizard has been pounding the mountain with lightning for the past hour. Jataan reports that the entrance we used to get in here has collapsed but the passages go deeper into the mountain, so there may be another way out."

"Is everyone all right?" Alexander asked.

"Evelyn was injured by the revenant's bite," Lucky said. "She fell unconscious but woke several minutes after I applied healing salve to her wound. I gave her a healing draught and she's resting quietly. You, on the other hand, are not healing and I'm worried that my magic isn't powerful enough to overcome the revenant's bite."

Alexander shook his head. "We have to kill the one that bit me. Otherwise, I'll turn into one of them."

"That might be a problem," Anatoly said. "We're trapped down here and we've heard the scream of at least one more revenant from the chambers below."

The ground shook again, showering Alexander with a coating of dust.

"And the wizard hasn't given up on us yet. How are you feeling?" Anatoly asked.

"I've been better," Alexander replied as he sat up. The wound on his neck still hurt but what worried him more was the feeling of numbing cold spreading from the bite into the rest of his body.

Chloe flew up and hovered a foot from his face. "I'm worried about you, My Love. I can feel the darkness growing within you."

"Me too, Little One," Alexander said. "It's supposed to take a month for the transformation to run its course. Hopefully, the soldiers or the wizard out there will kill the revenant for us and solve my problem."

"If they don't, what then?" Anatoly asked.

"It doesn't like the light, so it'll look for another way back underground before dawn," Alexander said. "I doubt it'll abandon its lair so easily. My guess is we'll have another run-in with the thing. Hopefully, it won't get the best of me next time."

Jataan returned with Boaberous in tow. "It's good to see you awake again, Lord Reishi. We've searched this level and found several rooms that look like they were once libraries or workrooms, but everything has long since turned to dust. There's a staircase leading to another level below but we thought it best not to venture too far."

"Good, I want to take a look at those rooms," Alexander said as he got to his feet. He was weak and chilled and felt sick but he forced himself to focus on the task at hand in spite of the magic working to transform him into a monster. "We'll be back in a few minutes."

Alexander raised his vial of night-wisp dust to illuminate the narrow corridor. It was made from stone blocks cut carefully and expertly set without mortar. The place was ancient but fresh revenant tracks were visible in the dust covering the floor. Alexander quickly evaluated the other rooms with his second sight for some hint of anything magical but saw nothing. They were exactly what Jataan said they were, the broken remains of long-abandoned workrooms.

On their way back to the room nearest the collapsed entrance, the old man in robes stepped out of one of the rooms they had already inspected and faced Alexander with a look of appraisal. Jataan stepped forward but Alexander stilled him with a hand on his shoulder.

"Who are you?" Alexander asked. He could see the man with his eyes but his magical sight told him something very different. There was no aura of life or magic. To Alexander's second sight, the man wasn't even there.

"Are you worthy?" the man asked, then shimmered out of existence.

"I guess we're going to find out," Alexander muttered.

When they returned to the others, Evelyn was awake and sitting up. Alexander appraised the weary looks on the faces around him and decided that his quest for knowledge about his calling could wait. Everyone was exhausted and they were in as safe a place as possible, given the situation.

"Everybody get some rest," Alexander said. "Place a vial of night-wisp dust in the hall outside the door and make sure that the person standing watch has one as well. The soldiers can't get to us without making enough noise to wake the dead, so the revenant in the lower chambers is the real concern.

"Also, keep an eye out for the illusions we've been seeing. Jataan and I just saw that man again in the hallway. I don't know what he has to do with anything, but I do know he's not really there. Don't let him lure you away from the group."

Alexander slept fitfully, waking frequently with dark and menacing nightmares. He'd never suffered from terror in his dreams before. He was starting to dread the idea of sleep because he knew it would bring the fear. It was different than real, rational fear. This was the all-encompassing fear of a dream that offered no escape and no means of resistance.

Just after his turn at watch sometime in the middle of the night, the lightning strikes stopped and the room fell quiet save for Lucky's gentle snoring and the rhythmic breathing of everyone else.

Alexander sat on a clear space on the floor and traced the outline of a magic circle around him in the dust. It took several minutes to quiet his mind. The numbing cold of the revenant bite was a constant distraction but he managed to overcome it with some effort. Once he found himself floating on the firmament, he focused on his task. The world rushed by in a blur and he found himself floating over the bed of Abel Ithilian. He was sleeping fitfully and his wife lay awake staring at the ceiling.

Alexander drifted into Abel's dreams and found him fighting a terrible monster that was about to devour his daughter. Alexander imposed his will on Abel's dreams, dispelling the imaginary enemy and leaving the two of them sitting in Abel's favorite study.

Abel looked all around with sudden dismay and confusion. "What's happening?" he asked.

"Abel, it's me, Alexander. I'm using my magic to communicate with you in your dreams. I've rescued Evelyn. The enemy is pursuing. Begin your attack into Grafton."

Abel woke with a start and Alexander found himself floating against the ceiling of his bedchamber.

"Sofia," Abel said excitedly, "Alexander has rescued Evelyn. I have to go speak with General Kishor."

Sofia hugged her husband fiercely and sobbed into his nightshirt for several moments before she gained some composure.

"Make those bastards pay for what they've done to her," she said through her tears.

Alexander returned to the firmament and then to the room where he sat meditating quietly. Chloe sat on his knee watching over him nervously while Jack sat against a wall watching the door and listening for any hint of danger.

He drifted out of the room and down to the level below. There was a long hall leading to three rooms, all equally dilapidated and abandoned. There were no signs of the revenant or the secrets that Alexander had come so far to find. He searched farther but realized that, even with his clairvoyance, he needed light to see some things. He knew there was probably another hidden door somewhere in one of the three rooms, but he would have to search for it with light to have any chance of finding it.

He floated through the stone of the ruins above and into the night sky. The stars were shining and the angry clouds conjured by the wizard were gone. Alexander drifted out over the enemy encampment and saw a scene of battle unfolding that was at once terrible and satisfying.

Two revenants flew over the soldiers below, periodically swooping down to snatch a victim from the feast arrayed before them, then carrying the screaming soldier into the night sky while feeding on his life force. With such a plentiful bounty to choose from, they didn't bother to draw the life completely out of any given soldier, just the vitality of the moment. When they were finished, they dropped the soldier to his death, crashing into those below and spreading terror through the ranks.

In the center of the encampment stood the wizard, casting lightning from his hands when the opportunity presented itself but missing most of the time. The single bolt of lightning that did strike home elicited a shriek of anger from the revenant but little more. Alexander knew from Malachi's description of the monsters that they were difficult to kill, especially if they had fed recently. Judging by the number of broken bodies littering the camp, these two had fed well. It was clear that the soldiers would probably not be able to kill either of them.

Alexander returned to his body and opened his eyes. Chloe looked up at him and smiled.

"I'm glad you're back, My Love," she said in his mind. "It always worries me when you leave like that."

"I know, Little One, but it was necessary. I sent word to Abel to begin his attack and then I took a look at our enemies outside. The soldiers are not faring well against the revenants, which poses a problem for me. The one that bit me needs to be killed before we leave this place and I was hoping the soldiers would do it for me. Hopefully, it'll find its way back down here."

"What happens if it runs away?" Chloe asked silently.

Alexander shrugged. "I'll have to hunt it down. It's the only way."

He lay on his bedroll and tried not to think about the night terrors as he drifted off to sleep. By morning he was not fully rested, but he was feeling slightly stronger for the few hours of sleep he'd gotten.

They ate a cold breakfast and made ready to search the lower level of the ruined fortress. As they were hoisting their packs into place, they heard a noise coming from the direction of the collapsed entrance. Alexander went to the pile of rubble filling the hole in the ceiling where the staircase had once stood and closed his eyes. He reached out with his all around sight and stretched to see through the ceiling up to the level above but couldn't reach far enough with his magical vision through all of the debris.

"I can go see what is happening above, My Love," Chloe said in his mind.

Alexander was a little chagrinned that he hadn't thought to enlist her aid in the first place.

"Thank you, Little One," he said with a sheepish smile.

She spun into a ball of light and was gone.

Alexander closed his eyes and linked his mind with hers as she floated up through the stone of the ceiling and the mound of rubble covering the entrance. As he looked through her eyes, it reminded him of how it felt to use his clairvoyance: a disembodied presence able to see but not be seen.

She surfaced amid dozens of soldiers working feverishly to clear the rocks and debris. It was just after dawn and the revenants were nowhere to be seen. The soldiers looked weary and exhausted from such a long night of defending against the onslaught from the sky. Their efforts to clear away the rubble were poorly directed and seemed more focused on finding some hint of where Alexander had gone rather than a deliberate effort to clear away the passage to the level below. Alexander breathed a sigh of relief. They still had time before the enemy poured into the underground chambers beneath the ruins. He meant to make good use of that time.

They descended into the chambers below with deliberate caution. Alexander expected that the other revenants had returned underground, although he had no way of knowing if they'd found another lair to hole up in or if they had another way into the chambers beneath the ruins.

It was cold and quiet but with the light of the night-wisp dust, they could easily see the tracks left by the revenants' comings and goings. The two rooms to either side of the long corridor were empty and abandoned but the room at the end of the hall had a multitude of revenant tracks leading to and fro. Alexander took a few minutes to inspect the two side rooms but came away empty-handed. Both rooms were vacant of anything of use or interest, having been exposed to the ravages of time for so many centuries.

The room at the end of the hall looked like it had once been a large study, though the furniture was nothing more than dust stains on the bare stone floor. There was a hearth on the far wall and evidence that once, long ago, the walls had been lined with bookshelves.

The floor was marred by the clawed footsteps of the revenants all leading to a place on one wall and then to the right of the hearth. Alexander inspected the wall carefully but found nothing, even with his second sight.

"I don't understand," he said with frustration. "It's obvious they came through here and it looks pretty clear that they came to this place in the wall and then went through a hidden door over there."

"Why not just cut your way through?" Conner asked. "You had no trouble getting through the wall to Grafton Keep. This not-so-hidden door shouldn't pose a problem for the Thinblade."

Alexander nodded. "The thought occurred to me, but we've got an army trying to find its way down here. The longer we can delay them the better our chances of escaping without a fight. If we can find a way to open the door, we can keep them looking that much longer."

"Perhaps a fresh pair of eyes might help," Jack said.

"Have at it," Alexander said, stepping aside for the bard.

Jack carefully inspected the wall, looking closely at each stone. He poked and prodded until he found a stone that moved ever so slightly when he pressed on it. Nodding, he held the stone down and carefully inspected all of the other stones near enough to reach. After several minutes of very systematic inspection, he found that another stone near his left foot pushed in just a slight bit as well. With both stones depressed, he began the process again, balancing on his right foot, until he found another stone that gave under pressure with a loud click. A section of wall next to the hearth swung inward, revealing a dark passage leading to a spiral staircase cut into the stone.

"Nicely done, Jack," Alexander said as he drew the Thinblade.

"You aren't seriously going to go down there, are you?" Evelyn asked.

"We all are," Alexander said. "The enemy is digging through the rubble looking for us. It's only a matter of time before they find the passage and clear the entrance. I'm not leaving anyone behind and I need to see what's down there—so we all go."

Evelyn started to say more but Conner put his hand on her shoulder and shook his head.

Alexander looked to the rest of his companions and nodded his approval as, one by one, they indicated their readiness to proceed. Jataan led the way, followed by Alexander with his light held high. Anatoly brought up the rear and closed the door behind them. Slowly and cautiously, they made their way down the winding staircase as it corkscrewed through the stone of the mountain, taking them ever deeper. They stopped every twenty steps or so, listening for the revenant. It was obvious from the clawed footprints on the stairs that the unnatural beasts had passed this way frequently.

They descended for nearly half an hour before they heard the scream of a revenant reverberate through the bedrock of the mountain. It sounded distant but still too near for comfort. Alexander reminded himself that he needed to kill the one that had bitten him or all would be lost. He steeled his resolve and nodded for Jataan to continue. The stair led down for another hundred feet or so. They were now deep within the mountain. The stone was cold and the air was still. Alexander idly wondered to himself what the ancient adept wizard who'd created this keep could have possibly wanted so deep within the stone of the mountain.

Jataan signaled that there was something just around the next turn in the stairs, and they heard the scream of the revenant again. It was concentrated and focused by the stone of the staircase and sent a chill of terror coursing through Alexander. He froze in place for only a moment before the creature came around the corner. With one wing it shielded its eyes from Alexander's light as it snatched Jataan and escaped back down the stairs. Alexander broke free of the paralyzing fear and darted down after the dark creature.

Alexander held up his light to illuminate a circular room with a domed ceiling thirty feet across. There were three exits aside from the staircase. Jataan had broken through the paralyzing fear of the revenant's scream and was struggling to free himself from its supernatural grip. He was on his back with the beast pinning him to the ground. He had one arm free and was stabbing the revenant repeatedly in the side of the chest, but with each new wound, the previous injury quickly healed over. The revenant was struggling to keep control over Jataan while shielding itself from the glare of the light.

Alexander swept into the room and slashed at the beast in a diagonal arc, slicing one wing in half. The severed portion of membranous batlike wing fell over Jataan and covered his face, making it difficult for him to judge the aim of his knife as he repeatedly stabbed the revenant. The revenant shrieked in pain even as the severed edge of its wing began to heal over. In the face of the light and the sudden assault, the revenant started to release Jataan in preparation to retreat, but Alexander was faster. He brought his blade back up and across the creature, slicing cleanly through its shoulder, across its body below the neck and out the top of its other shoulder. The revenant fell into pieces on top of Jataan who quickly thrust the remains of the creature off him.

The battle mage gained his feet and drew his sword in one fluid motion searching for an enemy. Failing to find one, he composed himself, drew himself up to his full height of five and a half feet, and nodded his thanks to Alexander.

A moment later Boaberous entered the room ready. He surveyed the scene and took a position watching the far door without even a grunt for the carnage that lay in the middle of the room. Everyone else entered on his heels.

Anatoly gave Alexander a grim nod of approval and a clap on the shoulder as he went to stand guard at the nearest door while motioning for Conner to take the third and final exit to the little room.

Conner headed for the door with a quip for his sister, "Told you they can be killed."

As if in answer, another revenant screamed from somewhere down one of the passages leading from the entry hall.

"Are you injured, Commander P'Tal?" Lucky asked.

"Not seriously," he replied as Lucky handed him a towel to wipe the dark blood of the foul beast from his face and hands.

"Take a minute and get cleaned up, Jataan," Alexander said. "There's no telling what their blood might do to you and I'd rather not find out."

Jataan frowned, then nodded as he unslung his pack and started changing clothes.

"Why do you think the wizard who built this place went so deep underground?" Jack mused as he looked all around the entry hall for anything of note.

"I don't know but I don't like it down here," Evelyn said as she poked the dead revenant in the eye with her sword. "I do feel better knowing these things can die though."

"Unfortunately, I don't think this is the one that bit me," Alexander muttered.

"How can you be sure?" Lucky asked.

"I still feel the cold seeping into me from the bite," Alexander said.

"Well, there's at least one more down here," Anatoly said. "So either you're right about there being another way in or there are a lot more of these things than we first suspected."

Jataan finished changing his clothes and packed his pack. He was dressed in an identical set of black pants, black shirt, and black cloak. He rolled his blood-soaked clothes in his other cloak and discarded them.

"I'm ready to proceed, Lord Reishi," he said.

Before Alexander could decide on a course of action, a man walked out of the shadows of the passage being guarded by Boaberous. The giant gave a fierce battle cry as he lunged at the man with his war hammer but it passed through him as if he wasn't even there. The man in grey robes proceeded to walk straight through Boaberous and stopped in the middle of the room, facing Alexander. He had no colors but Alexander could see him as plain as day.

"Many have tried, but you are the first to come this far," he said. "Are you worthy?"

"Who are you?" Alexander asked as his friends tensed for battle.

"I am what you've come here for," the man replied. Then he turned to black smoke that evaporated in seconds.

Alexander felt a thrill of anticipation in spite of the numbing cold emanating from the bite on his neck and the fatigue from so many days without sleep. He would find answers to some of his most pressing questions—and soon.

"I for one, would like to know what he's all about," Jack said.

Alexander nodded his agreement. "We'll try that one first," he said, pointing to the corridor to the right of the staircase entrance.

Jataan led, sword in hand, with Alexander behind him and Anatoly bringing up the rear. The corridor was cut from the stone of the mountain and ran straight for thirty feet before it opened into a room. The last few feet of the hallway transformed from bedrock granite to crystal that caught the light of Alexander's night-wisp dust and glittered like a wall of diamonds. When they entered the chamber, Alexander was speechless.

The room was about forty feet across and it was cut from the heart of a giant vein of crystal. The floor, walls, and arched ceiling were all translucent and polished. The light of the night-wisp dust danced and glittered off every surface as Alexander walked to the center of the room. A magic circle twenty feet in diameter was set into the floor in gold, but otherwise the room was completely empty and there were no other exits.

The splendor of the place was magnified by the slight aura of magic that radiated from every surface.

"I've never seen anything like this place," Evelyn whispered. "Isn't it beautiful?"

"Very much so," Jack said. "I wonder at its purpose but I suspect my previous question has been answered. As with most questions, the answer has only served to produce many more questions."

"I wonder if this is what I'm looking for," Alexander said. "If it is, I have no idea what to do with it. Any thoughts, Lucky?"

"I've read about wizards who use crystals to magnify or stabilize their connection to the firmament," Lucky said. "But this takes the practice to a whole new level and if the wizard who built this place was an adept, there's no telling what he might have used this room for."

"I wonder if the Reishi Sovereigns might know what it is," Alexander mused.

"Couldn't hurt to ask," Jack suggested, but before Alexander could make a decision, they heard the bloodcurdling scream of a revenant. The terrifying shriek was too far away to have the paralyzing effect it did up close, but it still sent a chill up Alexander's spine and evoked a primal and irrational fear that he struggled for a moment to overcome.

"Maybe we should deal with that before you start meditating," Anatoly suggested.

"Good idea," Alexander said.

They left the splendorous room in single file and reached the entry hall without encountering another revenant. Alexander motioned for Jataan to take the exit to the right and directly across from the staircase entrance. Jataan nodded and was headed that way when a thick black fog started to flow out of the passage. He stopped and raised his sword. Alexander held his light higher and scrutinized the fog. It quickly flowed into the room and surrounded them with darkness about three feet deep.

"I don't like this," Evelyn said.

"Me neither, but we have to press on," Alexander said. "Keep going, Jataan."

They slowly and cautiously moved through the thick black fog until the corridor opened into a large room. When they entered, a revenant screamed at them from across the room. Jataan and Alexander broke through the fear in just a few seconds and spread out to face the monster. Lucky came in behind them holding his light high to better illuminate the room and to keep the creature from escaping down the corridor filled with his paralyzed companions.

The revenant ducked below the level of the black fog, disappearing from view. Alexander could just make out the dark but powerful aura of the creature and struck out at it a moment before it reached him, but his strike only wounded the beast. The revenant grasped him by the legs and knocked him to the ground.

For the first time in his life, Alexander was truly blinded. The thick black fog totally obscured his vision as well as his second sight and even his all around sight. He felt a moment of panic. The revenant clambered on top of him, pinning him to the ground with its superior strength and took hold of his sword arm at the wrist. Alexander struggled as the beast sank its fangs into the side of his neck, not far from his previous wound.

Once again, he felt the numbing cold of his life energy being drained. His strength began to flow away as he struggled to free his sword arm. The end of his strength was fast approaching, so he changed his tactics. Rather than struggle to free his sword arm, he slipped his belt knife free with his left hand and plunged the blade into the beast's side with all of his remaining strength. As Alexander twisted the blade, the revenant released its bite and straightened up to scream in pain from the deep wound.

When its head broke the surface of the thick black fog, Jataan struck with precision and terrifying speed. The creature's head came free and it collapsed on top of Alexander. The thick black fog dissipated within seconds of the creature's death, and the rest of Alexander's friends rushed into the room. Anatoly snatched the corpse of the foul beast off Alexander and tossed it aside. Lucky went to work tending to Alexander's wounds as he slipped into unconsciousness.

After a dreamless sleep, he woke to Chloe sitting on his chest.

"How do you feel, My Love?"

"Beat up," he whispered.

"Lie still," Lucky said. "You took quite a beating and that thing drained a great deal of your strength. Let me have a look at your wound."

Lucky carefully removed the bandage and smiled with relief. "I believe that was the one that bit you in the first place. Your wounds are healing nicely. Do you still feel the numbing cold you described before?"

Alexander thought about it for a moment and shook his head. He was exhausted and felt like at least one of his ribs was broken but the dark magic of the creature was gone.

"Good, now drink this and try to get some sleep," Lucky said as he held up a vial of healing draught.

Alexander obeyed and was soon sleeping deeply. He dreamt of Isabel and woke several hours later feeling better than he had in days.

They were in a room about fifty feet square with two doors leading out. It was clear from the human remains scattered about the room that this had served as the lair of the revenants for quite some time. It looked like the room was once a wizard's workshop, while the other two smaller rooms were a bedchamber and a storage room.

"How long have I been out?" Alexander asked as he got to his feet. He was still stiff and it hurt to breathe but he was greatly relieved that the numbing cold of the revenant was no longer seeping into his body.

"Quite a while," Anatoly said. "We've held position in these rooms and searched pretty thoroughly but found nothing of any use."

Alexander scanned the place and instantly saw what he was looking for. One wall just a few feet from the corner had a single stone that glowed with the faint aura of magic. He went straight to it and pushed on it—but nothing happened. With a frown, he pushed harder but it didn't budge. When he sent his all around sight into the wall to see what lay beyond, the stone glowed brightly for a moment before a section of the wall vanished completely, opening a passageway to a staircase leading still farther down.

"It must have been triggered by magic," Alexander said. "Before we go any farther, have you heard any other revenants or any sign of the soldiers above?"

"No on both counts," Anatoly said. "But we still haven't looked into the third passage leading from the entry hall."

"I suspect that's our way out," Alexander said. "The one that bit me had to get back in here somehow and I'll bet it was down that hall. Stay alert. There's at least one left and it might be waiting for us."

With that he held up the night-wisp dust and drew the Thinblade before starting down the stairs.

Chapter 30

"Lord Reishi, please allow me to go first," Jataan said. "It is my place."

"Not this time, Jataan," Alexander said.

The long staircase ended in a small circular room about twenty feet in diameter. Standing in the center of the room was the old man in robes who had been haunting them. Alexander stopped a few paces from the apparition and waited. Jataan took a position to Alexander's left but didn't advance further.

"Your magic is sufficient or you would not have reached this chamber," the man said. "Your courage is sufficient or you would have not continued in the face of the threats I presented to you. That leaves only one question: Are you worthy?"

"Who are you?" Alexander asked.

"I am the guardian of Benesh Reishi's final resting place," the man said. "It is for me to decide if you are worthy."

"Worthy of what?" Alexander asked. "I've come here looking for information about my calling. The Reishi Sovereigns told me that I'm an adept, but I don't know how to use my magic very well. I've come here in search of any knowledge left here by the adept who built this place."

"The adept you speak of is Benesh Reishi, brother of Constantine Reishi, the Third Reishi Sovereign," the man said. "And who are you?"

"I'm Alexander Reishi, the Seventh Sovereign," he said as he withdrew the Sovereign Stone from under his armor shirt and let it fall against his chest.

The man smiled. "Very well then, you may attempt to claim the sword. But I must warn you, if you are deemed unworthy, it will be most unpleasant and possibly fatal, depending on the content of your character and the strength of your will."

"What sword are you talking about?" Alexander asked.

"Mindbender," the man said just before he turned to black smoke and evaporated.

A moment later the wall opposite the staircase entrance vanished, opening the way to a chamber beyond. Alexander stepped up to the threshold and peered in. It was a burial chamber with a single stone sarcophagus resting in the center. The domed ceiling glowed softly, illuminating the final resting place of Benesh Reishi.

Resting lengthwise atop the sarcophagus was a long sword. A stone chest sat at the foot. Alexander felt the age of the place in his bones. No one had set foot in this crypt in thousands of years, yet there was very little dust. Aside from the slight enchantment in the ceiling that illuminated the room, there was only one thing that caught Alexander's second sight.

Mindbender.

It glowed brightly to his aura reading, but unlike most magical items that Alexander had seen in the past, this sword had complexity and depth to its aura, almost like a person.

He approached cautiously, walking full circle around the sarcophagus and inspecting the entire chamber with his magical vision. Once he was satisfied that the room held no traps or other magical surprises, he carefully lifted the heavy stone lid of the chest at the foot of the sarcophagus.

His friends were assembled at the threshold of the room and looked on with quiet curiosity.

What Alexander found made his heart skip a beat. There were four books, each carefully wrapped in a square of soft leather. They were completely intact in spite of the centuries that had passed since they were placed inside the chest.

Alexander carefully unwrapped one of the books and found that it was written in a language that he couldn't read. It stood to reason, but it was still frustrating. He'd come searching for answers and now that he held what might be the key to unlocking his magic, it was still just out of reach.

"Lucky, come take a look at this," Alexander said over his shoulder.

The master alchemist knelt down and frowned as he examined the words on the first page of the book.

"It's written in a long-dead language that looks like a dialect of old Ithilian. Before the rise of the Reishi, each of the islands had its own language. The First Reishi Sovereign spent considerable time and effort to create a common language throughout the entire Seven Isles. Some wizards use the old languages as a way of limiting access to their works. I suspect we might find a way to translate these in the library at Blackstone Keep."

Alexander sighed. "I guess I shouldn't be disappointed but I was really hoping to find something I could put to use more quickly."

"Perhaps you have," Jack said, as he stood, arms crossed, staring at the sword. "It seems that the man who's been haunting us was standing watch over the sword rather than those books. Does your sight tell you anything interesting about it?"

Alexander nodded as he stood. "Its magic is nearly as great as the magic bound up in a Thinblade but considerably more complex. Its aura almost looks like the colors of a powerful wizard."

Lucky finished packing the books into his bag and stood up next to Alexander. "That would make it a very potent weapon."

"Why don't you just pick it up?" Evelyn asked as she walked toward it with clear intention.

Conner stopped her with a hand on her arm.

"I'm thinking about it," Alexander said. "Remember what the man said? His warning was pretty pointed and I have no way of knowing what kind of magic this sword has. It may be harmless or it may be deadly. I know from personal experience that some swords are only usable by certain people. The Thinblades are a good example. If you tried to wield my sword, it would probably kill you."

"Well, we can't just leave it here," Evelyn said.

"She has a point," Jack said. "I wouldn't want it falling into Phane's hands."

"There is that," Alexander said with a frown. "I suspect it's only a matter of time before that wizard finds his way down here and we have no way of knowing if he can get into this chamber or not."

Somewhere off in the distance, they heard the scream of a revenant.

"I'm getting really tired of those things," Anatoly growled.

Boaberous grunted his agreement.

"Hopefully, that's the last one," Alexander said. "I'd like to put an end to Malachi's abomination once and for all."

"Quiet," Jack whispered.

Everyone froze and listened intently to the silence of the crypt. The faint sounds of boots on stone could be heard from somewhere up the staircase.

"Looks like they've found their way in," Alexander said. He sized up the sword and took a deep breath, then grasped the hilt with his right hand.

The pain was shocking and paralyzing all at once. It radiated up his arm and into the core of his being, freezing him to the spot with the intensity of the agony that shot through him. He was helpless to resist the onslaught of the sword's magic. He retreated into the place within his psyche where the witness lived and focused his mind on regaining control over his body in spite of the overwhelming agony. For what seemed like a very long time, he stood frozen in place as he struggled with the sword for supremacy over his body. In the end, he won the battle. Through the fog of pain, he reached up with his left hand and took the scabbard from the top of the sarcophagus and drew the sword. It was as if a cool breeze washed over his soul, calming the torment of the previous few moments and soothing away the lingering sensitivity of the torture he'd just endured.

He slumped to his knees, vaguely aware of his friends gathered around him, exchanging words of concern and arguing about a course of action. Chloe buzzed in an orbit around his head. He saw his life flash before his mind's eye. Every meaningful event of his entire existence since the earliest days of his childhood came into clear focus, one after the next with impossible clarity. The emotions of each moment were fresh and real in his mind, but he didn't just feel his own feelings—Alexander also experienced the feelings he had created in the hearts and minds of the people he had interacted with in each situation. He felt the pain he'd caused in others from every petty and small thing he'd ever done. Dimly, somewhere in the back of his mind, he was grateful that he'd lived a relatively decent life. He'd never harmed anyone wantonly, but only out of ignorance or for a just cause. The times when his actions made others feel good, appreciated, and loved helped him weather the guilt he felt for the few less charitable things he'd done. The entire experience seemed to take only a second, but it also had a timeless quality to it. When it was over, Alexander knew himself better than he ever had before.

He staggered to his feet, still shaken from the experience.

His friends all fell silent.

"Well, at least it didn't kill me," he said weakly.

The sword was fashioned from steel and expertly balanced. Even after all these years it was sharp and gleamed in the light. The hilt felt good in his hand. The name of the sword was engraved on the crossbar. Carved along the first foot of the blade were the seven glyphs that gave a magic circle its power.

Alexander felt a link with the sword form within his mind. It felt alive, almost sentient . . . but not quite. He began to understand the complexity of its aura better. He wanted to spend the next hour just holding the sword and exploring his connection with the enchanted weapon, but he heard the sound of boots racing down the staircase into the small antechamber that opened into the crypt.

"Time's up," Anatoly said as he unslung his war axe.

Jataan and Boaberous flanked him as the enemy soldiers reached the base of the staircase. The first soldier into the room died quickly, cleaved nearly in two by Anatoly's axe, leaving his crumpled corpse for the next soldier to trip over. Jataan neatly sliced his throat as he fell over his companion. The next to enter was hit square in the chest with the top of Boaberous's war hammer in a powerful jabbing thrust that sent the man flying back into the soldiers behind him. Another man fell into him and the two of them tumbled into the antechamber at Anatoly's feet. He unceremoniously killed them both.

The two remaining men of the squad stopped before entering the room and turned to flee. Jataan tossed his knife with precision, driving the blade into one man's back and through his heart. He fell forward and slid down the stairs as the final man fled, running for his life and screaming for help.

The fight was over before Alexander could reach the room but he learned something in the process. As his friends fought the surprised enemy soldiers, Alexander knew what each of the soldiers was going to do before he did it. It was as if he could see into their minds as they formed their intentions and made their split-second decisions. He stood, mesmerized by the sensation. It was such a powerful advantage in a fight that he could hardly believe it was real.

Evelyn snapped him out of his trance. "What are we going to do now?" she complained. "We're trapped down here and the only way out is through hundreds of soldiers."

"The soldiers are of no concern," Jataan said.

Alexander grinned as Evelyn looked at the battle mage with incredulity.

"The wizard might be a problem, though," Anatoly said.

"True," Alexander said. "We make for the central chamber and then into the one passage we haven't tried yet. If I'm right, it's a way out. If not, then we're going to have to fight our way up that staircase. Use the confined quarters to our advantage and if you see the wizard, take a shot at him. Jataan, lead the way."

The battle mage nodded and produced a knife from somewhere under his cloak. As they headed up the staircase, they heard a revenant scream. At least the soldiers had something else to deal with, Alexander thought to himself.

They reached the top of the stairs and the room that used to be Benesh Reishi's workshop just as the one soldier who'd escaped returned with a platoon of reinforcements. Twenty soldiers flowed into the room with weapons drawn.

Jataan darted into the fray without hesitation, slipping past a soldier and slicing deeply into the inside of his arm on his way toward the only soldier wearing the insignia of an officer.

Boaberous let out a battle cry that reverberated throughout the room and literally stunned a few of the enemy soldiers before he crashed into the battle, flailing back and forth with his giant war hammer.

Anatoly entered the fight with his usual, measured deadliness, picking his target and dispatching him with deliberate precision and brute force before moving on to the next.

Alexander moved toward the nearest soldier and raised Mindbender. As the soldier charged, Alexander saw in his mind's eye the enemy's plan of attack. As the brief engagement unfolded, Alexander realized the profound power Mindbender gave him. The soldier did exactly as he expected him to do. The technique was executed competently but since Alexander knew exactly what was coming, he was able to calmly, almost routinely, place himself in precisely the right position to deliver a counter that slipped past the soldier's guard. Mindbender was quick and sharp. It drove through the man's armor and into his heart with relative ease—although nothing like the Thinblade.

With his all around sight, Alexander saw another man move to strike from behind. He ducked and whirled, slashing the man's thigh to the bone and sending him to the ground screaming. A quick step over the injured man brought him into position to kill another soldier who was moving toward Conner, Evelyn, and Lucky.

The enemy's thoughts came quickly and accurately as Alexander faced each one. In every case he knew exactly what they were thinking, what they intended to do even as they formed the idea. The sensation was slightly disorienting until he surrendered to it and allowed it to guide his hand in battle.

Within a minute the entire platoon lay dead or dying and Alexander and his friends were all unharmed, with the exception of a few nicks and bruises sustained by Boaberous and Anatoly.

Alexander nodded his satisfaction as he wiped the blood off Mindbender and strapped the scabbard to his back.

"Your new sword seems to work pretty well," Jack said as he took his hood down and flickered back into view.

"It's amazing," Alexander marveled. "I know what the enemy is going to do. It's like I'm inside their head, hearing their thoughts."

Anatoly whistled. "That's quite an advantage. I wondered why you didn't draw the Thinblade."

Alexander shrugged. "I didn't really think about it." He switched Mindbender to his left hand with the point down and drew the Thinblade. "Let's keep moving, maybe we'll get lucky and avoid that wizard."

They reached the central chamber and found a squad of soldiers standing guard all around the room as another squad reached the entrance from the long spiral staircase. Jataan had three dead before Alexander even reached the room. He dispatched the other three with ease. Knowing what the enemy was thinking coupled with the impossible sharpness of the Thinblade made for an unstoppable combination.

Boaberous reached the base of the staircase as a man from the second squad entered the room. He crushed him with one heavy blow from his hammer and waited for the next man to round the corner, but the soldier saw trouble and withdrew back around the bend in the spiral stair.

"Stand back," Lucky said as he tossed a shatter vial high into the staircase. The liquid turned to a thick green vapor when it made contact with the air and began to rise. Moments later, sounds of men choking and gagging drifted back down into the entry chamber.

"The cloud of vapor will rise up the staircase for several minutes before it dissipates," Lucky said. "I'm afraid the soldiers who inhale it won't survive."

Alexander smiled at Lucky and gave Jataan a nod to continue down the one passage that they hadn't yet explored. They heard the scream of a revenant from somewhere up ahead, but pressed on. The passage ran for a hundred feet or more before it opened into a natural cavern. There were several pillars of stone formed by the steady drip of water through the bedrock. Many surfaces were coated with luminescent green lichen that gave the place an eerie yet beautiful glow. A rivulet of water flowed down the far wall and fed a small underground lake that spilled over one edge and flowing into a natural passage leading into the bowels of the mountain at a slight downward angle. Under other circumstances, the place would have been beautiful . . . but not with the pitched battle taking place at the edge of the small lake.

A revenant stood its ground against a dozen soldiers backed up by the wizard. Two men were down with lurid red bite marks on their necks and another three were dead and broken on the floor of the cavern. The revenant screamed again and half of the men froze in place while several of the others managed to drop their weapons and cover their ears before the terrifying sound paralyzed them.

The wizard unleashed a bolt of lightning that struck the revenant squarely in the chest and blew it onto its back, but a moment later it sprang to its feet with inhuman quickness even as the burn on its chest healed over. It lashed out at the nearest soldier and raked deep gashes across his face and neck, sending him sprawling to the ground in a rapidly growing puddle of his own blood.

"Attack," Alexander commanded as he moved toward the wizard.

Boaberous launched a javelin just as the wizard became aware of their presence. He brought up a shield that deflected it and then started casting another spell.

The soldiers decided that they would rather face mortal enemies instead of the revenant. Several of them turned and rushed toward Alexander. He killed the first in passing on his way toward the wizard. Anatoly followed behind, guarding his back as Boaberous charged into the crowd of advancing soldiers, crushing any who got close to his giant war hammer.

Jataan headed for the revenant. It saw him coming and launched itself into the air toward him to meet the challenge. An instant before it came down on him, he darted to the side and neatly cleaved the beast's wing off. It wheeled and caught him squarely with a backhand, sending him sprawling. Before it could pounce, one of the enemy soldiers tried to stab it. The revenant batted his sword aside, grabbed the doomed man with both clawed hands by the shoulders, picked him up and sank his fangs into the man's neck.

Alexander was nearly to the wizard when lightning arced from the wizard's hand and struck Alexander square in the chest. He felt molten pain flow through his entire body from the middle of his chest to the ground where each foot met stone. He was held frozen for a second or more as the lightning tore through him. When the dazzling brilliance of the spell ended, he felt darkness claim him as he slumped to the ground.

A moment later, Jack drove his knife into the back of the wizard and through his heart. The wizard stiffened, then slumped forward and died.

Lucky raced to Alexander's side as Boaberous faced off against the revenant. The beast lunged at him and bore him to the ground but the giant was strong enough to grapple with the unnatural creature. They fought for several moments before Jataan rejoined the battle and neatly cleaved one of its arms off. It shrieked in pain and recoiled but Boaberous was strong enough to hold on. He clambered on top of it and smashed the back of its head into the stone floor over and over again until the creature stopped thrashing and lay still. When Boaberous rolled to his feet, Anatoly casually decapitated the revenant . . . just to be sure.

***

Alexander woke some time later. He hurt everywhere. It felt like molten metal had flowed through his veins and burned him from the inside. Lucky had removed his armored shirt, which was so hot from the lightning that it had burned his chest. He groaned and Chloe buzzed up to hover over his face.

"You have to stop getting hurt like that, My Love. I don't like it when you suffer."

"Me neither," he whispered through parched lips. "How long?"

"You've been out for a couple of hours," Lucky said. "I put some healing salve on your chest and the bottoms of your feet to help with the burns, but I think you really need a healing draught and a few more hours of sleep."

"Enemy?" he asked.

"They're still coming, a squad at a time," Jack said. "Jataan, Anatoly, and Boaberous are holding the entry hall and building quite a pile of bodies in the process."

"Revenant?"

"Boaberous beat its brains in and then Anatoly cut its head off," Jack said. "We're safe for the moment."

"Good. I hurt all over, especially on the inside," he whispered as he motioned for Lucky to give him the healing draught. He quaffed it and lay back down carefully. The magic of it claimed him quickly. He was happy to surrender to the succor of deep, dreamless sleep.

He woke sometime later feeling better but still tender from his injuries. He sat up and found Evelyn sitting by his side and Chloe curled up on his pack.

"How are you feeling?" Evelyn asked.

"Sore, but better," Alexander said as she handed him a waterskin. "What's been happening while I've been out?"

"The soldiers have stopped coming down the staircase for now, but Anatoly says they're probably just working on a new strategy. Aside from Conner and Anatoly who are watching the staircase, everyone else is resting."

"Good," Alexander said, easing himself back down on his bedroll. "You should get some sleep, too. Once we start moving again, it'll be at least a week before we reach safety."

"Thank you for rescuing me," she whispered.

Alexander smiled. "You're welcome."

"I realize how much you risked coming here, even if it wasn't just to get me, and how badly you were hurt. I feel bad that I sometimes don't think about how things affect other people. I just wanted you to know that I'm grateful."

"I do. All of this is a lot to endure for anyone. I don't blame you for feeling a bit overwhelmed. Now, get some rest, we'll be moving in a few hours."

When Alexander woke several hours later, Lucky was busy preparing a cold breakfast and the others were packing their bedrolls.

"Ah, you're awake," Lucky said with a smile. "How are you feeling?"

Alexander took a quick inventory of his injuries and found that he was still a bit tender, but the feeling of burning inside was mostly gone. The burns on his chest and feet were almost completely healed.

"Good, considering. And hungry."

Lucky chuckled and handed him a bowl of dried fruit and nuts.

After breakfast he went to see Anatoly and Conner in the entry hall. The scene was one of horror and carnage. There was a pile of corpses in front of the staircase taller than a man. Dozens of soldiers were dead. Alexander understood why they'd stopped to reconsider their approach.

"I thought we'd lost you for a minute there," Anatoly said grimly. "If your sister were here, she'd tell you to be more careful."

Alexander smiled and nodded. "I suspect she would. Who got to that wizard?"

"Jack stuck him in the back a moment after he zapped you," Anatoly said. "He's managed to bag two wizards on this trip. Not bad for a bard."

"Not bad at all," Alexander said. "We're about ready to move. That passage leading out of the cavern back there has air flowing into it so I'm hoping we can find a way out. If not, we're going to have to fight our way up these stairs."

"I wasn't even looking forward to walking up those stairs, never mind fighting my way to the top," Anatoly said.

They returned to the cavern and made ready. Evelyn had taken a pair of pants from one of the dead soldiers and put them on under her dress. Alexander couldn't help but smile at her. She had a sword strapped to her waist and wore a pair of heavy boots.

He adjusted his swords, putting the Thinblade on his back and Mindbender on his left hip so he could grasp the hilt with his left hand. He found that the magic of the sword didn't require the blade to be drawn.

Jataan led the way into the natural passage that drained the excess water from the small underground lake. It was slow going. The tunnel was about six feet high with a rivulet of water flowing down the center. Slime had formed along the floor, making it slippery and treacherous. After an hour of walking through the gloomy underground, Alexander was exhausted and chilled to the bone. He'd hit his head on the low stone ceiling several times but not nearly as often as Boaberous had. The giant was having a particularly difficult time negotiating through the cramped space. Alexander slipped and fell several times. He was wet and sore but determined to find a way out that didn't involve fighting through two hundred soldiers.

As they progressed deeper, the passage narrowed. In the distance they heard the sound of rushing water, and the air began to flow past them more quickly. They pressed on until they had to crawl through the constricted space with chilled water flowing through their clothes. Finally they reached a place where the water flowed over the edge and into another underground lake a dozen feet below.

Alexander peered over the edge and saw a pool of water with several inlets feeding it from a number of small underground streams. There was an opening on the far side with the faintest hint of light shining through. Alexander slipped over the edge and fell into the water.

The icy cold of the underground lake burned against his skin and his body temperature plunged even further. He was exhausted and his strength was failing, but he held onto the vial of night-wisp dust as he surfaced, looking desperately for a place out of the water. His light shimmered on wet stone and revealed a rock shelf a foot or so above running along one wall. His boots pulled at him and his clothes weighed him down, but after a struggle he made it to the shelf and crawled out of the water. Jataan reached the shelf next. With an act of will, Alexander rolled to a sitting position and brought his knees to his chest as he held the light high to illuminate the way for his friends.

One by one, they plunged into the icy water and swam for the shelf. Anatoly struggled under the weight of his armor but Jack was there to help him. Boaberous was the last man through, squeezing and struggling to fit his enormous body through the narrow gap until he slipped free and crashed into the water. Jack helped him remain afloat as well until all of Alexander's friends were huddled, soaking and freezing, on the wet stone shelf that ran alongside the little underground pool.

Jack crawled to the opening, looked out and swore. He returned, shivering and shaking his head.

"We're about forty feet over a small lake," he said through chattering teeth. "The water runs down the face of the cliff. The only way down is to risk sliding down the cliff into the lake, but there's no telling how deep it is or if there are any rocks we might hit on the way."

Alexander nodded and spoke to Chloe in his mind, "Can you scout the way ahead, Little One? We need a way out into the forest so we can make a fire and get warm."

"Of course, My Love," Chloe said.

She returned after only a minute. "The way is clear of stones but the water is very deep. You will need to swim to shore. Are you strong enough to make it, My Love?" she asked with worry.

"We don't have any choice," Alexander said.

He was shivering violently and wasn't looking forward to getting into the water again but he knew they needed to get to dry ground and make a fire or they wouldn't last the night.

Lucky started rummaging around in his bag. He pulled out six waterskins and a roll of cord. With shaking hands, he emptied the water from the skins and blew air into them, capping them quickly to keep them inflated. He tied two together with a length of cord and handed it to Anatoly. The next he gave to Boaberous and the final one he gave to Conner. Each of the three wore a breastplate that weighed him down enough to make the swim a struggle.

"Put the cord across your chest and the skins under your armpits to help you float," Lucky said.

"I don't know if I can make it," Evelyn said with tears in her voice. "I've never been so cold."

"We'll help you," Alexander said.

Jack went first, sliding on his backside for almost thirty feet down the water-slick cliff face, then over the edge to plunge from a height of about ten feet into the lake below.

Lucky was next. He strapped his bag to himself and carefully closed it to prevent water from getting inside, then went over the edge. Alexander heard a splash from below and waited a count of ten before he sent Evelyn.

She was clearly afraid and nearly in tears but she did as he instructed and was soon sliding down into the lake below.

One by one they went. Alexander could see with his second sight the colors of his friends as they struggled to make it to shore. Jack stayed in the water and helped each one reach the shallows before he returned for the next.

Alexander motioned for Jataan to go but he shook his head through his shivering. "You must go next, Lord Reishi. I will follow after a count of ten."

Alexander was too tired and cold to argue, so he nodded and slipped over the edge. The water at his back and the rushing air flowing over him chilled him even more. Then he hit the water and felt the burning cold of the mountain lake sap what little strength and warmth he had left. For what seemed like a long time, he struggled to orient himself and kick to the surface. His lungs burned with the need for air and his body felt heavy and spent but he finally broke through.

Lucky stood on the shore that looked very far away, holding his light high to guide everyone to safety. Alexander kicked his way clear of the shower of water raining down on him and struggled to swim toward the light. He felt like he was treading water without making any headway. Behind him he heard Jataan crash into the water, then he slipped under again.

With the sudden strength of panic, he kicked to the surface and started swimming toward shore again as Jack reached him and strapped a set of waterskins under his chest. Together, Jack, Jataan, and Alexander struggled to make it to the shallows where Anatoly and Boaberous pulled them from the freezing water and dragged them to shore.

Conner and Evelyn doggedly dragged a dead tree branch into the little lakeside meadow and Lucky produced a flask of oil. He dumped it on the wood and ignited it with a whoosh. They all huddled around the fire until it started to fade. Anatoly unbuckled his breastplate and dropped it before he stumbled into the woods to look for more wood. Boaberous went to help him. Between the two of them they carried a log into the fire pit and placed it atop the flames. It took a while for it to catch but when it did, it burned hot and bright.

Slowly, they began to regain some of their warmth and their clothes began to dry. After an hour or so, Alexander clumsily opened his pack and dumped the contents out in front of the fire. They struggled all night just to stay warm and to dry their things as best they could. When dawn came, they could see that they had traveled through the entire mountain and come out on the side opposite the ruined fortress. Alexander was glad for their position. They were far too exhausted to travel and they were still chilled, not to mention that their things were still wet and heavy. He hoped the enemy wouldn't find them before they had a chance to regain some of their strength.

They spent the day at their little makeshift camp feeding the fire. Alexander didn't feel warm until the middle of the afternoon and then only after he'd eaten three times and wrapped himself in every blanket he had.

His friends were in no better shape. Jack was especially worrisome. He didn't stop shivering until sometime in the early morning. Lucky wrapped him in an extra wool blanket and poured a healing draught into him. It wasn't until dinnertime when Jack woke that Alexander stopped worrying about his friend. For several hours, Alexander could see the colors of his aura waning and he feared for his life. Jack had spent more time in the water than any of them, swimming back and forth to make sure everyone got to shore. Without his help, Alexander was sure he would have drowned in the icy water.

By morning of the next day, everyone had recovered their strength and dried out their belongings. They set out an hour after dawn toward the east coast of Grafton Island. It was slow going and only got more difficult as the forest thickened. Just before dusk, they reached the road that connected the island's many small fishing villages and stopped to wait for dark. From their vantage point in the trees, they watched a patrol of a dozen soldiers on horseback pass by. The enemy was still looking for them.

An hour after dark they slipped across the road, one by one. Once on the other side, they headed for the coastline and then north. By midnight they saw the lights of a small village. They crept through the shadows and found a small dock with a fishing boat tied securely alongside.

"Jataan, make sure there's no one aboard," Alexander whispered. "Anatoly, help me with the ropes."

Once everyone was aboard, Alexander dropped his money purse on the dock. He wasn't sure the owner would have agreed to the sale, but he didn't like taking someone's property without paying for it, and he reasoned that the gold he left was a fair price and then some.

More importantly, the owner of the boat would be enslaved or worse if Alexander failed to prevent Phane from conquering Ithilian and the rest of the Seven Isles. He didn't like the circumstances but he needed to get off Grafton Island and couldn't risk hiring a boat for fear of being turned over to the soldiers.

The little fishing boat had a single sail and one pair of oars. It wasn't fast but the wind was blowing them in the right direction.

They weren't a thousand feet from the dock when they heard the cries of alarm coming from shore. Alexander just hoped the enemy didn't have a warship at any port near enough to give chase.

They rowed through the night, taking turns at the oars and tiller. By dawn they could see the shore of Grafton Province growing closer and a warship in the distance behind them closing fast. They were a hundred feet from shore when the first ranging shot from the warship's fore catapult splashed into the water fifty feet behind them. They made straight for the beach and ran aground in two feet of surf. The water was cold but not as bone chilling as the water of the mountain lake. They waded through the surf as the warship landed a direct hit with a firepot and the fishing boat caught fire with a whoosh.

Once onshore, they headed inland quickly through a pasture and a herd of cows grazing alongside the ocean. Alexander smiled at the sight. It seemed like it had been so long since he'd helped tend his father's herd. The smells of the grass and the cows mingled to remind him of his childhood. He snapped back to the present moment when he saw a dozen soldiers riding toward them.

He stopped and dropped his pack. "I hope they don't have crossbows," he said as he handed Jataan his bow and quiver. "It's a good bet they're not friendly. Kill as many as you can before they get too close."

Jataan nodded as he slung the quiver and nocked an arrow. He waited until they entered his range and then sent ten arrows at them one after the other with inhuman speed and deadly accuracy. Nine of the soldiers toppled from their horses. One managed to block the arrow with his shield. The three that survived the sudden onslaught turned and ran.

"Well done," Alexander said. "Let's round up those horses and get some distance on them before they send more men after us."

Chapter 31

Duncan Valentine stood atop the watch tower in the Ruathan Army main encampment and lamented his helplessness. The Regency had left two legions to guard the Gate and sent the remaining eight to attack New Ruatha, but when their scouts reported that the Ruathan Army was as large as theirs, they abruptly turned toward the coast and marched on Northport.

Duncan had anticipated the possibility, even half expected them to attack the undefended coastal city, but he hated it nonetheless. He'd ordered Northport to evacuate weeks ago and most of the people who lived there had obeyed, but there were always holdouts. His scouts reported that several thousand people were still holed up in the city, and from the looks of things, they were attempting to mount a defense. Duncan knew they were doomed and it turned his stomach.

They, no doubt, felt betrayed and abandoned. But Duncan knew there were more important things at stake than the homes and businesses of Northport. His first duty was to the people of Ruatha and he'd deployed his forces to ensure the survival of as many citizens as possible. Not all of them were happy with his efforts, but that was to be expected as well. War was inconvenient at best and blame for the difficulties it created was not always fairly placed.

"Take solace that we got most of the people out," Hanlon said to his old friend. "The Rangers guarding the forest road reported a huge number of refugees over the past week fleeing to Southport."

"Hanlon's right, General Valentine," Wizard Sark said. "Those who choose to remain were warned of the danger. Committing our forces to preserve a nearly empty city would be a grave mistake."

Duncan sighed. "I know, but I still hate it. Those people are just trying to defend their homes and they're going to die for it."

"We've done all we can, Duncan," Hanlon said. "The platoon of riders I sent will arrive a day ahead of the Regency outriders. They'll make it clear to the holdouts that they won't survive if they remain."

"We have three wizards within the city as well," Sark said. "They've been spreading word of the coming attack while they make preparations for the arrival of the Regency forces. I suspect the enemy will find the city less than hospitable."

"Just so long as the docks are destroyed before the wizards make their escape," Duncan muttered.

"I assure you, they will be," Sark said. "In fact, I suspect we'll be able to see the smoke from here. One of the wizards is very proficient with fire."

Duncan nodded as he watched the smudge of dust on the horizon that represented nearly a hundred thousand enemy soldiers marching across land he was charged with defending.

"How soon will they reach Northport?" he asked.

"My scouts estimate the cavalry will arrive at the walls by day after tomorrow, with the bulk of their forces arriving two days after that," Hanlon said.

"All things considered, we got lucky. Alexander's ruse managed to hold them at the Gate for a week. If they'd moved sooner, we might have faced some much harder decisions."

Duncan nodded sourly and fell silent for several long moments. He knew the answer to his question before he asked it but he couldn't help asking. "Any news of Alexander or Abigail?" he said very quietly.

"We've heard nothing," Sark said. "Erik has a squad of Rangers sleeping in shifts at Blackstone Keep but it's been weeks since Alexander has communicated with them."

"I imagine he's pretty busy," Hanlon said. "He'll send word when he has something to report."

Duncan didn't voice his real concern because he couldn't form the words without his voice breaking. He drew himself into the detached state of mind he'd first learned as a soldier and put his nagging concern for his children aside as much as he could manage.

"How is the evacuation of New Ruatha coming along?" he asked to take his mind off his real concern. He knew as well as any the state of affairs.

"Regent Cery has relocated to Headwater and taken command of the civil operations there. New Ruatha is a ghost town with the exception of a handful of wizards making preparations for abandoning the city and some constables patrolling the streets to deter any enterprising thieves. The population has relocated to Headwater and Blackstone Keep.

"We have sufficient food for the remainder of the summer and into autumn but this winter might be lean. Northport's crops are a total loss and Southport diverted so much manpower to building its navy that the yield from their lands will be about half that of a normal year. Kai'Gorn is struggling to salvage something of their crop, but General Talia says they'll need assistance to make it through next winter. Thankfully, Highlands Reach and the eastern territories are reporting a good crop so far."

Duncan nodded. "What's the latest report from Kevin in Southport?"

"He has the city working around the clock building those fast-attack boats he designed," Hanlon said. "I had him send a copy of the plans to us so the wizards could offer suggestions for improvements but they said the design was just about ideal for its purpose. The last report I received from him three days ago said they had a total of sixty-three ships including seventeen of the new attack boats built and crewed. They're running patrols up and down the coast and providing escort to the refugee ships from Northport.

"He mentioned that a few scout boats from Andalia made contact with his southernmost patrols but they turned and ran without a fight. Since Talia is sinking anything that gets close to Kai'Gorn, it's a good bet they're looking for another port to land their Lancers."

"I've been expecting something for a few weeks now," Duncan said. "Phane's been too quiet for too long. He's up to something and I'd rather not be caught flatfooted."

"The most likely possibility is a large scale naval invasion from Andalia," Sark said. "He would need time to assemble a fleet of troop transports and escort ships. If that's his plan, he will most likely attempt to use Northport as a stronghold to build his troop strength before he attacks."

"That's the one I can see coming," Duncan said wryly. "I'm a lot more worried about what I don't see. He's got way too much power at his disposal to be spending all his time supervising a shipyard. He's got to be working on something else."

"Mage Gamaliel has considerable resources devoted to determining Phane's next move," Sark said, "but so far, we have no new information. He's likely shielding his activities from our efforts."

"Any news from Duane?" Duncan asked.

"Last report has him about fifty leagues north of Blackstone Keep deployed along a scout line stretching east and west across the entire island," Hanlon said. "He has about half his force encamped somewhere on the southern edge of the northern wilds. For now, he says Rake and his soldiers are dug in deep in the highest reaches of the wilds. It'd be a fool's errand to go in there and try to get them. Rake has the high ground and good defenses. Duane's just keeping an eye on him for now."

"Have the reinforcements arrived at Blackstone Keep?" Duncan asked.

"They should be there by now," Hanlon said. "I sent the two legions from Buckwold to augment Erik's forces as soon as I got word that two legions from Southport were due to arrive.

"I'm a bit concerned about southern Ruatha. We have just three legions south of the forest with the exception of the Highlands Reach home guard. General Talia has his hands full occupying Kai'Gorn, so he can't spare any more troops and Kevin needs his entire legion to maintain control of Southport and the surrounding area. If Phane finds a way to land troops down south, we'll have a hard time getting enough soldiers through the forest fast enough to do any good."

"War is a lot like running a ranch," Duncan said. "Too many needs making demands on too few resources. We've deployed our forces as best we can given what we face. For now, all we can do is wait for Phane to make his move and use the time we have to fortify our position and protect our people. How's the Striker company coming along?"

"Well enough," Hanlon said. "Mage Gamaliel is working night and day to create enough breastplates for the hundred soldiers we selected. They've been training all day, every day, since we put the unit together. Captain Sava took to his new command with dedication and a single-minded drive to create the most lethal company of soldiers Ruatha has ever fielded. They're drilling relentlessly with every weapon imaginable. All of the soldiers have seen combat recently, most in the engagement with Headwater, and all of them are committed to victory. They're ready for duty now, but I'd like to give them a week or two more before we put them in the field."

"We have some time yet," Duncan said. "Phane's commanders are smart. They know we're nearly evenly matched as far as numbers go, so they won't make a move against us until they get reinforcements."

***

A week later a squad of scouts returned from Northport with a report. They were accompanied by Wizard Dinh, one of the three that Mage Gamaliel had sent to the city to destroy the docks and lay traps for the enemy. Duncan convened his war council in his command tent and presided over a very somber meeting.

"Northport has fallen and the remaining residents are being rounded up and summarily executed," the scout reported. "Their attempt at resistance ultimately proved futile because of the strategy employed by the enemy."

Wizard Dinh sighed and shook his head. "We should have seen it coming but we didn't. Rather than attack with their soldiers as we expected, they sent a company of men in to provide a guard force for the wizard commanding the scourgling and then used it to attack any who remained within the city. That thing is terrifying. Once it has a target in view, it runs it down and tears it apart. Both Edan and Hale died trying to escape. I was helpless to do anything but watch and stay hidden." His voice broke. "I feel so guilty for not going to their aid but I knew my sacrifice would be for nothing."

"You did the right thing," Wizard Sark said. "Wizards Edan and Hale will be sorely missed. I'll send word to Mage Gamaliel with the next courier to Blackstone Keep."

Wizard Dinh nodded and composed himself. "Once the scourgling had scoured the city for any remaining citizens and triggered most of the traps we set, the soldiers entered the city unopposed and began ransacking the place. They looked like they were setting up for an extended stay and seemed to be directing resources to the docks."

"How thoroughly were the docks damaged before you withdrew?" Duncan asked.

"Quite thoroughly," Wizard Dinh said. "Hale was very good with fire and he spent several hours directing his power toward the docks and shipyard. They were completely ablaze when the scourgling entered and began its rampage."

"At least there's that," Duncan muttered. "Anything you can tell me about their fortifications?"

"They manned the walls of the city but didn't seem to be working to augment their defenses any more than that," Wizard Dinh said. "I got the impression that they don't expect to be attacked any time soon, which stands to reason considering our troop strength relative to theirs, not to mention the scourgling."

"Unfortunately, they're right about that," Duncan said. "A full assault at this point would probably destroy them but it would also cost us the bulk of our forces. For now, all we can do is watch and wait. Hanlon, forward deploy a legion of Rangers in a loose cordon around Northport to keep an eye on them and make sure they don't get any resupply."

Chapter 32

They rode north for four days from first light to full dark, pausing only to feed and water the horses. The enemy had their scent and was on the hunt. Alexander estimated a force of a thousand soldiers were in pursuit less than a half day behind. He suspected the commanders of the force occupying Grafton and the lone surviving wizard were desperate for something positive to report to Phane. His capture would redeem them even if they weren't able to hold Grafton.

Thankfully, the majority of the invading force was concentrated in and around the city of Grafton and not deployed throughout the province or they would have had a much harder time making their escape. As it stood, the people they encountered were mostly farmers working their fields or merchants transporting their wares.

Alexander knew their horses couldn't take much more before one came up lame and then the enemy would catch up to them. Against even a company they had a chance but a thousand soldiers was something else altogether. He felt a tremendous sense of relief when they crested a rise in the gently rolling grasslands and saw an army marching straight toward them flying the banner of Ithilian. Abel was making good time considering the number of troops he was moving, along with all of the supply trains and support personnel required to sustain an army in the field.

As they approached, a platoon of outriders broke from the main force and sprinted ahead to meet them. Alexander stopped and waited for the soldiers to come to them. They charged up with spears at the ready until they saw Conner and Evelyn. The commander of the unit gave a crisp salute and brought his men to a halt.

"Prince Conner, Princess Evelyn, your father will be very happy to see you," he said. "He's with the main force. Allow us to ride escort and we'll take you to him straightaway."

Conner returned the salute with a smile. "Lead on, Commander."

An hour later they arrived at the site of the command tents being hastily set up for the night. Abel's tent was already erected and a number of soldiers stood guard around it signifying that the King was within.

"Why don't you and your sister go see your father," Alexander suggested. "I'm sure he'll want a few minutes alone with you before we discuss business."

Conner dismounted and faced Alexander. "Thank you, Lord Reishi. There were many times in the past few weeks that I was terrified, but in every case you and your people carried the day. I see why my father placed his trust in you."

Evelyn came to him and stood on her toes to kiss him on the cheek. "Thank you," she whispered, then turned and went with her brother to their father's tent.

Later that evening, Alexander and his companions were summoned to the King's table for an evening meal and council meeting.

Abel met Alexander outside the tent. "Thank you, Alexander. Evelyn and

Conner told me the story of all you went through to bring her home to me. I am in your debt and Ithilian is at your disposal."

"I'm just glad we made it," Alexander said. "There were a few times I wasn't sure we would."

"Come, you must be hungry," Abel said, motioning to his tent. "A hot meal will do you good."

After the meal, Abel summoned General Kishor and Mage Lenox.

"I have three legions in this force, mostly infantry with about six thousand heavy cavalry and two thousand archers," Abel said. "What can you tell us about the enemy forces?"

"When last I looked, they had about two thousand Andalian Lancers, another six thousand Karth infantry and two or three thousand soldiers from Grafton," Alexander reported. "The Governor of Grafton is dead as are two of the three wizards Phane sent to support his army."

"What happened to the Governor of Grafton?" General Kishor asked.

Alexander shrugged, "I cut his head off along with that of the general commanding Phane's forces."

"Sounds like they might have leadership problems," General Kishor said with a chuckle. "That will definitely work to our advantage."

"I'm still concerned about the Lancers," Abel said. "I hear they're fearsome on the battlefield."

"Speaking from personal experience, their lances are as powerful as you've heard," Alexander said. "A full charge will break through the lines of nearly any army, so we'll need a strategy to deal with them that doesn't involve a head-to-head fight."

"That might be difficult, considering we're advancing on their position," Anatoly said. "They have the opportunity to pick their battlefield and make preparations prior to our arrival."

"True, but we do have a significant advantage in terms of sheer numbers," General Kishor said. "I'm confident of victory; my only concern is the cost."

"Agreed. Unfortunately, the terrain surrounding Grafton lends itself to a cavalry charge," Abel said. "My question is, will they attack such a large force or will they retreat and cause mischief elsewhere. Two thousand Lancers could cause significant damage if they got out of Grafton and went on a rampage."

"I suspect our strategy will come into clearer focus once we get closer and see how the enemy reacts to our advance," Jataan said.

Abel nodded his agreement. "We're about a week away at this pace. I'll keep my scouts out as far as I dare. As soon as we have better information, we'll firm up our strategy. For now, I think the archers are the best chance we have of thinning out the Lancers before they reach us."

Stifling a yawn, Alexander felt all of the stress and strain of the past several weeks catch up with him. More than anything, he needed rest and he knew his companions were in bad shape as well.

"Let's see if your tents are ready yet," Abel said. "I suspect you're exhausted and we still have four or five days before we're likely to encounter any significant enemy presence. We'll have plenty of time to come up with a battle plan in the coming days."

Alexander nodded with a self-conscious smile.

An aid led them to a set of well-appointed tents with several field cots set up and piled with ample blankets. The floor was layered with rugs at odd angles to completely cover the bare dirt beneath. Several free-standing brass lamps stood around the room providing ample illumination. Abel had assigned a platoon of soldiers to stand guard around the tent and assured Alexander that he was safe within the army encampment.

As he lay down, he thought how good it felt to be in a bed. He was asleep within minutes and didn't wake until well after dawn. Lucky was still snoring and Anatoly had only just woken. Jack was up at the desk writing on a sheet of parchment under the light of a small lamp that he had carefully adjusted to ensure it wouldn't disturb anyone still sleeping. Chloe sat cross-legged on Alexander's pillow. She smiled tenderly when he opened his eyes.

"Good morning, Little One," he whispered.

"Good morning, My Love," she said. "Did you rest well?"

He nodded, then stretched and yawned.

When he stepped out of the tent, he found Jataan standing guard at the entrance with his hands clasped easily behind him.

"I'm told the bulk of the army is already on the move," Jataan reported. "The supply and support forces will be moving within the hour."

The pace would be slow because they were marching with so many men, but it gave Alexander time to think about the coming conflict. He had so many concerns to weigh against one another that he wasn't sure where to direct his attention. The shades worried him because of the horrific threat they represented, but he was sure that Mage Lenox would have brought word if there was any news regarding their movements or progress toward opening the Nether Gate.

He was concerned about the coming battle, not for fear of defeat but for fear of losing great numbers of soldiers to a Lancer charge. He worked the problem over in his mind as they rode with the army toward the battle for Grafton.

He was worried about Ruatha. By now the enemy would have surely made a move against New Ruatha and may even be occupying the city. Alexander only hoped that his ruse had given his father enough time to save the people.

Then there was his worry for Isabel and Abigail. By now Isabel would have taken the mana fast and either emerged a witch or died in the process. He felt a pang of guilt for not looking in on her sooner but he consoled himself with the reality of the past few weeks. He'd been too busy working toward the security of Ithilian that he hadn't spared the time to check on his loved ones.

By evening he was tired from the long slow ride over the lush green rolling hills of southern Ithilian but not too tired to take a few minutes to gather some much-needed information and relay word to his father of his progress and intentions.

After clearing a patch of ground outside his tent near the cook fire where Lucky was happily preparing the evening meal, Alexander drew a magic circle in the dirt with his knife. He smiled at the familiar feel of the hilt in his hand. His father had given him the knife when he turned seven and he'd carried it every time he'd been away from Valentine Manor ever since. Lately it had been at his side every day. Once the circle was cut into the dirt, he carefully cleaned the blade and inspected it before returning it to its sheath on his belt.

When he sat down in the circle, Chloe landed on his knee and frowned at him but didn't say a word. Instead she sat down cross-legged to watch over him. He closed his eyes and quieted his mind for several moments before beginning the process of shifting his awareness into the firmament. After a while of focused effort on quieting his mind and releasing his tension, he slipped free of his physical being and found his awareness floating gently on the firmament.

He had come to know the sound of creation and found it beautiful, if somewhat overwhelming, but he'd also found that he could judge the collective state of the world by the level of discord and tension in the impossibly complex music. Today it revealed a level of fear and angst that he'd never heard before. Battle and hardship were raging across the Seven Isles and the distress of millions of innocent people caught in the result of murderous ambition gave a hint of hysteria and panic to the music of the firmament.

Alexander felt a surge of anger at the injustice of it all. So many people who just wanted to live their lives were cast into chaos and jeopardy for the selfish desires of just a few ruthless people.

With an effort, he let go of his anger and focused on the long list of things he needed to do. First he thought of the fortress island, or more precisely, he formed an image of the place seen from a thousand feet overhead. He floated gently down to the balcony of the chambers that Isabel and Abigail shared. He approached as close as he dared and peered into the well-lit room. His wife and sister sat in their sitting room with the waifish girl that Alexander had seen before.

He took comfort in the knowledge that they were alive and well until he saw the lurid yellow bruises across Abigail's face and neck. His anger returned with full force. He had no way of knowing what had happened to her, but he knew it was probably not the result of an accident. His protective instincts fed his anger and he almost lost his connection to the firmament. With an effort of will, he melted back into the source of creation and focused his mind on Grafton Province.

His awareness coalesced high over the main city. He searched around and found that the bulk of the soldiers from Karth were within the city walls while the two thousand Lancers were in a small valley a day's ride to the northwest. They were in a perfect position to flank any direct assault against the fortified city, or failing that, run to the west toward the cover of the mountain wilds. Either way they would be a problem.

Next he directed his attention to the Isle of Fellenden and the world passed him by in a blur. He floated down into the city of Fellenden. What he saw threatened to make him sick and overwhelmed him with rage all at once. The streets were littered with broken bodies. A woman lay face down with her infant child not far from her. The baby had the back of its head smashed in. Alexander drifted through the scene of a nightmare.

The army that had attacked Fellenden had long since left the city. Most of the buildings were burned-out hulks. There wasn't a person left alive. A pack of dogs loped along the street until it came to the mother and her dead baby. When they stopped to pick at her bones, Alexander withdrew back into the firmament.

He had to school his mind for several long minutes while he struggled with rage, heartache, and shame that he was of the same species as the animals that had savaged the innocent people of Fellenden.

He thought of Ruatha and brought his awareness into being over the

Reishi Gate. There were at least two legions of Regency soldiers encamped around the Gate. They had constructed a rough stone wall in a semicircle around the front joined by a straight wall running behind the Gate. A company of archers stood watch atop the wall. They were certainly ready for him to return home.

He directed his focus to the city of New Ruatha. The countryside between the Gate and the city was destroyed. Every farmhouse had been burned to the ground. Bodies littered the landscape. The invading army had burnt the crops and killed what livestock they left behind. None of the farms in their path had been spared. When he arrived at New Ruatha, he found the city mostly dark, yet intact. As he looked around the surrounding countryside, he saw the encampment a few miles to the northwest of the city. In a blink he was there and was greatly relieved to see that it was his army and it looked stronger than he had any right to hope it might be.

He sent his mind to the message board in Blackstone Keep and saw several messages for him. The first asked how he had dealt with the scourgling. The second asked if there was any news of Isabel and Abigail. And the third said the enemy had taken Northport but the city had been mostly evacuated prior to their arrival.

Alexander shifted to the sleeping room where he found several Rangers awaiting his message. He floated into the mind of the nearest and stepped into the man's dreams. The Ranger was startled at first but then came to attention and saluted, fist to heart. They were standing in a meadow within the valley of Glen Morillian and it was a bright and sunny day. Alexander smiled at his memories of the secluded valley's beauty.

"Deliver my report to Mage Gamaliel and to my father," Alexander said to the Ranger. "I know of no way to defeat the scourgling. It was only through the Fairy Queen's assistance that we were able to send it back to the netherworld. Isabel and Abigail are alive and still in the custody of the Reishi Coven, and I believe they are making progress toward enlisting their aid. I hope to lead a force of four legions through the Gate from Ithilian in two or three weeks' time. Begin making preparations for a battle at the Gate. Once we've routed the enemy forces there, we'll turn our attention to their forces in Northport."

"I will deliver your message," the Ranger said proudly.

Alexander slipped out of the man's sleeping mind and back into the firmament. He opened his eyes and winked at Chloe before he touched the Sovereign Stone.

He sat down at the Reishi Council table and smiled at Malachi Reishi.

"I thought you'd like to know that I killed your revenants," he said.

Malachi frowned angrily, which was just the reaction Alexander was looking for.

"What has transpired since we last spoke?" Balthazar asked.

"I went to the island on the southern tip of Ithilian, rescued Abel's daughter and found the ruins of the adept's keep. The revenants had taken up residence there, so we had a difficult time finding the crypt where Benesh Reishi was buried but we made it eventually."

Constantine leaned in with interest. "What did you find there?"

"Four books and a sword called Mindbender," Alexander answered.

Constantine looked at Alexander sharply. "Have you grasped the hilt of the sword? Did it accept you?"

Alexander nodded. "It tested me in a way I never expected. I think that test helped me understand myself better than I ever have before."

"You have discovered one of the most potent weapons ever created during the reign of the Reishi," Constantine said. "My brother was very powerful within the limits of his magic. He assembled a number of arch mage wizards to help him construct Mindbender. The first several attempts failed, but he was persistent. He succeeded by channeling his link with the firmament into the sword. Sadly, that link drained away his vitality. As a result, Benesh died within the year."

Alexander was stunned. He knew Mindbender was powerful but he had no idea how much its creation had cost.

"I'm sorry, Constantine."

Constantine smiled sadly and nodded his thanks for the condolences. "Benesh was stubborn and driven. He was always trying to push the limits of magic. When he died, we assumed the sword was lost because it was created using his link to the firmament. Have you used the weapon in battle?"

"I have—and it's remarkable," Alexander said. "I can hear the thoughts and understand the intentions of my enemies. I know what they're going to do the moment they decide to act. I didn't believe any sword could rival the power of the Thinblade, but now I'm not so sure."

"Mindbender is capable of much more than that," Constantine said. "Not only does the sword allow you to hear the thoughts of your opponents but it also gives you the power to create illusions of great power. You can literally make others see and hear nearly anything you wish or even not see what is right before them."

Alexander was stunned. He'd only used the sword a few times and had found that it didn't work unless he was actually in a fight. The idea of creating illusions was more than he ever considered. The scope of the sword's power was breathtaking.

"How?" Alexander asked. "So far, I can only make it work in a fight. I tried to listen to the thoughts of those around me in other circumstances but I couldn't."

Constantine nodded. "Mindbender only works during battle—however that condition is met within the mind of the wielder. If you believe that you're in a fight, the sword will too. As for the illusion capability, I'm not entirely sure how to make it function. The sword was bound to my brother, so it wouldn't function for anyone else. I would suggest you visualize the outcome you wish your enemy to see and then release it into the sword in much the same way a wizard releases the vision of their intended outcome into the firmament."

Alexander nodded thoughtfully. "We also found four books in the crypt but they're written in an ancient language that I can't read."

"I suspect it's ancient Ithilian," Constantine said. "Benesh had an affinity for that particular language and often used it to obscure his research. Translating them may be a challenge although there may be a few works in the private library within the Reishi Keep that would be of great help."

Alexander frowned, shaking his head. "All of the books we found in the Reishi Keep had long ago rotted to dust."

"The private library should still be intact," Balthazar said. "It exists within a place out of time, much like a Wizard's Den, although it cannot be opened from any location other than the doorway. You can find the library within the Keep using the Stone. The door will recognize you and allow you entrance."

"That's encouraging, except there's a demon loose in the Reishi Keep," Alexander said. "I'm not sure how to defeat it."

Malachi chuckled. "The tentacle demon is still there, after all these years?" He tipped his head back and laughed. "I'm sure it's in a very foul mood by now."

All of the men at the table turned to glower at the despotic culmination of their family legacy.

Demetrius Reishi shook his head sadly. "You are a disappointment, my son."

Before Malachi could respond, Alexander silenced him with a hand. "Malachi, you will not speak unless asked a direct question."

Malachi crossed his arms and scowled.

"Any thoughts what the books we found might contain?" Alexander asked.

"I suspect there will be at least some of my brother's research on his very rare calling," Constantine said. "He was always fascinated about his way of interacting with the firmament and did a great deal of work to discover how to use his magic as well as to better understand why he was different from most other wizards. Besides that, it's hard to say. Benesh was a very curious man and a careful observer of those things that caught his interests. You may find a treasure within those books or you may find a collection of very esoteric research that ultimately proves unimportant."

"What's the state of the war with Phane?" Balthazar asked.

"He has an army on Ruatha that's taken Northport, but he doesn't have enough forces to do much else. My father is leading the Ruathan Army and he outnumbers the enemy forces by a couple of legions, which is not enough to ensure victory in an outright battle without sustaining severe losses. Phane also has a small force in Grafton Province on Ithilian. I'm currently with the Ithilian Army headed to destroy his forces there and secure the Isle of Ithilian to ensure that he isn't able to disrupt food production this summer. Since Ruatha's harvest will be limited, I need to make sure that Ithilian has food to spare for this winter."

"A wise precaution," Balthazar said, nodding.

"I'm concerned about the Andalian Lancers," Alexander said. "There are about two thousand with Phane's forces in Grafton. Is there anything you can tell me about them?"

Darius Reishi sat forward. "The Andalian King created the Lancers during my reign. He had a small faction of nobles who tried to establish their own kingdom within his territory. They abandoned the Old Law, so I sanctioned Andalian military action against them.

"The Lancers were created to tip the balance of power decisively in his favor. The rhone steeds they ride are indigenous to Andalia. But the Lancers' real power comes from their force lances, which are created with a magical forge located deep under the central city of Andalia and are tied to the crown itself. I meant it as a failsafe, but I can see now that it didn't work.

"I reasoned that by requiring the Lancers to serve the one who wore the crown and by linking the crown to the Andalian bloodline, I could maintain control over such a potent army through my power over the Thinblade. Since Malachi destroyed the Andalian Thinblade, that leverage no longer exists."

"So the lances themselves are tied to the crown worn by the Andalian King?" Alexander asked to confirm his understanding.

"Yes, if the crown is taken or destroyed, the lances will cease to function," Darius said. "Or at least that's how they operated during my time as the Reishi Sovereign."

"Is there any defense against them, aside from that?" Alexander asked.

"None that I'm aware of," Darius answered. "Some wizards were able to erect shields that protected against them for a short time, and solid fortifications are effective as well, but the Lancers proved to be devastating against troops or cavalry in the open. I would strongly advise that you not engage them in a head-on battle, particularly if they have the opportunity to mount a charge."

"I was afraid of that," Alexander said. "I guess I'll have to come up with another way. Thank you, gentlemen." With that, Alexander left the Reishi Council Chamber and opened his eyes to find Chloe still sitting on his knee watching over him.

He briefed his friends during dinner on everything he'd learned from his clairvoyance and his visit with the Reishi Council. Then he asked Anatoly and Jataan to think about a strategy to deal with the Lancers. He had a few ideas but they were risky and he wanted as much input as possible before he decided on a course of action.

***

Three days later they reached the outskirts of town. Alexander checked to find that the Lancers were still encamped a league to the east in a small valley. During the slow march, Alexander had made his decision and shared his plan with Abel and his generals. They didn't like it but had to admit that it was better than the alternatives.

They made camp and created the impression that they were digging in for a siege. Not a terribly effective strategy given Grafton's port and the substantial fleet of merchant ships at their disposal, but, given the size of the Ithilian Army relative to the number of Regency soldiers, certainly a worrisome development for those within the city.

That night, under the cover of darkness, Alexander and his friends took a force of four thousand cavalry and headed first north and then east. They rode for the better part of the night until they reached a small canyon that offered good cover. They made a cold and quiet camp for the day and moved on again at dusk.

Alexander had instructed Abel to make overtures of peace and offer the town every chance to surrender, knowing full well that Phane's forces would never accept the offer but would gladly take the time it bought them. The delay was what he was after. He needed to get his forces into position to strike.

The night was cold and dark and they moved slowly. It wasn't long before a scout returned to the head of the column and warned that they were approaching the outer edge of the enemy's encampment. Alexander called a halt and spoke briefly to the four unit commanders before each regiment of a thousand cavalry moved off into the night to encircle the enemy position.

Carefully and quietly, they formed a half circle around the western edge of the camp and waited through the early morning hours for the first light of dawn. Alexander nodded to the commander in the growing light. He gave the order and a whistler arrow shattered the quiet of the morning.

The Lancers were just stirring but many were still in their tents and bedrolls. Only a few moments passed after the whistler went up before the alarm bells began to toll. Alexander's cavalry charged to within striking range and loosed its first volley of arrows into the camp. From four positions arrayed around the periphery of the enemy encampment, thousands of arrows sailed into the sky and came down into the Lancers. Panic erupted within the camp as the Lancers struggled to strap on their armor and grab their weapons.

The second volley went up. Torches had been lit and soldiers were riding the length of each row of archers, igniting the tips of arrows tightly wrapped with oil-soaked burlap. Fire and death rained down on the Lancers. The gentle orange glow of flame began to color the air over the camp and smoke rose into the quickly lightening sky.

Another volley followed and then another.

Many of the rhone panicked and broke free of their pickets to run into the early morning gloom, trying to escape the fire and chaos. Some Lancers managed to reach their mounts, but they were few and didn't pose a real threat in the face of a sustained barrage of arrows. Alexander's men followed their instructions and loosed a total of twenty volleys into the enemy camp before they charged into the soldiers who remained. The battle was brief and very one-sided. A few of Alexander's men fell from the magical blasts of a Lancer's weapon here or there, but the Lancers were so disorganized and unprepared that they couldn't manage to mount an effective attack. They fell quickly as they were swarmed by the superior numbers surrounding them.

A force of two or three hundred managed to rally and turned to charge the regiment that Alexander was riding with. He smiled at the opportunity it provided to test the power of his new sword. Sitting atop his big mare, he gripped the hilt of Mindbender and focused his mind. He thought of the black shadow dragon that had feigned an attack from the walls of the ruined keep. He saw the terrifying creature in every detail and deliberately sent the image into the connection he had with his sword. The air overhead in the dim morning light swirled and coalesced into a giant black dragon that swooped down toward the rapidly advancing enemy.

Amid shrieks and cries, the Lancers broke and scattered in every direction to avoid the descent of the supernatural monster. Alexander was dumbstruck with the power he had just wielded. It had no substance, couldn't actually attack, but it could create a belief within the mind of the enemy. He smiled at the power of one of his father's favorite principles of battle taking shape before him. The enemy believed they were about to be attacked by a dragon, so they ran for their lives. That the dragon wasn't real made no difference. Their belief was as real as it needed to be to cause them to act.

With their spirit broken, the remaining Andalians escaped the scene of the battle and headed east toward the city of Grafton. Alexander had made preparations in case they chose to flee in that direction. Two thousand archers were deployed in units a thousand strong and carefully concealed in the tall grass on either side of the road.

Alexander's cavalry chased the Lancers into the kill zone, where they were met by arrows falling in their midst like a deadly rain. After the third volley, the entire enemy force littered the battlefield.

Alexander doubled back with the bulk of his soldiers to collect the force lances that had fallen and to round up the rhone steeds that were still alive.

By evening, Alexander had destroyed the entire force of Andalian Lancers to a man, confiscated their supplies, and collected nearly all of their lances. He knew they would be of no use to his soldiers since they were tied to the oath of loyalty that each Lancer gave to the Andalian crown, but he wanted to see if Mage Gamaliel could find a use for them.

They managed to round up nearly five hundred uninjured rhone as well, which were far more useful. The oversized horse-like creatures were fearless and trained to charge into an enemy. Alexander had plans to put them to use against the Regency Army on Ruatha.

By dusk of the following day they reached the Ithilian camp and found the city of Grafton locked down and surrounded. When Alexander entered the command tent, he was met by Abel, along with his general staff and Mage Lenox.

Abel smiled warmly at Alexander and offered him his hand in congratulations. "I hear the Lancers are no longer a threat."

"We managed to destroy them completely," Alexander said as he approached the map table. "Thankfully, we were able to catch them by surprise."

"Your gift of sight has proven to be much more powerful than I would have ever imagined," Abel said. "As for the soldiers within the city, they have refused to surrender, as predicted."

"Good, let's end this tonight," Alexander said, pointing at the main gate. "I'll open the gate and send up a signal arrow. When you see it, send in the cavalry, followed by the infantry. Flood into the city and kill anyone wearing the crest of the Reishi Army Regency. Show them no mercy and give them no quarter."

"What of the soldiers and people of Grafton?" Abel asked with a tinge of worry to his voice.

"Capture the soldiers and treat the people with courtesy and respect," Alexander said. "They had no say in the treachery of their leaders or the occupation of their home."

Abel nodded his approval of the plan.

"How do you plan to open the gate? The enemy has several hundred soldiers with bows atop the gatehouse walls. They'll pick you apart before you can get close," General Kishor said.

Alexander shook his head. "They won't even see me coming. We attack in one hour. By morning we'll own the city and we can be on our way north to the Gate."

Alexander returned to his friends and briefed them on his plan of attack.

"I don't much like the idea of you approaching that gatehouse all by yourself," Anatoly said.

"I will accompany Lord Reishi," Jataan said.

"You're both missing my point," Anatoly said. "You made some spectacular magic with that new sword of yours this morning," he said to Alexander, "but how can you be sure it can conceal you from all of the soldiers on that wall?"

"I'll know before we make our approach," Alexander said. "If it doesn't work, we'll fall back and come up with another plan."

"So if it does work, then I'm coming with you," Anatoly said. "If you can make two people invisible, three shouldn't be a problem."

"Actually, I wasn't planning on making us invisible," Alexander said. "I was thinking about creating a thick fog to cover our approach."

"Even better. Everyone can come along," Anatoly said. "But if that's your plan, then we should probably all be carrying a heavy shield. If I was on that guard tower, I know what I'd do if the approach to the gate was suddenly shrouded in fog."

"Good point," Alexander said.

It was late and he was tired, but what he'd seen in Fellenden and Northport was wearing on him. He felt a gnawing urge to speed up his plans and get back to Ruatha as quickly as possible. The time to strike was now, even if he was too tired to think as clearly as he'd like.

Alexander led his friends to the edge of bow range and appraised the walls of Grafton. The interior of the city was enclosed but there was still a shantytown built up around the walls, although the people had evacuated into the city itself.

Alexander grasped the hilt of Mindbender and focused on the fight. Even though he wasn't under attack, he knew he soon would be. His concentration narrowed down to the present moment the way it always did when he was in a fight. He envisioned the result he wanted and released it into the sword. Slowly at first, the air around the gate began to thicken in the dark of night. Within a few moments, a thick shroud of illusionary fog blanketed the area in front of the main gate. Alexander led the way with a shield held over his head. His friends followed in single file. They could hear the alarm bell begin to toll and saw the fiery streaks of flaming arrows cut through the obscuring mist and catch some nearby shacks on fire. Alexander pressed on.

As they got closer to the walls, arrows began to rain down around them. The heavy shields they carried deflected the projectiles but the experience was still harrowing. Alexander picked up the pace and soon reached the large double doors of the main gate. They stood twelve feet tall and were barred and locked with stout pins top and bottom. Alexander drew the Thinblade and sliced through the door in a number of places, cutting the bar, the lower locking pins and the hinges, then slicing crisscross through the door. Chunks began to fall away, eliciting cries of alarm from within the gatehouse itself. Soldiers rushed to defend. Alexander stepped through the newly formed hole in the door and assessed his environment. He stood in the gatehouse with a broken door behind him and a portcullis before him. A dozen soldiers armed with crossbows were preparing to fire.

"Hold," Alexander shouted to Anatoly as he crouched down behind his shield. The soldiers fired a volley of crossbow bolts. Most hit the broken door behind him. A few drove into his shield and a few inches further, but one found its mark, penetrating his shield and stabbing through his forearm and out the other side. Alexander cried out in pain. It was such a sudden shock that it took his breath away and left him momentarily nauseated.

At the sound of his cry, several more sections of the door broke away and fell into the gatehouse under an assault by Anatoly and Boaberous. Jataan slipped in behind Alexander and quickly assessed the situation. Seeing the soldiers protected behind the portcullis, he snapped an order.

"Boaberous, Anatoly, raise the bars."

The giant and the man-at-arms raced for the portcullis. They each took hold and heaved on the tremendously heavy iron bars. Between Boaberous's natural strength and the magical strength conferred on Anatoly by the belt he wore, the bars came up several feet. Jataan darted under into the dozen soldiers.

At first they were incredulous that one man would face them all, but then he killed two men with blinding speed, leaving them to bleed out on the floor as he moved toward his next target.

Lucky came to Alexander's aid a moment later. "You'll be all right, Alexander. Use the Thinblade to lop off the head of the crossbow bolt so I can pull it back through your arm and the shield."

With gritted teeth, Alexander did as he was told. Lucky gave him a look that spoke volumes and then pulled the bolt free. Alexander screamed at the pain but composed himself quickly and unbuckled the shield.

A dull grinding sound echoed through the gatehouse hall over the sounds of combat between the battle mage and the overconfident soldiers. Alexander looked up to see the portcullis lift out of Anatoly and Boaberous's hands. He glanced across to the other side of the gatehouse and saw Jack's colors at the portcullis winch.

Boaberous and Anatoly didn't miss a beat. Both slipped under the heavy iron gate and joined the battle beside Jataan. Alexander let Lucky wrap a quick bandage around his wounded left arm, then turned and found the pull cords for the locking pins at the top of the doors. Once they were released, he shoved the doors open and sheathed the Thinblade, handing Lucky his bow and a whistler arrow. With the signal sent, he turned to see the inner gates opening for a company of enemy soldiers that had mustered to defend the gatehouse.

"Withdraw!" Alexander commanded.

His friends fought an orderly retreat until the sound of hoof beats could be heard coming from behind. They pressed against the walls as a column of heavy cavalry poured past them and into the city. The enemy infantry were driven back quickly, leaving the soldiers atop the walls of the gatehouse as the only organized resistance left.

Alexander raced along the wall toward the staircase. His friends, seeing his objective, fell in line behind him as the soldiers continued to pour past on horseback. Once they reached the top of the gatehouse, Boaberous and Anatoly took the wall to one side of the gatehouse while Alexander and Jataan took the other. They crashed into the line of soldiers firing arrows down into the column of cavalry.

Within a few moments the archers tried to turn their bows against them, but lined up along the wall, only the nearest archer had a clear shot. Alexander cut the first in half with a single stroke. Before the man behind him could get his shot off, Jataan darted past him and neatly cut his bowstring and then the left side of his throat before moving on to the next man in line.

On the other side, Boaberous rushed the first man and tossed him off the wall, then barreled into the next with a sweeping blow from his hammer. The archer's broken body fell twenty feet to the ground below. Within a very short time, the remaining archers broke and ran, leaving a clear path for the cavalry charging into the city.

Chapter 33

By morning the battle was over. What resistance the enemy was able to mount was quickly overpowered by the superior numbers of the Ithilian Army, leaving only small pockets of holdouts. The soldiers of Grafton were only too happy to surrender and pledge their undying loyalty to Abel once it was clear what had happened. The soldiers from the Regency were less willing to give up but that suited Alexander just fine. He had long since decided that those who chose to side with Phane deserved what they got.

Most of the people of Grafton were relieved to be back under the banner of Ithilian—the rule of the Regency soldiers had been less than gentle. Abel put General Kishor in charge and left a legion of infantry to ensure Grafton would remain under his command and to root out what enemy remained in the outer parts of the province and on Grafton Island. The other two legions left the next morning for the Reishi Gate.

It would be a long walk for the infantry and archers, probably taking the better part of two weeks, so Alexander and Abel rode ahead to Ithilian with an honor guard of a thousand cavalry. They arrived several days later to the sound of the city's horns blaring notice of their return.

Queen Sofia was standing at the gate with tears streaming down her face when they arrived. Evelyn bounded off her horse and ran to her mother. Alexander smiled at the emotional reunion. This was at the core of his fight: protecting people's right to live and love as they chose and protecting the innocent from experiencing the heartache of needless loss at the hands of would-be tyrants.

Not long after Alexander and his friends were shown to their chambers, a messenger arrived with an invitation to a private banquet in celebration of the return of Princess Evelyn. Alexander was tired but knew it would be impolite to refuse, so he reluctantly changed into his finery. He felt a little conspicuous strapping two swords to his belt, but he wasn't about to let either of the weapons out of his sight.

When they arrived, it was just the family along with Mage Lenox. There were no courtiers or delegates and the dining hall was much smaller than the banquet hall they used for the more formal gatherings. Alexander was grateful for the informality. He had no desire to put up with the self-importance and pretension of nobles or delegates. Matters of far greater importance were weighing on his mind and his anxiousness was beginning to build.

The meal was simple and well prepared. Lucky seemed to enjoy himself as usual and offered effusive praise for the chef, which Sofia was only too happy to accept. Conversation revolved around Evelyn's retelling of her adventure. Alexander thought she embellished just a bit but he was content to listen to the young woman recount her view of the ordeal she'd just lived through.

Sofia gasped and cringed when Evelyn told about the first revenant attack. Abel was far more stoic about the story. It was clear to Alexander that the Ithilian King knew just how close he'd come to losing his daughter and there was an undercurrent of anger boiling just beneath the profound relief he felt for her return.

The dishes were cleared and the wine poured when the doors burst open and Cassius Ithilian strode in, trailing an aid and two palace guards. The soldiers looked nervous as they hurried after the Chancellor.

Cassius was furious. He came to a stop with his fists planted on his hips and stared at his brother with rage flashing in his eyes.

"I'm told you've invaded Grafton without the approval of the assembly and after you promised in good faith to negotiate a truce with them."

Alexander remained silent and watched Abel's colors flare into anger. Before anyone else spoke, Evelyn stood up and faced her uncle.

"Hello, Uncle Cassius," she said sweetly.

He looked stricken and surprised all at once. Alexander saw a flare of fear wash through his colors before he quickly regained his composure. His furtive glance took in all who sat at the table.

"Evelyn, I'm so happy you've been returned to us," he said with feigned relief. "We've all been so worried about you."

Alexander glanced to Conner who looked like he was angry enough to draw his sword. He caught the prince's eye and shook his head subtly to stay his hand.

"How is it that you came to be returned to us?" Cassius asked his niece.

"Lord Reishi rescued me," she answered with a smile of gratitude for Alexander.

He returned her smile innocently.

Once again, fear and guile shot through the Chancellor's colors. Alexander schooled his expression and let the exchange play out. He wasn't sure if he could still use Cassius against Phane but he decided that keeping the option available was better than dispensing justice immediately.

Cassius frowned and his initial anger started to return as he faced Alexander. "I don't understand. The assembly was told that you would be leading soldiers from Ithilian through the Reishi Gate to Ruatha. How is it that you changed your plans so abruptly and risked my niece's life with an ill-advised rescue?"

Cassius was shrewd and experienced at dealing with liars. Alexander realized that the circumstances would soon reveal the truth to Cassius regardless of Alexander's attempts at deception and any chance of using him against Phane would be lost. If he was to use the Chancellor, he had to act now. His mind raced to find a way to make use of the situation. When it hit him, he almost smiled.

"Abel and I felt that the fewer who knew of our plan, the better the chances of it succeeding," Alexander said with a casual shrug. "No one knew our intent until we were well on our way."

Cassius shook his head with feigned sadness. "I should have been apprised of the plan. If I had been, I could have given you legal sanction to act as you did. Even though I'm grateful that you've returned Evelyn to us, I must report your actions to the constable for investigation. I fear you are in violation of several very serious laws. I trust you will surrender your weapons while the situation is looked into."

Jataan started to tense. Alexander stilled him with a glance.

"That's not going to happen and you know it, Cassius," Abel said hotly. "Alexander is my guest and he was acting under my authority. There will be no investigation."

"I'm afraid, dear brother, that your authority doesn't extend to pursuing criminals, even if they abducted your own daughter. Apprehension of such criminals is the exclusive purview of the constable. Vigilantism cannot be tolerated, even to save my own niece."

Alexander smiled at Cassius even as his golden eyes glittered with building anger.

"You forget *my* authority," Alexander said.

Cassius looked almost startled but quickly covered by shaking his head. "You have no authority on Ithilian. We have not recognized your treaty and so you are a visiting dignitary, nothing more. The law is the law."

"Indeed it is," Alexander said. "But I wasn't speaking of the treaty, I was speaking of this." Alexander withdrew the Sovereign Stone from under his tunic and allowed it to fall against his chest. "I am the Sovereign of the Seven Isles, protector of the Old Law and I claim authority over all who would choose to govern others—including you, Cassius."

"Well, that's just absurd," Cassius sputtered. "That old relic hardly counts anymore. The Reishi Empire fell millennia ago. You can't expect such a ridiculous claim to be taken seriously just because you happened to find some ancient trinket."

The air was growing tense. Alexander could see the anger building within both Abel and Conner. Anatoly was carefully assessing his surroundings the way he usually did before violence broke out, but it was Jataan who stood.

"You are mistaken, Chancellor Cassius," he said calmly, which only served to heighten the menace in his voice. "Lord Reishi is the Sovereign of the Seven Isles. The Island Kings are subject to him, as are you."

"Nonsense," Cassius said. "Guards, take this man into custody until a constable can be summoned."

The two soldiers who'd followed Cassius into the dining hall looked around like they didn't know what they should do, clearly not wanting to refuse the Chancellor's order but unsure if obedience was the correct course either.

Abel stood up, unable to tolerate his brother any longer. "Wait outside and close the door," he said to the guards.

They nodded curtly and obeyed their King without hesitation.

"You are interfering with my authority to enforce the law," Cassius said to Abel. "This will not be tolerated." He turned to his aid. "Go and fetch a constable, tell him to bring a sizable force immediately."

"Stop!" Abel commanded the aid.

The man looked around a little wild-eyed until he saw the look of fury Cassius directed at him. He nodded quickly and hurried for the door only to stop dead in his tracks when Abel drew his Thinblade and barred the man's path. The aid's eyes went wider still.

"Sit down," Abel commanded quietly, pointing to a chair at the table.

The aid scurried to the chair without a word, trying to avoid the furious look Cassius was giving him.

"You won't get away with this," Cassius said. "I'll see to it that you're brought up on charges and stripped of your title."

"Enough of this," Alexander said as he stood and faced the traitorous Chancellor. "How long have you been in league with Phane?"

"What? Why that's just ridiculous," Cassius said. "I'm a loyal servant of Ithilian. You can't make such a baseless claim without evidence."

Alexander smiled at the man's arrogance. He still thought his laws and rules would save him from his treason. He clearly lived in a fantasy world where he believed reality would conform to his wishes simply because he wished the world to be a certain way.

Alexander knew better.

"I know you're working with Phane because my familiar watched you talking to his little demon," Alexander said.

"Wait—what are you saying?" Evelyn asked with urgency in her voice.

Alexander saw Conner silence his sister with a hard look.

"What did he promise you?" Alexander asked amiably. "The throne of Ithilian? The Thinblade?"

Cassius suddenly realized that the rules had changed. He looked around a little wildly. "I don't know what you're talking about. I don't have to put up with this. You're the one who broke the law."

When Cassius turned toward the door, Abel shook his head slowly, still holding the Thinblade. Cassius stopped and looked around in genuine fear.

"What's the wizard's name?" Alexander asked. "The one who summoned Phane's imp."

"How . . . I don't know what you're taking about," he said. "This is absurd. I'm the Chancellor of Ithilian. Any thought of a treaty is dead without my approval."

Alexander chuckled at his bluster, shaking his head. "Did you help the enemy abduct Evelyn?"

Cassius's head snapped to look at Alexander and then to Evelyn. Her face was stricken with betrayal that slowly morphed into fury. He did his best to school his growing fear, but Alexander could see the turmoil in his colors.

"Of course not. I would never do such a thing," Cassius lied.

Alexander nodded to himself. "Did you know that I'm a wizard?" Cassius blanched at the question. "In fact, one of my talents is the ability to see when someone lies to me."

"You have no proof of any of this," Cassius sputtered. "All of your allegations are your word against mine. No court would convict based on the unsubstantiated word of a guest of Ithilian."

Alexander nodded again with a mirthless smile. "You're exactly right, Chancellor. But fortunately, I don't need a court because I am the protector of the Old Law. And I don't need proof because I can see the truth."

Cassius shook his head back and forth in denial of what he was hearing, almost as if by refusing to believe it, he could negate the reality of it.

"I find you guilty of conspiring to abduct Princess Evelyn for use as leverage in war against the Old Law and the people of the Seven Isles. By violating her right to liberty, you forfeit your rights to life, liberty, or property."

"You can't do this!" Cassius shouted.

"You are mistaken," Alexander said. "Now, I will spare your life under two conditions. First, you will tell me the name of the wizard who summoned Phane's imp and where I can find him. Second, you will confess your crimes to the assembly."

"This is madness," Cassius said as he moved toward the door, only to stop in his tracks when Abel leveled the Thinblade at him.

"We were friends when we were boys, Cassius, but you have betrayed me. You have betrayed my family. You have betrayed my country. I highly recommend you accept Lord Reishi's generous offer."

"You have no right!" Cassius shouted. "This is a violation of the law of Ithilian. I am entitled to a trial before any punishment. Take me before the assembly. I'll see you dragged out in chains."

Alexander grasped the hilt of Mindbender with his left hand. He was angry, but more than that he felt the rush of a fight coursing through his veins even though there was no real threat from the Chancellor. He formed the image of a revenant in his mind's eye and released it into the sword. The air before the Chancellor swirled in blackness, then coalesced into the seven-foot-tall form of the ancient beast, complete with batlike wings spread wide, a crown of horns, and long fangs protruding from its mouth.

Everyone in the room froze. Alexander stilled his friends with a wave of his right hand, but the Chancellor saw nothing except the monster standing before him. He cowered up against the wall and started to whimper.

"Your niece was bitten by a creature such as this," Alexander said. "You will answer my questions or it will tear you apart."

Cassius wet himself as he sank to the floor in abject terror. "Please don't let it kill me. I did it. I helped Phane's agents abduct Evelyn. I told them how to get her out of the city unnoticed. I sent Phane word of your plans. Please, I don't want to die." He broke down in tears, cowering under the threat of such a horrible death. "I'll do whatever you want, just don't let it kill me," he sobbed.

Alexander willed the illusion away and it vanished in a swirl of black smoke. The room fell deadly silent.

"That looked so real," Evelyn said.

"You mean it wasn't?" Sofia asked, visibly shaken.

"It was just an illusion," Alexander said.

Cassius looked up with a mixture of confusion and defeat that quickly morphed into blind rage. He surged to his feet, drawing a knife from his robes and lunged at Alexander. In a blur, Jataan darted into his path and caught his hand by the wrist, twisting hard and forcing his knife hand around behind his back, wrenching his shoulder in the process. The Chancellor gasped in pain, then froze when Jataan put a blade to his throat.

"Not quite yet, Jataan," Alexander said. "He may yet redeem his life." Cassius's face went white. "Sit him down and strap him to a chair."

Jataan walked him to a nearby chair with the blade to his throat. Anatoly handed Jataan a leather strap and went to work tying one of the Chancellor's wrists to the arm of the chair. Once he was secure, Alexander regarded him with a grim expression for a long moment.

"Lord Reishi, he doesn't deserve to live," Sofia said. "He helped people take my Evelyn. Such a thing is beyond evil. I can't even explain the pain, fear, and horror I felt from worry for her life."

"I understand how you feel, Sofia, but it may serve a higher purpose to honor my offer, provided Cassius holds up his end of the bargain," Alexander said.

"I will. I'll do whatever you want, just please don't kill me," Cassius pleaded, but Alexander could still see the dirty smudge of deceit in his colors.

"Name the wizard who summoned Phane's imp," Alexander demanded.

"Wizard Petronius," he said quickly.

"Impossible!" Mage Lenox said hotly. "I know Wizard Petronius. He's no traitor."

Alexander turned to the mage. He'd been quiet all evening, even during the confrontation with Cassius.

"Can you describe Wizard Petronius?" Alexander asked as he called Chloe from the aether. She buzzed into existence in a bright ball of light, then flitted over to land on the table a few feet from the mage. "Chloe has seen him and will be able to verify if we have the right man."

Mage Lenox frowned deeply but nodded his agreement. "Wizard Petronius is average height, slightly rotund with black hair and no beard. He customarily wears brown robes with a gold hem."

"That's the man I saw," Chloe said. "He crushed a small stone and the imp appeared a few moments later."

"Lady Chloe, I would not question your account, but Wizard Petronius has been a member of my order for many years," Lenox said.

Her dragonfly wings bobbled as she shrugged. "You described the man I saw."

"Did he have any more of the stones, Little One?"

"Yes, My Love. He had a small pouch that appeared to contain several."

Alexander nodded with a grim smile, his decision made. "Mage Lenox, please escort us to the Wizards Guild. Abel, hold your brother here in the keep, quietly, until morning when we can convene the assembly and he can confess his crimes."

"What about him?" Abel asked, motioning to Cassius's aid.

Alexander turned to the aid. "Did you have any knowledge of the Chancellor's treason?"

"N . . . no," he stammered. "I'm loyal to Ithilian." His colors rang true.

"Very well then, you will be the guest of the King for the evening," Alexander said. "Once we've settled this matter, you will be released unharmed."

"I'll see that his quarters are comfortable," Abel said.

"What are you going to do?" Cassius asked, his curiosity getting the better of his good sense.

Alexander smiled with deliberate menace. "I'm going to hurt Phane the worst way I can at the moment."

It was well past dark when they arrived at the Wizards Guild, but mage Jalal was still up and reading quietly in his study. He was surprised to see so many people but happy to hear them out.

"I have reason to believe that Wizard Petronius is in league with Phane," Alexander said bluntly. "I'd like you to summon him here so that I may question him."

Mage Jalal thought the request over for several long moments. "I must say, I doubt your claim, but you would not have come to me with it unless you had good reason. I will do as you request. However, I have a condition. If he is a traitor, then the Wizards Guild will dispense justice."

"Very well," Alexander said.

While they waited for Wizard Petronius, they recounted the journey to Grafton for Mage Jalal. After nearly half an hour, there was a knock at the door and two men entered. The first was very young, from the look of his colors an apprentice who had yet to undergo the mana fast. The second was a wizard fitting the description Mage Lenox had given.

"That's the man I saw," Chloe said in Alexander's mind from her hiding place in the aether. "The little green pouch on his belt is where he got the stone for the summoning."

Wizard Petronius looked a little alarmed when he saw who was in the room but he schooled his expression and tried to remain calm.

"May I ask the reason for your summons, Mage Jalal," he said.

"Lord Reishi has some questions for you," Jalal said, nodding to Alexander.

"How is it that you came to be in league with Phane?" Alexander asked, watching his colors carefully. They flared with alarm but rather than attempt to lie his way out of the predicament, he chose to attack.

He started casting a spell as he raised his hand toward Alexander but stopped abruptly when Jataan, who had been standing next to the door behind him, slipped up and put a blade to his throat.

"Wizard Petronius, I'd like to introduce Battle Mage Jataan P'Tal," Alexander said. "No matter how quick you think you are, I assure you, he's quicker."

Mage Jalal stood up, leaning heavily on his walking stick, and shook his head sadly. "You have been with our order for many years. Why would you betray us?"

Petronius looked on the verge of panic.

Mage Jalal peered into his eyes, then frowned deeply. "Perhaps it is not betrayal," he said, then cast a spell with a few words and a hand to Petronius's forehead, rendering him unconscious. Jataan lowered him to the floor.

"What are you suggesting?" Alexander asked.

"I believe he may be under the influence of a possession spell," Jalal said. "I will need to do some work with him to be sure. It may take several hours."

Alexander knelt down and untied the little pouch from the wizard's belt and dumped the contents onto the table. Five small stones scattered across the surface. Each was black as soot and shot through with cracks. They glowed slightly with an aura of dark magic.

"Did he say anything when he broke the stone?" Alexander asked Chloe within his mind.

"No, My Love," she answered without speaking. "He put it on the floor and stomped on it. Nothing more."

Alexander picked up one of the stones and tossed it on the floor, then drew the Thinblade before stomping on the stone.

"What's your plan?" Anatoly asked.

Before Alexander could answer, the air before him started to darken. The darkness swirled into a vortex and, with a thump, Kludge appeared.

Its wings beat furiously to keep it afloat and its hateful eyes went wide when it saw Alexander smiling at it. Alexander brought the Thinblade up and through the horrible little creature, cleaving it in half from hip to shoulder. Both halves fell to the ground with a thud and the black blood that coursed through its veins flowed out onto the stone floor.

"I suspect Phane's going to be pretty upset about that," Jack said with a chuckle.

"More importantly, that little monster can't run messages for him anymore," Anatoly said with an approving smile.

"It's much more than that," Jataan said. "He used his familiar to transport demons through the netherworld to any place in the Seven Isles. That was how he delivered the scourgling to your doorstep at Blackstone Keep."

"Well done, Alexander," Lucky said with a broad smile.

Alexander turned to Mage Jalal, who was watching with a mixture of distaste for the dead little monster and appraisal of Alexander.

"Sorry about your floor," he said with a shrug.

Mage Jalal chuckled. "No matter. You've dealt a grievous blow to the enemy and I applaud you for it. I will investigate the circumstances surrounding our apparent betrayal by Wizard Petronius and send word of my findings."

By the time Alexander arrived at his rooms, he was dead tired. He felt jubilant at having struck such a damaging blow against Phane but also slightly worried that he had just provoked him in a way that was so personal. Phane *was* an arch mage, after all. He may have been focusing his attention on other matters, but now Alexander had no doubt that he would direct all of his energy to the purpose of revenge.

"Be wary, Little One," he told Chloe as he readied for bed. "Phane will be more dangerous than ever now."

"I'm glad that little monster is dead," she said. "It made my skin crawl."

* * *

Mage Lenox entered the dining hall midway through breakfast the next morning with Wizard Petronius close on his heels. Alexander and his friends were sharing the morning meal with Abel and his family as they discussed their next moves.

Wizard Petronius stopped and faced the table, bowing humbly. "Lord Reishi, Lord Abel, Queen Sofia, and especially Princess Evelyn, you have my most sincere apologies for any part that I played in Phane's plot against Ithilian."

Mage Lenox waved off a barrage of questions as he stepped up next to Wizard Petronius. "Please allow me to explain. Wizard Petronius was indeed under the influence of a possession spell. Mage Jalal succeeded in identifying the binding object, in this case a ring. With the help of several other wizards, we were able to sever the link between the binding object and Wizard Petronius, thereby undoing the spell and freeing him of Phane's influence."

"That's some pretty powerful magic," Jack remarked.

"Indeed it is," Mage Lenox said. "The spell is cast over an item of fine craftsmanship. A complex potion is then concocted that requires a number of very rare ingredients. The target of the spell must be subdued and rendered unconscious. Then the item is placed on his person, the potion is forced down his throat, and a triggering spell is cast that activates the possession. When the subject awakens, he is given a set of goals. He will work toward those goals faithfully with all of the capabilities at his disposal."

"I don't like that at all," Alexander muttered.

"Nor do we," Wizard Petronius said. "Mage Jalal has ordered all members of the Wizards Guild to submit to an examination. Since he knows what he's looking for, it will be a simple matter to determine if any others have been compromised."

"Can either of you cast the necessary spell to identify a possessed person?" Alexander asked.

"I can," Mage Lenox said.

"I guess we'd better test Cassius before we parade him before the assembly," Alexander said.

Abel looked sharply at Alexander. Hope and concern mixed with wariness and distrust in his eyes but he nodded his agreement. It wasn't long before two guards brought the Chancellor into the dining hall. He wore a calculating look and seemed to be scheming a way out of his predicament.

Mage Lenox looked to Abel, who nodded his approval. He began casting the spell. Cassius watched with worry and curiosity. When Lenox shook his head, Abel sighed.

"I was hoping you might be redeemed after all, Cassius. But it seems you have betrayed us of your own free will, unlike Wizard Petronius here."

"But he's the one who came to me with Phane's offer," Cassius protested. "Surely he bears some guilt for his actions as well."

"He was under the influence of a spell that guided his actions against us," Abel said. "You chose betrayal—he did not."

Later that morning as they filed into the well of the assembly hall, amid considerable muttering from the delegates in the gallery. Alexander surveyed the scene and saw a mixture of wariness and fear in the colors of the representatives of the various communities of Ithilian. Their concern heightened when the soldiers of Abel's personal guard filed into the room and took up stations around the walls. The chamber fell deathly silent when Cassius entered in chains.

Abel stepped up to the podium and surveyed the large round room. Light fell through the windows in the high domed ceiling and shone brightly on the marble pillars.

"Delegates, I have called you here this morning to reveal the treachery of my brother, Cassius Ithilian." He paused to let the statement sink in but not long enough that the long-winded delegates could start talking.

"Wizard Petronius, under the influence of a possession spell, enlisted my brother's assistance in the abduction of my daughter Evelyn. Cassius then worked to provide information about our intentions to Prince Phane. I am satisfied of his guilt, but this is an extraordinary situation that our system of governance is ill-prepared to accommodate. It is for that reason that I have brought him before you, so that you may hear his confession for yourselves."

With that he stepped aside and nodded to the two men escorting Cassius to lead him to the podium. He looked all around like an animal caught in a cage. Alexander saw the colors of fury and desperation play across his aura and knew that he would not relinquish power easily. When he reached the podium, he seemed to come to a decision and his demeanor calmed.

"Fellow delegates, I have been wrongly accused. My brother lusts for even more power. He is spreading lies to discredit me and this honorable institution in the hopes of seizing total power for himself."

Abel started to move toward his brother but Alexander stopped him with a look.

Emboldened, Cassius continued. "I have served Ithilian faithfully for my entire life and I demand that our laws be obeyed. I am innocent and willingly submit to an investigation by the office of the constable. But, I must also insist that my brother submit to an investigation as well. He has held me against my will," he raised the shackles on his wrists to emphasize the point, "and that is a crime that cannot go without scrutiny."

Cassius seemed to hit his stride. Phony passion and conviction oozed from him as he basked in the attention of his country's most influential people.

"Our system depends on the rule of law. Exceptions cannot be made for any man or woman no matter their station or title. How can we expect our citizens to obey a law that we of the highest rank ignore? We cannot. The law is the law and it must be enforced.

"Sadly, I must report another crime. One committed by Alexander Reishi, kin of the most murderous tyrant to ever walk the Seven Isles. He led a force of foreigners to the Province of Grafton, where he murdered the Governor of Grafton. Such crimes cannot go unpunished. They must not be tolerated, no matter the claim of station made by the perpetrators.

"We stand at a crossroads. Will Ithilian hold to our noble principles and obey the rule of law or will we succumb to the dreadful pressure to do what is expedient rather than what is right? I beg you to choose honor and law over thuggery and the tyranny of the powerful.

"I implore you, call in the constable and let us resolve these serious allegations properly—with evidence, a jury, and due process." He hung his head in feigned sorrow as he finished his impassioned plea.

Alexander saw the colors of triumph and exhilaration wash over the Chancellor and also saw that many in the chamber were in agreement with him. Deception was the most dangerous weapon on the battlefield, even if no blood would ever be spilled. Cassius Ithilian was a masterful deceiver.

The room broke out in murmurings as the delegates began discussing what they had just heard. It took several moments for one of them to realize that no one had stepped forward to speak for the assembly. The delegate who took the initiative puffed up with self-importance before he spoke.

"Lord Abel, this is most irregular. I am inclined to agree with the Chancellor and I must request that his shackles be removed immediately. You of all people know we are governed by the rule of law and it must be obeyed by all. I move that the constable be summoned to investigate the charges that have been leveled here today."

"I second," another delegate said over the din of the crowd.

"All in favor?" the first said, followed by a chorus of "Aye!"

"All opposed?" he said. The room fell silent.

Abel looked a little worried. The assembly was playing into Cassius's hands but Alexander didn't care. He had known it would probably come to this and he welcomed the opportunity to make a demonstration.

As he approached the podium, Cassius gave him a look of triumph that faltered when he saw the golden anger glittering in his eyes. With a flinch, Cassius stepped aside and gave Alexander the floor.

He gazed across the gallery and took in the colors of the delegates. Most were corrupt or self-serving. All knew that the status quo protected them and any change to a different process of dispensing justice, especially against one of their own, would be a threat to their power, not to mention to their wealth and freedom.

Alexander knew that many in the room were political allies of the Chancellor and stood to lose influence themselves if the balance of power were altered. He didn't care about their balance of power. The room grew silent under his withering glare. When the delegates started to fidget nervously, he began.

"Cassius Ithilian is a liar and a traitor. I know this because I have seen him associate with Prince Phane's imp familiar. He provided the enemy information about our battle plans. Can I prove this to your satisfaction? No, but then you have a vested interest in maintaining the status quo.

"I know that he is a traitor because I have heard the account of his treachery offered by Wizard Petronius, who while under the influence of dark magic, colluded with Cassius Ithilian to facilitate an invasion of your homeland by a hostile enemy force. Would his testimony persuade you? No, but then your power is at stake in this matter.

"I know that he is a traitor because I have heard him confess his crimes. He admitted that he conspired to abduct Princess Evelyn. He admitted that he provided Phane with our battle plans. He revealed the participation of Wizard Petronius in the plot, leading us to summon and then kill Phane's familiar. Would the corpse of the demon that Phane used to deliver orders to his agents all around the Seven Isles convince you of these allegations? No, but then you don't want to be convinced.

"You are on trial here as much as Cassius Ithilian."

One of the delegates started to object but Alexander silenced him with a challenging glare.

"You have all enjoyed wealth and privilege because of the offices you hold. You are all so desperate to maintain your hold on what power you have that you have forgotten your duty to serve the people. You claim fealty to the law and hold it up as sacred while you defile it in the shadows. You have forgotten that there is a law higher than the statutes that you pass to benefit some at the expense of others. You have willfully chosen to ignore the Old Law, to subvert it at every turn, to scorn the limitations on your power that the Old Law demands."

Alexander withdrew the Sovereign Stone and let it fall against his tunic. It glowed with a soft, deep-red aura of power.

"This confers upon me the title of Sovereign of the Seven Isles, but that is not the title I call upon here as my authority to resolve this matter. I claim the title of Champion of the Old Law. I claim it because the Old Law must have a defender. I claim it because I don't want power but it has been thrust upon me in spite of my wishes. I claim it because I see injustice rule and deceit reign and it makes me angry. I claim the title of Champion of the Old Law because no one else will, and there must be someone to stand for those most basic principles that underlie any civilization worthy of being called *civil*.

"Hear me now. Let it be known throughout the Seven Isles that all who choose to govern over others, all who choose to rule and all who claim any noble title are subject to my authority and my justice."

With blinding speed he drew the Thinblade and lopped off Cassius Ithilian's head in a single stroke.

The room gasped and then fell silent as Alexander pointed the bloody sword at the now terrified delegates. The Chancellor's head rolled to a stop and blood began to pool around it, bright red in the fall of sunlight through the skylights as his body crumpled to the floor.

"You will obey the Old Law or I will take your heads. For those who seek power over others, you will face my justice and mine alone. You will have no trial. You will receive no jury. I will judge you and decide your punishment and my sentence will be final."

He gave the room one last sweeping gaze, then turned and strode out without looking back. His friends trailed behind him along with Abel and his royal guard.

***

An hour later they were riding toward the Gate with Conner and his honor guard. Abel remained in the city to deal with the aftermath of Alexander's actions. The assembly was shocked and frightened at the sudden turn of events. Many demanded that Alexander be brought to trial, but Abel dismissed their demands and instead established a board of inquiry composed of a number of wizards and several ranking officers from his army to investigate any further corruption within the assembly. Alexander's aggressive approach had blunted any criticism and sent the delegates into a scramble to cover their own corruption.

Chapter 34

Alexander arrived at the Reishi Gate late in the afternoon just ahead of the two legions marching from Grafton Province. The Gate legions were busy making preparations for the assault into Ruatha. The soldiers in the encampment had been idle for so long that they were eager for the opportunity to fight. Alexander knew all too well that their enthusiasm would soon be dampened by the very real horror of war.

They were met at the Gate by a young officer who escorted them to their tents.

Alexander sat down to meditate and soon found his awareness floating on the firmament. He moved his focus to Ruatha. From high over the enemy position he assessed their defenses. They had constructed a stone wall in a semicircle around the front of the Gate, joined by a straight wall that ran just behind the Gate with a ramp on either end allowing access to the top of the wall. Atop the wall were several heavy ballistae and at least two hundred archers, all well stocked with arrows.

Alexander drifted in closer and saw that the ground enclosed by the front wall was covered with wooden stakes pounded in at an angle with their sharp points facing the Gate. Upon closer inspection he found that the points of the stakes were coated with dung and that the ground around the stakes was layered with several inches of oil-soaked straw. The entire Gate platform was haphazardly covered in boards riddled with six-inch nails pointing upward.

Outside the wall was a horde of twenty thousand soldiers. First heavy infantry, then a band of archers surrounded by the remaining soldiers, who were all facing outward. The entire position was encircled with a hastily constructed berm lined with wooden spikes and ringed by a trench.

Alexander shifted his focus high overhead and found the position of the Ruathan assault force not two miles away. They were camped with Blackstone Keep to their backs and still working to prepare for the battle to come.

Alexander next shifted his awareness into the Keep and looked at his message board. There was only one message: "We are ready to attack." He moved to the sleeping room. His message was short: "Attack at dawn."

When he opened his eyes, Chloe was sitting on his knee watching him and Jataan was standing several feet away, hands clasped behind his back. Alexander stood up and left the tent, trailed by Jataan. Jack caught up a few moments later as Alexander headed for the Gate.

"What's happening?" Jack asked.

"I'm going to stir up the enemy," Alexander said.

"Can I watch?" Jack asked with a broad smile.

Alexander just chuckled.

As he stopped at the Gate and stared at it for a long moment, several of Lieutenant Wyatt's Rangers formed up around him. Tomorrow he would lead an army through the Gate into his homeland and begin the battle for the survival of

Ruatha. For now, he just wanted to give the enemy something to worry about. The entire ancient gateway was made from black stone and consisted of a gently sloping platform thirty feet square with a wall jutting up from the side opposite the ramp. Cut into the stone wall was the outline of an archway. Etched into the right side of the outline was a map of the Seven Isles and an indentation in the form of the Glyph of the House of Reishi that exactly matched the butt of the Thinblade.

"Everyone stand to the side of the Gate," Alexander ordered. "They're probably going to send quite a few arrows through as soon as it opens."

He took a torch from one of the Rangers and handed it to Jataan. "Stand here," he said, motioning to the very edge of the arch, "and throw that torch through as soon as the Gate opens. Make sure you throw it hard enough to clear the stone platform."

Jataan nodded and took his position. Alexander went to the opposite side of the Gate arch and looked to Jataan for confirmation before he touched the outline of Ruatha. A moment later the stone shimmered briefly and then disappeared, opening a passageway to Ruatha.

Jataan tossed the torch through.

Alexander waited for just a moment until he saw the oil-soaked straw ignite with a whoosh. He touched the straight bar etched into the Gate arch beneath the map of the Seven Isles. With a shimmer, the stone wall returned, closing the Gate.

"I doubt they'll get much sleep tonight," Jack said with a chuckle.

"Let's hope not," Alexander said. "We need to talk to General Brand about our strategy. We're going to lose a lot of men trying to break through the wall they built around the Gate."

"Perhaps we should capture the wall, rather than break through it," Jataan suggested. "If we could get our archers onto the wall, we could do significant damage to the infantry beyond while risking few of our forces."

"They still have a lot of archers within range of the Gate," Alexander said. "Even if we take the wall, they can put more than enough arrows into the air to kill everyone on or inside the wall."

"Mage Dax might be able to offer a solution," Jack suggested. "I've spoken to Lieutenant Wyatt at length about his time here. He speaks highly of the mage."

Alexander nodded. "Better go find him. We need a plan or tomorrow is going to be bloody."

They found Mage Dax with Conner and General Brand along with a dozen other senior advisors and Lieutenant Wyatt in the command tents standing over a sketch map of northern Ruatha.

"Ah, Lord Reishi," Conner said. "My messenger was quicker than I expected."

Alexander shook his head. "I didn't receive a message. I just came from the Gate. We need to develop a plan for the initial thrust into Ruatha."

He stepped up to the map with Jack beside him. Jataan took up a position a step or two behind, watching the other officers for any sign of danger to his charge. Alexander took a piece of charcoal and quickly drew the wall and the positions of the enemy soldiers as well as the location of the Ruathan forces that were ready to attack.

"The area inside the wall has been prepared with spikes and oil-soaked straw. We just set it on fire, so the ground might be a bit less dangerous by tomorrow morning," Alexander said. "The wall is lined with archers and ballistae. Once we take the wall, the archers surrounding the Gate are at perfect range to send a sustained barrage of arrows at us from all sides.

"Ruathan forces will attack at dawn and attempt to drive a wedge to the Gate, but they'll meet heavy resistance, so we should view their attack as a distraction. We need a plan, and I'm open to suggestions since you know your capabilities better than I do."

They debated their options late into the night, considering every possibility and exploring every option at their disposal. After an exhaustive evaluation of every imaginable plan, Alexander selected elements from a number of suggestions and formulated his battle strategy.

He went to bed with the understanding that his plan wasn't perfect, but it was the best chance they had under the circumstances. He only hoped that he hadn't missed something but knew that he most likely had. He also knew that the enemy was making plans, and as good as his sight was, he couldn't see everything. Good people were going to die tomorrow on his order.

He drifted off to sleep, nursing his anger toward Phane for inflicting his narcissistic ambitions on the world.

***

He was up before dawn and took care strapping on his weapons and armor. He wore a baldric with Mindbender on his left hip and the Thinblade strapped across his back with the hilt over his right shoulder. He checked the blade of each to be sure they were clear in their scabbards. His wear-worn long knife on the right side of his belt and a throwing knife strapped onto the back of his belt completed his armaments. He left his bow and quiver with his pack to be carried through the Gate by the supply wagons that would bring up the rear of the assault force.

He emerged from his tent to find Lucky cheerfully cooking breakfast over a small fire. Then he saw Jataan P'Tal and almost faltered.

The battle mage was dressed in armor. He had always worn a simple tunic and fought with knives, but this morning he was dressed very differently. He wore a breastplate, greaves, bracers, gauntlets, and a helmet. He had a sword strapped to his belt and a spear thrust into the ground next to him with a large round shield resting against it.

Alexander took it in for a moment, then glanced over to Anatoly.

"A little disconcerting, isn't it?" the big man-at-arms said.

Alexander could only nod his agreement.

"In large scale battle, danger can come from any direction without warning," Jataan said. "I generally find armor cumbersome and anything more than a knife unnecessary, but given the circumstances, I believe it's warranted."

Jack whipped out his tablet and started writing furiously while nodding to himself.

The sky was just starting to turn deep blue and the stars were dimming when they finished their breakfast and went to the Gate. Conner, General Brand,

and Mage Dax were already there.

Alexander surveyed the scene. Soldiers were staged for as far as he could see. Several units were lined up close to the Gate waiting to play their part in the initial push into Ruatha, while many more waited farther out for the order to move. Three units of a thousand men each stood the closest. The first were heavy infantry. Men selected for their strength and size as well as their experience and reputation for skill in battle. The second were heavy cavalry, armed with heavy spears, javelins, and long swords. Half rode big and powerful warhorses while the rest were mounted on the captured rhone steeds. The final unit was composed of archers equipped with long bows and a hundred arrows each.

During the night, a pile of boulders had been stacked on the Gate platform and a battering ram was waiting off to one side.

Alexander nodded good morning to Conner and his senior advisors, then drew a magic circle in the dirt before the Ithilian Gate. There was some murmuring from the troops when Alexander sat down and started meditating. He ignored them. Within a few minutes his awareness was floating above the Ruathan Gate. Dawn was just breaking over the horizon. The sky was clear and the battle flags flapped lazily in the gentle breeze.

Off in the distance he saw a cloud of dust rising into the air from the movement of his army. They were beginning to advance toward the enemy line. The battle would be joined within the hour.

He looked closely at the wall enclosing the Gate and saw that the enemy hadn't taken the time to place new stakes in the ground or lay more oil-soaked straw. He floated amongst the archers lining the tops of the wall. They looked tired and nervous but they were alert and watching for any sign of movement. When he reached the spot on the straight wall that ran behind the Gate, he found a wizard, as expected. He returned to his body and stood up.

"There's a wizard on the wall behind the Gate," he said. "Our plan doesn't change. Mage Dax, please proceed."

The mage began casting a spell. It took several minutes to complete and, judging from the swell of his colors, required an unrestrained connection with the firmament. Once he completed his spell, the pile of boulders stacked on the Gate platform began to move. Slowly, the boulders took on a life of their own. Within a few minutes they were arranged in the form of a giant man. Flickerings of magical energy could be seen in the spaces between the stones. Once it was fully assembled, standing twelve feet tall, Mage Dax nodded to Alexander.

He went to the Gate controls and touched the outline of Ruatha on the little map. The Gate shimmered and then opened. A second later, arrows rained down through the Gate but none found their mark. The angle of attack from the wall made it impossible to shoot through the Gate any farther than a few feet.

With a word from Mage Dax, the creature of stone and magic started moving forward, gathering terrifying speed in just a few steps. It hit the wall facing the Gate with a thunderous crash, then began smashing the hastily built fortification with its giant stone fists. Arrows rained down on the magical creature with no effect. Alexander watched from a safe distance, marveling at the virtually limitless capacity of magic.

A bubble of liquid fire splashed against the back of the stone juggernaut and ignited with a whoosh, splattering droplets of flame all around, but still the magical creature continued to pound the wall. Stones began to break free and crash to the ground. Alexander smiled to himself when he saw the creature snatch up a block of stone and incorporate it into itself. As more stones fell, it gathered them up, adding to its size and bulk. As it grew, the blows to the stone wall grew in power and more stones fell. Sounds of shouting and alarm could be heard from the archers as the wall began to lose structural integrity.

By now the stone monster was twenty feet tall and the section of wall in front of it was nearly broken through. With one final blow, the wall shattered, sending stones scattering into the enemy infantry beyond. With the break in the wall, the stone creature was able to gather even more boulders up and add them to its mass and size. It started dismantling the wall piece by piece as the soldiers surrounding the fortification looked on in shock and amazement.

It quickly opened a twenty-foot gap in the stone wall and grew to thirty feet in height. Mage Dax gave a command and the creature turned and barreled into the corner of the semicircular wall where it met the straight wall running behind the Gate. Alexander heard shouted commands as the enemy commanders marshaled their forces to pour through the breach and into the enclosed space in front of the Gate.

As he gripped the hilt of Mindbender, his focus sharpened and his senses heightened the way they always did when he was in a fight. He created the image of a giant dragon in his mind and released it into the sword. With a flicker, the air before them condensed and a terrifying creature of bone and fang appeared.

Alexander's army gasped in surprise.

The illusionary dragon roared in fury, then folded its wings and started squeezing through the Gate. Soldiers on the other side cried out in alarm at the threat of a dragon in their midst. They fell back, giving the stone giant more time to work on the wall.

The dragon stood guard on the other side of the Gate, sending the enemy into a mad scramble to regroup and form some sort of strategy capable of dealing with such a terrifying threat. A hail of arrows descended on the illusionary creature and the stone giant from all directions but had no effect.

"Prepare the cavalry," Alexander said.

General Brand nodded and signaled to the cavalry commander.

Alexander smiled when he saw the shadow of the stone giant fall over the front of the Gate. It was nearing forty feet tall and gaining size rapidly from the stone blocks it was cannibalizing from the crumbling wall. It stepped into view and swept down with a mighty two-fisted blow onto the top of the wall. The weakened wall shuddered under the weight of the blow, then crumbled into rubble with a thunderous rolling crash.

Alexander focused on his dragon and it leapt up onto the remaining section of the semicircular wall and roared, sending nearby soldiers scrambling to escape the terrifying beast.

With the wall broken down, Mage Dax spoke another word of command and the now fifty-foot-tall rock monster waded out into the surrounding army, thrashing this way and that. Broken bodies of enemy soldiers flew through the air, sending the rest of the nearby soldiers into a panic. Mage Dax's creation cut a wide swath of destruction through the enemy ranks, sending them into disarray and confusion. With a final word of command, the magical jumble of stones stopped and drew itself up to a full sixty feet, then abruptly exploded, sending boulders half the size of a man flying through the air in every direction, crashing into the enemy with deadly force.

"Well done, Mage Dax," Alexander said.

"Send in the cavalry and prepare the infantry," he said to General Brand.

A column of heavy cavalry ten-wide thundered past and through the Gate. They charged through the breach in the wall and into the chaotic field of enemy soldiers. A few of their infantry tried to organize a resistance but the leading soldiers mounted on the rhone trampled over them on their way to the ring of archers two hundred feet from the Gate.

The enemy archers were concentrating their fire on the dragon still perched atop the wall and roaring ferociously at the nearby infantry. By the time they saw the column of Ithilian cavalry coming for them, it was too late. The horsemen trampled into the ranks of archers, crushing them under hoof and striking them down with their heavy spears, then wheeling right and continuing their charge. The lightly armored archers were no match for the heavy armor and momentum of the cavalry crashing through their ranks and leaving a trail of carnage and broken bodies in their wake.

As the cavalry moved around the band of archers, they left the area where the stone giant had caused the most damage and the heavy infantry on both sides began to offer some resistance.

Squads of men rushed into the flanks of the charging column and drove spears into the sides of their steeds, then pulled the men down and stabbed them to death. But the cavalry didn't stop—they had their orders and knew the risks. When one horse fell, the others closed ranks and filled in the gap to continue their charge through the archers.

Alexander sent Chloe through the Gate to scout for him. She floated in the aether high above and scanned the scene, while Alexander surveyed the battlefield through her eyes. The enemy had abandoned the broken wall and the soldiers in the immediate area were in disarray. They didn't know what to make of the dragon and seemed to be waiting for it to attack. His cavalry were halfway around the circle of archers, leaving nothing but wreckage in their path. It saddened him that they had lost nearly two hundred of their number, but the necessity of eliminating the archers outweighed the cost.

On the outer perimeter of the Regency encampment, Alexander saw another battle unfolding as three legions of Ruathan soldiers attacked. They'd already breached the defensive ditch and berm in two places and were pouring into the encampment.

"Stay high and remain in the aether, Little One," Alexander said to Chloe through his link with her mind.

"Be careful, My Love," she said.

"Send in the infantry and prepare the archers," Alexander commanded.

A thousand heavy infantry marched past twenty-wide and spread out as they entered the partially enclosed area in front of the Gate. Even though they all knew the dragon was nothing but an illusion, most couldn't help but look up when it roared.

The enemy soldiers that had taken the brunt of the stone giant's attack were scrambling to reorganize and present a coordinated resistance. Alexander's infantry weren't interested in fighting them. Instead they moved to seize what was left of the wall. Once on the other side of the Gate, they wheeled left and drove straight for the ramp leading up to the top of the long straight wall behind it. As they neared the base of the ramp, they met heavy resistance from an infantry unit that had managed to regroup. The fighting was fierce. Alexander watched as his soldiers fought to a standstill against the crush of superior numbers. The enemy commanders had regained control and were driving their forces toward the Gate to choke off the flow of Ithilian soldiers.

"It's time," Alexander said, drawing the Thinblade with his right hand and Mindbender with his left.

Anatoly unslung his war axe, Jataan strapped on his shield and took up his spear, Boaberous hefted his giant war hammer over his shoulder, and the thirteen Rangers commanded by Lieutenant Wyatt drew long swords as one. Jack and Lucky looked torn. They were staying behind until the area could be secured and neither looked happy about it.

"Wait for my signal, then send in the archers," Alexander said to Conner. "Once they're through, make sure the second wave is ready to go at a moment's notice."

"Good luck, Lord Reishi," Conner said with a salute.

Alexander turned and stepped through the Gate and onto Ruathan soil for the first time in months. He and his men moved to the left of the Gate toward the infantry that had fought to a stalemate. His soldiers had planted their heavy shields in the dirt, forming an interlocking wall to defend against the throng pressing in toward them. Bodies were piling up in front of them as they stabbed past their shields with swords and spears, wounding or killing those in the first ranks of the enemy counterattack.

Alexander scanned the scene and found the spot where he would make his thrust. He found a company commander coordinating the attack that had suddenly turned into a desperate defense.

"Captain, we're going to push through the line right there," Alexander said, pointing to the spot with the Thinblade. "Spread the word to your men to fold in on my command and open a gap in the line for us. Have another hundred men ready to follow us through."

The captain looked like he thought the plan was madness but he didn't argue the point. Instead, after only the briefest of hesitation, he grabbed a nearby sergeant and told him to spread the order.

Alexander and Jataan formed the point of a wedge with Boaberous and Anatoly on their flanks. The Rangers filled out the rear ranks. They moved into position and Alexander shouted the order. In unison, two soldiers unlocked their shields and a section of ten men along the hastily formed shield-wall separated and folded inward like two gates swinging open.

The enemy took advantage of the sudden opening and rushed in. Alexander could hear the thoughts of the nearby enemy soldiers through Mindbender. He released the illusion of the dragon and narrowed his focus. He was in a fight and he had a blade in his hand. Everything else faded away as he met the enemy.

He pushed forward with measured speed, using Mindbender to block enemy weapons and to see their intentions as they attacked. When they stepped into range, he cut them down with the Thinblade. The ground soaked up the blood. Alexander stepped over the severed body parts of those enemy soldiers who had been unfortunate enough to face off against him.

Jataan fought with speed and precision, using his shield to defend against attack and his spear to stab into the enemy, usually driving through their breastplates and into their hearts or simply slipping the point into their throats. Men fell away with each carefully placed thrust.

Anatoly fought with his usual deliberate style, waiting for the enemy to step just close enough before feinting to draw them into his kill zone or striking at their weapon to move it out of position before delivering a deadly blow with his war axe.

Boaberous was a study in bottled rage. He maintained formation but it was obvious that he wanted to wade into the enemy. He kept his hammer high and struck with deceptive speed and terrible force at any soldier close enough. Each smashing blow broke bones, rent armor, and crushed the life out of the man facing him.

The Rangers covered the rear and flanks as they steadily drove through the crush of enemy soldiers along the wall toward the ramp. A column of infantry flowed into the trail of carnage, then turned to attack the Regency soldiers in the twenty feet between the swath Alexander had cut and the wall that ran along the back of the Gate. When Alexander's assault reached the base of the ramp, he pushed out just a dozen feet and held position while soldiers poured past him up the ramp and onto the wall.

Alexander sent Chloe with the order for the archers to come through as the Ithilian infantry extended its shield-wall to enclose the area from the point opposite the Gate where the stone giant had first attacked the wall out to the base of the ramp leading to the top of the wall.

The slaughter of so many soldiers by Alexander and his friends had sent a wave of hesitation through the enemy that the Ithilian infantry used to their advantage to widen the foothold they had on the battlefield.

Within a minute of sending the order, the first of the Ithilian archers started to file behind the fierce fighting taking place in front of the infantry's shield-wall and up onto the wall. A contingent of infantry had killed any enemy soldiers that remained on top of the wall and cast their bodies down into the midst of their comrades. Once the wall was secure, they took a position at the top of the opposite ramp, forming a shield-wall with a row of pike men behind them to present a bristling defensive position that could defend against a push to retake the wall from that side.

Alexander pulled back as infantry with heavy shields took their place, creating an unbroken line of soldiers joining half of the semicircular wall around in front of the ramp and a dozen feet to the other side. Archers took positions along the top of the wall and immediately began firing into the crowd of soldiers below, thinning their ranks and putting them on the defensive.

Alexander raced up onto the wall and scanned the battlefield. Ithilian infantry were creating a space within the remains of the wall surrounding the Gate where his soldiers could be staged for the next push. A steady stream of arrow-laden archers was moving through the Gate and lining the top of the wall. They immediately began firing as soon as they reached their position, adding to the growing barrage of arrows falling on the enemy infantry.

The cavalry had completely routed the band of enemy archers surrounding the Gate and were making a charge into the infantry toward the Gate. It looked like about six hundred remained of the thousand he'd sent into the fray. He swallowed hard at the human toll his orders had exacted before he turned his attention to the battle raging a mile away between the Regency forces and the Ruathan Army.

Smoke rose from many of the Regency's fortifications, and their defenses had completely failed in four places. Pitched battles were taking place between their forces and the Ruathan soldiers pushing into their encampment.

Alexander nodded his satisfaction at their progress and returned to the battle raging all around him.

"Captain," he called down from the top of the wall. When the man turned and looked up at him, he pointed out across the battle toward the column of cavalry charging through the enemy soldiers. "Prepare to open a gap for our cavalry."

The captain saluted and turned to issue orders to his men.

Alexander spoke to Chloe through his mental link with her, "Tell Conner that our cavalry is returning, Little One."

"I will, My Love," she said in his mind.

Archers lining the top of the wall were busy sending a steady rain of arrows into the enemy surrounding them on all sides. Alexander saw a column of enemy cavalry charging through their own infantry toward the opposite ramp leading to the top of the wall. Some of the soldiers were too slow to avoid being trampled by the heavy horses.

Alexander brought the image of the dragon back into his mind and released it into Mindbender, calling it into being high overhead. He directed it down in a dive toward the onrushing cavalry, flaring its wings and roaring with deafening fury as it descended on them. The cavalry panicked at the threat the illusion presented and the column scattered, trying desperately to avoid the terrifying creature.

The Ithilian cavalry reached the shield line, which opened a gap for them to pour through, then closed it again once the last horseman had passed. They rode back through the Gate into Ithilian.

"Send the next regiment of infantry and more arrows," Alexander told Chloe in his mind.

"Yes, My Love,"

Not a minute later, another thousand infantry started to move through the Gate to relieve some of the soldiers still holding the line against the Regency soldiers and to help wounded soldiers retreat through the Gate. The crush of enemy soldiers was much less with the steady rain of arrows falling into their midst.

Alexander surveyed the battlefield again. He saw that the Ruathan soldiers were making headway against the Regency soldiers, having pushed through their defensive barriers and formed up into company-sized units to face the soldiers in pitched battles.

From behind and to his right, Alexander heard a whoosh followed by terrible screaming. He turned to see the squad of soldiers holding the far ramp leading to the top of the wall engulfed in bright, angry fire. He scanned the sea of enemy soldiers and found his target. A single man stood atop a wagon, well out of bow range. The wizard. His colors glowed brightly as he cast another spell.

Alexander snatched a bow from the nearest archer and handed it to Jataan, pointing at his target. The battle mage nodded as Alexander moved to reinforce the far ramp with Anatoly and Boaberous right behind him. As he moved along the wall, he watched a stream of a dozen arrows sail in a high arc from Jataan's bow toward the wizard.

When the first of the arrows neared the wizard, he abandoned his liquid-fire spell and threw up a flame screen to defend against the sudden attack. The first arrow charred as it passed through the plane of heat and flew off course. The second ignited in midair but still hit him in the shoulder, breaking his concentration and diminishing the heat of his frantically erected shield. The arrows that followed struck him in the chest one after the other until he toppled off the back of the wagon.

Enemy soldiers were advancing up the ramp toward the burning pool of liquid fire and charred bodies. Archers posted along the semicircular section of wall shifted fire to thin their ranks. Alexander stopped short of the flames and waited. The first soldier through caught on fire and turned to see the flames racing up his cloak. He spun to try to put it out, chasing around after his own cloak. Alexander kicked him back into the pool of fire. He fell screaming as the searing heat of the magical fire engulfed him.

Another squad of infantry raced up behind Alexander and took up the position in front of the flames. Alexander stepped back and assessed the situation yet again. Things were moving quickly and the circumstances dictated his strategy more than anything else.

There was a lull in the battle as the enemy fell back to regroup. Soldiers behind and to the right of the Gate formed up into units several hundred feet away and prepared to advance under the cover of shields. Bodies were scattered everywhere and the groans of dying soldiers suddenly filled the air as the din of battle faded.

The Regency soldiers in front of the Gate had turned to meet the advance of the Ruathan Army that had broken through their lines and were now pushing toward the Gate. To the left of the Gate, the enemy army was still pressing in on the shield line but not with nearly the pressure they brought to bear when the battle had begun.

Reinforcements from farther out in the sprawling encampment were moving toward the Gate. Alexander knew he needed to seize the moment and fill the void left on the battlefield with his forces before the enemy was able to find their footing and strike back.

"Little One, send in five thousand infantry, as quick as you can," he said to Chloe in his mind.

"Right away, My Love" she said in his mind. "Stay safe."

Soldiers started pouring into the space behind his shield-wall. The captain coordinating the defensive effort saw the new soldiers and looked up to Alexander for orders.

"Push out," Alexander called to him, motioning for him to expand the shield-wall. "Surround the Gate."

The captain saluted and started calling out orders to his sergeants. The men manning the oversized, interlocking shields lifted as one, pulling the grounding spikes out of the blood-soaked dirt, and shoved forward. At the same time, a line of spearmen just behind them lashed out at the soldiers trying to break the line, driving them back. The shield-wall expanded one step at a time. The enemy troops still trying to break through were caught between defending against the arrows steadily raining down on them and the spears and swords of the soldiers manning the shield-wall. They broke and retreated in favor of regrouping with other soldiers farther back.

"Advance!" Alexander shouted. The soldiers manning the shield-wall disconnected their shields and lumbered forward as many more men poured into the field behind them and raced in to fill the gaps in the shield line as their foothold expanded. Once they'd gained a hundred feet of ground, one well-seasoned sergeant called for them to stop, planting his shield in the dirt and signaling for the men around him to form a line. They locked their shields together and drove the grounding stakes into the dirt, lending stability and strength to their shield-wall.

Men poured through from Ithilian and filled the newly captured ground with soldiers eager for their taste of the glory of battle.

The stench of the blood and burned bodies made Alexander's stomach turn, but he kept his focus on the ebb and flow of the fight. Every turn of events presented opportunities and dangers that had to be seized or avoided.

When he saw the regiment of Rangers flanking the enemy to the north, he saw an opportunity.

"Stop the infantry, send all the cavalry in one column, Little One," he said in his mind. "Tell them to drive through to the north and punch a hole through the enemy forces until they join with the Ruathan cavalry. Have the infantry ready to follow on their heels."

"Yes, My Love," Chloe said.

He called out to get the captain's attention.

"Captain, clear a path wide enough for a cavalry charge," he yelled over the heads of a throng of soldiers. "Prepare the men at the shield-wall to fold in and let them through."

The small ocean of soldiers parted and a path opened just wide enough for ten horses, running abreast. Minutes later, cavalry started coming through the Gate. The commander saw his path and charged into the battle through the opening in the shield-wall.

The river of horses flowed out of the Gate and thundered across the battlefield stretching for a hundred feet, then a thousand and more. They crashed into the Regency infantry unit and trampled hundreds of soldiers under hoof.

Alexander scanned for other threats and saw a unit of archers forming up well out of bow range, but it was clear that they planned to move closer and begin an archery assault. Once they got close enough, it would be too late to stop them and they would be able to overpower the limited number of archers Alexander had deployed on the wall. Worse, he saw no immediate means of countering the threat.

He weighed the idea of diverting part of the cavalry from their course but decided against it. More than anything he needed a channel through the enemy encampment so he could move his entire army through the Gate. As things stood, there just wasn't enough space for all of his soldiers and they were still completely surrounded.

He watched the progress of the heavy-cavalry charge. The last of the horses thundered through the Gate onto the battlefield. The shield-wall closed after them, presenting a solid front to the enemy scrambling to regroup after being cut down by the horse charge. Infantry followed after the last of the horses.

"Push out," Alexander called down to the captain commanding the soldiers. "Fill in the gap left by the horses."

Soldiers started to push forward again, creating a narrow wedge pointing into the trail of broken bodies left by the cavalry charge and creating room for yet more soldiers to move through the Gate.

The Rangers saw the Ithilian cavalry coming toward them and shifted tactics to break through the enemy line. Since they were riding lighter horses that weren't suited to crashing into the enemy, they moved at a measured pace and attacked with spears in the front line of their advance while those behind used short bows to thin the ranks of the enemy soldiers.

As the two cavalry forces neared one another, a unit of enemy archers off to the side loosed a volley of arrows. Alexander watched the arrows rise into the air and held his breath as they rained down on his forces. Men toppled off their horses and were trampled. The momentum of the heavy-cavalry charge faltered, but the commanders quickly focused their men on the task before them and they resumed crashing through the field of infantry.

Then Alexander saw something he didn't expect. From within the ranks of the Rangers, a whirlwind formed. It started small but grew quickly, holding its position until it became a tornado. Then it abruptly hopped over the Rangers, floated over the enemy infantry and touched down in the ranks of the archers, scattering them haphazardly about the battlefield. The tornado scoured the ground, sucking men into its vortex and tossing them away with terrible force until the threat posed by the archers was eliminated. It lifted off the ground again and headed straight for Alexander. He watched with a mixture of tension and wonder.

"Hold," he said to those around him who were preparing to meet an attack.

The tornado calmed into a whirlwind, then touched down on top of the wall, sending archers scrambling to avoid the spot where it lighted. It whipped around for a moment more, then the swirl of air transformed into Wizard Sark.

"It's good to see you well, Lord Alexander . . . or should I say Lord Reishi?"

"Wizard Sark, your timing is excellent," Alexander said, pointing to the archers that were advancing into range. "Can you do something to stop them?"

"I can indeed," Wizard Sark said. He faced the enemy unit still many hundreds of feet away and began casting a spell. It took some time, but Alexander could see that it was working from the bright flare of Sark's colors. "That should do it," he said.

"I don't see anything," Anatoly growled as the first volley of arrows rose into the sky.

"Perhaps not, but that doesn't mean it isn't there," Wizard Sark said.

The arrows reached the apex of their flight and began to fall toward Alexander's foothold. At about fifty feet from the ground, they suddenly encountered a strong circular wind. The entire volley of arrows was caught up in the spell and sent whipping out away from the Gate to fall into the surrounding enemy.

"Huh," Anatoly said. "Not bad."

The archers didn't stop, but their efforts were useless against the shield of wind stirred up by Wizard Sark. With that threat neutralized, Alexander turned his attention to his rapidly growing army around the Gate. As the infantry poured through, the wedge of soldiers following the path of the cavalry extended farther toward the perimeter of the enemy encampment. In the distance, Alexander watched the Ranger regiment part and allow the column of heavy cavalry to pass between their ranks. The Rangers pressed forward until they met the wedge of infantry in the middle, creating a swath through the enemy encampment.

Several powerful explosions in the distance caught Alexander's attention. He scanned the battle raging between the Regency forces and the main body of the Ruathan Army and saw plumes of smoke rising in a line running through densely packed enemy units. He didn't know what had caused the detonations but he could see, even at this distance, that the attack had caused massive casualties. Alexander felt the tide turn. As if on cue, a horn sounded and the enemy began to retreat to the southwest, away from the Gate and the advancing Ruathan Army.

Alexander's forces pressed the attack into the fleeing army, doing significant damage until their orderly retreat turned into a rout. When he saw them break formation and flee, he ordered his infantry to consolidate and begin cleaning up any remaining soldiers still within their area of control.

Shortly after the fighting around the Gate ended, Erik rode up with a platoon of Rangers. He dismounted with a broad smile and strode up to Alexander.

"It's good to see you, Alexander," he said. "Your parents will be so relieved to have you home." He swallowed and looked around at the battlefield for a moment as if searching for the right words.

"I looked in on her just the other day," Alexander said. "Isabel is alive and well. And just as soon as I secure Ruatha, I'm going to go get her and my sister and bring them home."

Erik nodded his thanks without a word.

"For now, I have a job for you," Alexander said.

"Of course." Erik was once again all business.

"Take your Rangers and harass that army all the way to Northport," Alexander said. "Don't engage them, just pick at them. Bleed them a little at a time."

Erik nodded. "They've caused a lot of suffering and hardship for a lot of people. It's about time they felt the consequences of their crimes."

Alexander clapped him on the shoulder. "Very soon, they will all pay dearly for what they've done to our people."

By dark the Gate was closed and four legions of Ithilian soldiers were encamped a mile south of the gruesome battlefield. Alexander ordered the fallen cleared and buried, and the weapons, armor, and supplies of the dead collected and put to use where needed. He consolidated the Ithilian legions with two of the Ruathan legions into one force and placed Conner in command.

He lay down long after dark and thought of Isabel as he drifted off to sleep.

Chapter 35

Isabel wheeled high above the practice target. Wind rushed past, drowning out everything but her pounding heartbeat. Anger coursed through her as she balanced the demands of riding Asteroth with the act of supreme will required to cast a spell.

She released her vision into the firmament and argent-white light ignited around her outstretched hand and streaked to the target below, burning a hole clear through the wood-and-straw mannequin and several inches into the ground beneath it. Her spell released, she shifted her focus to guiding Asteroth into a steep dive. She leaned into her steed's strong neck and coaxed him on toward the target. At the last moment Asteroth extended his wings and pulled up hard, crushing Isabel into her saddle. She felt the jolt reverberate through his body when he snapped his tail like a whip and shattered the practice target into splinters. Isabel looked back with satisfaction at the mock carnage left behind by her practice run.

The witches and Sky Knights of the fortress island had taken on an entirely different view of her after she killed Gabriella. Her success in the challenge against the third triumvir guaranteed her acceptance within the secluded community. The fact that she had commanded Gabriella's steed to strike the final blow stunned the onlookers and conferred near reverence upon her in the eyes of the Sky Knights.

Since that day, Isabel had been training to ride Asteroth. She found that her horse-riding skills transferred somewhat to the practice of riding a wyvern and her unique ability to telepathically communicate and even command animals gave her a distinct advantage over other Sky Knights. She learned quickly and worked diligently at the new skills she was attempting to master. Her single-minded focus was driven by a very real need. She knew with certainty that she would soon be riding Asteroth into battle and she wanted to be as prepared as possible when that day came.

She had set aside the study of any new spells in favor of her aerial combat training, reasoning that Asteroth would give her a greater advantage more quickly than any of the spells she might learn in the time she had. Even as she guided her steed in a wide arc heading for the landing bay, she felt another pang of anxiousness. Alexander was out there and he needed her.

She needed him.

Darkness fell as she crossed the threshold into the enclosed landing bay. Abigail was behind and to her right riding Kallistos. Both wyverns flared their wings in unison and slowed to light gently on the smooth stone floor. Isabel yanked on the release cord, pulling a dozen locking bolts free, unbinding her riding armor from her saddle. It took much longer to make ready for flight than it did to dismount. She slid off her steed and ran a hand down his long neck, giving him an affectionate pat on the jaw on her way to the meat cart. With a grunt, she hefted the haunch of a steer from the cart and tossed it on the ground in front of Asteroth. He hesitated until she nodded, then snatched up the snack with gusto. A squad of handlers went to work removing his saddle and checking for any injury as was standard practice for returning wyverns.

She smiled at Abigail as she approached, slinging her bow.

"That was a good ride," Isabel said. "I think we're finally starting to get the hang of this."

"I never imagined how much more difficult or how much more effective it would be to maintain formation in a fight. Takes a lot of thought to anticipate where you're going to go next but I'm starting to understand your approach." Abigail smiled brightly. All of the discoloration from her injury was gone and her skin was as clear and perfect as ever. "Alexander is going to be impressed."

"Still looking to one-up your brother?" Isabel asked teasingly.

"Always," Abigail said with a grin.

A Sky Knight was waiting for them and approached as soon as they finished with their steeds.

"Lady Reishi, Mistress Magda has news from the patrols," he said respectfully.

"Thank you, Knight," Isabel said, then turned to Abigail. "Finally. They've been out all day."

They didn't bother stopping by their chambers to change out of their riding armor but went straight to the triumvirate's private council chamber. Magda and Cassandra were waiting for them, or more precisely, they were waiting for Isabel.

Since she had killed Gabriella, she'd taken on the title and duties of third triumvir which entailed casting her vote on any decision of importance concerning the function and operation of the fortress island, the Reishi Coven, or the Sky Knights.

"Lady Reishi, Abigail, please come in," Magda said when the guard opened the door. "We have word of war on Ruatha. Our scouts have just returned from their survey of the west coast and the news is most grave."

Isabel steeled herself for the report. She gave a glance to Abigail, whose face was set, anger dancing in her pale blue eyes.

They took their seats around the table. It was customary that only the three triumvirs met in the council chamber, but Isabel had insisted that Abigail be allowed to attend important meetings that concerned Ruatha. Magda and Cassandra had finally relented but steadfastly refused to give her any more than an advisory role.

"The northern scouts report that Northport has been occupied by a sizable army of Regency soldiers," Magda began. "It appears that there was little resistance and that the majority of the civilian population was evacuated prior to the assault. The city is remarkably intact with the exception of the ports which have been completely destroyed by fire. It appears that the occupying soldiers are cannibalizing materials from the nearby buildings in an effort to repair the docks.

"The central scouting party reports that Southport has deployed a sizable fleet for reconnaissance, with the bulk of their warships anchored not far offshore. They appear to be preparing for a naval battle, which brings me to the report from the southern scouting party.

"There is an armada of warships and troop transports moving north along the coast of Ruatha. They're flying the Andalian flag and I anticipate they will arrive at the Southport blockade sometime late tomorrow afternoon."

Isabel and Abigail shared a look.

"At least Kevin is taking the initiative," Abigail said.

"My brother never did like to wait around to be told what to do next," Isabel said.

Cassandra frowned in confusion. "Who are you referring to?"

"My brother Kevin is the Regent of Southport," Isabel said. "Alexander killed the previous Regent after he tried to assassinate him and wound up poisoning me instead. He put Kevin in charge because he wanted someone there that he trusted."

"I see," Cassandra said.

Isabel found that she was often at odds with the second triumvir, but she had come to respect the woman for her deliberate thought process and careful attention to detail. Cassandra liked facts and was often reluctant to make a decision when she felt there was still information to be gathered.

"What are the strength estimates of the two fleets?" Isabel asked.

"The armada from Andalia is more than twice the size of the Southport fleet," Magda said. "Over half of their ships are troop transports that are slow and clumsy. The rest are oversized longboats equipped with banks of oars, two masts, and a ram. The attack boats look big enough to carry fifty men including crew.

"The Southport fleet contains a handful of large warships equipped with multiple ballistae and a few catapults, but the majority of the fleet is made up of fast-attack boats armed with a single ballista on the foredeck. There is also a hodgepodge of merchant ships fitted with weapons."

Isabel held each of the other triumvir's eyes for a moment before she nodded to herself. "How many Sky Knights can we put in the air tomorrow?"

"What are you suggesting?" Cassandra asked with a hint of alarm.

"I'm suggesting we fly out and sink that Andalian fleet before it can reach Northport," Isabel said. "Kevin will do his best, but from the sounds of it, the warships will engage his fleet while the troop transports slip past. If they reach Northport and offload the Lancers they're carrying, then Ruatha is in real trouble."

"I'm not sure that would be wise," Cassandra said. "Perhaps we should conserve our strength and look for an opportunity to strike at Phane directly."

"Look, the Seven Isles are at war," Isabel said hotly. This wasn't the first time they'd had this argument. "You can either sit by and watch Phane grind the world to dust or you can get in the fight. Now is the time to strike. Those Lancers are vulnerable while they're on the water but they're deadly beyond measure once they make landfall. The people of Ruatha, and the rest of the Seven Isles for that matter, can't wait. They're dying now. We can help them."

"Perhaps it's time we change our thinking," Magda said. "For so long now we've maintained a defensive position here and protected the Reishi Isle. It may be that we've become blinded to other options because we're doing what we've always known."

"What about our patrol rotation?" Cassandra asked. "If we deploy a sizable force, we'll be spread too thin to defend the Reishi Isle."

Isabel huffed in exasperation. The other two triumvirs were much older. They both carried themselves with scrupulous attention to decorum. Isabel didn't care about any of that.

"Scrap the patrols," she said emphatically. "Who cares if someone wants to land on the Reishi Isle? The Sovereign Stone isn't there anymore. It's out there," she pointed to the wall for effect, "around my husband's neck. And he needs our help. If you want to fulfill your mission and live up to your duty to the Seven Isles, there's only one way to do that now. Get into this fight with everything you have."

"She does have a point," Magda said. "If nothing else, our assistance might spare the people of Ruatha great hardship."

Isabel waited. She'd made her case. Cassandra was always very thorough in her thought process but her reasoning was usually sound. Isabel respected that, so she waited for the triumvir to reach a decision.

"Perhaps a measured response that doesn't jeopardize our position here," Cassandra said.

Isabel bit her tongue. She wanted to scream but knew it wouldn't do any good.

"What did you have in mind?" Magda asked.

"Two flights," Cassandra said. "More than that and the fortress island is vulnerable."

Isabel wanted more but she knew some was better than none. She could probably persuade Magda to go along with a larger force but she knew it was better to find consensus. Contention within the triumvirate over one decision could easily spill over into future decisions. Isabel only hoped it would be enough.

"I'll take it," she said.

"Very well then," Magda said. "We will send two flights to Southport tomorrow to assist in the battle against the Andalian fleet. Who should we choose to lead the force?"

Isabel frowned in surprise and blurted out, "Me!"

"A triumvir shouldn't lead our forces in battle," Cassandra said. "You must learn that your place is here, making the important decisions for our people."

Isabel shook her head. "Cassandra, things are changing. I'm going to lead our forces into battle tomorrow and then I'm going to find my husband. Once we've had a chance to talk things over, then I may or may not return here, but I won't be staying for long. The way things were is at an end. The enemy is on the march and we won't win this war from here. We have to get out there and attack when and where we can."

Cassandra sighed. "This is all happening so quickly. For centuries we've chosen our course with deliberate care and careful consideration of all the foreseeable consequences of our actions. Now you would have us rush to judgment before all of the facts are known."

"Yes," Isabel said intently. "We're at war. We no longer have the luxury of time. The enemy is moving against those who hold the same values as we do, our natural allies. Once they fall, Phane will turn his attention here. There is only one path to salvation: Victory. We win or we die and we won't win through cautious deliberation. Only bold action will carry the day."

"I will think on what you've said," Cassandra said. "You speak with the passion and conviction of youth but I fear you lack the wisdom that comes with long years. For the time being, I will accept your choice to lead our forces even though I believe it is rash and ill-advised."

Isabel smiled gently and bowed her head slightly to Cassandra. "Thank you. I know I'm headstrong and willful. I know it's been difficult to accept the change I represent but I also know that, in time, you will come to see the enemy as I do and your fear for the future will lead you to make the kind of desperate choices that will be necessary to survive the storm that's coming."

***

As soon as Isabel left the triumvirate council chamber she dispatched two Sky Knights with a letter for Kevin in Southport. She didn't want his sailors turning their weapons on the wyverns out of fear and surprise. They stood a far better chance of success if they worked together against the Andalian armada.

By morning the entire fortress island was abuzz with activity as everyone pitched in to help with preparations for the coming battle. Isabel had briefed the commanders the night before and they had all spoken with their Sky Knights to ensure that everyone knew their target and the purpose of their mission. Communicating while airborne was difficult at best. The Sky Knights used a set of hand signals but those depended on alert riders and strict adherence to unit formation. Careful coordination beforehand made the process much easier by giving each rider a clear idea of their objectives prior to launch so they could anticipate the orders of their Wing Commanders.

Most of the Sky Knights were excited by the opportunity to fight, but some, mainly the older and more experienced, were more reserved. They circulated through the staging areas and flight decks now packed with Sky Knights checking their saddles and double checking their weapons, offering pointers and words of encouragement to the younger Knights.

Isabel stood with Abigail on an observation deck and struggled to impose some order on her feelings. She had arrived here as a prisoner and was leaving in command of half their forces. She knew the battle could well decide the fate of Ruatha. If the Lancers made landfall, they would be a deadly threat to the Ruathan Army, especially out in the open plains of northern Ruatha. The best chance they had was to destroy the Lancers at sea.

More than the anxiousness of impending battle, she knew that today would bring her one day closer to reuniting with Alexander. She missed him terribly. It felt like they'd been apart for ages even if it had only been a few months.

Flight Commanders Bianca and Constance ascended the stairs to the observation deck and nodded respectfully.

"All wings report ready," Bianca said.

"Very well," Isabel said. "Launch your Sky Knights."

Both saluted and turned crisply to relay the order to their Wing Commanders. Within minutes the launch deck bell sounded and the first four wyverns spread their wings and slipped over the edge into the sky. What followed was an exercise in ordered chaos. Handlers scrambled to get each wyvern into position to launch after each wave of Sky Knights took to the air while still other handlers rushed the wyverns deeper within the fortress island out to the launch bays. Within an hour, the entire force was airborne and flying in formation toward Southport.

Isabel floated high over the ocean with Abigail to her right. Two experienced Sky Knights who were also members of the coven were assigned as her personal guard at the insistence of both Magda and Cassandra. They flanked Isabel and Abigail and maintained careful watch of the glistening waters far below.

It was several hours before they could see the coastline of Ruatha on the horizon. Isabel felt a thrill of anticipation when she caught the first glimpse of land. She had never been away from Ruatha until she had gone with Alexander to the Reishi Isle and now she was finally going home.

As they got closer she started to see smoke rising from the ocean not far off the coastline . . . the battle was already in progress. She tipped her head back and looked through Slyder's eyes.

The warships from Southport were fighting a fierce battle with the escort ships of the Andalian armada, while the troop transports were skirting the battle and making best speed for Northport. A few of Kevin's fast-attack boats had broken the Andalian line and were sprinting across the water in pursuit of the troop transports, but they would be too little too late.

Isabel took the image of the enemy she saw thorough Slyder's eyes and fixed it in her mind. With an act of will she made contact with all of the wyverns flying toward the battle and sent them the image of the target. As one, the entire airborne strike force shifted north and began their descent.

The Wing Commanders understood the implicit command and signaled for their Knights to break into squads and begin their attack runs.

They caught the enemy by surprise with their initial attack as each squad formed up into single file and dove toward their target ship. The strategy was as simple as it was effective. Wyverns hurtled out of the sky only to break their dive and whip-strike at the masts and sails of the enemy vessels with their bone-bladed tails. One after another the dragon-like beasts pounded their targets in an effort to disable the sails and render the boats helpless to move under any power other than oars.

Each squad of eight targeted a single troop transport with the full force of their attack. Within minutes, twenty-four enemy ships were slowing. Two were taking on water and the rest were struggling to put their oars in the water and gain control of their direction.

The two fast-attack boats that had broken through the Andalian line raced up to the stalled troop transports and launched clay pots into the air. The fire pots sailed in a graceful arc and came crashing down onto the decks of two of the disabled ships, shattering on impact and splashing flaming oil into the torn sails and broken rigging. Each of the two ships erupted into flames.

Isabel assessed the situation and knew in an instant that she needed to change her strategy. The Sky Knights could cause damage to the troop transports, disable their sails and even sink a few ships, but they couldn't use fire with nearly the same effect because of the rushing wind. They needed to rely on the power of their wyverns and the accuracy of their javelins.

She had remained high overhead to observe the initial strike. She scanned the sky and picked out Bianca and her escort rider. With a hand signal, she indicated that she was breaking off to engage the warships that were fighting to contain the Southport fleet. Bianca signaled back and wheeled toward one of her

Wing Commanders.

Isabel glanced over her shoulder and saw the squads gaining altitude and wheeling around for another pass against a new set of targets. By now, the troop transports were aware of the threat from above and they'd put oars into the water to increase their speed while calling soldiers to the decks to repel the attackers. Bianca was moving toward the nearest Wing Commander, signaling for him to form up on her. Satisfied that reinforcements were on the way, Isabel turned her attention to the line of warships engaging the Southport fleet.

The Andalian warships were armed primarily with battering rams and soldiers. Their strategy was to ram the larger ships and then board with soldiers or to engage the smaller attack boats with archers. So far their strategy was proving effective in keeping the Southport fleet engaged. Isabel knew she needed to break a hole in the Andalian line to allow some of the fast-attack boats through so they could sink the troop transports.

She picked the ship she wanted to sink and signaled Abigail for a high pass. Her escorts formed up on her and they floated slowly toward the battle raging on the ocean below. Isabel started casting a light-lance spell, allowing the rage of battle to build within her as she approached her target.

The man at the wheel on the deck of the ship stiffened when Abigail's arrow drove into his neck at the shoulder and down into his torso. He fell dead amidst shouts of alarm from the soldiers aboard the ship. Abigail had scored the first kill.

Isabel smiled fiercely and released her spell. Light shot forth from her hand and burned through the sails and into the deck of the ship, opening a hole in the hull to let in the sea. Two flashes of light lanced out of the sky from each of Isabel's escort riders and burned two more holes into the deck of the ship.

As they floated over the raging battle, Abigail killed three more sailors. They coaxed their wyverns into an ascent to gain altitude then wheeled and lined up for the next pass.

Isabel watched Bianca and her escort rider float over the next ship in the line. Her escort rider cast a light-lance spell that burned a hole through the hull, while Bianca brought a small bubble of liquid fire into existence and cast it down onto the ship. It splashed magical fire across the deck, igniting the sails with a whoosh. Trailing behind her were three squads of Sky Knights lined up to attack the next three ships.

A group of fast-attack boats flying Southport's flag used the opening to guide their vessels toward the weak spot in the enemy line. Isabel surveyed the battle. Several of the larger Southport warships were taking on water and listing badly. Two had been rammed and become entangled with attacking vessels. Fierce battles were unfolding on their decks. The Angellica caught her eye. It was holding back and directing fire from its heavy ballistae and catapults toward a cluster of enemy ships that were engaging a number of fast-attack boats. An enemy warship was building speed for a battering-ram attack against her.

Isabel pointed it out and began her attack run. Abigail fell in on her lead, sending arrows out ahead of them. Isabel was focused on casting her light-lance spell when she saw a bubble of liquid fire streak up toward her from the deck of the warship. She abandoned her spell and rolled left, diving sharply out of the path of the enemy wizard's spell. It passed within ten feet of Asteroth's wingtip. She pulled hard on the reins and brought her wyvern into a steep rolling dive, corkscrewing around to bring her in line for an attack.

Arrows lifted off the deck of the ship toward her but she was moving so fast that they passed just behind her. She pulled up at the last moment and Asteroth brought his claws into strike position. As they crashed into the side railing, the sudden weight of the wyvern crushed a huge section of the ship. The ship listed and sailors lost their footing, many flying overboard. Asteroth pushed off and launched himself into the air with a mighty downward thrust of his wings. The ship capsized under the sudden assault. Isabel watched over her shoulder as it slipped beneath the waves. Abigail and her escort formed up above her and covered her ascent as she gained altitude for another attack run.

The three squads of Sky Knights made attack runs against three ships on the flank of the Andalian line. One after another they dove toward the ships, pulling up at the last moment and whipping their wyvern's bone-bladed tails into the enemy vessels. Isabel watched two wyverns take a volley of arrows from the deck of the ships they were attacking, falter after their attack runs, and then splash into the ocean. The Sky Knights that came next were clear to strike, one after the other. When the last of the squad had passed, the three ships were taking on water.

Two Sky Knights broke formation to provide overwatch for the two Sky Knights that had splashed into the ocean while two fast-attack boats moved toward their position to rescue the riders.

The Angellica adjusted her sails, put her oars into the water, and turned toward the fleeing troop transports. She shifted her ballistae and catapults to guard her escape while providing cover fire for a small force of fast-attack boats that were taking advantage of the opening to head for the transports.

Several of the Andalian warships fell back and regrouped to give chase after the Southport attack boats.

Isabel shifted her focus to covering the contingent of the Southport fleet heading for the transports. She turned and began her attack run. Bianca followed her lead, picking the ship off the port flank of the lead ship to target with magical fire. Her spell streaked past from high overhead and the ship went up in a whoosh as Isabel released her spell and caught the lead ship afire. The archers on deck released a volley, but she was too high to be in danger.

Three squads of Sky Knights followed, each taking aim at another ship in the group. Two more fell into the water from a barrage of arrows. But most of the warships racing to catch up with the Southport fast-attack boats were damaged badly and taking on water.

Isabel signaled to provide overwatch for the ten ships racing toward the battle raging between the transports and the bulk of the Sky Knights. Bianca and her wing circled over the small fleet of attack boats, gaining altitude with each pass.

As Isabel neared the scene of the other battle she saw that several of the wyverns were in the water and struggling to get enough distance from the transports to avoid further attack. The rest of the Sky Knights had changed strategies to attack from much higher. When she got closer, she saw dozens of Lancers on the deck of each ship pointing their magical lances at the sky. She understood immediately why so many of the wyverns were in the water.

Those still airborne were making higher passes with javelins and concentrating their fire on one ship at a time to thin the ranks on the deck before the final squad in the formation made a tail-strike run at the ship. Nearly two-thirds of the Andalian troop transports had been disabled and were moving under oar power as they struggled to flee the battle.

Southport's fast-attack boats gained on them quickly and when they were in range, they didn't waste a moment. The first volley of fire pots rose into the air in a long arc reaching out to the limits of the ballistae range and crashed into the decks of ten ships. Flame flashed with each strike and grew quickly. The Southport ships abandoned caution and raced forward, trusting the wyverns overhead to cover their flank.

The refined strategy of the Sky Knights was slower at disabling the enemy ships but it was also much less risky. After fifty or more javelins peppered the deck of a ship, sending the Lancers scattering, a squad of Sky Knights would strike with their wyverns' tails and break the masts, then escape out of range.

The battle lasted for over an hour. Isabel was exhausted by the time she landed Asteroth on the field north of Southport but she was also exhilarated. They had sunk the entire troop transport fleet to a ship. All of the Lancers bound for Northport were drowned and gone.

Her two flights were landing all around and tending to their wyverns' wounds when Bianca and Constance found her.

"Well done," Isabel said through the fog of fatigue. "Report."

"Twenty-three wyverns dead, seventeen injured," Bianca said somberly. "Nine Sky Knights dead, and twenty-eight injured, though none seriously. All of the witches are accounted for. Scout riders report that the troop transports have all been sunk and what remains of the fleet of warships has withdrawn south. Southport's fleet took heavy losses with several of their larger ships sunk but most of the smaller attack boats still seaworthy."

They heard the sound of horses approaching and turned to see a platoon of Rangers coming fast. Some of the Sky Knights looked on with concern as they calmed their steeds. Isabel waved to the Rangers, smiling broadly. When she saw Kevin, she broke into a run and met her brother with a fierce hug as he dismounted.

"It's good to see you, Little Sister," Kevin said as he held her tight. "We've been so worried about you ever since we got word you'd been taken."

"I'm all right, Kevin. Better, even."

Abigail walked up with Bianca and Constance flanking her. "Hi Kevin, it's good to see you," she said with a smile.

"You too. Your abduction took its toll on our parents, so I sent word last night of your plan to attack the Andalian armada," Kevin said.

"Kevin, I'd like to introduce Flight Commanders Bianca and Constance," Isabel said. "They led the Sky Knights in the battle against the troop transports."

Kevin bowed formally to the two formidable women. "Thank you for your timely assistance. Without you we wouldn't have been able to stop those Lancer transports. What do you need for your people and your steeds?"

Bianca smiled slightly. "To the point, I like that. Our steeds need food. A small herd would do nicely, say fifty head."

"I'll see to it right away," Kevin said, then turned to his Second and nodded. The man saluted and spurred his horse into a gallop. "I can offer barracks for your people tonight and better accommodations tomorrow."

"That won't be necessary," Constance said. "We will remain with our wyverns tonight and be on our way tomorrow."

Kevin frowned, "Where are you going?"

"Back to the fortress island," Constance said. "We have accomplished our mission and so we will return home."

"Then you don't know?" Kevin asked, turning to Isabel.

"Know what?" Isabel asked.

"Alexander is back on Ruatha. He led four Legions from Ithilian through the Gate five days ago," Kevin said. "He's gathering his forces for an assault on Northport tomorrow. Two legions from Blackstone Keep are moving south with the four Ithilian legions while the remaining ten legions in northern Ruatha are moving west from New Ruatha. They're planning a coordinated assault against Northport at dawn tomorrow morning."

Isabel and Abigail shared a look of hope and fierce triumph. Isabel hugged her brother again. "That's the best news I've heard in a very long time. I can't wait to see him."

"What are you considering, Lady Reishi?" Constance asked with a little concern.

She turned to the two Flight Commanders and drew herself up. "We're not going back to the fortress island tomorrow. We're going north to help Alexander against the Regency Army."

"This is most unusual," Bianca said. "The triumvirate has not approved this plan. Are you sure it's wise without deliberation?"

"We're at war, Bianca," Isabel said. "You've lived your whole life protecting the Sovereign Stone. Now I'm asking you to protect the one wearing it. He's fighting for the people of the Seven Isles and we can help him. I'm not going to order you to go against what you believe to be your duty, but I am going to leave you with a hard choice. Tomorrow, I'm flying north to find my husband. I'm going to fight at his side no matter the cost. I hope you'll come with me, but I understand if you decide to go home."

Constance grinned a little at the choice they'd been given.

Bianca chuckled.

"We can hardly let you go into battle alone," Constance said.

"I imagine Magda and Cassandra have their hands full with you," Bianca said. "They're not accustomed to bold moves and they will not be happy about your decision but I'm duty bound to stand with you."

"Good," Isabel said with a grateful smile. "See to your Sky Knights. We'll send Magda and Cassandra a message tomorrow morning when we leave for Northport. I'm going to spend some time with my brother. I need to know what's been going on during the past few months."

Chapter 36

Alexander stood next to his command tent on top of a little hillock. His forces stretched away in all directions, sprawling across the plain to the northeast of Northport. It was late in the afternoon of what had been a fine summer day until about an hour ago. Now there was a dark and angry cloud swirling over Northport. Lightning flickered and danced in the angry darkness. Alexander frowned. He'd seen this spell before.

"What do you make of it?" Duncan asked.

Alexander's reunion with his parents had been tearful and joyous, but now they were focused on the task that lay ahead. The Regency had withdrawn into the walled city and fortified it heavily. This battle wouldn't take place out in the open where cavalry charges and shield-walls decided the day. It would take place in the streets and buildings of Northport. Alexander knew it would be a deathtrap for all concerned.

"One of their wizards is preparing to call lightning from the sky," Alexander said. "If we send troops in under that dark cloud, he'll kill them by the thousands."

"I agree," Mage Gamaliel said. "But I suspect he's just providing us with a demonstration to give us pause. I doubt he can wield such power except directly over his position, so we have nothing to fear from his spell as long as we aren't under those clouds ourselves."

"So is he trying to stall us because he knows we have the strength to destroy him or is he expecting help from somewhere?" Duncan asked.

"When I looked in on them this morning, they were working on the docks," Alexander said. "It's a good bet they're expecting help."

"Probably more of those Lancers," Hanlon said. "That could be a problem."

"If it's Lancers he's expecting, Kevin will be the first to face them," Duncan said. "Hopefully those boats he's been building will work. From General Talia's report, it sounds like the Andalians could do some serious damage if we let them set foot on dry land."

"He's right about that," Alexander said. "We can't let more Lancers make landfall. Any word from Kevin?"

"I sent him a message letting him know you had arrived but I haven't heard from him since," Hanlon said. "Given the time it takes to make the trip, I don't expect a message rider for a day or two though."

Alexander looked out at Northport and shook his head in frustration. "That city is a deathtrap. I have no doubt we can defeat them but at what cost?"

"I know how you feel, Son, but I don't see that we have much choice," Duncan said. "They have to be dealt with and sooner would be better than later."

"I agree. But we can't afford to grind our army into dust doing it," Alexander said. "We need a better strategy than an all-out assault, because I guarantee this isn't going to be the last battle we fight before this war is over."

"Sleep on it, Son," Duncan said. "Maybe things will be clearer in the morning."

Alexander spent the rest of the afternoon circulating through the vast army encampment. Jataan trailed silently behind him as he talked with the soldiers. He wanted to gauge their determination and morale but also wanted to thank them for their sacrifice and service. He was humbled by their willingness to face the enemy no matter the cost, but he also knew that much of their enthusiasm was born of inexperience. The younger soldiers who had yet to step onto the battlefield were the most eager to prove themselves. Those who had recently fought in the battle of Headwater or at the Gate were more somber and reserved, although no less dedicated.

Alexander returned to his command tents with renewed determination to limit his army's casualties as much as possible. After dinner he listened silently to a lively debate between his general officers and a number of wizards, including the Guild Mage. They presented options and strategies for assaulting the city, exploring every possible capability they could bring to bear. Many of the strategies hinged on the unique magic of one wizard or another, while other plans of attack were more blunt and direct, depending on the sheer size of his army to overwhelm the defenses of the enemy.

In the cases of the wizards, Alexander knew they would be able to do significant damage to the wall and even to the enemy forces but nowhere near enough to overpower a force of a hundred thousand soldiers dug into a walled city. The strategies that relied on the brute force of numbers would be far more costly than he was willing to accept in terms of lives lost.

He lay awake in his bed with a growing feeling of dread. So many lives hung in the balance. The future of tens of thousands of souls rested on the choices he would make in the coming days.

"I don't know if I can do this, Little One," he said silently to Chloe. "So many lives—how can I decide their fate? What gives me the right?"

"It isn't your right, My Love, it's your duty," she said. "The enemy fights for ambition and power. You fight for the Old Law and the protection it guarantees to the innocent of the world who simply wish to live in peace. If you fail, many more will suffer."

"But how can I send so many soldiers into that city knowing that most will die?"

"It does not matter how the enemy dies, My Love, only that they do," Chloe said in his mind. "Battle is not always the best way to kill those who must die."

Alexander felt a great weight lift as he settled on a strategy. "Thank you, Little One. I think I can finally fall asleep now."

***

He woke with a start in the dead of night. There was commotion outside his tent. He sat up and reached for his baldric when he heard it. An inhuman howl like a cross between a dying pig's squeal and metal scraping against metal. He'd heard the sound before and his blood ran cold.

Chloe buzzed into a ball of bright light and was suddenly hovering a few feet in front of him.

"Darkness comes, My Love."

Alexander was pulling on his boots when Jataan entered his tent.

"We're under attack," he said.

"I know," Alexander growled. "It's nether wolves. Send out the word to cut off their heads. Arrows are useless against them, but they don't like bright light."

Jataan nodded and left the tent.

Alexander stepped out into the night and was greeted by the distant sounds of chaos as the unnatural beasts wreaked havoc in the outskirts of his camp.

Anatoly came running up, with Jack and Lucky not far behind.

"Sounds familiar," Anatoly said, axe in hand.

Jataan returned with Boaberous. "Your orders have been given."

"Good. We need horses," he said, turning toward the stables.

Lieutenant Wyatt and his dozen men were strapping saddles on their mounts. Alexander's horse and a half dozen more were already prepared.

"I took the liberty," Wyatt said as he cinched the last of his saddle straps into place and mounted.

"Well done," Alexander said, then turned to Jataan. "You'll need a sword."

Within moments they were riding through a camp fraught with confusion and distress. These men were willing to fight enemies that they understood but this was something else. The very sound of a nether wolf's howl was enough to send shivers of fear into the heart of even the most battle-tested warrior. Alexander understood how they felt all too well.

As they neared the area of the attack, the chaos grew. Men screamed and ran into the night. Some huddled in groups of four or five with their backs to each other, brandishing torches to keep the night at bay. A few called out in challenge to the darkness to show itself and fight. Still others cowered in the shadows, hoping that the darkness wouldn't find them. Men lay broken and bleeding all around.

Then Alexander saw the eyes that he remembered only in his nightmares. The hate in those eyes was visceral and timeless. His horse caught a whiff of the unnatural monsters and became skittish and afraid. He dismounted, turned his horse away from the enemy and slapped it on the rump, sending it running off into the night.

The first nether wolf came with terrifying speed, but Alexander held his ground.

Several more of the foul creatures in the darkness abandoned the frantic soldiers they had been stalking and turned to attack their real prey.

He drew the Thinblade in his right hand and Mindbender in his left. He didn't know if he would be able to hear the thoughts of the nether wolves or if he even wanted to, but having another blade in hand couldn't hurt.

His friends and the Rangers all dismounted. They drew swords in anticipation of the attack, all except Boaberous who was armed with his giant war hammer and Anatoly who always fought with his war axe if given a choice.

"Take their heads," Alexander said to the small army surrounding him.

The lead nether wolf leapt through the air, black as night with colors darker still. Alexander waited calmly until it reached just the right range, then slipped to the side and brought the Thinblade up fast. The beast's head came free and its body crashed to the ground in a broken heap of bleached bone and dried-out hide.

The next came quickly out of the shadows behind Alexander. Jataan was covering his flank. When he saw the beast, he raised his blade, waiting for the right moment to strike. The nether wolf ignored him in its path to Alexander and lost its head for the miscalculation. Then the remaining wolves were all around, peering from the darkness and waiting for their opening to strike.

Another bounded out of the darkness from the flank. Anatoly didn't have the angle to get a clean stroke at the creature's neck, so he swung horizontally at its foreleg. His axe blade sliced deeply into the side of the beast but that didn't stop it from crashing into Alexander.

He saw it coming but not quickly enough to bring the Thinblade down on it. Instead, he brought Mindbender up and across his body to shield against the powerful, oversized jaws, snapping and snarling, as it bore him to the ground. When he went down, several more of the beasts darted into the fray from all sides.

Boaberous met the first. His downward stroke hit the beast just behind the head on the center of its neck, driving it to the ground in a broken heap. But the one just beside it crashed into the giant, knocking him to the ground and landing on top of him.

A Ranger fell and died quickly when a nether wolf knocked him to the ground and ripped out his throat. It looked up in a frenzy and leapt toward another terrified Ranger.

There were at least a dozen all around and they were coming too quickly.

The one on Alexander bore into his chest with one claw and pinned his right arm to the ground with the other as it tried to tear into his throat with its fangs. Somehow he managed to get Mindbender into its mouth. With the point of the sword against the ground beside him, he leveraged it up to push the monster away as much as possible.

With his all around sight, he watched Jataan face off against another beast. It seemed to be toying with him, distracting him from helping Alexander in his desperate fight against the one on top of him.

Anatoly drove the top spike of his axe into the rump of the nether wolf trying to kill Alexander but only succeeded in shifting the monster's weight a little. It didn't waver from its single-minded effort to kill Alexander. As it bore down on him, Mindbender cut deeply into the sides of its mouth but it didn't seem to care. Alexander could feel the coldness of its breath. The rotting stench of it made him gag.

Then there was light flooding into the area all around him. Jack and Lucky held their night-wisp dust high and pure white light flooded into the desperate battle. The nether wolves suddenly turned into thick black smoke that sank to the ground and seeped into the dirt to escape.

At least two nether wolves outside the field of light howled in rage and frustration. Alexander rolled to his feet and surveyed the scene. Three of the Rangers commanded by Lieutenant Wyatt were dead. His men had paid such a high price for their loyalty. Many more were bruised and battered. Boaberous had a deep gash on his left arm.

Alexander looked off into the darkness and found the two pairs of eyes. "Anatoly, Jataan, you're with me," he said. "Jack, Lucky, hold your position. Everyone else, stay in the light."

He stalked toward the darkness and the creatures of the night that awaited him. When he reached the edge of the darkness, they attacked with snarling rage.

He met them with righteous anger. The two leapt in unison. Alexander killed one with the Thinblade in midair. The second came for Anatoly. He crouched as he planted the butt of his axe in the dirt and aimed the top spike into the chest of the nether wolf. The creature sailed over him and crashed into the ground. Jataan darted in and cleaved its head from its body in a stroke.

The next hour was spent carefully moving the light of the night-wisp dust to allow just one of the nether wolves at a time to rematerialize in a spot flanked by soldiers waiting to cut it to pieces. Word of the battle rippled through the camp and a crowd gathered to watch Alexander and his men destroy the fearsome beasts, one by one.

They gasped when each materialized from thin air and cheered as each fell. When they'd killed the last of them, Alexander ordered his war council to assemble. It was still hours from dawn but he was angry and filled with deadly purpose. The enemy needed to die. They needed to die today.

He strode into the command tent and found it was full. His father and mother, Hanlon, Conner, Erik, Wizards Gamaliel, Sark, and Dax, Generals Markos and Brand all sat around the table. Two dozen commanders and a few other wizards sat in chairs around the walls of the tent.

He took his chair and waited for Anatoly, Jack, Wyatt, and Lucky to sit as well. Jataan remained standing just behind him while Boaberous had taken a position just outside the door. Chloe buzzed into a ball of light as she materialized from the aether. She stood on the table in front of Alexander and surveyed those in attendance as if assessing their worthiness before she sat down cross-legged in front of him. Her appearance quieted the room and drew everyone's attention to Alexander.

"Northport dies today," he said with anger still flashing in his golden eyes. "The necromancer within those walls called forth more than a dozen nether wolves and sent them into our midst in the night. Hundreds of our men are dead. Such attacks can't break the strength of our army but they can weaken the morale and resolve of our soldiers."

"I take it you've decided on a strategy then," Duncan said.

Alexander nodded gravely. "Fire. We're going to surround the city at a safe distance and burn it to the ground. None of the enemy will be spared. They are all guilty of treason against the Old Law and I sentence them to death."

The room fell silent as the magnitude of Alexander's pronouncement sank in.

"Speak your mind," Alexander said. "If you're in this room, then I value your counsel and I will not fault you for presenting your opinion."

The silence lingered on for several moments until Duncan smiled grimly.

"Northport is an ancient city," he said. "Must it be destroyed?"

Alexander understood the tone of his father's question. He'd heard it countless times during his lessons when Duncan had wanted him to think more deeply on his answer, but this time his question was a prompt meant to give Alexander a reason to explain himself.

"I've heard every conceivable battle plan we can employ," Alexander said. "Either we can cause some damage to the enemy with limited risk or we can destroy the enemy but lose half of our army—or more. Neither option is acceptable. The city is just buildings, stone and timber. It can be rebuilt. Our soldiers are flesh and blood. Their lives cannot be replaced.

"Yet, we must defeat this army or risk night after night of attack by creatures called forth from the netherworld. They will come in the darkness and sap our will and our courage until we are cowering in our tents awaiting the next attack while the enemy sleeps secure and safe behind the walls of Northport.

"Eventually, they will get reinforcements by sea. Southport can't stop everything Phane can send. Kevin will do his best but the resources of both Karth and Andalia will be put to use building ships. Kevin can't match what they'll send against him. A prolonged siege will only lead to a more deadly battle in the future against a larger army."

"I'm saddened that it's come to this," Kelvin said. "The city of Ruatha was destroyed in the final years of the Reishi war. I've read some of Mage Cedric's journal entries about that battle. He struggled with the decision mightily but eventually came to the same conclusion that you have. The city is just buildings and they can be replaced. I only hope that Northport isn't left to become a haunted ruin like Ruatha was."

"It won't be," Alexander said. "We'll rebuild it because we have to. Since we control the Gates, the enemy will need to build ships to wage their war. We can't let them gain control of the seas, so we must begin construction of a navy capable of defending our shores against any fleet they send. Northport will be essential to those efforts—but for now, it must fall."

He surveyed the room and saw resolve and determination in the colors of his commanders. Satisfied with their reaction to his strategy, he began laying out his plan. By an hour before dawn, the entire army was up and breaking camp in preparation to move into position for the assault against Northport.

As the stars faded into the deep blue of the coming dawn, Alexander stood on his little hillock overlooking the valley below and watched his army begin to move. Four legions went to the south across the Ruatha River to block the enemy's retreat into the forest. Four legions moved north and west to cut off any escape along the coastline. The remaining six legions deployed to assault the city. The leading two legions made up the primary assault force with reserves in the rear to be deployed where needed.

Alexander had ordered an archery legion armed with longbows and three dozen flame arrows each to be paired with a heavy infantry legion all equipped with large round shields. Each archer was assigned an infantryman to cover them against enemy attack. The force of twenty thousand lumbered forward with scores of heavy ballistae in their midst to augment the firepower of the archers.

The light of day broke over the horizon on a clear sky. Not ten minutes later, a dark and angry cloud began to form over the city. Horns could be heard in the distance calling the enemy to stand ready.

Alexander felt a mixture of excitement and dread. He watched his army execute his battle plan and felt the anxiety of command. The next hours would decide so much and yet he knew they wouldn't play out as he'd planned. No battle ever did.

"I feel like I should be down there with them," Alexander muttered.

"No, you shouldn't," Duncan said. "Generals who lead from the front lines fall in the opening minutes of the battle and leave their soldiers leaderless and demoralized. You're exactly where you should be. Let your plan unfold."

Alexander nodded. He'd grown up hearing lectures on the finer points of military leadership but those had been just lessons, abstract and without emotion or desperate need. This was something else. Men would die today. Men he'd sent into battle. The responsibility of it was crushing.

The sky over Northport grew darker and the lightning began to flicker through the clouds. The spell was nearly ready to begin dealing death to his advancing army. He took a deep breath and steeled himself to the ruin that was about to befall so many lives.

The first ranging arrows rose from the battlements of Northport's walls. Alexander's soldiers were still several hundred feet out of range. They marched forward into the killing field. A horn sounded in the distance and dozens of ballistae and catapults fired from the walls. Clay pots streaming trails of smoke behind them rose into the air in a graceful arc and came crashing down into the ranks of marching soldiers, shattering and spraying their burning contents into their midst. Men scattered and screamed but the commanders regained control with shouted orders and iron discipline.

His assault force started running forward to reach attack range more quickly. A volley of thousands of arrows rose from the walls. Officers called for cover. As one, the infantry raised their shields and the archers ducked behind them. The arrows clattered against the heavy shields with only a small number finding flesh. The unit dashed forward again. Another volley rose from the walls and again the assault force defended against the attack. Some fell, but most survived. One last sprint brought the entire force within range before they stopped and made ready for their assault, pausing only to defend against another volley from Northport's walls.

Loosely woven ropes of burlap drizzled in oil were strung out in front of each rank. Ballistae were loaded with clay pots filled with lamp oil. On command the burlap ropes were lit, as were the fuses on the clay pots. Archers used the flaming rope to ignite the tips of their arrows. A horn blew and the archers and ballistae fired at the city. They were ordered to overshoot the walls and reach the buildings behind. Once they'd loosed the first volley, they began to fire at will, sending a steady stream of fire into the city, stopping their attack only to take refuge under the upturned shields of their infantry protectors when the enemy arrows rained down on them.

It was only minutes before the fires could be seen over the walls of the city. The first bolt of lightning touched down with crashing thunder into the ranks of the assault force and scorched a patch of dirt three dozen feet wide. Men for fifty feet in every direction were sent sprawling while those closer to the point of impact were vaporized or burned so badly that they died where they fell.

Those farther away stopped for only a moment to recover their wits before they renewed their assault. The fires in Northport grew. Another bolt of lightning struck into the assault force and killed dozens more but the soldiers held their ground and continued the relentless barrage of flaming arrows and fire pots into the city. A plume of dark smoke rose from the flames toward the black clouds overhead.

Then the city gates opened and the scourgling came bounding out toward the assault force, followed by a column of cavalry. It was still a good distance off, but Alexander could see the darkness of its aura and knew in an instant what it was.

"Kelvin, we need a magic circle right there," he said urgently, pointing to the patch of ground at the base of the little hillock where they stood.

"There isn't time to make one in gold," Kelvin said. "I don't know that lines in the dirt will hold it."

"We don't have a choice," Alexander said. "If we don't contain it, we're lost. Deploy the cavalry to meet the charge coming toward us and send in two legions of infantry to reinforce the assault force," he said to his father as he turned toward the path to the base of the hillock.

"Where are you going?" Duncan asked urgently.

"I'm the bait," Alexander said. "The scourgling is coming for me. I have to be the one to lure it into place."

"Alexander, no!" Bella cried. She had been silent during most of their deliberations but now that her son was stepping into harm's way, she could hold her tongue no longer. "You have to run! We can't destroy that thing, so you have to run. Take a dozen horses and head for Blackstone Keep."

Alexander stopped and looked at his mother sadly, shaking his head slowly. "I can't, Mother. I've asked all of these men to face death. If I run, their spirit will be broken. I have to stand with them no matter the cost."

"But it will kill you," she pleaded.

"Perhaps Lady Valentine is right, Lord Reishi," Jataan said, glancing out across the distance to the monster charging across the field. "I do not believe I can protect you against such a thing."

"Trust me, Jataan, you can't," Alexander said. "Even the Thinblade is useless against it. Our only hope is to contain it within a magic circle and the only way we can do that is to lure it into the right spot—using me as bait."

"Listen to your protector, Alexander," Bella said. "The Maker knows I hate him for taking Darius from me, but he's right about this. You have to run!"

"No," Alexander said with finality. "I will not leave these men to wonder if the leader they follow is a coward who will abandon them to face the horrors of this war alone."

The scourgling crashed into the ranks of the archers and infantry, sending men sprawling or worse as it drove through their lines. Those who stood in its way were batted aside or trampled underfoot but it didn't stop to finish them or to disrupt their sustained barrage of flaming arrows. Instead it charged through the soldiers in a straight path toward Alexander.

He pointed out into the battlefield. "Even if I run, it will catch me. It's faster than any horse and stronger than any weapon we have. We have one chance and one chance only. I love you, Mom, but I have to do this."

Chloe buzzed into material existence from the aether in a scintillating ball of white light and floated a few feet in front of Alexander.

"I can send it away, My Love," she said.

"You'd die," he said.

"Yes, but you would live."

"Absolutely not! My decision is final," he said with anger flashing in his eyes. "Chloe, you will not risk your life against that thing. Kelvin, set the trap. We don't have much time."

"My wizards are already preparing the circle," he said. "I will stand with you against the scourgling. I may not be able to kill it but I suspect I can slow it down."

Alexander nodded, then turned to survey the scene of battle unfolding in the distance. The enemy cavalry had nearly reached the assault force. The archers had shifted fire to thin the ranks of the charging horses while the infantry was forming up a rank of shields and pikes to try to break the enemy's momentum. Alexander's legion of cavalry was still several minutes away. It wouldn't be long before his assault force was caught in a pitched battle well within arrow range of the walls of Northport.

The city was burning, but the dark clouds swirling over it had transformed into rain clouds and were starting to drizzle. His plan was failing. He knew from his fight on the ruins over Benesh Reishi's crypt that the same spell that called forth lightning could also bring heavy rain, enough to extinguish any fire they could set.

"Withdraw the assault force out of arrow range," he said to Duncan. "We've set all the fire we can for the moment."

Alexander heard the horns blow from behind him, signaling retreat as he made his way to the base of the little hillock. The ground was prepared with a magical circle and several wizards had assembled to stand with him, including Sark, Jahoda, Mage Gamaliel, and Mage Landi. Each was busy casting a spell, except Mage Gamaliel who was checking the straps on his dragon-plate armor.

Wizard Jahoda finished his spell and a jumble of rocks assembled into a nine-foot-tall stone giant. Alexander smiled at the creation. The last time he'd seen one in action, he'd been impressed, although he feared it wouldn't be a match for the scourgling.

Wizard Sark completed his spell and a whirlwind came into being, swirling a column of dust up into it. It didn't look very powerful but Alexander knew better. It could gain strength very quickly when Sark wanted it to.

Mage Landi completed his spell and the air started to glow, softly at first but then with an intensity that made Alexander look away. When he looked back he saw a creature like nothing he'd ever seen before. It stood six feet tall and looked almost like a man except it was made entirely of pure white light. It had no hair or facial features, which made it look like it was not quite finished. Its skin was smooth and shined gently with the kind of light Alexander expected to see when he died. It was beautiful and terrible all at once.

It turned to mage Landi. "For what purpose have you summoned me?" Its voice was hauntingly distant, as though it was calling out through a tunnel from very far away.

"A scourgling approaches. Will you help us fight it?"

It stood motionless for many moments. "I will help you, but a scourgling is beyond me."

"I know," Mage Landi said sadly, "but you are the most powerful creature of light I know of and we are desperate."

Everyone turned when they heard it coming. Soldiers who tried to engage it were smashed, trampled, or rent asunder as it thrashed through the crowd of men in its path. Others scrambled to avoid it as it charged through their midst.

Alexander stood at the edge of the magic circle and waited.

Chloe buzzed around his head, flaring into a ball of light every few moments.

"Are you mad at me, My Love," she asked.

"No, Little One. I love you and I don't want you to be hurt."

She buzzed into a ball of light momentarily, then flitted up to kiss him on the cheek before she disappeared into the aether.

The scourgling broke free of the soldiers and entered the clearing. It didn't even seem to notice the summoned creatures or wizards arrayed before it as it bore straight down on Alexander.

The creature summoned by Mage Landi reached it first, landing a powerful blow in the middle of the beast's chest. The scourgling staggered to a stop and shifted its attention to the being of light. It swatted with one hand and raked a series of gashes across the creature's chest. Scintillating white light poured out of the gashes, bright enough to make the scourgling back off a step or two before the creature of light disappeared, leaving everyone slightly dazzled.

The stone giant reached it next and attempted to grapple with the nine-foot-tall demon. They tumbled to the ground and rolled before the scourgling grabbed a single stone from its body and tore it free, tossing it aside. One at a time, the demon tore stones away until the stones that remained fell to the ground.

Mage Gamaliel stepped to within twenty feet of the scourgling and brought his magical hammer down on the ground with a battle cry. It struck with such force that Alexander staggered to keep his feet. A chasm opened up, splitting the earth from the point of impact for about thirty feet. The scourgling slipped into the crack and fell out of view.

Alexander held his breath, but he knew it was only a matter of time before the creature surfaced.

Sark's whirlwind intensified and landed in the chasm, pulling dirt in on top of the scourgling until it was completely buried.

"Think that'll hold it?" Anatoly asked.

"No," Alexander said, never taking his eyes off the spot where the demon was entombed.

He didn't have to wait long. Not a minute later, its clawed hand burst from the dirt and pulled it up out of the hole. Alexander held his ground and waited.

The scourgling started toward him again, gaining speed as it charged. When it entered the circle, Jahoda cast the spell that turned the magic circle into a device of confinement rather than a place of protection. The scourgling crashed into the invisible magical barrier as Alexander rolled aside.

It tried to push through but couldn't.

Alexander breathed a sigh of relief.

Then the scourgling started digging next to the edge of the circle. It wasn't a moment before the circle broke and the magic failed. The beast lunged at Alexander.

Anatoly shoved him aside and faced the beast. It swatted him in the chest, sending him sprawling. Jataan darted in and thrust so hard that his sword shattered against the creature. It brushed him aside and turned toward Alexander.

He didn't remember drawing the Thinblade but it was in his hand. The whole world narrowed down to that moment. He was in a fight for his life and he had a blade in his hand. Everything else faded away.

The scourgling lashed out at him with one clawed hand. He danced aside and slashed at its wrist. The Thinblade bounced off it the way a steel sword would bounce off stone. The scourgling turned and backhanded him hard in the chest. The Thinblade slipped out of his hand as he tumbled to the ground. The scourgling leaped into the air in an arc that would bring its giant taloned feet into the middle of him.

Everything seemed to slow down. He saw the deadly, otherworldly monster float through the air. He heard Chloe cry out in his mind and saw her buzz into existence, apparently trying to reach the demon before it reached him. He saw Jataan stumble to his feet, trying to shake off the haze from the blow he'd taken. He heard Anatoly groan in pain and watched Lucky pour a healing draught into his mouth. He thought of Isabel as he watched his death descend on him.

Then a shadow passed overhead. The scourgling was knocked backward through the air just a few feet before it would have landed right in the middle of him. When he looked up, he saw a sky full of wyverns. More than a hundred of the creatures were making attack runs into the enemy cavalry in the distance, but a dozen or more were circling directly overhead. He looked closer and felt his heart nearly stop when he saw a hawk flying in formation with the one that had just hit the scourgling with its tail. The next in line flew low enough to whip-strike the scourgling again, sending it sprawling across the ground. The flash of sunlight off the rider's silvery blond hair filled Alexander with hope.

The first rider wheeled quickly for another pass. He saw Isabel riding on the great beast. She reached out with her hand and sent a bolt of bright white light into the scourgling as it regained its feet. The light ran up its back but had no effect. Another wyvern floated overhead and a javelin bounced off the nine-foot-tall demon.

It started coming for Alexander again.

Kelvin used his hammer to open another rift in the earth and slow the beast's charge. It stumbled and went to ground before bouncing back to its feet. Two more wyverns wheeled overhead and sent light stabbing into the creature.

When it reached Alexander, he dove to the side and out of reach of its clawed hand. It turned and bounded toward him, landing over him with one foot on either side. He struggled to get out of the path of the demon's attack but he was trapped. Its hand came up poised for a kill strike and started to come down just as Isabel floated over again. This time the quality of the light that streaked from her hand was altogether different. Its color was that of pure love and life.

The argent-white light struck the scourgling square in the back. It stopped, frozen in place for just a moment before its skin burned off in a flash, leaving only a thick black smoke that seemed to flee the world of time and substance as if it knew it had no place there.

Isabel and Abigail landed in the little clearing and scrambled off their wyverns.

Alexander bounded to his feet and raced toward his wife. They crashed into each other and he held her tight as he spun her in a circle.

"I'm never going to let you out of my sight again," he said, hugging her fiercely.

"Promise?" she whispered.

When he let go of his wife, Abigail was standing a few feet away watching with a gentle smile.

"Told you he'd get into trouble without us," she said to Isabel.

Alexander grabbed his sister and hugged her. "I've missed you both so much."

"Easy, Big Brother, you'll break me," she said teasingly.

He let her go and held her out at arm's length. "Who hurt you? I saw that you were injured. Who?"

She and Isabel shared a smile before she shrugged. "Your wife already killed her."

Alexander looked over at Isabel and nodded approvingly as he slipped his arm around her waist and drew her close.

Jack stepped up and bowed formally to Isabel. "Lady Reishi . . ."

"Don't you start that with me, Jack," she said.

He smiled and winked. "I'm very glad you are well and have returned to us." Then he turned to Abigail and held out his hand. She looked a little taken aback but she gave him her hand nonetheless. He took it with a gentle smile and bowed to kiss it softly.

"There are many things I wish to say to you, Abigail," he said. "For now, just know that I've missed you terribly every single day that you've been gone."

She blushed. Alexander was glad. It was about time someone could fluster his sister.

Lucky came ambling up, a mixture of happiness and grief struggling to gain control of his face.

"I'm so glad to see you both, but I have terrible news," Lucky said, his voice breaking slightly.

"What is it?" Alexander said, suddenly alarmed. It took a lot to undo Lucky's composure.

"Anatoly has been gravely injured," Lucky said. "I've done all I can, but I fear he won't survive the day."

Alexander was suddenly stricken with a mixture of guilt and grief. He knew Anatoly had fallen to the scourgling but his joy at seeing Isabel and Abigail had driven the worry for his old man-at-arms from his mind. He raced to the place where Anatoly had fallen. Lucky had made him comfortable and treated his wounds as best he could, but there was a lot of damage. His breastplate lay nearby, crushed and rent where the demon had swatted him.

"Dear Maker," Alexander whispered as he knelt next to Anatoly. "You can't die, you stubborn old bull," he said, taking Anatoly's hand. His emotions crashed from the pure joy of seeing his wife and sister again to finding that his mentor and protector was dying.

"You have to fix him, Isabel," Abigail said through a sob.

Alexander wasn't sure what she was talking about and he didn't take the time to focus on anything other than his friend lying on the field where he'd fallen trying to protect him. The guilt threatened to crush him.

Isabel knelt next to Anatoly and smiled at Alexander. "He'll be all right," she said as she laid her hand gently on his chest and closed her eyes.

Alexander watched her colors turn pure white, the color of life itself, then her aura swelled and the light became visible around her hand. Anatoly stiffened slightly and then began to breathe easier as he drifted off to sleep.

"I don't understand," Alexander said. "What just happened?"

"She healed him," Abigail said through her tears.

"But how?" Lucky asked.

"With magic from the realm of light," Isabel said. "It's a long story better told at another time."

Lucky and Alexander both nodded, somewhat dumbfounded by the power Isabel had just displayed.

Everyone turned when Duncan, Bella, and Hanlon came rushing up. Once they were assured that Anatoly would be all right, they spent a few moments hugging their daughters while the sounds of battle raged in the distance.

Another wyvern landed not far off, sending soldiers scattering out of the way and looking at the giant beast warily. It folded its wings, and the rider waved to Isabel.

"The enemy cavalry have retreated back to the city. What are your orders, Lady Reishi?"

Isabel looked up to Alexander. "What were your plans?"

"We were trying to set Northport on fire, but it's not working," Alexander said. "I've ordered the assault force to retreat out of range of the archers for now."

Isabel nodded and turned to the woman rider. "Have the Sky Knights land behind the army. I'll send riders for you and Constance."

She nodded and her wyvern launched into the air gaining altitude with each powerful stroke of its wings. Asteroth and Kallistos launched into the air just after her and followed as she ascended toward the circling formation of Sky Knights overhead.

Alexander smiled at Isabel. "I want to hear about every single thing that's happened since you were taken from me, and I want to know how you destroyed that scourgling, but right now we have a battle to win. Let's go back to the command tents and decide what to do next. Lieutenant Wyatt, please go to the Sky Knights and escort their leaders back here."

He nodded and turned on his heel to tend to his orders.

"I'll stay with Anatoly," Lucky said. "It really is good to see the two of you. We were all quite worried when you were taken."

They both gave him a hug before everyone made their way up the winding path to the top of the hillock where they stopped for a moment to watch the fires dying down in the city from the heavy rain that was falling out of the conjured clouds.

"I should have anticipated that," Alexander said, shaking his head.

Isabel shrugged. "No plan ever survives contact with the enemy," she said, smiling up at him.

"You are very wise, Lady Reishi."

They turned away from the army sprawling before them and went into the command tent. Alexander was overjoyed that Isabel had returned. He knew he should be anxious or even worried that his plan had failed but he just couldn't bring himself to feel anything but happiness.

It wasn't long before Wyatt entered with two women wearing armor following behind him. They each carried themselves with confidence. Both had the colors of a witch.

"Alexander, these are Flight Commanders Bianca and Constance," Isabel said. "Ladies, this is my husband, Lord Alexander Reishi."

Both women bowed formally.

"Lord Reishi, it is an honor to meet you," Bianca said. "For my part, I hope we can put any past differences behind us and join forces against our common enemy."

"Well said. Please, sit. We have much to discuss."

Once everyone was seated around the council table, Chloe buzzed into existence. She floated up to Isabel and kissed her on the cheek.

"I'm so glad you've returned to Our Love," she said. "He's been most distraught since you were taken, but now his heart sings."

Bianca and Constance blinked, looked at each other and then back at Chloe.

"We heard the rumor that you had bonded with a fairy, but none of us believed it," Constance said.

Alexander smiled, then cocked his head to the side in recognition. "You're the one on the bridge. The one Jataan put a javelin through."

She looked a little startled. "I am," she said rubbing her shoulder. "That was a very dark day for us, Lord Reishi. We believed that we had failed the world when you recovered the Sovereign Stone."

"And now?" he asked, pointedly. He saw Jataan tense ever so slightly through his all around sight.

"Now, many of us are uncertain, though your wife and sister have impressed all who live within the fortress island. Many believe that a man can be measured by the quality of the women who love him. By that standard, you have earned our respect."

"Good enough, for now," Alexander said. "In time, I hope to win your friendship as well."

Both women seemed surprised by his response. Their colors shined with uncertainty.

Alexander smiled more broadly. "Not what you were expecting?"

"No," Bianca said. "Most who seek power tend to lord it over others, yet you speak of friendship rather than command. We expected you to demand our obedience and press our forces into service."

Alexander laughed, shaking his head. "I invited you here to listen to your counsel and ask for your assistance. As for seeking power, I didn't. It sought me and I'd gladly give it all up if I could take my wife home and raise a nice little herd of cattle. But I can't because Phane is out there plotting to kill everything and everyone I care about."

"We will gladly offer our counsel," Constance said. "As for our assistance, Lady Reishi, as the only triumvir of the Reishi Coven present, is the commander of our forces. We will follow her orders."

"Triumvir, huh?" Alexander said to Isabel. "I bet there's quite a story behind that one."

"You have no idea," Abigail said, rolling her eyes.

Isabel gave her a look but Abigail just shrugged.

"All right then," Alexander said, "does anyone have any suggestions for killing the hundred thousand or so enemy soldiers holed up in Northport without grinding our army into dust in the process?"

The table fell silent for a moment before Kelvin cleared his throat and sat forward. "I believe that I may have a way, with the assistance of the Sky Knights, to do immeasurable damage to the occupants of Northport."

Alexander gestured for Kelvin to continue and sat forward to listen.

"As you may recall, there were a number of powerful explosions during the battle at the Gate. Those were the result of a weapon that I created while you were away. The ones used by our forces during that battle were delivered with a very large catapult. I have created several more of much greater power, but they are very heavy and I had to leave them at Blackstone Keep until I could devise an effective means of delivering them into the midst of the enemy.

"If the Sky Knights can drop them into the city, I can detonate them. A dozen of the larger versions would devastate everything within the walls."

"All right, I like it. But that still leaves the problem of the weather wizard and his lightning," Alexander said. "I don't want to send anyone in under that dark cloud of his."

"We noticed the clouds over the city on our way here," Bianca said. "They are most unnatural. Am I to assume they're the result of a spell of some kind?"

"One of the wizards in Northport can control the weather," Alexander said. "He killed at least a hundred men today with lightning called down from the sky."

"I see," Bianca said. "How long does it take him to call lightning from the clouds?"

"Ah, simple solutions are always the best solutions," Alexander said. "It takes him a good twenty minutes. How heavy are these weapons of yours, Kelvin?"

"Easily the weight of a full-grown bison," the Guild Mage said.

"That's no problem for a wyvern," Isabel said.

Alexander nodded to himself, considering the plan and liking it more and more. "Dad, order the army to withdraw, and make a show about it. Isabel, send a couple of dozen Sky Knights to the flight deck on Blackstone Keep. Kelvin, which one of your wizards knows enough about these things to find them and move them up to the flight deck?"

"Wizard Hax would be the one to speak with," Kelvin said.

"Good, I'll send the message," Alexander said. "They should be ready by the time the Sky Knights arrive."

Alexander sent his orders into the dreams of a Ranger in the sleep room at Blackstone Keep. With his plan set in motion, he and his family spent the time talking and sharing stories of their past few months. Reports came to them from time to time but the enemy was quiet and seemed content to wait. Alexander was happy to learn that the reinforcements the Regency soldiers were expecting were never going to arrive. Lucky came and went to attend to Anatoly as needed, but he reported that the big man-at-arms was resting and would recover from his wounds.

By midafternoon a report came with news that the wing of Sky Knights had returned from Blackstone Keep with the weapons. Kelvin rode out to the staging area where the wyverns had landed and prepared his magically constructed weapons. The weather wizard had let his spell lapse and the sky had returned to the clear blue of a warm summer afternoon. By the time Kelvin returned to the command tents, the wyverns were just passing overhead, carrying the large, barrel-shaped weapons in their talons.

Alexander stood with his arm around Isabel's waist, flanked by his family and friends as the Sky Knights released the weapons to fall indiscriminately into the city of Northport. Within moments of their passage over the city, dark clouds began to form overhead. The wing of wyverns circled out from under the conjured clouds and set a course for the staging area behind Alexander's army.

"I haven't tested this version of the weapon," Kelvin said. "I'll be interested to see just how powerful it actually is."

The wing of Sky Knights floated overhead and out of harm's way.

"It's time," Alexander said.

Kelvin nodded and set a handful of twelve little pebbles on a nearby table and corralled them into one spot. He raised his hammer and gently brought it down onto the dozen stones, crushing them into powder. Alexander saw the telltale flare of magic as the stones shattered. There was a sudden stillness in the air, followed by a bright flash of light. A fiery cloud of smoke and debris rose from within the walls of Northport. A moment later the sound hit them. It was a stunning shock to hear something so loud. Even thunder didn't compare with the fury unleashed by the Guild Mage's enchanted weapons. Everyone stepped back when the shock wave hit them. The ground shook beneath their feet. The plates and cups on the table rattled as a great ball of flaming smoke lifted into the air and formed a massive cloud of destruction over the city.

"I have never in all my life seen such power," Bianca said with a mixture of awe and fear.

"I know what you mean," Alexander said. "Well done, Kelvin, but let's hope we never have to use those things again."

The Guild Mage nodded somberly.

Here Ends Mindbender
Sovereign of the Seven Isles: Book Three

www.SovereignOfTheSevenIsles.com

The Story Continues…

Blood of the Earth
Sovereign of the Seven Isles: Book Four

Made in United States
North Haven, CT
17 March 2022

17237271R00183